I0592025

Friedrich Schiller

Schiller and Horace

Friedrich Schiller

Schiller and Horace

ISBN/EAN: 9783743373709

Manufactured in Europe, USA, Canada, Australia, Japa

Cover: Foto ©Andreas Hilbeck / pixelio.de

Manufactured and distributed by brebook publishing software (www.brebook.com)

Friedrich Schiller

Schiller and Horace

SCHILLER

AND

HORACE

Translated

BY

THE RIGHT HON. LORD LYTTON

LONDON
GEORGE ROUTLEDGE AND SONS
THE BROADWAY, LUDGATE
NEW YORK: 416 BROOME STREET
1875

LONDON :

BRADBURY, AGNEW, & CO., PRINTERS, WHITEFRIARS.

PREFATORY NOTE TO THE KNEBWORTH EDITION.

———◆———

A QUARTER of a century divided from each other the two labours of love the fruits of which are here for the first time placed side by side.

It was in 1844 that Sir Edward Lytton's version of the "Poems and Ballads of Schiller" was, in its original piecemeal issue, drawn to a conclusion in the pages of *Blackwood's Magazine;* while it was in the April, May, July, and August numbers, for 1868, of the same periodical, that the earliest specimens of the metrical translation of the " Odes and Epodes of Horace " by Lord Lytton were tentatively put forth, without the slightest hint being afforded at the moment as to their authorship. What was avowedly aimed at in each instance was a line for line equivalent. Towards the accomplishment of this object no amount of toil or thought was grudged by the translator. In order to recognise this in the instance of the Schiller translation, it is only necessary to compare the first edition (that of 1845) with the second (that of 1852), both published by the Messrs. Blackwood. The scrupulous care taken in the revision of the Horace Translation may in the same way be the most readily appreciated upon a comparison of the first edition, that published in 1869 by the Messrs. Blackwood, with the second, that published in 1870 by the Messrs. Longmans. Here more conspicuously than ever was rendered apparent the fact underlying all Lord Lytton's labours in literature, that he himself was his sevt.'est critic. Wherever in these carefully-elaborated versions of Schiller and Horace he has departed from his otherwise invariable practice of translating line by line, and, as far as might be in any way possible, word for word, he has done so only where it seemed expedient to care rather for the poet's leading idea or inner meaning than for his verbal manner of expressing it.

It was in the accomplishment of the second of these two scholarly achievements that Lord Lytton gave signal evidence in his maturity of his readiness to modify upon reconsideration one of his long-cherished preferences. When, a quarter of a century before, employing in his version of "The Walk" of Schiller the boldest alternations of rhyme in lieu of the long rhymeless metre of the German original, he had spoken almost disdainfully of the latter as of a "spurious classical metre," which he would not have employed even in the translation of Ovid and Tibullus. When undertaking, long afterwards, however, to express in familiar English the thoughts and words of the master-lyrist of antiquity, Lord Lytton employed those purely rhythmical and strictly rhymeless measures which were but an adaptation to the crucial task of translating Horace, of the metrical experiments already adventured upon by him in his "Lost Tales of Miletus."

CONTENTS.

POEMS AND BALLADS OF SCHILLER.

CONTENTS.

FIRST PERIOD; or, EARLY POEMS.

ODES AND EPODES OF HORACE.

THE ODES.

BOOK I.

THE EPODES.

THE POEMS AND BALLADS

OF

SCHILLER.

THE DIVER.

A BALLAD.

[The original of the story on which Schiller has founded this ballad, matchless perhaps for the power and grandeur of its descriptions, is to be found in Kircher. According to the true principles of imitative art, Schiller has preserved all that is striking in the legend, and ennobled all that is commonplace. The name of the Diver was Nicholas, surnamed the Fish. The King appears, according to Hoffmeister's probable conjectures, to have been either Frederic I. or Frederic II., of Sicily. Date from 1295 to 1377.]

"Oh, where is the knight or the squire so bold,
　As to dive to the howling charybdis below?—
I cast in the whirlpool a goblet of gold,
　And o'er it already the dark waters flow;
Whoever to me may the goblet bring,
Shall have for his guerdon that gift of his king."

He spoke, and the cup from the terrible steep,
　That, rugged and hoary, hung over the verge
Of the endless and measureless world of the deep,
　Swirl'd into the maëlstrom that madden'd the surge,
"And where is the diver so stout to go—
I ask ye again—to the deep below?"

And the knights and the squires that gather'd around,
　Stood silent—and fix'd on the ocean their eyes;
They look'd on the dismal and savage Profound,
　And the peril chill'd back every thought of the prize.
And thrice spoke the monarch—"The cup to win,
Is there never a wight who will venture in?"

And all as before heard in silence the king—
　Till a youth with an aspect unfearing but gentle,
'Mid the tremulous squires—stept out from the ring,
　Unbuckling his girdle, and doffing his mantle;
And the murmuring crowd as they parted asunder,
On the stately boy cast their looks of wonder.

As he strode to the marge of the summit, and gave
　One glance on the gulf of that merciless main;
Lo! the wave that for ever devours the wave,
　Casts roaringly up the charybdis again;
And, as with the swell of the far thunder-boom,
Rushes foamingly forth from the heart of the gloom.

And it bubbles and seethes, and it hisses and roars,*
　As when fire is with water commix'd and contending,
ﾠnd the spray of its wrath to the welkin up-soars,
　And flood upon flood hurries on, never-ending.
ﾠd it never *will* rest, nor from travail be free,
ﾠke a sea that is labouring the birth of a sea.

ﾠt, at length, comes a lull o'er the mighty commotion,
　As the whirlpool sucks into black smoothness the swell
ﾠ the white-foaming breakers—and cleaves thro' the ocean
　ﾠ path that seems winding in darkness to hell.
ﾠﾠnd and round whirl'd the waves—deeper and deeper
　　still driven,
ﾠﾠe a gorge thro' the mountainous main thunder-riven!

ﾠﾠ youth gave his trust to his Maker! Before
ﾠﾠhat path through the riven abyss closed again—
ﾠﾠk! a shriek from the crowd rang aloft from the shore,
　ﾠnd, behold! he is whirl'd in the grasp of the main!
　o'er him the breakers mysteriously roll'd,
　ﾠ the giant-mouth closed on the swimmer so bold.

ﾠ Und es wallet, und siedet, und brauset, und zischt," &c. Goethe
ﾠﾠ ﾠrticularly struck with the truthfulness of these lines, of which his
ﾠﾠal observation at the Falls of the Rhine enabled him to judge.
ﾠﾠ ﾠr modestly owns his obligations to Homer's descriptions of Charybdis,
ﾠﾠ l. 12. The property of the higher order of imagination to reflect
ﾠﾠﾠ, though not familiar to experience, is singularly illustrated in this
description. Schiller had never seen even a Waterfall.

O'er the surface grim silence lay dark; but the crowd
  Heard the wail from the deep murmur hollow and fell;
They harken and shudder, lamenting aloud—
  "Gallant youth—noble heart—fare-thee-well, fare-thee-
    well!"
More hollow and more wails the deep on the ear—
More dread and more dread grows suspense in its fear.

If thou shouldst in those waters thy diadem fling,
  And cry, " Who may find it shall win it and wear;"
God wot, though the prize were the crown of a king—
  A crown at such hazard were valued too dear.
For never shall lips of the living reveal
What the deeps that howl yonder in terror conceal.

Oh, many a bark, to that breast grappled fast,
  Has gone down to the fearful and fathomless grave;
Again, crash'd together the keel and the mast,
  To be seen, toss'd aloft in the glee of the wave.—
Like the growth of a storm ever louder and clearer,
Grows the roar of the gulf rising nearer and nearer.

And it bubbles and seethes, and it hisses and roars,
  As when fire is with water commix'd and contending;
And the spray of its wrath to the welkin up-soars,
  And flood upon flood hurries on, never ending;
And as with the swell of the far thunder-boom,
Rushes roaringly forth from the heart of the gloom.

And, lo! from the heart of that far-floating gloom,*
  What gleams on the darkness so swanlike and white?
Lo! an arm and a neck, glancing up from the tomb!—
  They battle—the Man's with the Element's might.
It is he—it is he! in his left hand behold,
As a sign—as a joy!—shines the goblet of gold!

And he breathèd deep, and he breathèd long,
  And he greeted the heavenly delight of the day.
They gaze on each other—they shout, as they throng—
  "He lives—lo the ocean has render'd its prey!

* The same rhyme as the preceding line in the original.

And safe from the whirlpool and free from the grave,
Comes back to the daylight the soul of the brave!"

And he comes, with the crowd in their clamour and glee,
    And the goblet his daring has won from the water,
He lifts to the king as he sinks on his knee ;—
    And the king from her maidens has beckon'd h
        daughter—
She pours to the boy the bright wine which they bring,
And thus spake the Diver—"Long life to the king !

"Happy they whom the rose-hues of daylight rejoice,
    The air and the sky that to mortals are given!
May the horror below never more find a voice—
    Nor Man stretch too far the wide mercy of Heaven!
Never more—never more may he lift from the sight
The veil which is woven with Terror and Night !

"Quick-brightening like lightning—it tore me along,
    Down, down, till the gush of a torrent, at play
In the rocks of its wilderness, caught me—and strong
    As the wings of an eagle, it whirl'd me away.
Vain, vain was my struggle—the circle had won me,
Round and round in its dance, the wild element spun me

"And I call'd on my God, and my God heard my prayer
    In the strength of my need, in the gasp of my breath-
And show'd me a crag that rose up from the lair,
    And I clung to it, nimbly—and baffled the death!
And, safe in the perils around me, behold
On the spikes of the coral the goblet of gold.

"Below, at the foot of the precipice drear,
    Spread the gloomy, and purple, and pathless Obscure
A silence of Horror that slept on the ear,
    That the eye more appall'd might the Horror endure !
Salamander—snake—dragon—vast reptiles that dwell
In the deep—coil'd about the grim jaws of their hell.

"Dark-crawl'd—glided dark the unspeakable swarms,
    Clump'd together in masses, misshapen and vast—
Here clung and here bristled the fashionless forms—
    Here the dark-moving bulk of the Hammer-fish pass'd

And with teeth grinning white, and a menacing motion,
Went the terrible Shark—the Hyæna of Ocean.

" There I hung, and the awe gather'd icily o'er me,
    So far from the earth, where man's help there was none!
The One Human Thing, with the Goblins before me—
    Alone—in a loneness so ghastly—ALONE !
Fathom-deep from man's eye in the speechless profound,
With the death of the Main and the Monsters around.

" Methought, as I gazed through the darkness, that now
    IT * saw—the dread hundred-limbed creature—its prey !
And darted—O God! from the far flaming-bough
    Of the coral, I swept on the horrible way;
And it seized me, the wave with its wrath and its roar,
It seized me to save—King, the danger is o'er ! "

On the youth gazed the monarch, and marvell'd ; quoth he,
    " Bold Diver, the goblet I promised is thine,
And this ring will I give, a fresh guerdon to thee,
    Never jewels more precious shone up from the mine ;
If thou'lt bring me fresh tidings, and venture again ;
To say what lies hid in the *innermost* main ? "

Then outspake the daughter in tender emotion :
    " Ah ! father, my father, what more can there rest ?
Enough of this sport with the pitiless ocean—
    He has served thee as none would, thyself has confest.
If nothing can slake thy wild thirst of desire,
Let thy knights put to shame the exploit of the squire ! "

The king seized the goblet—he swung it on high,
    And whirling, it fell in the roar of the tide :
" But bring back that goblet again to my eye,
    And I'll hold thee the dearest that rides by my side ;
And thine arms shall embrace, as thy bride, I decree,
The maiden whose pity now pleadeth for thee."

* " ——da kroch's heran," &c.
The *It* in the original has been greatly admired. The poet thus vaguely
represents the fabulous misshapen monster, the Polypus of the ancients.

In his heart, as he listen'd, there leapt the wild joy—
   And the hope and the love through his eyes spoke in fire,
On that bloom, on that blush, gazed delighted the boy;
   The maiden—she faints at the feet of her sire!
Here the guerdon divine, there the danger beneath ;
He resolves!   To the strife with the life and the death!

They hear the loud surges sweep back in their swell,
   Their coming the thunder-sound heralds along!
Fond eyes * yet are tracking the spot where he fell:
   They come, the wild waters, in tumult and throng,
Roaring up to the cliff—roaring back, as before,
But no wave ever brings the lost youth to the shore.

This ballad is the first composed by Schiller, if we except his early and ruder lay of " Count Eberhard, the Quarreller," which really, however, has more of the true old ballad spirit about it than those grand and artistic tales elaborated by his riper genius and belonging to a school of poetry, to which the ancient Ballad singer certainly never pretended to aspire. . . The old Ballad is but a simple narrative, without any symbolical or interior meaning. . . But in most of the performances to which Schiller has given the name of Ballad, a certain purpose, not to say philosophy, in conception, elevates the Narrative into Dramatic dignity. . . . Rightly, for instance, has " The Diver" been called a Lyrical Tragedy in two Acts—the first act ending with the disappearance of the hero amidst the whirlpool; and the conception of the contest of Man's will with physical Nature, ... together with the darkly hinted moral, not to stretch too far the mercy of Heaven, . . . belong in themselves to the design and the ethics of Tragedy.

There is another peculiarity in the art which Schiller employs upon his narrative poems.—Though he usually enters at once on the interest of his story, and adopts, for the most part, the simple and level style of recital, he selects a subject admitting naturally of some striking picture, upon which he lavishes those resources of description that are only at the command of a great poet; . . . thus elevating the ancient ballad not only into something of the Drama, by conception, but into something of the Epic by execution.—The reader will recognise this peculiarity in the description of the Charybdis and the Abyss in the Ballad he has just concluded—in that of the Storm in " Hero and Leander "—of the Forge and the Catholic Ritual in " Fridolin "—of the Furies in the " Cranes of Ibycus," &c. . . . We have the more drawn the reader's notice to these distinctions between the simple ballad of the ancient minstrels, and the artistical narratives of Schiller—because it seems to us, that our English critics are too much inclined to consider that modern Ballad-writing succeeds or fails in proportion as it seizes merely the spirit of the ancient. . . . But this would but lower genius to an exercise of the same imitative ingenuity which a school-boy or a college prizeman displays upon Latin Lyrics . . . in which the merit consists in the avoidance of originality. The Great Poet cannot be content with only imitating what he studies : And he succeeds really in proportion not

<hr />

* Viz.: the King's Daughter.   Hoffmeister, Sup. iv. 301.

to his fidelity but his innovations ... that is, in proportion as he improves upon what serves him as a model.

In the ballad of "The Diver," Schiller not only sought the simple but the sublime.—According to his own just theory—"The Main Ingredient of Terror is the Unknown." He here seeks to accomplish as a poet what he before perceived as a critic. ... And certainly the picture of his lonely Diver amidst the horrors of the Abyss, dwells upon the memory amongst the sublimest conceptions of modern Poetry.

THE GLOVE.

A TALE.

[The original of this well-known story is in St. Foix—(*Essai sur Paris*) date the reign of Francis I.]

BEFORE his lion-court,
To see the griesly sport,
  Sate the king ;
Beside him group'd his princely peers,
And dames aloft, in circling tiers,
  Wreath'd round their blooming ring.
King Francis, where he sate,
Raised a finger—yawn'd the gate,
And, slow from his repose,
A LION goes !
Dumbly he gazed around
The foe-encircled ground ;
And, with a lazy gape,
He stretch'd his lordly shape,
And shook his careless mane,
And—laid him down again !

  A finger raised the king—
And nimbly have the guard
A second gate unbarr'd ;
  Forth, with a rushing spring,
    A TIGER sprung !
Wildly the wild one yell'd
When the lion he beheld ;
And, bristling at the look,
With his tail his sides he strook,
    And roll'd his rabid tongue ;

In many a wary ring
He swept round the forest king,
  With a fell and rattling sound ;—
  And laid him on the ground,
    Grommelling !
The king raised his finger ; then
Leap'd two LEOPARDS from the den
  With a bound ;
And boldly bounded they
Where the crouching tiger lay
  Terrible !
And he griped the beasts in his deadly hold ;
In the grim embrace they grappled and roll'd ;
  Rose the lion with a roar !
  And stood the strife before ;
  And the wild-cats on the spot,
  From the blood-thirst, wroth and hot,
    Halted still !

Now from the balcony above,
A snowy hand let fall a glove :—
Midway between the beasts of prey,
Lion and tiger ; there it lay,
  The winsome lady's glove !

Fair Cunigonde said, with a lip of scorn,
To the knight DELORGES—" If the love you have sworn
Were as gallant and leal as you boast it to be,
I might ask you to bring back that glove to me ! "

The knight left the place where the lady sate ;
The knight he has pass'd thro' the fearful gate ;
The lion and tiger he stoop'd above,
And his fingers have closed on the lady's glove !

All shuddering and stunn'd, they beheld him there—
The noble knights and the ladies fair ;
But loud was the joy and the praise the while
He bore back the glove with his tranquil smile !

With a tender look in her softening eyes,
That promised reward to his warmest sighs,

Fair Cunigonde rose her knight to grace,
He toss'd the glove in the lady's face!
"Nay, spare me the guerdon, at least," quoth he;
And he left for ever that fair ladye!

THE KNIGHT OF TOGGENBURG.

[In this beautiful ballad, Schiller is but little indebted to the true legend
of Toggenburg, which is nevertheless well adapted to Narrative Poetry.
Ida, wife of Henry Count of Toggenburg, was suspected by her husband of
a guilty attachment to one of his vassals, and ordered to be thrown from a
high wall. Her life, however, was miraculously saved; she lived for some
time as a female hermit in the neighbouring forest, till she was at length
discovered, and her innocence recognised. She refused to live again with
the Lord whose jealousy had wronged her, retired to a convent, and was
acknowledged as a saint after her death. This Legend, if abandoned by
Schiller, has found a German Poet not unworthy of its simple beauty and
pathos. Schiller has rather founded his poem, which sufficiently tells its
own tale, upon a Tyrolese Legend, similar to the one that yet consecrates
Rolandseck and Nonnenwörth on the Rhine. Hoffmeister implies that,
unlike "The Diver," and some other of Schiller's Ballads, "The Knight
of Toggenburg" dispenses with all intellectual and typical meaning, draws
its poetry from feeling, and has no other purpose than that of moving the
heart. Still upon Feeling itself are founded those ideal truths which make
up the true philosophy of a Poet. In these few stanzas are represented the
poetical chivalry of an age—the contest between the earthly passion and
the religious devotion, which constantly agitated human life in the era of
the Crusades. How much of deep thought has been employed to arouse the
feelings—what intimate conviction of the moral of the middle ages, in the
picture of the Knight looking up to the convent—of the Nun bowing calmly
to the vale!]

"KNIGHT, a sister's quiet love
    Gives my heart to thee!
Ask me not for other love,
    For it paineth me!
Calmly could'st thou greet me now,
    Calmly from me go;
Calmly ever,—why dost thou
    Weep in silence, so?"

Sadly—(not a word he said!)—
    To the heart she wrung,
Sadly clasp'd he once the maid,
    On his steed he sprung!
"Up, my men of Swisserland!"
    Up awake the brave!
Forth they go—the Red-Cross band,
    To the Saviour's grave!

High your deeds, and great your fame,
  Heroes of the tomb !
Glancing through the carnage came
  Many a dauntless plume.
Terror of the Moorish foe,
  Toggenburg, thou art !
But thy heart is heavy ! Oh,
  Heavy is thy heart !

Heavy was the load his breast
  For a twelvemonth bore :
Never can his trouble rest !
  And he left the shore.
Lo ! a ship on Joppa's strand,
  Breeze and billow fair,
On to that beloved land,
  Where she breathes the air !

Knocking at her castle-gate
  Was the pilgrim heard ;
Woe the answer from the grate !
  Woe the thunder-word !
"She thou seekest lives—a Nun !
  To the world she died !
When, with yester-morning's sun,
  Heaven received a Bride !"

From that day, his father's hall
  Ne'er his home may be ;
Helm, and hauberk, steed and all,
  Evermore left he !
Where his castle-crownèd height
  Frowns the valley down,
Dwells unknown the hermit-knight,
  In a sackcloth gown.

Rude the hut he built him there,
  Where his eyes may view
Wall and cloister glisten fair
  Dusky lindens through.*

* In this description (though to the best of our recollection, it has escaped the vigilance of his many commentators) Schiller evidently has his

There, when dawn was in the skies,
   Till the eve-star shone,
Sate he with mute wistful eyes,
   Sate he there—alone !

Looking to the cloister, still,
   Looking forth afar,
Looking to her lattice—till
   Clink'd the lattice-bar.
Till—a passing glimpse allow'd—
   Paused her image pale,
Calm and angel-mild, and bow'd
   Meekly tow'rds the vale.

Then the watch of day was o'er,
   Then, consoled awhile,
Down he lay, to greet once more,
   Morning's early smile.
Days and years are gone, and still
   Looks he forth afar,
Uncomplaining, hoping—till
   Clinks the lattice-bar :

Till,—a passing glimpse allow'd,—
   Paused her image pale,
Calm, and angel-mild, and bow'd
   Meekly tow'rds the vale.
So, upon that lonely spot,
   Sate he, dead at last,
With the look where life was not
   Tow'rds the casement cast !

eye and his mind upon the scene of his early childhood at Lorch, a scene to
which in later life he was fondly attached.

   The village of Lorch lies at the foot of a hill crowned with a convent,
before the walls of which springs an old linden or lime tree. The ruined
castle of Hohenstaufen is in the immediate neighbourhood.

THE MEETING.

[This poem and the two that immediately follow, appear to have been inspired by Charlotte von Lengefeld, whom Schiller afterwards married.]

I.

I SEE her still, with many a fair one nigh,
  Of every fair the stateliest shape appear:
Like a lone sun she shone upon my eye—
  I stood afar, and durst not venture near.
Seized, as her presence brighten'd round me, by
  The trembling passion of voluptuous fear,
Yet, swift, as borne upon some hurrying wing,
The impulse snatch'd me, and I struck the string!

II.

What then I felt—what sung—my memory hence
  From that wild moment would in vain invoke—
It was the life of some discover'd sense
  That in the heart's divine emotion spoke;
Long years imprison'd, and escaping thence
  From every chain, the SOUL enchanted broke,
And found a music in its own deep core,
Its holiest, deepest deep, unguess'd before.

III.

Like melody long hush'd, and lost in space,
  Back to its home the breathing spirit came:
I look'd, and saw upon that angel face
  The fair love circled with the modest shame;
I heard (and heaven descended on the place)
  Low-whisper'd words a charmèd truth proclaim—
Save in thy choral hymns, O spirit-shore,
Ne'er may I hear such thrilling sweetness more!

IV.

"I know the worth within the heart which sighs,
  Yet shuns, the modest sorrow to declare;
And what rude Fortune niggardly denies,
  Love to the noble can with love repair.
The lowly have the birthright of the skies;
  Love only culls the flower that love should wear;

And ne'er in vain for love's rich gifts shall yearn
The heart that feels their wealth—and can return!"*

THE ASSIGNATION.

[NOTE.—In Schiller the eight long lines that conclude each stanza of
this charming love-poem, instead of rhyming alternately, as in the translation, chime somewhat to the tune of Byron's *Don Juan*—six lines rhyming
with each other, and the two last forming a separate couplet. In other
respects the translation, it is hoped, is sufficiently close and literal.]

I.

HEAR I the creaking gate unclose ?
    The gleaming latch uplifted ?
No—'twas the wind that, whirring, rose,
    Amidst the poplars drifted !

Adorn thyself, thou green leaf-bowering roof,
    Destined the Bright One's presence to receive,
For her, a shadowy palace-hall aloof
    With holy Night, thy boughs familiar weave.
And ye sweet flatteries of the delicate air,
    Awake and sport her rosy cheek around,
When their light weight the tender feet shall bear,
    When Beauty comes to Passion's trysting-ground.

II.

Hush ! what amidst the copses crept—
    So swiftly by me now ?
No—'twas the startled bird that swept
    The light leaves of the bough !

Day, quench thy torch ! come, ghost-like, from on high,
    With thy loved Silence, come, thou haunting Eve,
Broaden below thy web of purple dye,
    Which lullèd boughs mysterious round us weave.
For love's delight, enduring listeners none,
    The froward witness of the light will flee ;
Hesper alone, the rosy Silent One,
    Down-glancing may our sweet Familiar be !

* This is the only one of Schiller's poems that reminds us of the Italian
poets.—It has in it something of the sweet mannerism of Petrarch.

III.

What murmur in the distance spoke,
  And like a whisper died?
No!—'twas the swan that gently broke
  In rings the silver tide!

Soft to my ear there comes a music-flow;
  In gleesome murmur glides the waterfall;
To Zephyr's kiss the flowers are bending low;
  Through life goes joy, exchanging joy with all.
Tempt to the touch the grapes—the blushing fruit,*
  Voluptuous swelling from the leaves that hide;
And, drinking fever from my cheek, the mute
  Air sleeps all liquid in the Odour-Tide!

IV.

Hark! through the alley hear I now
  A footfall?   Comes the maiden?
No,—'twas the fruit slid from the bough,
  With its own richness laden!

Day's lustrous eyes grow heavy in sweet death,
  And pale and paler wane his jocund hues,
The flowers too gentle for his glowing breath,
  Ope their frank beauty to the twilight dews.
The bright face of the moon is still and lone,
  Melts in vast masses the world silently;
Slides from each charm the slowly-loosening zone;
  And round all beauty, veilless, roves the eye.

V.

What yonder seems to glimmer?
  Her white robe's glancing hues?—
No,—'twas the column's shimmer
  Athwart the darksome yews!

O, longing heart, no more delight-upbuoy'd
  Let the sweet airy image thee befool!
The arms that would embrace her clasp the void:
  This feverish breast no phantom-bliss can cool.

* The Peach.

O, waft her here, the *true*, the *living* one !
  Let but my hand *her* hand, the tender, feel—
The very shadow of her robe alone !—
  So into life the idle dream shall steal !

*   *   *   *   *

As glide from heaven, when least we ween,
  The rosy hours of bliss,
All gently came the maid, unseen :—
  He waked beneath her kiss !

THE SECRET.

And not a word by her was spoken ;
  For many a listener's ear was by,
But sweetly was the silence broken,
  For eye could well interpret eye.
Soft to thy hush'd pavilion stealing,
  Thou fair, far-spreading Beech, I glide,
Thy favouring veil our forms concealing,
  And all the garish world denied.

From far, with dull, unquiet clamour,
  Labours the vex'd and busy day,
And, through the hum, the sullen hammer
  Comes heaving down its heavy way.
Thus man pursues his weary calling,
  And wrings the hard life from the sky.
While happiness unseen is falling
  Down from God's bosom silently.

O, all unheard be still the lonely
  Delights in our true love embrac'd.
The hearts that never loved can only
  'Disturb the well they shun to taste.
The world but searches to destroy her,
  The Bliss conceal'd from vulgar eyes—
In secret seize, in stealth enjoy her,
  Ere watchful Envy can surprise.

Soft, upon tiptoe, comes she greeting,
  Thro' silent night she loves to stray,
A nymph, that fades to air, if meeting
  One gaze her mysteries to betray.
Roll round us, roll, thou softest river,*
  Thy broad'ning stream, a barrier given,
And guard with threat'ning waves for ever
  This one last Heritage of Heaven!

TO EMMA.

I.

AMIDST the cloud-grey deeps afar
  The Bliss departed lies;
How linger on one lonely star
  The loving wistful eyes!
Alas—a star in truth—the light
Shines but a signal of the night!

II.

If lock'd within the icy chill
  Of the long sleep, thou wert—
My faithful grief could find thee still
  A life within my heart;—
But, oh, the worse despair to see
Thee live to earth, and die to me!

III.

Can those sweet longing hopes, which make
  Love's essence, thus decay?
Can that be love which doth forsake?—
  That love—which fades away?
That earthly gifts are brief, I knew—
Is that all heaven-born mortal too?

* Probably the river Saale, on the banks of which Schiller was accustomed to meet his Charlotte.

THE POET TO HIS FRIENDS.

(WRITTEN AT WEIMAR.)

I.

FRIENDS, fairer times have been
(Who can deny?) than we ourselves have seen;
And an old race of more majestic worth.
Were History silent on the Past, in sooth,
A thousand stones would witness of the truth
   Which men disbury from the womb of earth.
But yet that race, if more endowed than ours
   Is past!—no joy to death can glory give;
But we—we *are*—to us the breathing hours,
   They have the best—who live!

II.

Suns are of happier ray
Than where, not ill, we while our life away,
If the far-wandering traveller speaks aright;
   But much which Nature hath to us denied
   Hath not kind Art, the genial friend, supplied,
And our hearts warm'd beneath her mother-light!
Tho' native not beneath our winters keen,
   Or bays or myrtle—for our mountain shrines
And hardy brows, their lusty garlands green
   Weave the thick-clustering vines.

III.

Well may proud hearts take pleasure
Where change four worlds their intermingled treasure,
And Trade's great pomp the wanderer may behold,
   Where, on rich Thames, a thousand sails unfurl'd
   Or seek or leave the market of the world—
And throned in splendour sits the Earth-god,—GOLD.
But never, in the mire of troubled streams,
   Swell'd by wild torrents from the mountain's breast,
But on the still wave's mirror, the soft beams
   Of happy sunshine rest.*

* These lines afford one of the many instances of the peculiar tenacity with which Schiller retained certain favourite ideas. At the age of

Prouder and more elate
Than we o' the North, beside the Angel's Gate *
The beggar basking views eternal Rome!
   Round to his gaze bright-swarming beauties given,
    And, holy in the heaven, a second heaven,
The world's large wonder, hangs St. Peter's Dome.
But Rome in all her glory is a grave,
The Past, that ghost of power, alone is hers,
Strew'd by the green Hours, where the young leaves wave
  · Breathes all the life that stirs!

Elsewhere are nobler things
Than to our souls our scant existence brings :
The *New* beneath the sun hath never been.
   Yet still the greatness of each elder age
    We see—the conscious phantoms of the stage—
As the world finds its symbol on the scene.†
Life but repeats itself, all stale and worn;
   Sweet Phantasy alone is young for ever;
What ne'er and nowhere on the earth was born ‡
   Alone grows aged never.

EVENING.

(FROM A PICTURE.)

SINK, shining god—tired Nature halts; and parch'd
Earth needs the dews; adown the welkin arch'd
    Falter thy languid steeds;—
    Sink in thy ocean halls!
Who beckons from the crystal waves unto thee?
Knows not thy heart the smiles of love that woo thee?
    Quicken the homeward steeds!
    The silver Thetis calls!

seventeen he had said, "Not on the stormy sea, but on the calm and glassy stream, does the sun reflect itself."—See Hoffmeister, Part iv., p. 39.

  * St. Peter's Church.

  † The signification of these lines in the original has been disputed—we accept Hoffmeister's interpretation.—Part vi., p. 40.

  ‡ " The light that never was on sea or land,
    The Consecration and the Poet's Dream."—WORDSWORTH.

Swift to her arms he springs, and, with the bridle
Young Eros toys—the gladdening steeds (as idle
        The guideless chariot rests)
    The cool wave bend above ;
And Night, with gentle step and melancholy,
Breathes low through heaven ; with her comes Love the
    holy—
        Phœbus the lover rests,—
        Be all life, rest and love !

THE LONGING.

From out this dim and gloomy hollow,
    Where hang the cold clouds heavily,
Could I but gain the clue to follow,
    How blessed would the journey be !
Aloft I see a fair dominion,
    Through time and change all vernal still ;
But where the power, and what the pinion,
    To gain the ever-blooming hill ?

Afar I hear the music ringing—
    The lulling sounds of heaven's repose,
And the light gales are downward bringing
    The sweets of flowers the mountain knows.
I see the fruits, all golden-glowing,
    Beckon the glossy leaves between,
And o'er the blooms that there are blowing
    Nor blight nor winter's wrath hath been.

To suns that shine for ever, yonder,
    O'er fields that fade not, sweet to flee :
The very winds that there may wander,
    How healing must their breathing be !
But lo, between us rolls a river—
    O'er which the wrathful tempest raves ;
I feel the soul within me shiver
    To gaze upon the gloomy waves.

A rocking boat mine eyes discover,
  But, woe is me, the pilot fails !—
In, boldly in—undaunted over !
  And trust the life that swells the sails !
Thou must *believe*, and thou must *venture*,
  In fearless faith thy safety dwells ;
 * By miracles alone men enter
  The glorious Land of Miracles !

THE PILGRIM.

YOUTH's gay spring-time scarcely knowing
  Went I forth the world to roam—
And the dance of youth, the glowing,
  Left I in my Father's home.
Of my birthright, glad-believing,
  Of my world-gear took I none,
Careless as an infant, cleaving
  To my pilgrim staff alone.
For I placed my mighty hope in
  Dim and holy words of Faith,
" Wander forth—the way is open
  Ever on the upward path—
Till thou gain the Golden Portal,
  Till its gates unclose to thee.
There the Earthly and the Mortal,
  Deathless and Divine shall be ! "
Night on Morning stole, on stealeth,
  Never, never stand I still,
And the Future yet concealeth,
  What I seek, and what I will !
Mount on mount arose before me,
  Torrents hemm'd me every side,
But I built a bridge that bore me
  O'er the roaring tempest-tide.
Towards the East I reach'd a river,
  On its shores I did not rest ;
Faith from Danger can deliver,
  And I trusted to its breast.

---

* " Wo kein Wunder geschicht, ist kein Beglückter zu sehn."
                  SCHILLER, *Das Glück*.

·Drifted in the whirling motion,
    Seas themselves around me roll—
Wide and wider spreads the ocean,
    Far and farther flies the goal.
While I live is never given
    Bridge or wave the goal to near—
Earth will never meet the Heaven,
    Never can the THERE be HERE !

The two poems of "The Longing" and "The Pilgrim" belong to a class which may be said to allegorise *Feeling*, and the meaning, agreeably to the genius of allegory or parable, has been left somewhat obscure. The commentators agree in referring both poems to the illustration of the *Ideal*. "The Longing" represents the desire to escape from the real world into the higher realms of being. "The Pilgrim" represents the active labour of the idealist to reach "the Golden Gate." The belief in what is beyond Reality is necessary to all who would escape from the Real; and in "The Longing" it is intimated that that belief may attain the end. But "The Pilgrim," after all his travail, finds that the earth will never reach the heaven, and the *There* never can be *Here*. The two poems are certainly capable of an interpretation at once loftier and more familiar than that which the commentators give to it. They are apparently intended to express the natural human feeling—common not to poets alone, but to us all —the human feeling which approaches to an instinct, and in which so many philosophers have recognised the inward assurance of a hereafter, viz., the desire to escape from the coldness and confinement, "the valley and the cloud" of actual life, into the happier world which smiles, in truth, evermore upon those who *believe* that it exists : the desire of the poet is identical with the desire of the religious man. He who longs for another world— only to be attained by abstraction from the low desires of this—longs for what the Christian strives for. And if he finds, with Schiller's Pilgrim, that in spite of all his longing and all his labour, the goal cannot be reached below, still, as Schiller expresses it elsewhere, "He has had *Hope*—his belief has been his reward." That Heaven which "The Longing" yearns for, which "The Pilgrim" seeks, may be called "The Ideal," or whatever else refiners please; but, in plain fact and in plain words, that Ideal is the Hereafter—is Heaven!

THE DANCE.

SEE how like lightest waves at play, the airy dancers fleet ;
And scarcely feels the floor the wings of those harmonious feet.
Oh, are they flying shadows from their native forms set free ?
Or phantoms in the fairy ring that summer moonbeams see ?

As, by the gentle zephyr blown, some light mist flees in
 air,
As skiffs that skim adown the tide, when silver waves are
 fair,
So sports the docile footstep to the heave of that sweet
 measure,
As music wafts the form aloft at its melodious pleasure,
Now breaking through the woven chain of the entangled
 dance,
From where the ranks the thickest press, a bolder pair
 advance,
The path they leave behind them lost—wide opes the path
 beyond,
The way unfolds or closes up as by a magic wand.
See now, they vanish from the gaze in wild confusion
 blended;
Ah, in sweet chaos whirl'd again, that gentle world is
 ended!
No!—disentangled glides the knot, the gay disorder
 ranges—
The only system ruling here, a grace that ever changes.
For aye destroy'd—for aye renew'd, whirls on that fair
 creation;
And yet one peaceful law can still pervade in each mu-
 tation.
And what can to the reeling maze breathe harmony and
 vigour,
And give an order and repose to every gliding figure?
That each a ruler to himself doth but himself obey,
Yet through the hurrying course still keeps his own ap-
 pointed way.
What, would'st thou know? It is in truth the mighty
 power of Tune,
A power that every step obeys, as tides obey the moon;
That threadeth with a golden clue the intricate employ-
 ment,
Curbs bounding strength to tranquil grace, and tames the
 wild enjoyment.
And comes THE WORLD'S wide harmony in vain upon thine
 ears?
The stream of music borne aloft from yonder choral
 spheres?

And feel'st thou not the measure which Eternal Nature
    keeps ?
The whirling Dance for ever held in yonder azure deeps ?
The suns that wheel in varying maze ?—*That* music thou
    discernest ?
No ! Thou canst honour that in sport which thou for-
    gett'st in earnest.

NOTE.—This poem is very characteristic of the noble ease with which
Schiller often loves to surprise the reader, by the sudden introduction of
matter for the loftiest reflection, in the midst of the most familiar subjects.
What can be more accurate and happy than the poet's description of the
national dance, as if such description were his only object—the outpouring,
as it were, of a young gallant, intoxicated by the music, and dizzy with the
waltz ? Suddenly and imperceptibly the reader finds himself elevated from
a trivial scene. He is borne upward to the harmony of the spheres. He
bows before the great law of the universe—the young gallant is transformed
into the mighty teacher ; and this without one hard conceit—without one
touch of pedantry. It is but a flash of light ; and where glowed the playful
picture, shines the solemn moral.

THE SHARING OF THE EARTH.

" TAKE the world," cried the God from his heaven
    To men—" I proclaim you its heirs ;
To divide it amongst you 'tis given,
    You have only to settle the shares."

Each takes for himself as it pleases,
    Old and young have alike their desire ;
The Harvest the Husbandman seizes,
    Throrgh the wood and the chase sweeps the Squire.

The Merchant his warehouse is locking—
    The Abbot is choosing his wine—
Cries the Monarch, the thoroughfares blocking,
    " Every toll for the passage is mine ! "

All too late, when the sharing was over,
    Comes the Poet—He came from afar—
Nothing left can the laggard discover,
    Not an inch but its owners there are.

" Woe is me, is there nothing remaining,
    For the son who best loves thee alone ! "
Thus to Jove went his voice in complaining,
    As he fell at the Thunderer's throne.

"In the land of the dreams if abiding,"
    Quoth the God—"Canst thou murmur at ME?
Where wert *thou*, when the Earth was dividing?"
    "I WAS," said the Poet, "BY THEE!"

"Mine eye by thy glory was captur'd—
    Mine ear by thy music of bliss,
Pardon him whom *thy* world so enraptur'd—
    As to lose him his portion in this!"

"Alas," said the God—"Earth is given!
    Field, forest, and market, and all!—
What say you to quarters in Heaven?
    We'll admit you whenever you call!"

THE INDIAN DEATH-DIRGE.

[The idea of this Poem is taken from Carver's Travels through North
America. Goethe reckoned it amongst Schiller's best poems of the kind,
and wished he had made a dozen such. But, precisely because Goethe
admired it for its *objectivity*, William von Humboldt, found it wanting in
ideality. See Hoffmeister, pp. 3, 311.]

SEE on his mat—as if of yore,
    All life-like, sits he here!
With that same aspect which he wore
    When light to him was dear.
But where the right hand's strength?—and where
    The breath that loved to breathe,
To the Great Spirit aloft in air,
    The peace-pipe's lusty wreath?
And where the hawk-like eye, alas!
    That wont the deer pursue,
Along the waves of rippling grass,
    Or fields that shone with dew?
Are these the limber, bounding feet,
    That swept the winter snows?
What stateliest stag so fast and fleet?
    Their speed outstript the roe's!
These arms that then the sturdy bow
    Could supple from its pride,
How stark and helpless hang they now
    Adown the stiffen'd side!

Yet weal to him—at peace he strays
    Where never fall the snows ;
Where o'er the meadows springs the maize
    That mortal never sows :
Where birds are blithe on every brake—
    Where forests teem with deer—
Where glide the fish through every lake—
    One chase from year to year !
With spirits now he feasts above ;
    All left us—to revere
The deeds we honour with our love,
    The dust we bury here.
Here bring the last gifts !—loud and shrill
    Wail, death-dirge for the brave !
What pleased him most in life may still
    Give pleasure in the grave.
We lay the axe beneath his head
    He swung, when strength was strong—
The bear on which his banquets fed—
    The way from earth is long !
And here, new-sharpen'd, place the knife
    That sever'd from the clay,
From which the axe had spoil'd the life,
    The conquer'd scalp away !
The paints that deck the Dead, bestow—
    Yes, place them in his hand—
That red the Kingly Shade may glow
    Amidst the Spirit-Land !

THE LAY OF THE MOUNTAIN.

[The scenery of Gotthardt is here personified.]
The three following ballads, in which Switzerland is the scene, betray
their origin in Schiller's studies for the drama of William Tell.

To the solemn abyss leads the terrible path,
    The life and the death winding dizzy between ;
In thy desolate way, grim with menace and wrath,
    To daunt thee the spectres of giants are seen ;
That thou wake not the Wild One,* all silently tread—
Let thy lip breathe no breath in the pathway of Dread !

* The avalanche--the *équivoque* of the original, turning on the Swiss

High over the marge of the horrible deep
  Hangs and hovers a Bridge with its phantom-like span,*
Not by man was it built, o'er the vastness to sweep;
  Such thought never came to the daring of Man!
The stream roars beneath—late and early it raves—
But the bridge which it threatens, is safe from the
    waves.

Black-yawning a Portal, thy soul to affright,
  Like the gate to the kingdom, the Fiend for the king—
Yet beyond it there smiles but a land of delight,
  Where the Autumn in marriage is met with the
    Spring.
From a lot which the care and the trouble assail,
Could I fly to the bliss of that balm-breathing vale!

Through that field, from a fount ever hidden their birth,
  Four Rivers in tumult rush roaringly forth;
They fly to the fourfold divisions of earth—
  The sunrise, the sunset, the south, and the north.
And, true to the mystical mother that bore,
Forth they rush to their goal, and are lost evermore.

High over the races of men in the blue
  Of the ether, the Mount in twin summits is riven;
There, veil'd in the gold-woven webs of the dew,
  Moves the Dance of the Clouds—the pale Daughters of
    Heaven!
There, in solitude circles their mystical maze,
Where no witness can hearken, no earthborn surveys.

August on a throne which no ages can move,
  Sits a Queen, in her beauty serene and sublime,†
The diadem blazing with diamonds above
  The glory of brows, never darken'd by time,

word *Lawine*, it is impossible to render intelligible to the English reader.
The giants in the preceding line are the rocks that overhang the pass which
winds now to the right, now to the left, of a roaring stream.
  * The Devil's Bridge. The Land of Delight (called in Tell "a serene
valley of joy") to which the dreary portal (in Tell the black rock gate) leads,
is the Urse Vale. The four rivers, in the next stanza, are the Reus, the
Rhine, the Tessin, and the Rhône.
  † The everlasting glacier. See William Tell, act v. scene 2.

His arrows of light on that form shoots the sun—
And he gilds them with all, but he warms them with
   none !

THE ALP HUNTER.

[Founded on a legend of the Valley of Ormond, in the Pays de Vaud.]

" WILT thou not, thy lamblings heeding,
   (Soft and innocent are they !)
Watch them on the herbage feeding,
   Or beside the brooklet play ? "
" Mother, mother, let me go,
   O'er the mount to chase the roe."

" Wilt thou not, around thee bringing,
   Lure the herds with lively horn ?—
Gaily go the clear bells ringing,
   Through the echoing forest borne ! "
" Mother, mother, let me go,
   O'er the wilds to chase the roe."

" Wilt thou not (their blushes woo thee !)
   In their sweet beds tend thy flowers ;
Smiles so fair a garden to thee,
   Where the savage mountain lours ? "
" Leave the flowers in peace to blow ;
Mother, mother, let me go ! "

On and ever onwards bounding,
   Scours the hunter to the chase,
On and ever onwards hounding
   To the mountain's wildest space.—
Swift, as footed by the wind,
Flies before the trembling hind.

Light and limber, upwards driven,
   On the hoar crag quivering,
Or through gorges thunder-riven
   Leaps she with her airy spring !
But behind her still the Foe—
Near, and near the deadly bow !

Fast and faster on—unslack'ning;
　Now she hangs above the brink,
Where the last rocks, grim and black'ning,
　Down the gulf abruptly sink.
Never pathway there may wind,
Chasms below—and death behind!

To the hard man—dumb-lamenting,
　Turns she with her look of woe;
Turns in vain—the Unrelenting
　Meets the look—and bends the bow.—
Sudden—from the darksome deep,
Rose the Spirit of the Steep!—

And his godlike hand extending,
　From the hunter snatch'd the prey,
"Wherefore, woe and slaughter sending,
　To my solitary sway?—
Why should my herds before thee fall?—
THERE'S ROOM UPON THE EARTH FOR ALL!"

RUDOLF OF HAPSBURG.

A BALLAD.

[Hinrichs properly classes this striking ballad (together with the yet grander one of the "Fight with the Dragon") amongst those designed to depict and exalt the virtue of Humility. The source of the story is in Ægidius Tschudi, a Swiss chronicler; and Schiller appears to have adhered, with much fidelity, to the original narrative.]

At Aachen, in imperial state,
　In that time-hallow'd hall renown'd,
At solemn feast King Rudolf sate,
　The day that saw the hero crown'd!
Bohemia and thy Palgrave, Rhine,
Give this the feast, and that the wine;*

* The office, at the coronation feast, of the Count Palatine of the Rhine (Grand Sewer of the Empire and one of the Seven Electors) was to bear the Imperial Globe and set the dishes on the board; that of the King of Bohemia was cup-bearer. The latter was not, however, present, as Schiller himself observed in a note (omitted in the editions of his collected works), at the coronation of Rudolf.

The Arch Electoral Seven,
Like choral stars around the sun,
Gird him whose hand a world has won,
    The anointed choice of Heaven.

In galleries raised above the pomp,
    Press'd crowd on crowd their panting way;
And with the joy-resounding tromp,
    Rang out the million's loud hurra!
For closed at last the age of slaughter,
When human blood was pour'd as water—
    LAW dawns upon the world! *
Sharp force no more shall right the wrong,
And grind the weak to crown the strong—
    War's carnage-flag is furl'd!

In Rudolf's hand the goblet shines—
    And gaily round the board look'd he;
" And proud the feast, and bright the wines
    My kingly heart feels glad to me!
Yet where the Gladness-Bringer—blest
In the sweet art which moves the breast
    With lyre and verse divine?
Dear from my youth the craft of song,
And what as knight I loved so long,
    As Kaisar, still be mine."

Lo, from the circle bending there,
    With sweeping robe the Bard appears,
As silver white his gleaming hair,
    Bleach'd by the many winds of years;
" And music sleeps in golden strings—
Love's rich reward the minstrel sings,
    Well known to him the ALL
High thoughts and ardent souls desire!
What would the Kaisar from the lyre
    Amidst the banquet-hall?"

---

* Literally,." *A judge* (*ein Richter*) was again upon the earth." The
word substituted in the translation is introduced in order to recall to the
reader the sublime name given, not without justice, to Rudolf of Hapsburg,
viz., "THE LIVING LAW."

The Great One smiled—"Not mine the sway—
 The minstrel owns a loftier power—
A mightier king inspires the lay—
 Its host—THE IMPULSE OF THE HOUR!"
As through wide air the tempests sweep,
As gush the springs from mystic deep,
 Or lone untrodden glen;
So from dark hidden fount within,
Comes SONG, its own wild world to win
 Amidst the souls of men!"

Swift with the fire the minstrel glow'd,
 And loud the music swept the ear:—
"Forth to the chase a Hero rode,
 To hunt the bounding chamois-deer;
With shaft and horn the squire behind;—
Through greensward meads the riders wind—
 A small sweet bell they hear.
Lo, with the HOST, a holy man,—
Before him strides the sacristan,
 And the bell sounds near and near.

"The noble hunter down-inclined
 His reverent head and soften'd eye,
And honour'd with a Christian's mind
 The Christ who loves humility!
Loud through the pasture, brawls and raves
A brook—the rains had fed the waves,
 And torrents from the hill.
His sandal shoon the priest unbound,
And laid the Host upon the ground,
 And near'd the swollen rill!

"'What wouldst thou, priest?' the Count began,
 As, marvelling much, he halted there;
'Sir Count, I seek a dying man,
 Sore-hungering for the heavenly fare.
The bridge that once its safety gave,
Rent by the anger of the wave,
 Drifts down the tide below.
Yet barefoot now, I will not fear
(The soul that seeks its God, to cheer)
 Through the wild wave to go!'

" He gave that priest the knightly steed,
 He reach'd that priest the lordly reins,
That he might serve the sick man's need,
 Nor slight the task that heaven ordains.
He took the horse the squire bestrode;
On to the chase the hunter rode,
 On to the sick the priest!
And when the morrow's sun was red,
The servant of the Saviour led
 Back to its lord the beast.

"'Now Heaven forfend!' the Hero cried,
 'That e'er to chase or battle more
These limbs the sacred steed bestride
 That once my Maker's image bore;
If not a boon allow'd to thee,
Thy Lord and mine its Master be,
 My tribute to the King,
From whom I hold, as fiefs, since birth,
Honour, renown, the goods of earth,
 Life and each living thing!'

"'So may the God, who faileth never
 To hear the weak and guide the dim,
To thee give honour here and ever,
 As thou hast duly honour'd Him!
Far-famed ev'n now through Swisserland,
Thy generous heart and dauntless hand;
 And fair from thine embrace,
Six daughters bloom,* six crowns to bring,
Blest as the daughters of a KING,
 The mothers of a RACE!"

The mighty Kaisar heard amazed!
 His heart was in the days of old;
Into the minstrel's heart he gazed,
 That tale the Kaisar's own had told.

---

* At the coronation of Rudolf was celebrated the marriage-feast of three of his daughters—to Ludwig of Bavaria, Otto of Brandenburg, and Albrecht of Saxony. His other three daughters married afterwards Otto, nephew of Ludwig of Bavaria, Charles Martell, son of Charles of Anjou, and Wenceslaus, son of Ottocar of Bohemia. The royal house of England numbers Rudolf of Hapsburg amongst its ancestors.

Yes, in the bard the priest he knew,
And in the purple veil'd from view
 The gush of holy tears !
A thrill through that vast audience ran,
And every heart the godlike man
 Revering God—reveres !

THE FIGHT WITH THE DRAGON.

WHO comes ?—why rushes fast and loud,
Through lane and street the hurtling crowd,
Is Rhodes on fire ?—Hurrah !—along
Faster and fast storms the throng !
High towers a shape in knightly garb—
Behold the Rider and the Barb !
Behind is dragg'd a wondrous load ;
Beneath what monster groans the road ?
The horrid jaws—the Crocodile,
 The shape the mightier Dragon, shows—
From Man to Monster all the while—
 The alternate wonder glancing goes.

Shout thousands, with a single voice,
" Behold the Dragon, and rejoice,
Safe roves the herd, and safe the swain !
Lo !—there the Slayer—here the Slain !
Full many a breast, a gallant life,
Has waged against the ghastly strife,
And ne'er return'd to mortal sight—
Hurrah, then, for the Hero Knight ! "
So to the Cloister, where the vow'd
 And peerless brethren of St. John
In conclave sit—that sea-like crowd,
 Wave upon wave, goes thundering on.

High o'er the rest, the chief is seen—
There wends the Knight with modest mien ;
Pours through the galleries raised for all
Above that Hero-council Hall,
The crowd—And thus the Victor One :—
" Prince—the knight's duty I have done.

The Dragon that devour'd the land
Lies slain beneath thy servant's hand ;
Free, o'er the pasture, rove the flocks—
  And free the idler's steps may stray—
And freely o'er the lonely rocks,
  The holier pilgrim wends his way ! "

A lofty look the Master gave :
" Certes," he said, " thy deed is brave ;
Dread was the danger, dread the fight—
Bold deeds bring fame to vulgar knight ;
But say, what sways with holier laws
The knight who sees in Christ his cause,
And wears his cross ? "—Then every cheek
Grew pale to hear the Master speak ;
But nobler was the blush that spread
  His face—the Victor's of the day—
As bending lowly—" Prince," he said ;
  " His noblest duty—TO OBEY ! "

" And yet that duty, son," replied
The chief " methinks thou hast denied
And dared thy sacred sword to wield,
For fame in a forbidden field."
" Master, thy judgment, howso'er
It lean, till all is told, forbear—
Thy law, in spirit and in will,
I had no thought but to fulfil,
Not rash, as some, did I depart
  A Christian's blood in vain to shed ;
But hoped by skill, and strove by art,
  To make my life avenge the dead.

" Five of our Order, in renown
The war-gems of our saintly crown,
The martyr's glory bought with life ;
'Twas then thy law forbade the strife.
Yet in my heart there gnaw'd, like fire,
Proud sorrow, fed with stern desire :
In the still visions of the night,
Panting I fought the fancied fight ;

And when the morrow glimmering came,
   With tales of ravage freshly done,
The dream remember'd, turn'd to shame,
   That night should dare what day should shun.

"And thus my fiery musings ran—
'What youth has learn'd should nerve the man;
How lived the great in days of old,
Whose fame to time by bards is told—
Who, heathens though they were, became
As gods—upborne to heaven by fame?
How proved they best the hero's worth?
They chased the monster from the earth—
They sought the lion in his den—
   They pierced the Cretan's deadly maze—
Their noble blood gave humble men
   Their happy birthright—peaceful days.

"'What! sacred, but against the horde
Of Mahound, is the Christian's sword?
All strife, save one, should he forbear?
No! earth itself the Christian's care.—
From every ill and every harm,
Man's shield should be the Christian's arm.
Yet art o'er strength will oft prevail,
And mind must aid where heart may fail!'
Thus musing, oft I roam'd alone,
   Where wont the Hell-born Beast to lie;
Till sudden light upon me shone,
   And on my hope broke victory!

"Then, Prince, I sought thee with the prayer
To breathe once more my native air;
The license given—the ocean past—
I reach'd the shores of home at last.
Scarce hail'd the old beloved land,
Than huge, beneath the artist's hand,
To every hideous feature true,
The Dragon's monster-model grew,
The dwarf'd, deform'd limbs upbore
   The lengthen'd body's ponderous load;
The scales the impervious surface wore,
   Like links of burnish'd harness, glow'd.

" Life-like, the huge neck seem'd to swell,
And widely, as some porch to hell,
You might the horrent jaws survey,
Griesly, and greeding for their prey.
Grim fangs and added terror gave,
Like crags that whiten through a cave.
The very tongue a sword in seeming—
The deep-sunk eyes in sparkles gleaming.
Where the vast body ends, succeed
   The serpent spires around it roll'd—
Woe—woe to rider, woe to steed,
   Whom coils as fearful o'er enfold!

" All to the awful life was done—
The very hue, so ghastly, won—
The grey, dull tint :—the labour ceased,
It stood—half reptile and half beast!
And now began the mimic chase ;
Two dogs I sought, of noblest race,
Fierce, nimble, fleet, and wont to scorn
The wild bull's wrath and levell'd horn ;
These, docile to my cheering cry,
   I train'd to bound, and rend, and spring,
Now round the Monster-shape to fly,
   Now to the Monster-shape to cling!

" And where their gripe the best assails,
The belly left unsheath'd in scales,
I taught the dexterous hounds to hang
And find the spot to fix the fang ;
Whilst I, with lance and mailèd garb,
Launch'd on the beast mine Arab barb.
From purest race that Arab came,
And steeds, like men, are fired by fame.
Beneath the spur he chafes to rage ;
   Onwards we ride in full career—
I seem, in truth, the war to wage—
   The monster reels beneath my spear !

" Albeit, when first the *destrier* * eyed
The laidly thing, it swerved aside,

       * War-horse.

Snorted and rear'd—and even they,
The fierce hounds, shrank with startled bay;
I ceased not, till by custom bold,
After three tedious moons were told,
Both barb and hounds were train'd—nay, more,
Fierce for the fight—then left the shore !
Three days have fleeted since I prest
    (Return'd at length) this welcome soil,
Nor once would lay my limbs to rest,
    Till wrought the glorious crowning toil.

"For much it moved my soul to know
The unslack'ning curse of that grim foe.
Fresh rent, men's bones lay bleach'd and bare
Around the hell-worm's swampy lair;
And pity nerved me into steel :—
Advice ?—I had a heart to feel,
And strength to dare !   So, to the deed.—
I call'd my squires—bestrode my steed,
And with my stalwart hounds, and by
    Lone secret paths, we gaily go
Unseen—at least by human eye—
    Against a worse than human foe !

"Thou know'st the sharp rock—steep and hoar ?—
The abyss ?—the chapel glimmering o'er ?
Built by the Fearless Master's hand,
The fane looks down on all the land.
Humble and mean that house of prayer—
Yet God hath shrined a wonder there :—
Mother and Child, to whom of old
The Three Kings knelt with gifts, behold !
By three times thirty steps, the shrine
    The pilgrim gains—and faint, and dim,
And dizzy with the height, divine
    Strength on the sudden springs to him !

"Yawns wide within that holy steep
A mghty cavern dark and deep—
By blessed sunbeam never lit—
Rank fœtid swamps engirdle it;

And there by night, and there by day,
Ever at watch, the fiend-worm lay,
Holding the Hell of its abode
Fast by the hallow'd House of God.
And when the pilgrim gladly ween'd
   His feet had found the healing way,
Forth from its ambush rush'd the fiend,
   And down to darkness dragged the prey.

"With solemn soul, that solemn height
I clomb, ere yet I sought the fight—
Kneeling before the cross within,
My heart, confessing, clear'd its sin.
Then, as befits the Christian knight,
I donn'd the spotless surplice white,
And, by the altar, grasp'd the spear :—
So down I strode with conscience clear—
Bade my leal squires afar the deed,
   By death or conquest crown'd, await—
Leapt lightly on my lithesome steed,
   And gave to God his soldier's fate!

"Before me wide the marshes lay—
Started the hounds with sudden bay—
Aghast the swerving charger slanting
Snorted—then stood abrupt and panting—
For curling there, in coilèd fold,
The Unutterable Beast behold!
Lazily basking in the sun.
Forth sprang the dogs. The fight's begun!
But lo! the hounds, in cowering, fly
   Before the mighty poison-breath—
A fierce yell, like the jackal's cry,
   Howl'd, mingling with that wind of death.

"No halt—I gave one cheering sound,
Lustily springs each dauntless hound—
Swift as the dauntless hounds advance,
Whirringly skirrs my stalwart lance—
Whirringly skirrs ; and from the scale
Bounds, as a reed aslant the mail.
Onward—but no!—the craven steed

Shrinks from his lord in that dread need—
　　Smitten and scar'd before that eyo
Of basilisk horror, and that blast
　　Of death, it only seeks to fly—
And half the mighty hope is past!

" A moment, and to earth I leapt ;
Swift from its sheath the falchion swept ;
Swift on that rock-like mail it plied—
The rock-like mail the sword defied :
The monster lash'd its mighty coil—
Down hurl'd—behold me on the soil !
Behold the hell-jaws gaping wide—
When lo ! they bound—the flesh is found ;
　　Upon the scaleless parts they spring !
Springs either hound ;—the flesh is found—
　　It roars ; the blood-dogs cleave and cling !

" No time to foil its fast'ning foes—
Light, as it writhed, I sprang, and rose ;
The all-unguarded place explored,
Up to the hilt I plunged the sword—
Buried one instant in the blood—
The next, upsprang the bubbling flood !
The next, one Vastness spread the plain—
Crush'd down—the victor with the slain ;
And all was dark—and on the ground
　　My life, suspended, lost the sun,
Till waking—lo my squires around—
　　And the dead foe !—my tale is done."

Then burst, as from a common breast,
The eager laud so long supprest—
A thousand voices, choral-blending,
Up to the vaulted dome ascending—
From groinèd roof and banner'd wall'
Invisible echoes answering all—
The very Brethren, grave and high,
Forget their state, and join the cry.
" With laurel wreaths his brows be crown'd,
　　Let throng to throng his triumph tell ;
Hail him all Rhodes !"—the Master frown'd,
　　And raised his hand—and silence fell.

" Well," said that solemn voice, " thy hand
From the wild-beast hath freed the land.
An idol to the People be !
A foe our Order frowns on thee !
For in thy heart, superb and vain,
A hell-worm laidlier than the slain,
To discord which engenders death,
Poisons each thought with baleful breath !
That hell-worm is the stubborn Will—
   Oh ! What were man and nations worth
If each his own desire fulfil,
   And law be banish'd from the earth ?

" *Valour* the Heathen gives to story—
Obedience is the Christian's glory ;
And on that soil our Saviour-God
As the meek low-born mortal trod.
We the Apostle-knights were sworn
To laws thy daring laughs to scorn—
Not *fame*, but *duty* to fulfil—
Our noblest offering—man's wild will.
Vain-glory doth thy soul betray—
   Begone—thy conquest is thy loss :
No breast too haughty to obey,
   Is worthy of the Christian's cross ! "

From their cold awe the crowds awaken,
As with some storm the halls are shaken ;
The noble Brethren plead for grace—
Mute stands the doom'd, with downward face ;
And mutely loosen'd from its band
The badge, and kiss'd the Master's hand,
And meekly turn'd him to depart :
A moist eye follow'd, " To my heart
Come back, my son ! "—the Master cries :
   " Thy grace a harder fight obtains ;
When Valour risks the Christian's prize,
   Lo, how Humility regains ! "

In the poem just presented to the reader, Schiller designed, as he wrote to
Goethe, to depict the old Christian chivalry—half knightly, half monastic.
The attempt is strikingly successful. Indeed, "The Fight of the Dragon"
appears to us the most spirited and nervous of all Schiller's narrative poems,

with the single exception of "The Diver;" and if its interest is less intense than that of the matchless "Diver," and its descriptions less poetically striking and effective, its interior meaning or philosophical conception is at once more profound and more elevated. In "The Fight of the Dragon," is expressed the moral of that humility which consists in self-conquest—even merit may lead to vain-glory—and, after vanquishing the fiercest enemies without, Man has still to contend with his worst foe,—the pride or disobedience of his own heart. "Every one," as a recent and acute, but somewhat over-refining critic has remarked, "has more or less—his own 'fight with the Dragon'—his own double victory (without and within) to achieve." The origin of this poem is to be found in the Annals of the Order of Malta—and the details may be seen in Vertot's History. The date assigned to the conquest of the Dragon is 1342. Helion de Villeneuve was the name of the Grand Master—that of the Knight, Dieu-Donné de Gozon. Thevenot declares that the head of the monster (to whatever species it really belonged), or its effigies, was still placed over one of the gates of the city in his time.—Dieu-Donné succeeded De Villeneuve as Grand Master, and on his gravestone were inscribed the words "Draconis Exstinctor."

DITHYRAMB.*

Believe me, together
The bright gods come ever,
      Still as of old;
Scarce see I Bacchus, the giver of joy,
Than comes up fair Eros, the laugh-loving boy;
      And Phœbus, the stately, behold!

      They come near and nearer,
         The Heavenly Ones all—
      The Gods with their presence
         Fill earth as their hall!

Say, how shall *I* welcome,
      Human and earthborn,
         Sons of the Sky?
Pour out to me—pour the full life that ye live!
What to you, O ye gods! can the mortal-one give?

      The Joys can dwell only
         In Jupiter's palace—
      Brimm'd bright with your nectar,
         Oh, reach me the chalice!

* This has been paraphrased by Coleridge.

" Hebe, the chalice
  Fill full to the brim !
Steep his eyes—steep his eyes in the bath of the dew,
Let him dream, while the Styx is concealed from his view,
    That the life of the Gods is for him ! "

        It murmurs, it sparkles,
            The Fount of Delight ;
        The bosom grows tranquil—
            The eye becomes bright.

THE KNIGHTS OF ST. JOHN.

Oh, nobly shone the fearful Cross upon your mail afar,
When Rhodes and Acre hail'd your might, O lions of the
    war !
When leading many a pilgrim horde, through wastes of
    Syrian gloom ;
Or standing with the Cherub's sword before the Holy
    Tomb.
Yet on your forms the Apron seem'd a nobler armour far,
When by the sick man's bed ye stood, O lions of the
    war !
When ye, the high-born, bow'd your pride to tend the
    lowly weakness,
The duty, though it brought no fame,* fulfilled by Christian
    meekness—
Religion of the Cross, thou blend'st, as in a single flower,
The twofold branches of the palm—HUMILITY AND POWER.

THE MAIDEN FROM AFAR.

(OR FROM ABROAD.)

WITHIN a vale, each infant year,
    When earliest larks first carol free,
To humble shepherds doth appear
    A wondrous maiden, fair to see.

* The epithet in the first edition is *ruhmlose.*

Not born within that lowly place—
    From whence she wander'd, none could tell ·
Her parting footsteps left no trace,
    When once the maiden sigh'd farewell.

And blessèd was her presence there—
    Each heart, expanding, grew more gay ;
Yet something loftier still than fair
    Kept man's familiar looks away.
From fairy gardens, known to none,
    She brought mysterious fruits and flowers—
The things of some serener sun—
    Some Nature more benign than ours.

With each, her gifts the maiden shared—
    To some the fruits, the flowers to some ;
Alike the young, the aged fared ;
    Each bore a blessing back to home.
Though every guest was welcome there,
    Yet some the maiden held more dear,
And cull'd her rarest sweets whene'er
    She saw two hearts that loved draw near.

NOTE.—It seems generally agreed that POETRY is allegorised in these
stanzas; though, with this interpretation, it is difficult to reconcile the
sense of some of the lines—for instance, the last in the first stanza. How
can Poetry be said to leave no trace when she takes farewell ?

THE TWO GUIDES OF LIFE—

THE SUBLIME AND THE BEAUTIFUL.

Two genii are there, from thy birth through weary life, to
    guide thee ;
Ah, happy when, united both, they stand to aid, beside
    thee !
With gleesome play, to cheer the path, the One comes
    blithe with beauty—
And lighter, leaning on her arm, the destiny and duty.

With jest and sweet discourse, she goes unto the rock
    sublime,
Where halts above the Eternal Sea,* the shuddering
    Child of Time.
The Other here, resolved and mute, and solemn claspeth
    thee,
And bears thee in her giant arms across the fearful sea.
Never admit the one alone!—Give not the gentle guide
Thy honour—nor unto the stern thy happiness confide!

THE FOUR AGES OF THE WORLD.

[This Poem is one of those in which Schiller has traced the progress
of Civilization, and to which the Germans have given the name of Culture-
Historic.]

BRIGHT-PURPLING the glass glows the blush of the wine—
    Bright sparkle the eyes of each guest;
The POET has enter'd the circle to join—
    To the good brings the Poet the best.
Ev'n Olympus were mean, with its nectar and all,
If the lute's happy magic were mute in the hall.

Bestow'd by the gods on the poet has been
    A soul that can mirror the world!
Whate'er has been done on this earth he has seen,
    And the future to him is unfurl'd.
He sits with the gods in their council sublime,
And views the dark seeds in the bosom of Time.

The folds of this life, in the pomp of its hues,
    He broadens all lustily forth,
And to him is the magic he takes from the Muse,
    To deck, like a temple, the earth.
A hut, though the humblest that man ever trod,
He can charm to a heaven, and illume with a god!

---

* By this, Schiller informs us elsewhere that he does not mean Death
alone; but that the thought applies equally to every period in life, when we
can divest our souls of the body, and perceive or act as pure spirits: we are
truly then under the influence of the Sublime.

As the god and the genius, whose birth was of Jove,[*]
  In one type all creation reveal'd,
When the ocean, the earth, and the star-realm above,
  Lay compress'd in the orb of a shield ;
So the poet, a shape and a type of the All,
From a sound, that is mute in a moment, can call.[†]

Blithe pilgrim! his footsteps have pass'd in their way,
  Every time, every far generation ;
He comes from the age when the Earth was at play
  In the childhood and bloom of Creation.
Four Ages of men have decay'd to his eye,
And fresh to the Fifth he glides youthfully by.

King Saturn first ruled us, the simple and true—
  Each day as each yesterday fair :
No grief and no guile the calm shepherd-race knew—
  Their life was the absence of care ;
They loved, and to love was the whole of their task—
Kind earth upon all lavish'd all they could ask.

Then the LABOUR arose, and the demi-god man
  Went the monster and dragon to seek ;
And the age of the hero, the ruler, began,
  And the strong were the stay of the weak.
By Scamander the strife and the glory had birth ;
But the Beautiful still was the god of the earth.

From the strife came the conquest; and Strength, like a
    wind,
Swept its way through the meek and the mild :
Still vocal the Muse, and in marble enshrined,
  The gods upon Helicon smiled.
Alas, for the age which fair Phantasie bore !—
It is fled from the earth, to return nevermore.

---

   * Vulcan—the allusion, which is exquisitely beautiful, is to the Shield of Achilles.—HOMER, Il. i. 18.
     "There Earth, there Heaven, there Ocean, he design'd."—POPE.
   † This line is obscure, not only in the translation, but so in the original. Schiller means to say that the Poet is the true generaliser of the infinite—a position which he himself practically illustrates, by condensing, in the few verses that follow, the whole history of the world. Thus, too, Homer is the condenser of the whole heroic age of Greece. In the Prologue to "Wallenstein," the same expressions, with little alteration, are employed to convey the perishable nature of the Actor's art.

The gods from their thrones in Olympus were hurl'd,
 Fane and column lay rent and forlorn ;
And—holy, to heal all the wounds of the world—
 The Son of the Virgin was born.
The lusts of the senses subdued or suppress'd,
Man mused on life's ends, and took THOUGHT to his
  breast.*

Ever gone were those charms, the voluptuous and vain,
 Which had deck'd the young world with delight ;
For the monk and the nun were the penance and pain,
 And the tilt for the iron-clad knight.
Yet, however that life might be darksome and wild,
Love linger'd with looks still as lovely and mild :

By the shrine of an altar yet chaste and divine,
 Stood the Muses in stillness and shade ;
And honour'd, and household, and holy that shrine—
 In the blush—in the heart of the maid :
And the sweet light of song burn'd the fresher and truer,
In the lay and the love of the wild Troubadour.

As ever, so aye, in their beautiful band,
 May the Maid and the Poet unite :
Their task be to work, and to weave, hand in hand,
 The zone of the Fair and the Right !
Love and Song, Song and Love, intertwined evermore,
Weary Earth to the suns of its youth can restore.

* " Der Mensch griff *denkend* in seine Brust,"
i. e. Man strove by reflection to apprehend the phenomena of his own being
—the principles of his own nature. The development of the philosophical,
as distinguished from the natural consciousness, forms a very important æra
in the history of civilization. It is in fact the great turning-point of
humanity, both individually and historically. Griff, Begriff—has a peculiar
logical significance in German.

THE MAIDEN'S LAMENT.

[The two first Stanzas of this Poem are sung by Thekla, in the third Act of
the " Piccolomini."]

THE wind rocks the forest,
  The clouds gather o'er;
The girl sitteth lonely
  Beside the green shore;
The breakers are dashing with might, with might:
And she mingles her sighs with the gloomy night,
    And her eyes are hot with tears.

" The earth is a desert,
  And broken my heart,
Nor aught to my wishes
  The world can impart.
To her Father in Heaven may the Daughter now go;
I have known all the joys that the world can bestow—
    I have lived—I have loved "—

" In vain, oh! how vainly,
  Flows tear upon tear!
Human woe never waketh
  Dull Death's heavy car!—
Yet say what can soothe for the sweet vanish'd love,
And I, the Celestial, will shed from above
    The balm for thy breast."

" Let ever, though vainly,
  Flow tear upon tear;
Human woe never waketh
  Dull Death's heavy ear;
Yet still when the heart mourns the sweet vanish'd love,
No balm for its wound can descend from above
    Like Love's own faithful tears ! "

THE IMMUTABLE.

TIME flies on restless pinions—constant never.
Be constant—and thou chainest time for ever.

THE VEILED IMAGE AT SAIS.

A YOUTH, whom wisdom's warm desire had lured
To learn the secret lore of Egypt's priests,
To Sais came.   And soon, from step to step
Of upward mystery, swept his rapid soul!
Still ever sped the glorious Hope along,
Nor could the parch'd Impatience halt, appeased
By the calm answer of the Hierophant—
"What have I, if I have not all," he sigh'd;
"And givest thou but the little and the more?
Does thy truth dwindle to the gauge of gold,
A sum that man may smaller or less small
Possess and count—subtract or add to—still?
Is not TRUTH *one* and indivisible?
Take from the Harmony a single tone—
A single tint take from the Iris bow,
And lo! what once was all, is nothing—while
Fails to the lovely whole one tint or tone!"

They stood within the temple's silent dome,
And, as the young man paused abrupt, his gaze
Upon a veil'd and giant IMAGE fell:
Amazed he turn'd unto his guide—"And what
Towers, yonder, vast beneath the veil?"

                                             "THE TRUTH,"

Answered the Priest.
                      "And have I for the truth
Panted and struggled with a lonely soul,
And yon the thin and ceremonial robe
That wraps her from mine eyes?"
                                         Replied the priest,
"There shrouds herself the still Divinity.
Hear, and revere her hest: 'Till I this veil
Lift—may no mortal-born presume to raise;
And who with guilty and unhallow'd hand
Too soon profanes the Holy and Forbidden—
He,' says the goddess"—
                         "Well?"
                             "'SHALL SEE THE TRUTH!'"

" A wond'rous oracle; and hast *thou* never
Lifted the veil ? "

               " No ! nor desired to raise ! "
" What ! nor desired ?   O strange incurious heart,
Here the thin barrier—there reveal'd the truth ! "
Mildly return'd the priestly master, " Son,
More mighty than thou dream'st of, Holy Law
Spreads interwoven in yon slender web,
Air-light to touch—lead-heavy to the soul ! "

    The young man, thoughtful, turn'd him to his home,
And the sharp fever of the Wish to Know
Robb'd night of sleep.   Around his couch he roll'd,
Till midnight hatch'd resolve—
                " Unto the shrine ! "

Stealthily on, the involuntary tread
Bears him—he gains the boundary, scales the wall,
And midway in the inmost, holiest dome,
Strides with adventurous step the daring man.

Now halts he where the lifeless Silence sleeps
In the embrace of mournful Solitude ;—
Silence unstirr'd,—save where the guilty tread
Call'd the dull echo from mysterious vaults !

High from the opening of the dome above,
Came with wan smile the silver-shining moon. .
And, awful as some pale presiding god,
Dim-gleaming through the hush of that large gloom,
In its wan veil the Giant Image stood.

    With an unsteady step he onwards past,
Already touch'd the violating hand
The Holy—and recoil'd ! a shudder thrill'd
His limbs, fire-hot and icy-cold in turns,
As if invisible arms would pluck the soul
Back from the deed.
          " O miserable man !
What would'st thou ? "   (Thus within the inmost heart
Murmur'd the warning whisper.)   " Wilt thou dare
The All-hallow'd to profane ?   ' No mortal-born

(So spake the oracular word) may lift the veil
Till I myself shall raise ! '   Yet said it not,
The same oracular word—' who lifts the veil
Shall see the truth ? '   Behind, be what there may,
I dare the hazard—I will lift the veil—"
Loud rang his shouting voice—"and I will see ! "

" SEE ! "

A lengthen'd echo, mocking, shrill'd again !
He spoke and rais'd the veil !   And ask'st thou what
Unto the sacrilegious gaze lay bare ?
I know not—pale and senseless, stretch'd before
The statue of the great Egyptian queen,
The priests beheld him at the dawn of day ;
But what he saw, or what did there befall,
His lips reveal'd not.   Ever from his heart
Was fled the sweet serenity of life,
And the deep anguish dug the early grave :
" Woe—woe to him "—such were his warning words,
Answering some curious and impetuous brain,
" Woe—for her face shall charm him never more !
Woe—woe to him who treads through Guilt to TRUTH ! "

THE CHILD IN THE CRADLE.

WITHIN that narrow bed, glad babe, to thee
  A boundless world is spread !
Unto thy soul, the boundless world shall be
  When man, a narrow bed ! " *

---

* This epigram has a considerable resemblance to the epitaph on
Alexander the Great :

> Sufficit huic Tumulus, cui non suffecerat orbis :
> Res brevis huic ampla est, cui fuit ampla brevis.

A little tomb sufficeth him whom not sufficed all :
The small is now as great to him as once the great was small.
Vide BLACKWOOD'S MAGAZINE, *April*, 1838, p. 556.

THE RING OF POLYCRATES.

A BALLAD.

Upon his battlements he stands—
And proudly looks along the lands—
        His Samos and the Sea !
" And all," he said, " that we survey,
Egyptian king, my power obey—
        Own, Fortune favours me ! "

" With thee the Gods their favour share,
And they who once thine equals were,
        In thee a monarch know !
Yet one there lives to avenge the rest,
Nor can my lips pronounce thee blest,
        While on thee frowns the Foe ! "

He spoke, and from Miletus sent,
There came a breathless man, and bent
        Before the tyrant there.
" Let incense smoke upon the shrine,
And with the lively laurel twine,
        Victor, thy godlike hair !

" The foe sunk, smitten by the spear ;
With the glad tidings sends me here,
        Thy faithful Polydore."
And from the griesly bowl he drew
(Grim sight they well might start to view !)
        A head that dripp'd with gore.

The Egyptian king recoil'd in fear,
" Hold not thy fortune yet too dear—
        Bethink thee yet," he cried,
" Thy Fleets are on the faithless seas ;
Thy Fortune trembles in the breeze,
        And floats upon the tide."

Ere yet the warning word was spoken—
Below, the choral joy was broken—
      Shouts ring from street to street !
Home-veering to the crowded shore—
Their freight of richest booty bore
      The Forests of the Fleet.

Astounded stood that kingly guest,
" Thy luck this day must be confest,
      Yet trust not the Unsteady !
The banners of the Cretan foe
Wave war, and bode thine overthrow—
      They near thy sands already ! "

Scarce spoke the Egyptian King—before
Hark, " Victory—Victory ! " from the shore,
      And from the seas ascended ;
" Escaped the doom that round us lower'd,
Swift storm the Cretan has devoured,
      And war itself is ended ! "

Shudder'd the guest—" In sooth," he falter'd,
" To-day thy fortune smiles unalter'd,
      Yet more thy fate I dread—
The Gods oft grudge what they have given,
And ne'er unmix'd with grief has Heaven
      Its joys on Mortals shed !

" No less than thine my rule has thriven,
And o'er each deed the gracious heaven
      Has, favouring, smiled as yet.
But one beloved heir had I—
God took him !—I beheld him die,
      His life paid fortune's debt.

" So, would'st *thou* 'scape the coming ill—
Implore the dread Invisible—
      Thy sweets themselves to sour !
Well ends his life, believe me, never,
On whom, with hands thus full for ever,
      The Gods their bounty shower.

" And if thy prayer the Gods can gain not
This counsel of thy friend disdain not—
    Thine own afflictor be!
And what of all thy worldly gear
Thy deepest heart esteems most dear,
    Cast into yonder sea!"

The Samian thrill'd to hear the king—
"No gems so rich as deck this ring,
    The wealth of Samos gave:
By this—O may the Fatal Three
My glut of fortune pardon me!"
    He cast it on the wave—

And when the morrow's dawn began,
All joyous came a fisherman
    Before the prince.—Quoth he,
"Behold this fish—so fair a spoil
Ne'er yet repaid the snarer's toil,
    I bring my best to thee!"

The cook to dress the fish begun—
The cook ran fast as cook could run—
    "Look, look!—O master mine—
The ring—the ring the sea did win,
I found the fish's maw within—
    Was ever luck like thine!"

In horror turns the kingly guest—
"Then longer here I may not rest,
    I'll have no friend in thee!
The Gods have marked thee for their prey,
To share thy doom I dare not stay!"
    He spoke—and put to sea.

NOTE.—This story is taken from the well-known correspondence between Amasis and Polycrates, in the third book of Herodotus. Polycrates—one of the ablest of that most able race, the Greek tyrants,—was afterwards decoyed into the power of Orœtes, Governor of Sardis, and died on the cross. Herodotus informs us, that the ring Polycrates so prized, was an emerald set in gold, the workmanship of Theodorus the Samian. Pliny, on the contrary, affirms it to have been a sardonyx, and in his time it was supposed still to exist among the treasures in the Temple of Concord. It is worth while to turn to Herodotus (c. 40—43, book 3), to notice the admirable art with which Schiller has adapted the narrative, and heightened its effect.

HOPE.

WE speak with the lip, and we dream in the soul,
   Of some better and fairer day;
And our days, the meanwhile, to that golden goal
   Are gliding and sliding away.
Now the world becomes old, now again it is young,
But " *The Better* " 's for ever the word on the tongue

At the threshold of life Hope leads us in—
   Hope plays round the mirthful boy;
Though the best of its charms may with youth begin,
   Yet for age it reserves its toy.
When we sink at the grave, why the grave has scope,
And over the coffin Man planteth—HOPE!

And it is not a dream of a fancy proud,
   With a fool for its dull begetter;
There's a voice at the heart that proclaims aloud—
   We are born for a something Better! "
And that Voice of the Heart, oh, ye may believe,
Will never the Hope of the Soul deceive!

THE SEXES.

SEE in the babe two loveliest flowers united—yet in truth,
While in the bud they seem the same—the virgin and the
   youth!
But loosen'd is the gentle bond, no longer side by side—
From holy Shame the fiery Strength will soon itself
   divide.
Permit the youth to sport, and still the wild desire to
   chase,
For, but when sated, weary strength returns to seek the
   grace.
Yet in the bud, the double flowers the future strife
   begin,
How precious all—yet nought can still the longing heart
   within.

In ripening charms the virgin bloom to woman shape hath
  grown,
But round the ripening charms the pride hath clasp'd its
  guardian zone;
Shy, as before the hunter's horn the doe all trembling
  moves,
She flies from man as from a foe, and hates before she
  loves!
From lowering brows this struggling world the fearless
  youth observes,
And, harden'd for the strife betimes, he strains the willing
  nerves;
Far to the armèd throng and to the race prepared to
  start,
Inviting glory calls him forth, and grasps the troubled
  heart:—
Protect thy work, O Nature now! one from the other
  flies,
Till thou unitest each at last that for the other sighs.
There art thou, mighty one! where'er the discord darkest
  frown,
Thou call'st the meek harmonious Peace, the godlike
  soother down.
The noisy chase is lull'd asleep, day's clamour dies afar,
And through the sweet and veilèd air in beauty comes the
  star.
Soft-sighing through the crispèd reeds, the brooklet glides
  along,
And every wood the nightingale melodious fills with
  song.
O virgin! now what instinct heaves thy bosom with the
  sigh?
O youth! and wherefore steals the tear into thy dreaming
  eye?
Alas! they seek in vain within the charm around be-
  stow'd,
The tender fruit is ripen'd now, and bows to earth its
  load.
And restless goes the youth to feed his heart upon its
  fire,
Ah, where the gentle breath to cool the flame of young
  desire!

And now they meet—the holy love that leads them lights
    their eyes,
And still behind the wingèd god the wingèd victory flies.
O heavenly Love!—'tis thy sweet task the human flowers
    to bind,
For aye apart, and yet by thee for ever intertwined !

HONOURS.

[DIGNITIES would be the better title, if the word were not so essentially
unpoetical.]

WHEN the column of light on the waters is glass'd,
    As blent in one glow seem the shine and the stream ;
But wave after wave through the glory has pass'd,
    Just catches, and flies as it catches, the beam :
So Honours but mirror on mortals their light ;
Not the MAN but the PLACE that he passes is bright.

POMPEII AND HERCULANEUM.

WHAT wonder this ?—we ask the lymphid well,
O Earth ! of thee—and from thy solemn womb
What yield'st thou ?—Is there life in the abyss—
Doth a new race beneath the lava dwell ?
Returns the Past, awakening from the tomb ?
Rome—Greece !—O, come !—Behold—behold !   For this
Our living world—the old Pompeii sees ;
And built anew the town of Dorian Hercules !
House upon house—its silent halls once more
Opes the broad Portico !—O, haste and fill
Again those halls with life !—O, pour along
Through the seven-vista'd theatre the throng !
Where are ye, mimes ?—Come forth, the steel prepare
For crown'd Atrides, or Orestes haunt,
Ye choral Furies with your dismal chaunt !
The Arch of Triumph !—whither leads it ?—still
Behold the Forum !—On the curule chair
Where the majestic image ?   Lictors, where
Your solemn fasces ?—Place upon his throne

The Prætor—here the Witness load, and there
Bid the Accuser stand!
              —O God! how lone
The clear streets glitter in the quiet day—
The footpath by the doors winding its lifeless way!
The roofs arise in shelter, and around
The desolate Atrium—every gentle room
Wears still the dear familiar smile of Home!
Open the doors—the shops—on dreary night
Let lusty day laugh down in jocund light!
See the trim benches ranged in order!—See
The marble-tesselated floor—and there
The very walls are glittering livingly
With their clear colours.   But the artist where?
Sure but this instant he hath laid aside
Pencil and colours!—Glittering on the eye
Swell the rich fruits, and bloom the flowers!—See all
Art's gentle wreaths still fresh upon the wall!
Here the arch Cupid slyly seems to glide
By with bloom-laden basket.   There the shapes
Of Genii press with purpling feet the grapes.
Here springs the wild Bacchante to the dance,
And there she sleeps [while that voluptuous trance
Eyes the sly faun with never-sated glance]
Now on one knee upon the centaur-steeds
Hovering — the Thyrsus plies. — Hurrah! — away she
        speeds!
Come—come, why loiter ye?—Here, here, how fair
The goodly vessels still!   Girls, hither turn,
Fill from the fountain the Etruscan urn!
On the wing'd sphinxes see the tripod.—
                        Ho!
Quick—quick, ye slaves, come—fire!—the hearth prepare!
Ha! wilt thou sell?—this coin shall pay thee—this,
Fresh from the mint of mighty Titus!—Lo!
Here lie the scales, and not a weight we miss!
So—bring the light!   The delicate lamp!—what toil
Shaped thy minutest grace!—quick, pour the oil!
Yonder the fairy chest!—come, maid, behold
The bridegroom's gifts—the armlets—they are gold,
And paste out-feigning jewels!—lead the bride
Into the odorous bath—lo, unguents still—

And still the crystal vase the arts for beauty fill!
But where the men of old—perchance a prize
More precious yet in yon papyrus lies,
And see ev'n still the tokens of their toil—
The waxen tablets—the recording style.
    The earth, with faithful watch, has hoarded all!
Still stand the mute Penates in the hall;
Back to his haunts returns each ancient God.
Why absent only from their ancient stand
The Priests?—waves Hermes his Caducean rod,
And the wing'd victory struggles from the hand.
Kindle the flame—behold the Altar there!
Long hath the God been worshipless—To prayer!

LIGHT AND WARMTH.

In cheerful faith that fears no ill
    The good man doth the world begin;
And dreams that all without shall still
    Reflect the trusting soul within.
Warm with the noble vows of youth,
Hallowing his true arm to the truth;

Yet is the littleness of all
    So soon to sad experience shown,
That crowds but teach him to recall
    And centre thought on self alone;
Till love, no more, emotion knows,
And the heart freezes to repose.

Alas! though truth may *light* bestow,
    Not always *warmth* the beams impart,
Blest he who gains the BOON TO KNOW,
    Nor buys the knowledge with the heart.
For warmth and light a blessing both to be,
Feel as the Enthusiast—as the World-wise see.

BREADTH AND DEPTH.

FULL many a shining wit one sees,
  With tongue on all things well-conversing;
The what can charm, the what can please,
  In every nice detail rehearsing.
Their raptures so transport the college,
It seems one honeymoon of knowledge.

Yet out they go in silence where
  They whilome held their learned prate;
Ah! he who would achieve the fair,
  Or sow the embryo of the great,
Must hoard—to wait the ripening hour—
In the least point the loftiest power.

With wanton boughs and pranksome hues,
  Aloft in air aspires the stem;
The glittering leaves inhale the dews
  But fruits are not conceal'd in *them*.
From the small kernel's undiscerned repose
The oak that lords it o'er the Forest grows.

THE PHILOSOPHICAL EGOIST.

HAST thou the infant seen that yet, unknowing of the
    love
Which warms and cradles, calmly sleeps the mother's heart
    above—
Wandering from arm to arm, until the call of passion
    wakes,
And glimmering on the conscious eye—the world in glory
    breaks?—
And hast thou seen the mother there her anxious vigil
    keep,
Buying with love that never sleeps the darling's happy
    sleep?
With her own life she fans and feeds that weak life's
    trembling rays,
And with the sweetness of the care, the care itself repays.

And dost thou Nature then blaspheme—that, both the child
    and mother
Each unto each unites, the while the one doth need the
    other?—
All self-sufficing wilt thou from that lovely circle stand—
That creature still to creature links in faith's familiar
    band?
Ah! dar'st thou, poor one, from the rest thy lonely self
    estrange?
Eternal Power itself is but all powers in interchange!

FRIDOLIN;

OR, THE MESSAGE TO THE FORGE.

[Schiller speaking of this Ballad, which he had then nearly concluded,
says that " accident had suggested to him a very pretty theme for a Ballad;"
and that " after having travelled through air and water," alluding to " The
Cranes of Ibycus" and "The Diver," " he should now claim to himself the
Element of Fire."—Hoffmeister supposes from the name of Savern, the
French orthography for Zabern, a town in Alsatia, that Schiller took the
material for his tale from a French source; though there are German
Legends analogous to it. The general style of the Ballad is simple almost
to homeliness, though not to the puerility affected by some of our own Ballad
writers.—But the pictures of the Forge and the Catholic Ritual are worked
out with singular force and truthfulness.]

A HARMLESS lad was Fridolin,
    A pious youth was he;
He served and sought her grace to win,
    Count Savern's fair ladye;
And gentle was the Dame as fair,
And light the toils of service there;
And yet the woman's wildest whim
In her—had been but joy to him.

Soon as the early morning shone,
    Until the vesper bell,
For her sweet hest he lived alone
    Nor e'er could serve too well.
She bade him oft not labour so:
But then his eyes would overflow. . .
It seemed a sin if strength could swerve,
From that one thought—her will to serve!

And so of all her House, the Dame
   Most favour'd him always;
And from her lip for ever came
   His unexhausted praise.
On him, more like some gentle child,
Than serving-youth, the lady smiled,
And took a harmless pleasure in
The comely looks of Fridolin.

For this, the Huntsman Robert's heart
   The favour'd Henchman cursed;
And long, till ripen'd into art,
   The hateful envy nursed.
His Lord was rash of thought and deed:
And thus the knave the deadly seed,
(As from the chase they homeward rode,)
That poisons thought to fury, sow'd—

"Your lot, great Count, in truth is fair,
   (Thus spoke the craft suppress'd;)
The gnawing tooth of doubt can ne'er
   Consume your golden rest.
He who a noble spouse can claim,
Sees love begirt with holy shame;
Her truth no villain arts ensnare—
The smooth seducer comes not there.

"How now!—bold man, what sayest thou?"
   The frowning Count replied—
"Think'st thou I build on woman's vow,
   Unstable as the tide?
Too well the flatterer's lip allureth—
On firmer ground my faith endureth;
The Count Von Savern's wife unto
No smooth seducer comes to woo!"

"Right!"—quoth the other—"and your scorn
   The fool enow the fool chastises,
Who though a simple vassal born,
   Himself so highly prizes;
Who buoys his heart with rash desires,
And to the Dame he serves aspires."

"How!" cried the Count, and trembled—"How!
Of One who lives, then, speakest thou?"

"Surely; can that to all reveal'd
    Be all unknown to you?
Yet, from your ear if thus conceal'd,
    Let me be silent too."
Out burst the Count, with gasping breath,
"Fool—fool!—thou speak'st the words of death!
What brain has dared so bold a sin?"
"My Lord, I spoke of Fridolin!

"His face is comely to behold"—
    He adds—then paused with art.
The Count grew hot—the Count grew cold—
    The words had pierced his heart.
"My gracious master sure must see
That only in her eyes lives he;
Behind your board he stands unheeding,
Close by her chair—his passion feeding.

"And then the rhymes..." "The rhymes!" "The
        same—
    Confess'd the frantic thought."
"Confess'd!" "Ay, and a *mutual* flame
    The foolish boy besought!
No doubt the Countess, soft and tender,
Forbore the lines to you to render, . . .
And I repent the babbling word
That 'scaped my lips—What ails my lord?"

Straight to a wood, in scorn and shame,
    Away Count Savern rode—
Where, in the soaring furnace-flame,
    The molten iron glow'd.
Here, late and early, still the brand
Kindled the smiths, with crafty hand;
The bellows heave and the sparkles fly,
As if they would melt down the mountains high.

Their strength the Fire, the Water gave,
   In interleagued endeavour;
The mill-wheel, whirl'd amidst the wave,
   Rolls on for aye and ever—
Here, day and night, resounds the clamour,
While measured beats the heaving hammer;
And, suppled in that ceaseless storm,
Iron to iron stamps a form.

Two smiths before Count Savern bend,
   Forth-beckon'd from their task.
" The first whom I to you may send,
   And who of you may ask—
' *Have you my lord's command obey'd ?* '
—Thrust in the hell-fire yonder made;
Shrunk to the cinders of your ore,
Let him offend mine eyes no more ! "

Then gloated they—the griesly pair—
   They felt the hangman's zest;
For senseless as the iron there,
   The heart lay in the breast.
And hied they, with the bellows' breath,
To strengthen still the furnace-death;
The murder-priests nor flag nor falter—
Wait the victim—trim the altar !

The huntsman seeks the page—God wot,
   How smooth a face hath he !
" Off, comrade, off ! and tarry not;
   Thy lord hath need of thee ! "
Thus spoke his lord to Fridolin,
" Haste to the forge the wood within,
And ask the serfs who ply the trade—
' *Have you my lord's command obey'd ?* ' "

" It shall be done "—and to the task
   He hies without delay.
Had *she* not hest ?—'twere well to ask,
   To make less long the way.
So, wending backward at the thought,
The youth the gracious lady sought.

"Ere I go to the forge, I have come to thee :
Hast thou any commands, by the road for me ? "

" I fain," thus spake that lady fair,
  In winsome tone and low,
" But for mine infant ailing there,
  To hear the mass would go.
Go thou, my child—and on the way,
For me and mine thy heart shall pray ;
Repent each sinful thought of thine—
So shall thy soul find grace for mine ! "

Forth on the welcome task he wends,
  Her wish the task endears,
Till, where the quiet hamlet ends,
  A sudden sound he hears.
To and fro the church-bell, swinging,
Cheerily, clearly forth is ringing ;
Knolling souls that would repent
To the Holy Sacrament.

He thought, " Seek God upon thy way,
  And he will come to thee ! "
He gains the House of Prayer to pray,
  But all stood silently.
It was the Harvest's merry reign,
The scythe was busy in the grain,
One clerkly hand the rites require
To serve the mass and aid the choir.

At once the good resolve he takes,
  As sacristan to serve :
" No halt," quoth he, " the footstep makes,
  That doth but heavenward swerve ! "
So, on the priest, with humble soul,
He hung the cingulum and stole,
And eke prepares each holy thing
To the high mass administ'ring.

Now, as the ministrant, before
  The priest he took his stand ;
Now towards the altar moved, and bore
  The mass-book in his hand.

Rightward, leftward kneeleth he,
Watchful every sign to see ;
Tinkling, as the *sanctus* fell,
Thrice at each holy name, the bell.

Now the meek priest, bending lowly,
 Turns unto the solemn shrine,
And with lifted hand and holy,
 Rears the cross divine.
While the clear bell, lightly swinging,
That boy-sacristan is ringing ;—
Strike their breasts, and down inclining,
Kneel the crowd, the symbol signing.

Still in every point excelling,
 With a quick and nimble art—
Every custom in that dwelling
 Knew the boy by heart !
To the close he tarried thus,
Till *Vobiscum Dominus ;*
To the crowd inclines the priest,
And the crowd have sign'd—and ceased !

Now back in its appointed place,
 His footsteps but delay
To range each symbol-sign of grace—
 Then forward on his way.
So, conscience calm, he lightly goes ;
Before his steps the furnace glows ;
His lips, the while, (the count completing,)
Twelve paternosters slow-repeating.

He gain'd the forge—the smiths survey'd,
 As there they grimly stand :
" How fares it, friends ?—*have ye obey'd,*"
 He cried, " *my lord's command ?* "
" Ho ! ho ! " they shout and ghastly grin,
And point the furnace-throat within :
" With zeal and heed, we did the deed—
The master's praise, the servants' meed."

On, with this answer, onward home,
　With fleeter step he flies;
Afar, the Count beheld him come—
　He scarce could trust his eyes.
" Whence com'st thou ? " " From the furnace." "So !
Not elsewhere ? troth, thy steps are slow;
Thou hast loiter'd long ! "—" Yet only till
I might the trust consign'd fulfil.

" My noble lord, 'tis true, to-day,
　I'd chanced, on quitting thee,
To ask my duties, on the way,
　Of her who guideth me.
She bade me, (and how sweet and dear
It was !) the holy mass to hear;
Rosaries four I told, delaying,
Grace for thee and thine heart-praying."

All stunn'd, Count Savern heard the speech—
　A wondering man was he;
"And when thou didst the furnace reach,
　What answer gave they thee ? "
" An answer hard the sense to win ;
Thus spake the men with ghastly grin,
' With zeal and heed, we did the deed—
The master's praise, the servants' meed.' "

" And *Robert ?* "—gasp'd the Count, as lost
　In awe, he shuddering stood—
"Thou must, be sure, his path have cross'd ?
　I sent him to the wood."
" In wood nor field where I have been,
No single trace of him was seen."
All deathlike stood the Count : " Thy might,
O God of heaven, hath judged the right ! "

Then meekly, humbled from his pride,
　He took the servant's hand;
He led him to his lady's side,
　She nought mote understand.
This child—no angel is more pure—
Long may thy grace for him endure ;

Our strength how weak, our sense how dim—
GOD AND HIS HOSTS ARE OVER HIM ! "

THE YOUTH BY THE BROOK.

[Sung in "The Parasite," a comedy which Schiller translated from Picard
—much the best comedy, by the way, that Picard ever wrote.]

BESIDE the brook the Boy reclin'd
    And wove his flowery wreath,
And to the waves the wreath consign'd—
    The waves that danced beneath.
" So fleet mine hours," he sighed, " away
    Like waves that restless flow :
And, so my flowers of youth decay
    Like those that float below.

" Ask not why I, alone on earth,
    Am sad in life's young time ;
To all the rest are hope and mirth
    When spring renews its prime.
Alas ! the music Nature makes,
    In thousand songs of gladness—
While charming all around me, wakes
    My heavy heart to sadness.

" Ah ! vain to me the joys that break
    From Spring, voluptuous are ;
For only ONE 'tis mine to seek—
    The Near, yet ever Far !
I stretch my arms, that shadow-shape
    In fond embrace to hold ;
Still doth the shade the clasp escape—
    The heart is unconsoled !

" Come forth, fair Friend, come forth below,
    And leave thy lofty hall,
The fairest flowers the spring can know
    In thy dear lap shall fall !
Clear glides the brook in silver roll'd,
    Sweet carols fill the air ;
The meanest hut hath space to hold
    A happy loving Pair ! "

TO THE IDEAL.

[To appreciate the beauty of this Poem,—the reader must remember that it preceded our own School—we will not say of Egotism, but of Self-expression; a school of which the great Byron is the everlasting master—and in which the Poet reveals the hearts of others, by confessing the emotions of his own. Of late years we have been overwhelmed with attempts at the kind of pathos which the following stanzas embody with melancholy tenderness—yet with manly resignation. But at the time Schiller wrote this elegy on departed youth, he had the merit of originality —a merit the greater, because the Poem expresses feelings which almost all of us have felt in the progress of life.—The only Poem written before it, which it resembles, is the "Ode on a Distant Prospect of Eton College," by our own illustrious Gray, whom the little critics of our day seek to depreciate.—Beautiful as the German's poem is (in his own language), the Englishman's excels it.]

THEN wilt thou, with thy fancies holy—
    Wilt thou, faithless, fly from me?
With thy joy, thy melancholy,
    Wilt thou thus relentless flee?
O Golden Time, O Human May,
    Can nothing, Fleet One, thee restrain?
Must thy sweet river glide away
    Into the eternal Ocean-Main?

The suns serene are lost and vanish'd
    That wont the path of youth to gild,
And all the fair Ideals banish'd
    From that wild heart they whilome fill'd.
Gone the divine and sweet believing
    In dreams which Heaven itself unfurl'd!
What godlike shapes have years bereaving
    Swept from this real work-day world!

As once, with tearful passion fired,
    The Cyprian Sculptor clasp'd the stone,
Till the cold cheeks, delight inspired,
    Blush'd—to sweet life the marble grown:
So youth's desire for Nature!—round
    The Statue, so my arms I wreathed,
Till warmth and life in mine it found,
    And breath that poets breathe—it breathed;

With my own burning thoughts it burn'd ;—
　Its silence stirr'd to speech divine ;—
Its lips my glowing kiss return'd—
　Its heart in beating answer'd mine !
How fair was then the flower—the tree !—
　How silver-sweet the fountain's fall !
The soulless had a soul to me !
　My life its own life lent to all !

The Universe of things seem'd swelling
　The panting heart to burst its bound,
And wandering Fancy found a dwelling
　In every shape—thought—deed, and sound.
Germ'd in the mystic buds, reposing,
　A whole creation slumbered mute,
Alas, when from the buds unclosing,
　How scant and blighted sprung the fruit !

How happy in his dreaming error
　His own gay valour for his wing,
Of not one care as yet in terror,
　Did Youth upon his journey spring ;
Till floods of balm, through air's dominion,
　Bore upward to the faintest star—
For never aught to that bright pinion
　Could dwell too high, or spread too far.

Though laden with delight, how lightly
　The wanderer heavenward still could soar,
And aye the ways of life how brightly
　The airy Pageant danced before !—
Love, showering gifts (life's sweetest) down,
　Fortune, with golden garlands gay,
And Fame, with starbeams for a crown,
　And Truth, whose dwelling is the Day.

Ah ! midway soon lost evermore,
　Afar the blithe companions stray ;
In vain their faithless steps explore,
　As one by 'one, they glide away.

Fleet Fortune was the first escaper—
  The thirst for wisdom linger'd yet;
But doubts with many a gloomy vapour
  The sun-shape of the Truth beset!

The holy crown which Fame was wreathing,
  Behold! the mean man's temples wore,
And but for one short spring-day breathing,
  Bloom'd Love—the Beautiful—no more!
And ever stiller yet, and ever
  The barren path more lonely lay,
Till scarce from waning Hope could quiver
  A glance along the gloomy way.

Who, loving, lingered yet to guide me,
  When all her boon companions fled,
Who stands consoling yet beside me,
  And follows to the House of Dread?
Thine FRIENDSHIP—thine the hand so tender,
  Thine the balm dropping on the wound,
Thy task, the load more light to render,
  O! earliest sought and soonest found!—

And Thou, so pleased, with her uniting,
  To charm the soul-storm into peace,
Sweet TOIL, in toil itself delighting,
  That more it laboured, less could cease,
Tho' but by grains thou aid'st the pile
  The vast Eternity uprears,
At least thou strik'st from Time the while
  Life's debt—the minutes, days and years.*

---

* Though the Ideal images of youth forsake us, the Ideal itself still remains to the Poet. It is his task and his companion—unlike the Phantasies of Fortune, Fame, and Love, the Phantasies of the Ideal are imperishable. While, as the occupation of life, it pays off the debt of Time, as the exalter of life it contributes to the Building of Eternity.

PHILOSOPHERS.

To learn what gives to every thing
    The form and life which we survey,
The law by which the Eternal King
Moves all Creation's order'd ring,
    And keeps it from decay—
When to great Doctor Wiseman we go—
If help'd not out by Fichté's Ego—
All from his brain that we can delve,
Is this sage answer—"Ten's not Twelve." *

The snow can chill, the fire can burn,
    Men when they walk on two feet go ;—
A sun in Heaven all eyes discern—
This through the senses we may learn,
    Nor go to school to know !
But the profounder student sees,
That that which burns—will seldom freeze ;
And can instruct the astonish'd hearer,
How moisture moistens—light makes clearer.

Homer composed his mighty song,
    The hero danger dared to scorn,
The brave man did his duty, long
Before—(and who shall say I'm wrong)—
    Philosophers were born !

*   " Wenn Ich nicht drauf ihm helfe
    Er heisst: zehn ist nicht zwölfe."
If the Ich in the text is correctly printed with a capital initial, the
intention of Schiller must apparently be to ridicule the absolute Ego of
Fichté—a philosopher whom he elsewhere treats with very little ceremony
—and thus Hoffmeister seems to interpret the meaning.—Hinrichs, on the
other hand, quoting the passage without the capital initial, assumes the
satire to be directed against the first great law of logic, which logicians call
the Principle of Contradiction, viz., that it is impossible for a thing to be
and not to be at the same time ; or, as Schiller expresses it, that it is
impossible for ten to be both ten and twelve ; a truth which is obvious to all
men, and which, precisely because it is obvious to all men, Philosophers can
state and explain. According to this interpretation, the sense of the
translation is not correctly given, and Schiller seems rather to say, "I
should call that man exceedingly clever who could explain to me the great
law of the Universe, if I did not first explain it to him by saying it is this,
Ten is not Twelve—i. e., No philosopher can tell a plain man anything
about a profound principle, which any plain man could not just as well have
told to the Philosopher."

Without Descartes and Locke—the Sun
Saw things by Heart and Genius done,
Which those great men have proved, on viewing,
The—possibility of doing !

Strength in this life prevails and sways—
    Bold Power oppresses humble Worth—
He who can nòt command obeys—
In short there's not too much to praise
    In this poor orb of earth.
But how things better might be done,
If sages had this world begun,
By moral systems of their own,
Most incontestably is shown!

" Man needs mankind, must be confest—
    In all he labours to fulfil,
Must work, or with, or for, the rest ;
'Tis drops that swell the ocean's breast—
    'Tis waves that turn the mill.
The savage life for man unfit is,
So take a wife and live in cities."
Thus *ex cathedrâ* teach, we know,
Wise Messieurs Puffendorf and Co.

Yet since, what grave professors preach,
    The crowd may be excused from knowing ;
Meanwhile, old Nature looks to each,
Tinkers the chain, and mends the breach,
    And keeps the clockwork going.
Some day, Philosophy, no doubt,
A better World will bring about :
Till then the Old a little longer,
Must blunder on—through Love and Hunger !

PUNCH SONG.

Four Elements, join'd in
    An emulous strife,
Fashion the world, and
    Constitute life.

From the sharp citron
  The starry juice pour ;
Acid to Life is
  The innermost core.

Now, let the sugar
  The bitter one meet ;
Still be life's bitter
  Tamed down with the sweet !

Let the bright water
  Flow into the bowl ;
Water, the calm one,
  Embraces the Whole.

Drops from the spirit
  Pour quick'ning within ;
Life but its life from
  The spirit can win.

Haste, while it gloweth,
  Your vessels to bring ;
The wave has but virtue
  Drunk hot from the spring !

PUNCH SONG.

TO BE SUNG IN THE NORTH.

On the free southern hills
  Where the full summers shine,
Nature quicken'd by sunlight,
  Gives birth to the vine !

Her work the Great Mother
  Conceals from the sight,
Untrack'd is the labour,
  Unfathom'd the might.

As the child of the sunbeam,
  The wine leaps to-day,
From the tun springs the crystal,
  A fountain at play.

All tho senses it gladdons,
  Gives Hope to the breast;
To grief a soft balsam,
  To life a new zest.

But, our zone palely gilding,
  The Sun of the North,
From the leaves it scarce tintoth
  No fruit ripens forth.

Yet life will ne'er freely
  Life's gladness resign:
Our vales know no vineyard—
  Invent we a wine!

But wan the libation,
  In truth must appear;
Living Nature alone gives
  The bright and the clear!

Yet draw from the dim fount,
  The Waters of Mirth!
For Heaven gave us Art,
  The Prometheus of Earth.

Wherever strength reacheth,
  What kingdoms await her!
From the Old, the New shaping,
  Art, ay—a Creator!—

The Elements' union
  Divides at her rod,
With the hearth-flame she mimics
  The glow of a god.

To Hesperidan Islands
  She sends the ship forth;
Lo, the southern fruits lending
  Their gold to the North!

So, this sap wrung from flame be
  A symbol-sign still,
Of the wonders man works with
  The Force and the Will!

PEGASUS IN HARNESS.

AT Smithfield * once, as I've been told,
Or some such place where beasts are sold,
A bard, whose bones from flesh were all free,
Put up for sale the Muses' palfrey.
His ears how cock'd, his tail how stiff!
Loud neigh'd the prancing Hippogriff.
The crowd grew large, the crowd grew larger:
"By Jove, indeed a splendid charger!
'T would suit some coach of state!—the king's!
But, bless my soul, what frightful wings!
No doubt the breed is mighty rare—
But who would coach it through the air?
Who'd trust his neck to such a flyer?"—
In short, the bard could find no buyer.
　At last a farmer pluck'd up mettle:
"Let's see if we the thing can settle.
These useless wings my man may lop,
Or tie down tight—I likes a crop!
'T might draw my cart; it seems to frisk it;
Come, twenty pounds!—ecod, I'll risk it."
I blush to say the bard consented,
And Hodge bears off his prize, contented.
The noble beast is in the cart;
Hodge cries, "Gee hup!" and off they start.
He scarcely feels the load behind,
Skirrs, scours, and scampers like the wind.
The wings begin for heaven to itch,
The wheels go devilish near the ditch!
"So ho!" grunts Hodge, "'tis more than funny;
I've got a penn'orth for my money.
To-morrow, if I still survive,
I have some score of folks to drive;—
The load of five the beast could drag on;
I'll make him leader to the wagon.
Choler and collar wear with time;
The lively rogue is in his prime."

* Literally "Haymarket."

All's well at first; a famous start—
Wagon and team go like a dart.
The wheelers' heavy plod behind him,
But doubly speeds the task assign'd him;
Till, with tall crest, he snuffs the heaven,
Spurns the dull road so smooth and even.
True the impetuous instinct to,
Field, fen, and bog, he scampers through.
The frenzy seems to catch the team;
The driver tugs, the travellers scream.
O'er ditch, o'er hedge, splash, dash, and crash on,
Ne'er farmer flew in such a fashion.
At last, all batter'd, bruised, and broken,
(Poor Hodge's state may not be spoken,)
Wagon, and team, and travellers stop,
Perch'd on a mountain's steepest top!
Exceeding sore, and much perplext,
" I fegs," the farmer cries, " what next?
This helter-skelter sport will never do,
But break him in I'll yet endeavour to;
Let's see if work and starving diet
Can't tame the monster into quiet! "
The proof was made, and save us! if in
Three days you'd seen the hippogriffin,
You'd scarce the noble beast have known,
Starved duly down to skin and bone.
Cries Hodge, rejoiced, " I have it now,
Bring out my ox, he goes to plough."
So said, so done, and droll the tether,
Wing'd horse, slow ox, at plough together!
The unwilling griffin strains his might,
One last strong struggle yet for flight;
In vain, for well inured to labour.
Plods sober on his heavy neighbour,
And forces, inch by inch, to creep,
The hoofs that love the air to sweep;
Until, worn out, the eye grows dim,
The sinews fail the founder'd limb,
The god-steed droops, the strife is past,
He writhes amidst the mire at last!
" Accursed brute! " the farmer cries;
And, while he bawls, the cart-whip plies,

" All use it seems you think to shirk
So fierce to run—so dull to work!
My twenty pounds!—Not worth a pin!
Confound the rogue who took me in ! "
He vents his wrath, he plies his thong,
When, lo! there gaily comes along,
With looks of light and locks of yellow,
And lute in hand, a buxom fellow;
Through the bright clusters of his hair
A golden circlet glistens fair.
" What's this—a wondrous yoke and pleasant ? "
Cries out the stranger to the peasant.
" The bird and ox thus leash'd together—
Come, prithee, just unbrace the tether:
But let *me* mount him for a minute—
That beast !—you'll see how much is in it."
The steed released—the easy stranger
Leaps on his back, and smiles at danger;
Scarce felt that steed the master's rein,
When all his fire returns again:
He champs the bit—he rears on high,
Light, like a soul, looks from his eye;
Changed from a creature of the sod,
Behold the spirit and the god:
As sweeps the whirlwind, heavenward springs
The unfurl'd glory of his wings.
Before the eye can track the flight,
Lost in the azure fields of light.

HERO AND LEANDER,

A BALLAD.

[We have already seen, in "The Ring of Polycrates," Schiller's mode of
dealing with classical subjects. In the poems that follow, derived from
similar sources, the same spirit is maintained. In spite of Humboldt, we
venture to think that Schiller certainly does not narrate Greek legends in
the spirit of an ancient Greek. The Gothic sentiment, in its ethical depth
and mournful tenderness, more or less pervades all that he translates from
classic fable into modern pathos. The grief of Hero, in the ballad subjoined, touches closely on the lamentations of *Thekla*, in "Wallenstein."
The Complaint of Ceres, embodies Christian Grief and Christian Hope.
The Trojan Cassandra expresses the moral of the Northern Faust. Even
the "Victory Feast" changes the whole spirit of Homer, on whom it is

founded, by the introduction of the Ethical Sentiment at the close, borrowed, as a modern would apply what he so borrows, from the moralising Horace. Nothing can be more foreign to the Hellenic Genius (if we except the very disputable intention of the " Prometheus"), than the interior and typical design which usually exalts every conception in Schiller. But it is perfectly open to the Modern Poet to treat of ancient legends in the modern spirit. Though he selects a Greek story, he is still a modern who narrates —he can never make himself a Greek, any more than Æschylus in the "Persæ" could make himself a Persian. But this is still more the privilege of the Poet in Narrative, or lyrical composition, than in the Drama, for in the former he does not abandon his identity, as in the latter he must—yet even this *must* has its limits. Shakespeare's wonderful power of self-transfusion has no doubt enabled him, in his Plays from Roman History, to animate his characters with much of Roman life. But no one can maintain that a Roman would ever have written plays, in the least resembling "Julius Cæsar," or "Coriolanus," or " Antony and Cleopatra." The Portraits may be Roman, but they are painted in the manner of the Gothic school. The Spirit of antiquity is only in them, inasmuch as the representation of Human Nature, under certain circumstances, is accurately, though loosely outlined. When the Poet raises the dead, it is not to restore, but to remodel.]

SEE you the towers, that, gray and old,
Frown through the sunlight's liquid gold,
   Steep sternly fronting steep?
The Hellespont beneath them swells,
And roaring cleaves the Dardanelles,
   The Rock-Gates of the Deep!
Hear you the Sea, whose stormy wave,
   From Asia, Europe clove in thunder?
That sea which rent a world can nòt
   Rend Love from Love asunder!

In Hero's, in Leander's heart,
Thrills the sweet anguish of the dart
   Whose feather flies from Love.
All Hebe's bloom in Hero's cheek—
And his the hunters's steps that seek
   Delight, the hills above!
Between their sires the rival feud
   Forbids their plighted hearts to meet;
Love's fruits hang over Danger's gulf,
   By danger made more sweet.

Alone on Sestos' rocky tower,
Where upward sent in stormy shower,
   The whirling waters foam,—

Alone the maiden sits, and eyes
The cliffs of fair Abydos rise
   Afar—her lover's home.
Oh, safely thrown from strand to strand,
   No bridge can love to love convey;
No boatman shoots from yonder shore,
   Yet LOVE has found the way.—

That Love, which could the Labyrinth pierce—
Which nerves the weak, and curbs the fierce,
   And wings with wit the dull;—
That Love which o'er the furrow'd land
Bow'd—tame beneath young Jason's hand—
   The fiery-snorting Bull!
Yes, Styx itself, that nine-fold flows,
   Has Love, the fearless, ventured o'er,
And back to daylight borne the bride,
   From Pluto's dreary shore!

What marvel then that wind and wave,
Leander doth but burn to brave,
   When Love, that goads him, guides!
Still when the day, with fainter glimmer,
Wanes pale—he leaps, the daring swimmer,
   Amid the darkening tides;
With lusty arms he cleaves the waves,
   And strives for that dear strand afar;
Where high from Hero's lonely tower
   Lone streams the Beacon-star.

In vain his blood the wave may chill,
These tender arms can warm it still—
   And, weary if the way,
By many a sweet embrace, above
All earthly boons—can liberal Love
   The Lover's toil repay,
Until Aurora breaks the dream,
   And warns the Loiterer to depart—
Back to the ocean's icy bed,
   Scared from that loving heart.

So thirty suns have sped their flight—
Still in that theft of sweet delight
   Exult the happy pair;
Caress will never pall caress,
And joys that gods might envy, bless
   The single bride-night there.
Ah! never he has rapture known,
  Who has not, where the waves are driven
Upon the fearful shores of Hell,
   Pluck'd fruits that taste of Heaven!

Now changing in their Season are,
The Morning and the Hesper Star;—
   Nor see those happy eyes
The leaves that withering droop and fall,
Nor hear, when, from its northern hall,
   The neighbouring Winter sighs;
Or, if they see, the shortening days
   But seem to them to close in kindness;
For longer joys, in lengthening nights,
   They thank the heaven in blindness.

It is the time, when Night and Day,
In equal scales contend for sway *
   Lone, on her rocky steep,
Lingers the girl with wistful eyes
That watch the sun-steeds down the skies,
   Careering towards the deep.
Lull'd lay the smooth and silent sea,
   A mirror in translucent calm,
The breeze, along that crystal realm,
   Unmurmuring, died in balm.

In wanton swarms and blithe array,
The merry dolphins glide and play
   Amid the silver waves.
In gray and dusky troops are seen,
The hosts that serve the Ocean-Queen,
   Upborne from coral caves:

* This notes the time of year—not the time of day—viz., about the 23rd
of September.—HOFFMEISTER.

They—only they—have witness'd love
  To rapture steal its secret way:
And Hecate * seals the only lips
  That could the tale betray!

She marks in joy the lullèd water,
And Sestos, thus thy tender daughter,
  Soft-flattering, woos the sea!
"Fair god—and canst thou then betray?
No! falsehood dwells with them that say
  That falsehood dwells with thee!
Ah! faithless is the race of man,
  And harsh a father's heart can prove;
But thee, the gentle and the mild,
  The grief of love can move!

"Within these hated walls of stone,
Should I, repining, mourn alone,
  And fade in ceaseless care,
But thou, though o'er thy giant tide,
Nor bridge may span, nor boat may glide,
  Dost safe my lover bear.
And darksome is thy solemn deep,
  And fearful is thy roaring wave;
But wave and deep are won by love—
  Thou smilest on the brave!

"Nor vainly, Sovereign of the Sea,
Did Eros send his shafts to thee:
  What time the Ram of Cold,
Bright Helle, with her brother bore,
How stirr'd the waves she wander'd o'er,
  How stirr'd thy deeps of old!
Swift, by the maiden's charms subdued,
  Thou cam'st from out the gloomy waves,
And, in thy mighty arms, she sank
  Into thy bridal caves.

"A goddess with a god, to keep
In endless youth, beneath the deep,
  Her solemn ocean-court!

* Hecate, as the mysterious Goddess of Nature.—HOFFMEISTER.

And still she smoothes thine angry tides,
Tames thy wild heart, and favouring guides
   The sailor to the port!
Beautiful Helle, bright one, hear
   Thy lone adoring suppliant pray!
And guide, O goddess—guide my love
   Along the wonted way!"

Now twilight dims the water's flow,
And from the tower the beacon's glow
   Waves flickering o'er the main.
Ah, where athwart the dismal stream,
Shall shine the Beacon's faithful beam
   The lover's eye shall strain!
Hark! sounds moan threat'ning from afar—
   From heaven the blessed stars are gone—
More darkly swells the rising sea—
   The tempest labours on!

Along the ocean's boundless plains
Lies Night—in torrents rush the rains
   From the dark-bosom'd cloud—
Red lightning skirs the panting air,
And, loosed from out their rocky lair,
   Sweep all the storms abroad.
Huge wave on huge wave tumbling o'er,
   The yawning gulf is rent asunder,
And shows, as through an opening pall,
   Grim earth—the ocean under!

Poor maiden! bootless wail or vow—
"Have mercy, Jove—be gracious, Thou!
   Dread prayer was mine before!
What if the gods have heard—and he,
Lone victim of the stormy sea,
   Now struggles to the shore!
There's not a sea-bird on the wave—
   Their hurrying wings the shelter seek;
The stoutest ship the storms have proved,
   Takes refuge in the creek.

"Ah, still that heart, which oft has braved
The danger where the daring saved,
  Love lureth o'er the sea ;—
For many a vow at parting morn,
That nought but death should bar return,
  Breathed those dear lips to me ;
And whirl'd around, the while I weep,
  Amid the storm that rides the wave,
The giant gulf is grasping down
  The rash one to the grave !

"False Pontus ! and the calm I hail'd,
The awaiting murder darkly veil'd—
  The lull'd pellucid flow,
The smiles in which thou wert array'd,
Were but the snares that Love betray'd
  To thy false realm below !
Now in the midway of the main,
  Return relentlessly forbidden,
Thou loosenest on the path beyond
  The horrors thou hadst hidden."

Loud and more loud the tempest raves,
In thunder break the mountain waves,
  White foaming on the rock—
No ship that ever swept the deep
Its ribs of gnarled oak could keep
  Unshatter'd by the shock.
Dies in the blast the guiding torch
  To light the struggler to the strand ;
'Tis death to battle with the wave,
  And death no less to land !

On Venus, daughter of the seas,
She calls the tempest to appease—
  To each wild-shrieking wind
Along the ocean-desert borne,
She vows a steer with golden horn—
  Vain vow—relentless wind !
On every goddess of the deep,
  On all the gods in heaven that be,
She calls—to soothe in calm, awhile,
  The tempest-laden sea !

"Hearken the anguish of my cries!
From thy green halls, arise—arise,
  Leucothoe the divine!
    Who, in the barren main afar,
Oft on the storm-beat mariner
  Dost gently-saving shine.
Oh, reach to him thy mystic veil,
  To which the drowning clasp may cling,
And safely from that roaring grave,
  To shore my lover bring!"

And now the savage winds are hushing,
And o'er the arch'd horizon, blushing,
  Day's chariot gleams on high!
Back to their wonted channels roll'd,
In crystal calm the waves behold—
  One smile on sea and sky!
All softly breaks the rippling tide,
  Low-murmuring on the rocky land,
And playful wavelets gently float
  A Corpse upon the strand!

'T is he!—who ev'n in death would still
Not fail the sweet vow to fulfil;
  She looks—sees—knows him there!
From her pale lips no sorrow speaks,
No tears glide down the hueless cheeks,
  Cold—numb'd in her despair—
She look'd along the silent deep,
  She look'd upon the bright'ning heaven,
Till to the marble face the soul
  Its light sublime had given!

"Ye solemn Powers men shrink to name,
Your might is here, your rights ye claim—
  Yet think not I repine:
Soon closed my course; yet I can bless
The life that brought me happiness—
  The fairest lot was mine!
Living have I thy temple served,
  Thy consecrated priestess been—
My last glad offering now receive
  Venus, thou mightiest queen!"

Flash'd the white robe along the air,
And from the tower that beetled there
    She sprang into the wave;
Roused from his throne beneath the waste,
Those holy forms the god embraced—
    A god himself their grave!
Pleased with his prey, he glides along—
    More blithe the murmur'd music seems,
A gush from unexhausted urns
    His Everlasting Streams!

THE PLAYING INFANT.

PLAY on thy mother's bosom, Babe, for in that holy isle
The error cannot find thee yet, the grieving, nor the guile;
Held in thy mother's arms above Life's dark and troubled
    wave,
Thou lookèst with thy fearless smile upon the floating
    grave.
Play, loveliest Innocence!—Thee, yet Arcadia circles
    round,
A charmèd power for thee has set the lists of fairy ground;
Each gleesome impulse Nature now can sanction and
    befriend,
Nor to that willing heart as yet the Duty and the End.
Play, for the haggard Labour soon will come to seize its
    prey,
Alas! when Duty grows thy law—Enjoyment fades away!

CASSANDRA.

[There is peace between the Greeks and Trojans—Achilles is to wed
Polyxena, Priam's daughter. On entering the Temple, he is shot through
his only vulnerable part by Paris.—The time of the following Poem is
during the joyous preparations for the marriage.]

AND mirth was in the halls of Troy,
    Before her towers and temples fell;
High peal'd the choral hymns of joy,
    Melodious to the golden shell.

The weary had reposed from slaughter—
  The eye forgot the tear it shed ;
This day King Priam's lovely daughter
  Shall great Pelides wed !

Adorn'd with laurel boughs, they come,
  Crowd after crowd—the way divine,
Where fanes are deck'd—for gods the home—
  And to the Thymbrian's * solemn shrine.
The wild Bacchantic joy is madd'ning
  The thoughtless host, the fearless guest ;
And there, the unheeded heart is sadd'ning
  One solitary breast !

Unjoyous in the joyful throng,
  Alone, and linking life with none,
Apollo's laurel groves among,
  The still Cassandra wander'd on !
Into the forest's deep recesses
  The solemn Prophet-Maiden pass'd,
And, scornful, from her loosen'd tresses,
  The sacred fillet cast !

" To all, its arms doth Mirth unfold,
  And every heart forgoes its cares—
And Hope is busy in the old—
  The bridal-robe my sister wears—
And I alone, alone am weeping ;
  The sweet delusion mocks not me—
Around these walls destruction sweeping,
  More near and near I see !

" A torch before my vision glows,
  But not in Hymen's hand it shines,
A flame that to the welkin goes,
  But not from holy offering-shrines ;
Glad hands the banquet are preparing,
  And near, and near the halls of state
I hear the God that comes unsparing,
  I hear the steps of Fate.

* Apollo.

"And men my prophet-wail deride!
　　The solemn sorrow dies in scorn;
And lonely in the waste, I hide
　　The tortured heart that would forewarn.
Amidst the happy, unregarded,
　　Mock'd by their fearful joy, I trod;
Oh, dark to me the lot awarded,
　　Thou evil Pythian god!

"Thine oracle, in vain to be,
　　Oh, wherefore am I thus consign'd
With eyes that every truth must see,
　　Lone in the City of the Blind?
Cursed with the anguish of a power
　　To view the fates I may not thrall,
The hovering tempest still must lower—
　　The horror must befall!

"Boots it the veil to lift, and give
　　To sight the frowning fates beneath?
For error is the life we live,
　　And, oh, our knowledge is but death!
Take back the clear and awful mirror,
　　Shut from mine eyes the blood-red glare;
Thy truth is but a gift of terror
　　When mortal lips declare.

"My blindness give to me once more* -
　　The gay dim senses that rejoice;
The Past's delighted songs are o'er
　　For lips that speak a Prophet's voice.
To me *the future* thou hast granted;
　　I miss *the moment* from the chain—
The happy Present-Hour enchanted!
　　Take back thy gift again!

"Never for me the nuptial wreath
　　The odour-breathing hair shall twine;
My heavy heart is bow'd beneath
　　The service of thy dreary shrine.

"Everywhere," says Hoffmeister truly, "Schiller exalts Ideal Belief
over real wisdom;—everywhere this modern Apostle of Christianity advo-
cates that Ideal, which exists in Faith and emotion, against the wisdom of
worldly intellect, the barren experience of life," &c.

My youth was but by tears corroded,—
  My sole familiar is my pain,
Each coming ill my heart foreboded,
  And felt it first—in vain !

" How cheerly sports the careless mirth,—
  The life that loves, around I see ;
Fair youth to pleasant thoughts give birth—
  The heart is only sad to me.
Not for mine eyes the young spring gloweth,
  When earth her happy feast-day keeps ;
The charm of life who ever knoweth
  That looks into the deeps ?

" Wrapt in thy bliss, my sister, thine
  The heart's inebriate rapture-springs ;—
Longing with bridal arms to twine
  The bravest of the Grecian kings.
High swells the joyous bosom, seeming
  Too narrow for its world of love,
Nor envies, in its heaven of dreaming,
  The heaven of gods above !

" I too might know the soft controul
  Of one the longing heart could choose,
With look which love illumes with soul—
  The look that supplicates and woos.
And sweet with him, where love presiding
  Prepares our hearth, to go—but, dim,
A Stygian shadow, nightly gliding,
  Stalks between me and him !

" Forth from the grim funereal shore,
  The Hell-Queen sends her ghastly bands ;
Where'er I turn—behind—before—
  Dumb in my path—a Spectre stands !
Wherever gayliest, youth assembles—
  I see the shades in horror clad,
Amidst Hell's ghastly People trembles
  One soul for ever sad !

" I see the steel of Murder gleam—
    I see the Murderer's glowing eyes—
To right—to left, one gory stream—
    One circling fate—my flight defies !
I may not turn my gaze—all seeing,
    Foreknowing all, I dumbly stand—
To close in blood my ghastly being
    In the far strangers' land ! "

Hark ! while the sad sounds murmur round,
    Hark, from the Temple-porch, the cries !—
A wild, confused, tumultuous sound !—
    Dead the divine Pelides lies !
Grim Discord rears her snakes devouring—
    The last departing god hath gone !
And, womb'd in cloud, the thunder, lowering,
    Hangs black on Ilion.

NOTE.—Upon this poem, Madame de Staël makes the following just and striking criticism.—*L'Allemagne*, Part II. c. 13. " One sees in this ode, the curse inflicted on a mortal by the prescience of a god. Is not the grief of the prophetess that of all who possess a superior intellect with an impassioned heart? Under a shape wholly poetic, Schiller has embodied an idea grandly moral—viz., that the true genius (that of the sentiment) is a victim to itself, even when spared by others. There are no nuptials for Cassandra : not that she is insensible—not that she is disdained, but the clear penetration of her soul passes in an instant both life and death, and can only repose in Heaven."

THE VICTORY FEAST.

[In this Lyric, Schiller had a notion of raising the popular social song from the prosaic vulgarity common to it—into a higher and more epic dignity.]

THE stately walls of Troy had sunken,
    Her towers and temples strew'd the soil;
The sons of Hellas, victory-drunken,
    Richly laden with the spoil,
Are on their lofty barks reclin'd
    Along the Hellespontine strand;
A gleesome freight the favouring wind
    Shall bear to Greece's glorious land;

And gleesome chaunt the choral strain,
  As towards the household altars, now,
  Each bark inclines the painted prow—
For Home shall smile again!

And there the Trojan women, weeping,
  Sit ranged in many a length'ning row;
Their heedless locks, dishevell'd, sweeping
  Adown the wan checks worn with woe.
No festive sounds that peal along,
Their mournful dirge can overwhelm;
  Through hymns of joy one sorrowing song
Commingled, wails the ruin'd realm.
  " Farewell, beloved shores!" it said,
    " From home afar behold us torn,
    By foreign lords as captives borne—
  Ah, happy are the dead!"

And Calchas, while the altars blaze,
  Invokes the high gods to their feast!
On Pallas, mighty or to raise
  Or shatter cities, call'd the Priest—
And Him, who wreathes around the land
  The girdle of his watery world,
And Zeus, from whose almighty hand
  The terror and the bolt are hurl'd.
Success at last awards the crown—
    The long and weary war is past;
    Time's destined circle ends at last—
  And fall'n the Mighty Town!

The Son of Atreus, king of men,
  The muster of the hosts survey'd,
How dwindled from the thousands, when
  Along Scamander first array'd!
With sorrow and the cloudy thought,
  The Great King's stately look grew dim—
Of all the hosts to Ilion brought,
  How few to Greece return with him!
Still let the song to gladness call,
    For those who yet their homes shall greet!—
    For them the blooming life is sweet:
  Return is not for all!

Nor all who reach their native land
  May long the joy of welcome feel—
Beside the household gods may stand
  Grim Murther with awaiting steel;
And they who 'scape the foe, may die
  Beneath the foul familiar glaive.
Thus He * to whose prophetic eye
  Her light the wise Minerva gave :—
  "Ah! blest whose hearth, to memory true,
    The goddess keeps unstain'd and pure—
    For woman's guile is deep and sure,
  And Falsehood loves the New!"

The Spartan eyes his Helen's charms,
  By the best blood of Greece recaptured;
Round that fair form his glowing arms—
  (A second bridal)—wreathe enraptured.
"Woe waits the work of evil birth—
  Revenge to deeds unblest is given!
For watchful o'er the things of earth,
  The eternal Council-Halls of Heaven.
  Yes, ill shall ever ill repay—
    Jove to the impious hands that stain
    The Altar of Man's Hearth, again
  The doomer's doom shall weigh!"

"Well they, reserved for joy to-day,"
  Cried out Oïleus' valiant son,
"May laud the favouring gods who sway
  Our earth, their easy thrones upon;
With careless hands they mete our doom,
  Our woe or welfare Hazard gives—
Patroclus slumbers in the tomb,
  And all unharm'd Thersites lives.
If Fate, then, showers without a choice
  The lots of luck and life on all,
  Let him on whom the prize may fall,—
Let him who lives—rejoice!"

* Ulysses.

"Yes, war will still devour the best!—
    Brother, remember'd in this hour!
His shade should be in feasts a guest,
    Whose form was in the strife a tower!
What time our ships the Trojan fired,
    Thine arm to Greece the safety gave—
The prize to which thy soul aspired,
    The crafty wrested from the brave.*
Peace to thine ever-holy rest—
        Not thine to fall before the foe!
    Ajax alone laid Ajax low:
    Ah—wrath destroys the best!"

To his dead sire—(the Dorian king)—
    The bright-hair'd Pyrrhus † pours the wine :—
" O'er every lot that life can bring,
    My soul, great Father, prizes thine.
Whate'er the goods of earth, of all,
    The highest and the holiest—FAME !
For when the Form in dust shall fall,
    O'er dust triumphant lives the Name !
Brave Man, thy light of glory never
        Shall fade, while song to man shall last;
    The Living soon from earth are pass'd,
    'THE DEAD—ENDURE FOR EVER!'"

" Since all are mute to mourn and praise
    In Victory's hour, the vanquish'd Man—
Be mine at least one voice to raise
    For HECTOR," Tydeus' son began :
" A Tower before his native town ;
    He stood—and fell as fall the brave. .
The conqueror wins the brighter crown,
    The conquer'd has the nobler grave!

---

* Need we say to the general reader, that allusion is here made to the
strife between Ajax and Ulysses, which has furnished a subject to the Greek
tragic poet, who has depicted, more strikingly than any historian, that
intense emulation for glory, and that mortal agony in defeat, which constituted the main secret of the prodigious energy of the Greek character?
The Tragic poet, in taking his hero from the Homeric age, endowed him
with the feelings of the Athenian republicans he addressed.
    † Neoptolemus, the son of Achilles.

He who brave life shall bravely close,
　For Home and Hearth, and Altar slain,
　If mourn'd by Friends, shall glory gain
Out of the lips of Foes!"

Lo, Nestor now, whose stately age
　Through threefold lives of mortals lives!—
The laurel'd bowl, the kingly sage
　To Hector's tearful mother gives.
"Drink—in the draught new strength is glowing,
　The grief it bathes forgets the smart!
O Bacchus! wond'rous boons bestowing,
　Oh how thy balsam heals the heart!
　Drink—in the draught new vigour gloweth,
　　The grief it bathes forgets the smart—
　　And balsam to the breaking heart,
　The healing god bestoweth.

" As Niobe, when weeping mute,
　To angry gods the scorn and prey,
But tasted of the charmèd fruit,
　And cast despair itself away;
So, while unto thy lips, its shore,
　This stream of life enchanted flows,
Remember'd grief, that stung before,
　Sinks down to Lethè's calm repose.
So, while unto thy lips, its shore,
　　The stream of life enchanted flows—
　　Drown'd deep in Lethè's calm repose,
　The grief that stung before! "

Seized by the god, behold the dark
　And dreaming prophetess arise,
She gazes from the lofty Bark
　Where Home's dim vapours wrap the skies—
" A vapour all of human birth
　Like mists ascending, seen and gone,
So fade Earth's great ones from the Earth
　And leave the changeless gods alone.
Behind the steed that skirs away;
　　And on the galley's deck—sits Care,
　　To-morrow comes, and we are where?
At least we'll live to-day! "

THE CRANES OF IBYCUS.

FROM Rhegium to the Isthmus, long
Hallow'd to steeds and glorious song,
Where, link'd awhile in holy peace,
Meet all the sons of martial Greece—
Wends Ibycus—whose lips the sweet
　　And ever-young Apollo fires;
The staff supports the wanderer's feet—
　　The God the Poet's soul inspires!

‛Soon from the mountain-ridges high,
The tower-crown'd Corinth greets his eye;
In Neptune's groves of darksome pine,
He treads with shuddering awe divine;
Nought lives around him, save a swarm
　　Of CRANES, that still pursued his way—
Lured by the South, they wheel and form
　　In ominous groups their wild array.

And "Hail! beloved Birds!" he cried;
"My comrades on the ocean tide,
Sure signs of good ye bode to me;
Our lots alike would seem to be;
From far, together borne, we greet
　　A shelter now from toil and danger;
And may the friendly hearts we meet
　　Preserve from every ill—the Stranger!"

His step more light, his heart more gay,
Along the mid-wood winds his way,
When, where the path the thickets close,
Burst sudden forth two ruffian foes;
Now strife to strife, and foot to foot!
　　Ah! weary sinks the gentle hand;
The gentle hand that wakes the lute
　　Has learn'd no lore that guides the brand.

He calls on men and Gods—in vain!
His cries no blest deliverer gain;
Feebler and fainter grows the sound,
And still the deaf life slumbers round—

"In the far land I fall forsaken,
  Unwept and unregarded, here;
By death from caitiff hands o'ertaken,
  Nor ev'n one late avenger near!"

Down to the earth the death-stroke bore him—
Hark, where the Cranes wheel dismal o'er him!
He hears, as darkness veils his eyes,
Near, in hoarse croak, their dirgelike cries.
"Ye whose wild wings above me hover,
  (Since never voice, save yours alone,
The deed can tell)—the hand discover—
  Avenge!"—He spoke, and life was gone.

Naked and maim'd the corpse was found—
And, still through many a mangling wound,
The sad Corinthian Host could trace
The loved—too well-remember'd face.
"And must I meet thee thus once more?
  Who hoped with wreaths of holy pine,
Bright with new fame—the victory o'er—
  The Singer's temples to entwine!"

And loud lamented every guest
Who held the Sea-God's solemn feast—
As in a single heart prevailing,
Throughout all Hellas went the wailing.
Wild to the Council Hall they ran—
  In thunder rush'd the threat'ning Flood—
"Revenge shall right the murder'd man,
  The last atonement—blood for blood!"

Yet 'mid the throng the Isthmus claims,
Lured by the Sea-God's glorious games—
The mighty many-nation'd throng—
How track the hand that wrought the wrong?—
How guess if that dread deed were done,
  By ruffian hands, or secret foes?
He who sees all on earth—the SUN—
  Alone the gloomy secret knows.

Perchance he treads in careless peace,
Amidst your Sons, assembled Greece—
Hears with a smile revenge decreed—
Gloats with fell joy upon the deed—
His steps the avenging gods may mock
  Within the very Temple's wall,
Or mingle with the crowds that flock
  To yonder solemn scenic * hall.

Wedg'd close, and serried, swarms the crowd—
Beneath the weight the walls are bow'd—
Thitherwards streaming far, and wide,
Broad Hellas flows in mingled tide—
A tide like that which heaves the deep
  When hollow-sounding, shoreward driven;
On, wave on wave, the thousands sweep
  Till arching, row on row, to heaven!

The tribes, the nations, who shall name,
That guest-like, there assembled came?
From Theseus' town, from Aulis' strand—
From Phocis, from the Spartans' land—
From Asia's wave-divided clime,
  The Isles that gem the Ægæan Sea,
To hearken on that Stage Sublime,
  The Dark Choir's mournful melody!

True to the awful rites of old,
In long and measured strides, behold
The Chorus from the hinder ground,
Pace the vast circle's solemn round.
So this World's women never strode,
  Their race from Mortals ne'er began,
Gigantic, from their grim abode,
  They tower above the Sons of Man!

Across their loins the dark robe clinging,
In fleshless hands the torches swinging,
Now to and fro, with dark red glow—
No blood that lives the dead cheeks know!

* The theatre.

Where flow the locks that woo to love
  On *human* temples—ghastly dwell
The serpents, coil'd the brow above,
  And the green asps with poison swell.

Thus circling, horrible, within
That space—doth their dark hymn begin,
And round the sinner as they go,
Cleave to the heart their words of woe.
Dismally wails, the senses chilling,
  The hymn—the FURIES' solemn song;
And froze the very marrow thrilling
  As roll'd the gloomy sounds along.

" And weal to him—from crime secure—
Who keeps his soul as childhood's pure;
Life's path he roves, a wanderer free—
We near him not—THE AVENGERS, WE!
But woe to him for whom we weave
  The doom for deeds that shun the light:
Fast to the murderer's feet we cleave,
  The fearful Daughters of the Night.

" And deems he flight from us can hide him ?
Still on dark wings We sail beside him !
The murderer's feet the snare enthralls—
Or soon or late, to earth he falls !
Untiring, hounding on, we go;
  For blood can no remorse atone !
On, ever—to the Shades below,
  And there—we grasp him, still our own ! "

So singing, their slow dance they wreathe,
And stillness, like a silent death,
Heavily there lay cold and drear,
As if the Godhead's self were near.
Then, true to those strange rites of old,
  Pacing the circle's solemn round,
In long and measured strides—behold,
  They vanish in the hinder ground !

Confused and doubtful—half between
The solemn truth and phantom scene,
The crowd revere the Power, presiding
O'er secret deeps, to justice guiding—
The Unfathom'd and Inscrutable
  By whom the web of doom is spun;
Whose shadows in the deep heart dwell,
  Whose form is seen not in the sun!

Just then, amidst the highest tier,
Breaks forth a voice that starts the ear;
"See there—see there, Timotheus;
Behold the Cranes of Ibycus!"
A sudden darkness wraps the sky;
  Above the roofless building hover
Dusk, swarming wings; and heavily
  Sweep the slow Cranes—hoarse-murmuring, over!

"Of Ibycus?"—that name so dear
Thrills through the hearts of those who hear!
Like wave on wave in eager seas,
From mouth to mouth the murmur flees—
"Of Ibycus, whom we bewail?
  The murder'd one! What mean those words?
Who is the man—knows *he* the tale?
  Why link that name with those wild birds?"

Questions on questions louder press—
Like lightning flies the inspiring guess—
Leaps every heart—"The truth we seize;
Your might is here, EUMENIDES!
The murderer yields himself confest—
  Vengeance is near—that voice the token—
Ho!—him who yonder spoke, arrest!—
  And him to whom the words were spoken!"

Scarce had the wretch the words let fall,
Than fain their sense he would recall.
In vain; those whitening lips, behold!
The secret have already told.

> Into their Judgment Court sublime
> The Scene is changed ;—their doom is seal'd !
> Behold the dark unwitness'd Crime,
> Struck by the light'ning that reveal'd !

The principal sources whence Schiller has taken the story of Ibycus (which was well known to the ancients, and indeed gave rise to a proverb) are Suidas and Plutarch. Ibycus is said by some to have been the Inventor of the Sambuca or triangular Cithera. We must observe, however—(though erudite investigation on such a subject were misplaced here), that Athenæus and Strabo consider the Sambuca to have originated with the Syrians, and this supposition is rendered the more probable by the similarity of the Greek word with the Hebrew, which in our received translation of the Bible is rendered by the word Sackbut. The tale, in its leading incidents, is told very faithfully by Schiller : it is the moral, or interior meaning, which he has heightened and idealised. Plutarch is contented to draw from the story a moral against loquacity. "It was not," says he, "the Cranes that betrayed the murderers, but their own garrulity." With Schiller the garrulity is produced by the surprise of the Conscience, which has been awakened by the Apparition and Song of the Furies. His own conceptions as to the effect he desired to create are admirable. "It is not precisely that the Hymn of the Furies" (remarks the poet) "has roused the remorse of the murderer, whose exclamation betrays himself and his accomplice ; that was not my meaning—but it has reminded him of his deed : his sense is struck with it. In this moment the appearance of the Cranes must take him by surprise ; he is a rude, dull churl, over whom the impulse of the moment has all power. His loud exclamation is natural in such circumstances." "That he feels no great remorse, in this thoughtless exclamation, is evident by the quick, snappish nature of it :—'See there, see there !' &c."—"In any other state of mind," observes Hoffmeister, "perhaps the Audience might not have attended to this ejaculation—but at that moment of deep inward emotion, produced by the representation of the fearful Goddesses, and an excited belief in their might, the name of the newly-murdered man must have struck them as the very voice of Fate, in which the speaker betrayed himself."—In fact the poem is an illustration of Schiller's own lines in "The Artists," written eight years before :—

> " Here secret Murder, pale and shuddering, sees
> Sweep o'er the stage the stern Eumenides ;
> Owns, where law fails, what powers to art belong,
> And, screened from justice, finds its doom in song !"

In the foregoing ballad POETRY (that is, the Dirge and dramatic representation of the Furies) acts doubly—first on the Murderer, next on the Audience ; it surprises the one into self-betrayal, it prepares in the other that state of mind in which, as by a divine instinct, the quick perception seizes upon the truth. In this double effect is nobly typified the power of Poetry on the individual and on the multitude. Rightly did Schiller resolve to discard from his design whatever might seem to partake of marvellous or supernatural interposition. The appearance of the Cranes is purely accidental. . . . Whatever is of diviner agency in the punishment of crime is found not in the outer circumstances, but in the heart within—the true realm in which the gods work their miracles. As it has been finely said—"The bad conscience (in the Criminal) is its own Nemesis, the good conscience in the Many—the audience—drags at once the bad before its forum and adjudges it." The history of the composition of this

Poem affords an instance of the exquisite art of Goethe, to which it is largely indebted. In the first sketch of the ballad, it was only one Crane that flew over Ibycus at the time he was murdered, and moreover this was only mentioned at the end of the piece. But Goethe suggested the enlargement of this leading incident—into "the long and broad phenomenon" of the swarm of Cranes, corresponding in some degree with the long and ample pageant of the Furies. Schiller at once perceived how not only the truthfulness, but the grandeur, of his picture was heightened by this simple alteration. . . . According to Goethe's suggestions, the swarm of Cranes were now introduced as the companions of Ibycus in his voyage. . . . The fine analogy between the human wanderer and his winged companions, each seeking a foreign land, was dimly outlined. . . . And the generous criticism of the one Poet finally gave its present fulness and beauty to the masterpiece of the other.—*See Goethe's Correspondence with Schiller. Hoffmeister. Heinrichs.*

THE HOSTAGE.

A BALLAD.

THE tyrant Dionys to seek,
  Stern Mœrus with his poniard crept;
  The watchful guards upon him swept;
The grim king mark'd his changeless cheek:
"What wouldst thou with thy poniard? Speak!"
"The city from the tyrant free!"—
"The death-cross shall thy guerdon be."

"I am prepared for death, nor pray,"
  Replied that haughty man, "to live;
  Enough, if thou one grace will give:
For three brief suns the death delay
To wed my sister—leagues away;
I boast one friend whose life for mine,
If I should fail the cross, is thine."

The tyrant mused,—and smil'd,—and said
  With gloomy craft, "So let it be;
  Three days I will vouchsafe to thee.
But mark—if, when the time be sped,
Thou fail'st—thy surety dies instead.
His life shall buy thine own release;
Thy guilt atoned, my wrath shall cease."

He sought his friend—" The king's decree
   Ordains my life the cross upon
   Shall pay the deed I would have done;
Yet grants three days' delay to me,
My sister's marriage-rites to see;
If thou, the hostage, wilt remain
Till I—set free—return again!"

His friend embraced—No word he said,
   But silent to the tyrant strode—
   The other went upon his road.
Ere the third sun in heaven was red,
The rite was o'er, the sister wed;
And back, with anxious heart unquailing,
He hastes to hold the pledge unfailing.

Down the great rains unending bore,
   Down from the hills the torrents rush'd,
   In one broad stream the brooklets gush'd.
The wanderer halts beside the shore,
The bridge was swept the tides before—
The shatter'd arches o'er and under
Went the tumultuous waves in thunder.

Dismay'd, he takes his idle stand—
   Dismay'd, he strays and shouts around;
   His voice awakes no answering sound.
No boat will leave the sheltering strand,
To bear him to the wish'd-for land;
No boatman will Death's pilot be;
The wild stream gathers to a sea!

Sunk by the banks, awhile he weeps,
   Then rais'd his arms to Jove, and cried,
   " Stay thou, oh stay the madd'ning tide!
Midway behold the swift sun sweeps,
And, ere he sinks adown the deeps,
If I should fail, his beams will see
My friend's last anguish—slain for me!"

More fierce it runs, more broad it flows,
  And wave on wave succeeds and dies—
  And hour on hour remorseless flies;
Despair at last to daring grows—
Amidst the flood his form he throws;
With vigorous arms the roaring waves
Cleaves—and a God that pities, saves.

He wins the bank—he scours the strand,
  He thanks the God in breathless prayer;
  When from the forest's gloomy lair,
With ragged club in ruthless hand,
And breathing murder—rush'd the band
That find, in woods, their savage den,
And savage prey in wandering men.

"What," cried he, pale with generous fear;
  "What think to gain ye by the strife?
  All I bear with me is my life—
I take it to the King!"—and here
He snatch'd the club from him most near:
And thrice he smote, and thrice his blows
Dealt death—before him fly the foes!

The sun is glowing as a brand;
  And faint before the parching heat,
  The strength forsakes the feeble feet:
"Thou has saved me from the robbers' hand,
Through wild floods given the blessed land;
And shall the weak limbs fail me now?
And *he*—Divine one, nerve me, thou!

Hark! like some gracious murmur by,
  Babbles low music, silver-clear—
  The wanderer holds his breath to hear;
And from the rock, before his eye,
Laughs forth the spring delightedly;
Now the sweet waves he bends him o'er,
And the sweet waves his strength restore.

Through the green boughs the sun gleams dying,
  O'er fields that drink the rosy beam,
  The trees' huge shadows giant seem.
Two strangers on the road are hieing;
And as they fleet beside him flying,
These mutter'd words his ear dismay:
"Now—now the cross has claim'd its prey!"

Despair his wingèd path pursues,
  The anxious terrors hound him on—
  There, redd'ning in the evening sun,
From far, the domes of Syracuse!—
When towards him comes Philostratus,
(His leal and trusty herdsman he,)
And to the master bends his knee.

"Back—thou canst aid thy friend no more,
  The niggard time already flown—
  His life is forfeit—save thine own!
Hour after hour in hope he bore,
Nor might his soul its faith give o'er;
Nor could the tyrant's scorn deriding,
Steal from that faith one thought confiding!"

"Too late! what horror hast thou spoken!
  Vain life, since it can nòt requite him!
  But death with me can yet unite him;
No boast the tyrant's scorn shall make—
How friend to friend can faith forsake.
But from the double-death shall know,
That Truth and Love yet live below!"

The sun sinks down—the gate's in view,
  The cross loom ismal on the ground—
  The eager crowd gape murmuring round.
His friend is bound the cross unto . . .
Crowd—guards—all-bursts he breathless through:
"Me! Doomsman, me!" he shouts, "alone!
His life is rescued—ho, mine own!"

Amazement seized the circling ring!
　Link'd in each other's arms the pair—
　Weeping for joy—yet anguish there!
Moist every eye that gazed ;—they bring
The wond'rous tidings to the king—
His breast Man's heart at last hath known,
And the Friends stand before his throne.

Long silent, he, and wondering long,
　Gaz'd on the Pair—" In peace depart,
　Victors, ye have subdued my heart!
Truth is no dream!—its power is strong.
Give grace to Him who owns his wrong!
'Tis mine your suppliant now to be,
Ah, let the band of Love—be THREE ! "

⌐This story, the heroes of which are more popularly known to us under
the names of Damon and Pythias (or *Phintias*), Schiller took from Hyginus,
in whom the friends are called Mœrus and Selinuntius. Schiller has somewhat amplified the incidents in the original, in which the delay of Mœrus is
occasioned only by the swollen stream—the other hindrances are of
Schiller's invention. The subject, like "The Ring of Polycrates," does not
admit of that rich poetry of description with which our author usually
adorns some single passage in his narratives. The poetic spirit is rather
shown in the terse brevity with which picture after picture is not only
sketched, but finished—and in the great thought at the close. Still it is not
one of Schiller's best ballads. His additions to the original story are not
happy. The incident of the Robbers is commonplace and poor. The delay
occasioned by the thirst of Mœrus is clearly open to Goethe's objection, (an
objection showing very nice perception of nature)—that extreme thirst was
not likely to happen to a man who had lately passed through a stream, on a
rainy day, and whose clothes must have been saturated with moisture—
nor in the traveller's preoccupied state of mind, is it probable that he
would have so much felt the mere physical want. With less reason has
it been urged by other Critics, that the sudden relenting of the Tyrant is
contrary to his character. The Tyrant here has no individual character at
all. ⌐He is the mere personation of Disbelief in Truth and Love—which
the spectacle of sublime self-abnegation at once converts. In this idea
lies the deep Philosophical Truth, which redeems all the defects of the
piece—for Poetry, in its highest form, is merely this—"Truth made
beautiful."⌐

THE COMPLAINT OF CERES.

It may be scarcely necessary to treat, however briefly, of the mythological
legend on which this exquisite elegy is founded; yet we venture to do so
rather than that the forgetfulness of the reader should militate against
his enjoyment of the poem. Proserpine, according to the Homeridæ (for
the story is not without variations), when gathering flowers with the

Ocean Nymphs, is carried off by Aidoneus, or Pluto. Her mother, Ceres, wanders over the earth for her in vain, and refuses to return to Heaven till her daughter is restored to her. Finally, Jupiter commissions Hermes to persuade Pluto to render up his bride, who rejoins Ceres at Eleusis. Unfortunately she has swallowed a pomegranate seed in the Shades below, and is thus mysteriously doomed to spend one-third of the year with her husband in Hades, though for the remainder of the year she is permitted to dwell with Ceres and the Gods. This is one of the very few mythological fables of Greece which can be safely interpreted into an Allegory. Proserpine denotes the seed corn one-third of the year below the earth; two-thirds (that is, dating from the appearance of the ear) above it. Schiller has treated this story with admirable and artistic beauty; and, by an alteration in its symbolical character, has preserved the pathos of the external narrative, and heightened the beauty of the interior meaning— associating the productive principle of the earth with the immortality of the soul. Proserpine here is not the symbol of the buried seed, but the buried seed is the symbol of her—that is, of the Dead. The exquisite feeling of this poem consoled Schiller's friend, Sophia La Roche, in her grief for her son's death.

I.

Does pleasant Spring return once more?
   Does Earth her happy youth regain?
Sweet suns green hills are shining o'er;
   Soft brooklets burst their icy chain:
Upon the blue translucent river
   Laughs down an all-unclouded day,
The winged west winds gently quiver,
   The buds are bursting from the spray;
While birds are blithe on every tree;
   The Oread from the mountain-shore
Sighs ' Lo thy flowers come back to thee—
   Thy Child, sad Mother, comes no more!'

II.

Alas! how long an age it seems
   Since all the Earth I wander'd over,
And vainly, Titan, task'd thy beams
   The lov'd—the lost one—to discover!
Though all may seek—yet none can call
   Her tender presence back to me!
The Sun, with eyes detecting all,
   Is blind one vanish'd form to see.
Hast thou, O Zeus, hast thou away
   From these sad arms my Daughter torn?
Has Pluto, from the realms of Day,
   Enamour'd—to dark rivers borne?

III.

Who to the dismal Phantom-Strand
　　The Herald of my Grief will venture?
The Boat for ever leaves the Land,
　　But only Shadows there may enter.—
Veil'd from each holier eye repose
　　The realms were Midnight wraps the Dead,
And, while the Stygian River flows,
　　No living footstep there may tread!
A thousand pathways wind the drear
　　Descent;—none upward lead to-day;—
No witness to the Mother's car
　　The Daughter's sorrows can betray.

IV.

Mothers of happy Human clay
　　Can share at least their children's doom;
And when the loved ones pass away,
　　Can track—can join them—in the tomb!
The race alone of Heavenly birth
　　Are banish'd from the darksome portals;
The Fates—have mercy on the Earth,
　　And death is only kind to mortals! *
Oh, plunge me in the Night of Nights,
　　From Heaven's ambrosial halls exil'd!
Oh, let the Goddess lose the rights
　　That shut the Mother from the Child!

V.

Where sits the Dark King's joyless bride,
　　Where midst the Dead her home is made:
Oh that my noiseless steps might glide,
　　Amidst the shades myself a shade!
I see her eyes, that search thro' tears,
　　In vain the golden light to greet;
That yearn for yonder distant spheres,
　　That pine the Mother's face to meet!
Till some bright moment shall renew
　　The severed Hearts' familiar ties;
And softened pity still in dew,
　　From Pluto's slow-relenting eyes!

* What a beautiful vindication of the shortness of human life!

VI.

Ah, vain the wish, the sorrow are!
  Calm in the changeless paths above
Rolls on the Day-God's golden Car—
  Fast are the fix'd decrees of Jove!
Far from the ever gloomy Plain,
  He turns his blissful looks away.
Alas! Night never gives again
  What once it seizes as its prey!
Till over Lethe's sullen swell,
  Aurora's rosy hues shall glow;
And arching thro' the midmost Hell
  Shine forth the lovely Iris-Bow!

VII.

And is there nought of Her;—no token—
  No pledge from that beloved hand?
To tell how Love remains unbroken,
  How far soever be the land?
Has love no link, no lightest thread,
  The Mother to the Child to bind?
Between the Living and the Dead,
  Can Hope no holy compact find?
No! every bond is not yet riven;
  We are not yet divided wholly;
To us the eternal Powers have given
  A symbol language, sweet and holy.

VIII.

When Spring's fair children pass away,
  When, in the Northwind's icy air,
The leaf and flower alike decay,
  And leave the rivell'd branches bare,
Then from Vertumnus' lavish horn
  I take Life's seeds to strew below—
And bid the gold that germs the corn
  An offering to the Styx to go!
Sad in the earth the seeds I lay—
  Laid at thy heart, my Child—to be
The mournful tokens which convey
  My sorrow and my love to Thee!

IX.

But, when the Hours, in measured dance,
  The happy smile of Spring restore,
Rife in the Sun-god's golden glance
  The buried Dead revive once more!
The germs that perish'd to thine eyes,
  Within the cold breast of the earth,
Spring up to bloom in gentler skies,
  The brighter for the second birth!
The stem its blossom rears above—
  Its roots in Night's dark womb repose—
The plant but by the equal love
  Of light and darkness fostered—grows!

X.

If half with Death the germs may sleep,
  Yet half with Life they share the beams;
My heralds from the dreary deep,
  Soft voices from the solemn streams,—
Like her, so them, awhile entombs,
  Stern Orcus, in his dismal reign,
Yet Spring sends forth their tender blooms
  With such sweet messages again,
To tell,—how far from light above,
  Where only mournful shadows meet,
Memory is still alive to love,
  And still the faithful Heart can beat!

XI.

Joy to ye children of the Field!
  Whose life each coming year renews,
To your sweet cups the Heaven shall yield
  The purest of its nectar-dews!
Steep'd in the light's resplendent streams,
  The hues that streak the Iris-Bow
Shall trim your blooms as with the beams
  The looks of young Aurora know.
The budding life of happy Spring,
  The yellow Autumn's faded leaf,
Alike to gentle Hearts shall bring
  The symbols of my joy and grief.

THE ELEUSINIAN FESTIVAL.

This, originally called the "Burger-Lay," is one of the poems which Schiller has devoted to his favourite subject—the Progress of Society.

I.

WIND in a garland the ears of gold,
 Azure Cyanes * inwoven be!
Oh how gladly shall eye behold
 The Queen who comes in her majesty.
Man with man in communion mixing,
 Taming the wild ones where she went;
Into the peace of the homestead fixing –
 Lawless bosom and shifting tent.†

II.

Darkly hid in cave and cleft
 Shy, the Troglodyte abode;
Earth, a waste, was found and left
 Where the wandering Nomad strode:
Deadly with the spear and shaft,
 Prowl'd the Hunter through the land;
Woe the Stranger, waves may waft
 On an ever-fatal strand!

III.

Thus was all to Ceres, when
 Searching for her ravish'd child,
(No green culture smiling then,)
 O'er the drear coasts bleak and wild,
Never shelter did she gain,
 Never friendly threshold trod;
All unbuilded then the Fane,
 All unheeded then the God!

---

* The corn-flowers.
† "This first strophe," observes Hoffmeister, "is opened by the chorus of the whole festive assembly. A smaller chorus, or a single narrator passes then to the *recitative*, and traces the progress of mankind through Agriculture."

IV.

Not with golden corn-ears strewed
　Were the ghastly altar-stones ;
Bleaching there, and gore-embrued,
　Lay the unhallow'd Human bones !
Wide and far, where'er she roved,
　Still reigned Misery over all ;
And her mighty soul was moved
　At Man's universal fall.

V.

" What ! can *this* be Man—to whom
　Our own godlike form was given—
Likeness of the shapes that bloom
　In the Garden-Mount of Heaven ?
Was not Earth on Man bestow'd ?
　Earth itself his kingly home !
Roams he thro' his bright abode,
　Homeless wheresoe'er he roam ?

VI.

" Will no God vouchsafe to aid ?—
　None of the Celestial choir—
Lift the Demigod we made
　From the slough and from the mire ?
No, the grief they ne'er have known,
　Calmly the Celestials scan !
I—The Mother—I, alone
　Have a heart that feels for Man !

VII.

" Let—that Men to Man may soar—
　Man and Earth with one another
Make a compact evermore—
　Man the Son, and Earth the Mother.
Let their laws the Seasons show,
　Time itself Man's teacher be ;
And the sweet Moon moving slow
　To the starry Melody ! "

VIII.

Gently brightening from the cloud,
   Round her image, veil-like, thrown ;
On the startled savage crowd
   Lo ! the Goddess-glory shone !
Soft, the Goddess-glory stole
   On their War-feast o'er the Dead ;
Fierce hands offered her the bowl
   With the blood of foemen red.

IX.

Loathing, turned the gentle Queen,
   Loathing, shuddering, turned—and said,
" Ne'er a Godhead's lips have been
   With the food of tigers fed.
Offering pure that ne'er pollutes,
   Be to purer Beings given,
Summer flowers and autumn fruits
   Please the Family of Heaven."

X.

And the wrathful spear she takes
   From the Hunter's savage hand,
With the shaft of Murder,—breaks
   Into furrows the light sand ;
From her spikèd wreath she singles
   Out a golden seed of corn,
With the earth the germ she mingles,
   And the mighty birth is born !

XI.

Robing now the rugged ground—
   Glints the budding lively green,
Now—a Golden Forest—round
   Waves the Mellow Harvest's Sheen !—
And the Goddess bless'd the Earth,
   Bade the earliest sheaf be bound—
Chose the landmark for a hearth,
   And serenely smiling round,

XII.

Spoke in prayer—" O Father King,
  On thine Ether-Hill'divine—
Take, O Zeus, this offering,
  Let it soften Thee to thine !
From thy People's eyes—away,
  Roll the vapour coil'd below ;
Let the hearts untaught to pray
  Learn the Father-God to know ! "

XIII.

And his gentle Sister's prayer,
  To the High Olympian came
Thundering thro' a cloudless air
  Flashed the consecrating flame ;—
On the holy sacrifice,
  Bright the wreathèd lightning leaps ;
And in circles thro' the skies,
  Jove's good-omened Eagle sweeps.

XIV.

Low at the feet of the great Queen, low *
  Fall the crowd in a glad devotion ;
First then, first the rude souls know
  Human channels of sweet emotion—
Cast to the Earth is the gory spear,
  Wakened a soft sense blind before ;
Hush'd in delight, from her lips they hear
  Mildest accents and wisest lore !

XV.

Thither from their thrones descending,
  All the Blest ones brightly draw ;
Sceptred Themis, order-blending,
  Metes the right and gives the law : †

* Here the Full chorus chime in again. . . The Art of Husbandry once
commenced, the chorus proceed to deduce from it the improvements of all
social life.—HOFFMEISTER.
 † Property begins with the culture of the Earth, Law with Property.

Teaches each one to respect
    What his Neighbour's landmarks girth ;
Bids attesting Styx protect
    What the mortal owns on earth.

XVI.

Hither limps the God, whom all*
    Life's inventive Arts obey,
Highly skill'd is he to call
    Shape from metal, use from clay !
Heave the bellows, rings the clamour
    Of the heavy Anvil, now ;
Fashion'd from the Forge-God's hammer
    O'er the Furrow speeds the Plough !

XVII.

And Minerva, towering proudly
    Over all, with lifted spear,
Calls in accents ringing loudly
    O'er the millions far and near—†
Calls the scattered tribes around ;—
    Soars the rampart—spreads the wall,
And the scattered tribes have found
    Bulwark each, and union all !

XVIII.

Forth she leads her lordly train,
    O'er the wide earth ;—and where'er
Prints her conquering step the plain,
    Springs another Landmark there !
O'er the Hills her empire sweeps ;
    O'er their heights her chain she throws,
Stream that thundered to the deeps
    Curb'd in green banks, gently flows.

XIX.

Nymph and Oread, all who follow
    The fleet-footed Forest-Queen,
O'er the hill, or through the hollow ;
    Swinging light their spears are seen.

* Vulcan. Then follow the technical Arts.
† Now come the Arts of Polity.

With a merry clamour trooping,
　　With bright axes—one and all
Round the doomèd forest grouping,
　　Down the huge pines crackling fall !

XX.

At the hest of Jòve's high daughter,
　　Heavy load and gròaning raft
O'er his green reed-margined Water
　　Doth the River Genius waft.
In the work, glad hands have found,
　　Hour on hour, light-footed, flies,
From the rude trunk, smooth and round,
　　Till the polish'd mast arise !

XXI.

Up leaps now the Ocean God,
　　Riving ribbèd Earth asunder ;
With his wondrous Trident-rod ;—
　　And the granite falls in thunder.
High he swings the mighty blocks,
　　As an Infant swings a ball—
Help'd by active Hermes, rocks
　　Heap'd on rocks—construct the wall.*

XXII.

Then from golden strings set free
　　(Young Apollo's charmed boon)
Triple flows the Harmony,
　　And the Measure, and the Tune !
With their ninefold symphonies
　　There the chiming Muses throng,
Stone on stone the walls arise
　　To the Choral Music-song.†

---

* This refers to the building of Troy.
† A felicitous allusion to the Walls of Thebes, built according to the
fable to the sound of the Muses.

XXIII.

By Cybele's cunning hand
  Set the mighty Portals arc ;
And the huge Lock's safety-band,
  And the force-defying Bar.
Swift from those divinest hands
  Does the Wondrous City rise—
Bright, amidst, the Temple stands
  In the pomp of sacrifice.

XXIV.

With a myrtle garland—there
  Comes the Queen,* by Gods obey'd,
And she leads the Swain most fair
  To the fairest Shepherd-maid !
Venus and her laughing Boy
  Did that earliest pair array ;
All the Gods, with gifts of joy
  Bless'd the earliest Marriage Day !

XXV.

Thro' the Hospitable Gate
  Flock the City's newborn sons,
Marshall'd in harmonious state
  By that choir of Holy ones.
At the Altar-shrine of Jove
  High—the Priestess Ceres stands
Folding, the mute Crowd above,
  Blessed and all-blessing hands !

XXVI.

In the waste the Beast is free,
  And the God upon his throne !
Unto each the curb must be
  But the nature each doth own.
Yet the Man—(betwixt the two)
  Must to man allied, belong ;
Only Law and Custom thro'
  Is the Mortal free and strong ! ”

* Juno, the Goddess presiding over marriage.

XXVII.

Wind in a garland the ears of gold,
  Azure Cyanes inwoven be ;
Oh how gladly shall eye behold
  'The Queen, who comes in her majesty !
Man to man in communion bringing,
  Hers are the sweets of Home and Hearth,
Honour and praise, and hail her, singing,
  " Hail to the Mother and Queen of Earth ! "

PARABLES AND RIDDLES.

I.

From Pearls her lofty bridge she weaves,
  A grey sea arching proudly over ;
A moment's toil the work achieves,
  And on the height behold her hover !
Beneath that arch securely go
  The tallest barks that ride the seas,
No burthen e'er the bridge may know,
  And as thou seek'st to near—it flees !
First with the floods it came, to fade
  As roll'd the waters from the land ;
Say where that wondrous arch is made,
  And whose the Artist's mighty hand ? *

II.

League after league it hurrieth thee,
  Yet never quits its place ;
It hath no wings wherewith to flee,
  Yet wafts thee over space !
It is the fleetest boat that e'er
  The wildest wanderer bore :
As swift as thought itself to bear
  From shore to farthest shore ;
'Tis here and there, and everywhere,
  Ere yet a moment's o'er ! †

* The Rainbow.
† The Sight, or perhaps Light.

K

III.

O'er a mighty pasture go,
    Sheep in thousands, silver-white;
As to-day we see them, so
    In the oldest grandsire's sight.
They drink (never waxing old)
    Life from an unfailing brook;
There's a Shepherd to their fold,
    With a silver-horned crook.
From a gate of gold let out,
    Night by night he counts them over;
Wide the field they rove about,
    Never hath he lost a rover!
True the DOG, that helps to lead them,
    One gay RAM in front we see;
What the Flock and who doth heed them,
    Sheep and Shepherd—tell to me! *

IV.

There is a Mansion vast and fair,
    That doth on unseen pillars rest;
No Wanderer leaves the portals there,
    Yet each how brief a guest!
The craft by which that mansion rose
    No thought can picture to the soul;
'Tis lighted by a Lamp which throws
    Its stately shimmer through the whole.
As crystal clear, it rears aloof
The single gem which forms its roof,
And never hath the eye survey'd
The Master who that Mansion † made.

V.

Up and down two buckets ply,
    A single well within;
While the one comes full on high,
    One the deeps must win;
Full or empty, never ending,
Rising now and now descending,

----

* The Moon and Stars.
† The Earth and the Firmament.

Always—while you quaff from this,
That one lost in the abyss,
From that well the waters living
Never both together giving.*

VI.

That gentle picture dost thou know,
    Itself its hues and splendour gaining?
Some change each moment can bestow,
    Itself as perfect still remaining;
It lies within the smallest space,
    The smallest framework forms its girth,
And yet that picture can embrace
    The mightiest objects known on Earth:
Canst thou to me that crystal name
    (No gem can with its worth compare)
Which gives all light, and knows no flame;
    Absorbed is all creation there!—
That ring can in itself enclose
    The loveliest hues that light the Heaven,
Yet from it light more lovely goes
    Than all which to it can be given! †

VII.

There stands a Building vast and wide,
    Built in eldest times of yore;
Round it may the Rider ride
    For a hundred days or more;
And however fast he speed,
Shall the pile outstrip the steed.
Many a hundred years have fled,
    'Gainst it Time and Storm have striven,
Stark and strong it rears its head
    Underneath the Vault of Heaven;
Soaring here the clouds to meet,
There the ocean laves its feet.

---

* Day and Night. It has also been interpreted as Youth and Age, or Past and Present.
† The Eye.

Not some pageant-pomp to lend
   Vaunting Pride, or flaunting Power,
But to shield and to defend
   Doth that Mighty Fabric tower.
Ne'er its like hath Earth survey'd,
Tho' a mortal hand hath made!*

VIII.

Amidst the Serpent Race is one
   That Earth did never bear;
In speed and fury there be none
   That can with it compare,—
With fearful hiss—its prey to grasp
   It darts its dazzling course;
And locks in one destroying clasp
   The Horseman and the Horse.
It loves the loftiest heights to haunt—
   No bolt its prey secures,
In vain its mail may Valour vaunt,
   For steel its fury lures!
As slightest straw whirl'd by the wind,
   It snaps the starkest tree;
It can the might of metal grind,
   How hard soe'er it be!
Yet ne'er but once the Monster tries
   The prey it threats to gain,†
In its own wrath consumed it dies,
   And while it slays is slain.‡

IX.

Six Sisters, from a wondrous pair,§
   We take our common birth;
Our solemn Mother—dark as Care,
   Our Father bright as Mirth,

* The Wall of China.
† " Hat zwei mal nur gedroht." For *nur* should be read *nie.*
‡ Lightning.
§ Black and White. Here Schiller adopts Goethe's theory of colours, and
supposes that they are formed from the mixture of Light and Darkness,--

Its several virtue each bequeathes;
   The soften'd shade—the merry glance;
In endless youth, around you wreathes
   Our undulating dance!
We shun the darksome hollow cave,
   And bask where daylight glows;
Our magic life to Nature gave
   The soul her beauty knows.
Blithe messengers of Spring, we lead
   Her jocund train,—we flee
The dreary chambers of the Dead,—
   Where life is—there are we!
To Happiness essential things,
   Where Man enjoys we live—
Whate'er the Pomp that blazons kings,
   'Tis ours the pomp to give! *

X.

What's that, the Poor's most precious Friend
   Nor less by kings respected—
Contrived to pierce, contrived to rend,
   And to the sword connected.
It draws no blood, and yet doth wound;—
   Makes rich, but ne'er with spoil;
It prints, as Earth it wanders round,
   A blessing on the soil.
Tho' eldest cities it hath built—
   Bade mightiest kingdoms rise, it
Ne'er fired to War, nor roused to guilt:
   Weal to the states that prize it! †

XI.

In a Dwelling of stone I conceal,
   My existence obscure and asleep;
But forth at the clash of the steel,
   From my slumber exulting I leap!

i. e., the Children of Night and Day. In his earlier poem of "The Artists,"
the noble image which concludes the Poem is taken from the different theory
of Newton. According to the former theory, the Colours are six in number
—according to the latter, seven.—HOFFMEISTER.
  * The Colours.
  † The Ploughshare.

At first, all too feeble for strife,
  As a dwarf I appear to thine eye;
A drop could extinguish my life—
  But my wings soon expand to the sky!
Let the might of my Sister * afford
  Its aid to those wings when unfurl'd,
And I grow to a terrible Lord,
  Whose anger can ravage the world.†

XII.

Revolving round a Disk I go,
  One restless journey o'er and o'er;
The smallest field my wanderings know,
  Thy hands the space could cover:
Yet many a thousand miles are past,
  In circling round that field so narrow;
My speed outstrips the swiftest blast—
  The strongest bowman's arrow! ‡

XIII.

It is a Bird—whose swiftness flees,
  Fast as an Eagle thro' the Air;
It is a Fish—and cleaves the seas,
  Which ne'er a mightier monster bear:
It is an Elephant, whose form
  Is crownèd with a castle-keep;
And now, all like the spider-worm,
  Spinning its white webs—see it creep!
It hath an iron fang; and where
  That fang is grappled hold doth gain,
It roots its rock-like footing there,
  And braves the baffled Hurricane.§

* Viz. :—The Air.
† Fire.

‡ The Shade on the Dial.
§ The Ship.

THE MIGHT OF SONG.

In the two Poems—"The Might of Song"—and that to which, in the translation, we have given the paraphrastic title "Honour to Woman" (Würde der Frauen), are to be found those ideas which are the well-streams of so much of Schiller's noblest inspiration :—1st, An intense and religious conviction of the lofty character and sublime ends of the true poet. 2nd, A clear sense of what is most lovely in woman, and a chivalrous devotion to the virtues of which he regards her as the Personation and Prototype. It is these two articles in his poetical creed, which constitute Schiller so peculiarly the Poet of *Gentlemen*—not the gentlemen of convention, but the gentlemen of nature—that Aristocracy of feeling and sentiment which are the flower of the social world; chivalrously inclined to whatever is most elevated in Art—chivalrously inclined to whatever is most tender in emotion. The Nobility of the North, which Tacitus saw in its rude infancy, has found in Schiller not only the voice of its mature greatness, but the Ideal of its great essentials.

A RAIN-FLOOD from the Mountain riven,
    It leaps in thunder forth to-day ;
Before its rush the crags are driven,
    The oaks uprooted whirl'd away !
Awed—yet in awe all wildly gladd'ning,
    The startled wanderer halts below ;
He hears the rock-born waters madd'ning,
    Nor wits the source from whence they go,—
So, from their high, mysterious Founts, along,
Stream on the silenced world the Waves of Song !

Knit with the threads of life, for ever,
    By those dread Powers that weave the woof,—
Whose art the singer's spell can sever ?
    Whose breast has mail to music proof ?
Lo, to the Bard, a wand of wonder
    The Herald * of the Gods has given :
He sinks the soul the death-realm under,
    Or lifts it breathless up to heaven—
Half sport, half earnest, rocking its devotion
Upon the tremulous ladder of emotion.

        * Hermes.

As, when in hours the least unclouded
  Portentous, strides upon the scene—
Some Fate, before from wisdom shrouded,
  And awes the startled souls of Men—
Before that Stranger from ANOTHER,
  Behold how THIS world's great ones bow
Mean joys their idle clamour smother,
  The mask is vanish'd from the brow—
And from Truth's sudden, solemn flag unfurl'd,
Fly all the craven Falsehoods of the World !

So, Song—like Fate itself—is given,
  To scare the idler thoughts away,
To raise the Human to the Holy,
  To wake the Spirit from the Clay ! *
One with the Gods the Bard : before him
  All things unclean and earthly fly—
Hush'd are all meaner powers, and o'er him
  The dark fate swoops unharming by ;
And while the Soother's magic measures flow,
Smooth'd every wrinkle on the brows of Woe!

Even as a child, that, after pining
  For the sweet absent mother—hears
Her voice—and, round her neck entwining
  Young arms, vents all his soul in tears ;—
So, by harsh Custom far estranged,
  Along the glad and guileless track,
To childhood's happy home unchanged,
  The swift song wafts the wanderer back—
Snatch'd from the cold and formal world, and prest
By the Great Mother to her glowing breast !

---

* This somewhat obscure, but lofty comparison, by which Poetry is
likened to some fate that rouses men from the vulgar littleness of sensual
joy, levels all ranks for the moment, and appals conventional falsehoods with
unlooked-for truth, Schiller had made, though in rugged and somewhat
bombastic prose, many years before,—as far back as the first appearance of
" The Robbers."

HONOUR TO WOMAN.

[Literally " Dignity of Women."]

HONOUR to Woman ! To her it is given
To garden the earth with the roses of Heaven !
   All blessed, she linketh the Loves in their choir—
In the veil of the Graces her beauty concealing,
She tends on each altar that's hallow'd to Feeling,
   And keeps ever-living the fire !

   From the bounds of Truth careering,
     Man's strong spirit wildly sweeps,
   With each hasty impulse veering,
     Down to Passion's troubled deeps.
   And his heart, contented never,
     Greeds to grapple with the Far,
   Chasing his own dream for ever,
     On through many a distant Star !

But Woman with looks that can charm and enchain,
Lureth back at her beck the wild truant again,
   By the spell of her presence beguiled—
In the home of the Mother her modest abode,
And modest the manners by Nature bestow'd
   On Nature's most exquisite child !

   Bruised and worn, but fiercely breasting,
     Foe to foe, the angry strife ;
   Man the Wild One, never resting,
     Roams along the troubled life ;
   What he planneth, still pursuing ;
     Vainly as the Hydra bleeds,
   Crest the sever'd crest renewing—
     Wish to wither'd wish succeeds.

But Woman at peace with all being, reposes,
And seeks from the Moment to gather the roses—
   Whose sweets to her culture belong.
Ah ! richer than he, though his soul reigneth o'er
The mighty dominion of Genius and Lore,
   And the infinite Circle of Song.

Strong, and proud, and self-depending,
   Man's cold bosom beats alone ;
Heart with heart divinely blending,
   In the love that Gods have known,
Souls' sweet interchange of feeling,
   Melting tears—he never knows,
Each hard sense the hard one steeling,
   Arms against a world of foes.

Alive, as the wind-harp, how lightly soever
If woo'd by the Zephyr, to music will quiver,
   Is Woman to Hope and to Fear ;
Ah, tender one ! still at the shadow of grieving,
How quiver the chords—how thy bosom is heaving—
   How trembles thy glance through the tear !

Man's dominion, war and labour ;
   Might to right the Statute gave ;
Laws are in the Scythian's sabre ;
   Where the Mede reign'd—see the Slave !
Peace and Meekness grimly routing,
   Prowls the War-lust, rude and wild ;
Eris rages, hoarsely shouting,
   Where the vanish'd Graces smiled.

But Woman, the Soft One, persuasively prayeth—
Of the life* that she charmeth, the sceptre she swayeth ;
   She lulls, as she looks from above,
The Discord whose Hell for its victims is gaping,
And blending awhile the for-ever escaping,
   Whispers Hate to the Image of Love !

THE WORDS OF BELIEF.

THREE Words will I name thee—around and about,
   From the lip to the lip, full of meaning, they flee ;
But they had not their birth in the being without,
   And the heart, not the lip, must their oracle be !
And all worth in the man shall for ever be o'er
When in those Three Words he believes no more.

  * Literally, " the Manners." The French word *mœurs* corresponds best
with the German.

Man is made FREE!—Man, by birthright is free,
   Though the tyrant may deem him but born for his
     tool.
Whatever the shout of the rabble may be—
   Whatever the ranting misuse of the fool—
Still fear not the Slave, when he breaks from his chain,
For the Man made a Freeman grows safe in his gain.

And VIRTUE is more than a shade or a sound,
   And Man may her voice, in this being, obey;
And though ever he slip on the stony ground,
   Yet ever again to the godlike way,
To the *science* of Good though the Wise may be blind,
Yet the *practice* is plain to the childlike mind.

And a GOD there is!—over Space, over Time,
   While the Human Will rocks, like a reed, to and fro,
Lives the Will of the Holy—A Purpose Sublime,
   A Thought woven over creation below;
Changing and shifting the All we inherit,
But changeless through all One Immutable Spirit!

Hold fast the Three Words of Belief—though about
   From the lip to the lip, full of meaning, they flee;
Yet they take not their birth from the being without—
   But a voice from within must their oracle be;
And never all worth in the Man can be o'er,
Till in those Three Words he believes no more.

THE WORDS OF ERROR.

THREE Errors there are, that for ever are found
   On the lips of the good, on the lips of the best;
But empty their meaning and hollow their sound—
   And slight is the comfort they bring to the breast.
The fruits of existence escape from the clasp
Of the seeker who strives but those shadows to grasp—

So long as Man dreams of some Age in *this* life
   When the Right and the Good will all evil subdue;
For the Right and the Good lead us ever to strife,
   And wherever they lead us, the Fiend will pursue.

And (till from the earth borne, and stifled at length)
The earth that he touches still gifts him with strength ! *

So long as Man fancies that Fortune will live,
    Like a bride with her lover, united with Worth ;
For her favours, alas ! to the mean she will give—
    And Virtue possesses no title to earth !
That Foreigner wanders to regions afar,
Where the lands of her birthright immortally are !

So long as Man dreams that, to mortals a gift,
    The Truth in her fulness of splendour will shine ;
The veil of the goddess no earth-born may lift,
    And all we can learn is—to guess and divine !
Dost thou seek, in a dogma, to prison her form ?
The spirit flies forth on the wings of the storm !

O, Noble Soul ! fly from delusions like these,
    More heavenly belief be it thine to adore ;
Where the Ear never hearkens, the Eye never sees,
    Meet the rivers of Beauty and Truth evermore !
Not *without* thee the streams—there the Dull seek them ; —
        No !
Look *within* thee—behold both the fount and the flow !

THE MERCHANT.

WHERE sails the ship ?—It leads the Tyrian forth
For the rich amber of the liberal North.
Be kind ye seas—winds lend your gentlest wing,
May in each creek, sweet wells restoring spring !--
To you, ye gods, belong the Merchant !—o'er
The waves, his sails the wide world's goods explore ;
And, all the while, wherever waft the gales,
The wide world's good sails with him as he sails !

* This simile is nobly conceived, but expressed somewhat obscurely. As Hercules contended in vain against Antæus, the Son of Earth,—so long as the Earth gave her giant offspring new strength in every fall,—so the soul contends in vain with evil—the natural earth-born enemy, while the very contact of the earth invigorates the enemy for the struggle. And as Antæus was slain at last, when Hercules lifted him from the earth, and strangled him while raised aloft, so can the soul slay the enemy (the desire, the passion, the evil, the earth's offspring), when bearing it from earth itself, and stilling it in the higher air.

THE GERMAN ART.

By no kind Augustus reared,
To no Medici endeared,
  German Art arose;
Fostering glory smil'd not on her,
Ne'er with kingly smiles to sun her,
  Did her blooms unclose.

No,—she went by Monarchs slighted—
Went unhonoured, unrequited,
  From high Frederick's throne;
Praise and Pride be all the greater,
That Man's genius did create her,
  From Man's worth alone.

Therefore, all from loftier mountains,
Purer wells and richer Fountains,
  Streams our Poet-Art;
So no rule to curb its rushing—
All the fuller flows it gushing
  From its deep—The Heart!

THE WALK.

This (excepting only "The Artists," written some years before) is the most elaborate of those Poems which, classed under the name of *Culture-Historic*, Schiller has devoted to the Progress of Civilisation. Schiller himself esteemed it amongst the greatest of the Poems he had thitherto produced—and his friends, from Goethe to Humboldt, however divided in opinion as to the relative merit of his other pieces, agreed in extolling this one. It must be observed, however, that Schiller had not then composed the narrative poems, which bear the name of Ballads, and which are confessedly of a yet higher order—inasmuch as the Narrative, in itself, demands much higher merits than the Didactic.* It is also reasonably to be objected to all Schiller's Poems of this Culture-Historic School (may we be pardoned the use of the German Barbarism), that the leading idea of the Progress of Civilisation, however varied as to form in each, is essentially repeated in all. Nor can we omit this occasion of inculcating one critical Doctrine, which seems to us highly important, and to which the theories of Schiller's intimate and over-refining friend, William Von Humboldt, were strongly opposed. The object of Poetry, differing essentially from that of abstract wisdom, is not directly to address the Reasoning faculty—but

---

* Schiller perhaps disclaimed the title of Didactic for this Poem, as for "The Artists"—yet Didactic both Poems unquestionably are.

insensibly to rouse it through the popular medium of the emotions. Science aims at Truth, and through Truth may arrive at Beauty. Poetry or Art aims at Beauty, and through Beauty it cannot fail to arrive at Truth. The fault of "The Walk," of "The Artists,"—more than all of "The Ideal and the Actual Life," not to specify some other Poems, less elaborately scholastic—is, that they strain too much the faculty with which Poetry has least to do, viz., the mere Reason. Poetry ought, it is true, to bear aloft and to sustain the mind in a state of elevation—but through the sentiment or the passion. It fails in something when it demands a high degree of philosophy or knowledge in the reader to admire—nay to comprehend it. It ought not to ask a prepared Audience, but to raise any audience it may address. Milton takes the sublimest theme he can find—he adorns it with all his stately genius, and his multiform learning; but, except in two or three passages (which are really defects in his great whole), he contrives to keep within reach of very ordinary understandings. Because the Poet is wise, he is not for that reason to demand wisdom from his readers. In the Poem of "The Walk," it is only after repeated readings that we can arrive at what seems to us its great and distinctive purpose—apart from the mere recital of the changes of the Social State. According to our notion, the purpose is this—the intimate and necessary connexion between Man and Nature—the Social State and the Natural. The Poet commences with the actual Landscape, he describes the scenery of his walk: Rural Life, viz.— Nature in the Fields—suggests to him the picture of the Early Pelasgian or Agricultural life—Nature is then the *Companion* of Man. A sudden turn in the Landscape shows him the popular avenues which in Germany conduct to cities. He beholds the domes and towers of the distant Town—and this suggests to him the alteration from the rural life to the civic—still Nature is his guide. But in cities Man has ceased to be the companion of Nature— he has become her *Ruler* (der Herrscher). In this altered condition the Poet depicts the growth of Civilisation, till he arrives at the Invention of Printing. Light then breaks upon the Blind—Man desires not only to be Lord of Nature, but to dispense with her. "Instead of Necessity and Nature he would appoint Liberty and Reason." Reason shouts for Liberty —so do the Passions, and both burst from the wholesome control of Nature. He then reviews the corruption of Civilisation under the old French Régime; he likens Man, breaking from this denaturalised state, to the tiger escaping from its den into the wilderness; and suggests the great truth, that it is only by a return to Nature, that he can regain his true liberty and re- demption. Not, indeed (as Hoffmeister truly observes), the savage Nature to which Rousseau would reduce Man—*that*, Schiller was too wise to dream of—and too virtuous to desire; but that Nature which has not more its generous liberty than its holy laws—that Nature which is but the word for Law—God's Law. He would not lead Man back to Nature in its infancy, but advance him to Nature in its perfection. The moral Liberty of a well- ordered condition of society is as different from the physical liberty lusted after by the French Revolutionists, as (to borrow Cowley's fine thought) "the solitude of a God from the solitude of a wild beast." And finally, after this general association of Nature with Mankind, the Poet awakens as from a dream, to find himself individually alone with Nature, and concludes, in some of the happiest lines he ever wrote, by insisting on that eternal youthfulness of Nature, which links itself with its companion Poetry. "The Sun of Homer smiles upon us still." In the original German, the Poem is composed in the long rhymeless metre, which no one has succeeded, or can succeed, in rendering into English melody. But happily, the true beauty of the composition, like most of Schiller's (unlike most of Goethe's), is independent of *form :*—consisting of ideas, not easily deprived of their effect, into what mould soever they may be thrown. . . . In the above

remarks we have sought to remove the only drawback the general reader
may find, to the pleasure to be derived from the Poem in the original—
to lighten the weight upon his intellect, and define the purpose of the
design. As to execution, even in translation, the sense of beauty must
be dull in those who cannot perceive the exquisite merits of the preliminary description—the rapid vigour with which what Herder called "the
World of Scenes," shifts and shimmers, and the grand divisions of Human
History are seized and outlined—and the noble reflections which, after
losing himself in the large interests of the multitude, Solitude forces upon
the Poet at the close.

Hail, mine own hill—ye bright'ning hill-tops, hail!
Hail, sun, that gild'st them with thy looks of love!
Sweet fields!—ye lindens, murmuring to the gale!
And ye gay choristers the boughs above!
And thou, the Blue Immeasurable CALM,
O'er mount and forest, motionless and bright,—
Thine airs breathe through me their reviving balm,
And the heart strengthens as it drinks thy light!
Thou gracious Heaven! man's prison-home I flee—
Loosed from the babbling world, my soul leaps up to thee!

Flowers of all hue are struggling into glow,
Along the blooming fields; yet their sweet strife
Melts into one harmonious concord. Lo,
The path allures me through the pastoral green,
And the wide world of fields!—The labouring bee
Hums round me; and on hesitating wing
O'er beds of purple clover quiveringly
Hovers the butterfly.—Save these, all life
Sleeps in the glowing sunlight's steady sheen—
Ev'n from the west, no breeze the lull'd airs bring.
Hark—in the calm aloft, I hear the skylark sing!

The thicket rustles near—the alders bow
Down their green coronals—and as I pass,
Waves, in the rising wind, the silvering grass.
Come, day's ambrosial night!—receive me now
Beneath the roof by shadowy beeches made,
Cool-breathing! Lost the gentler landscape's bloom!
And as the path mounts, snake-like, through the shade,
Deep woods close round me with mysterious gloom;
Still, through the trellice-leaves, at stolen whiles,
Glints the stray beam, or the meek azure smiles.
Again, and yet again, the veil is riven—

And the glade opening, with a sudden glare,
Lets in the blinding day !   Before me, heaven
With all its Far-Unbounded !—one blue hill
Ending the gradual world—in vapour !
                                        Where
I stand upon the mountain-summit, lo,
As sink its sides precipitous before me,
The stream's smooth waves in flying crystal flow
Through the calm vale beneath.   Wide Ether o'er me—
Beneath, alike, wide Ether endless still !
Dizzy, I gaze aloft—shuddering, I look below !—
A railèd path betwixt the eternal height—
And the eternal deep allures me on.
Still, as I pass—all laughing in delight,
The rich shores glide along ; and in glad toil,
Glories the pranksome vale with variegated soil.
Each feature that divides what labour's son
Claims for his portion from his labouring brother ;—
Broidering the veil wrought by the Mighty Mother.*
Hedge-row and bound—those friendly scrolls of law,—
Law, Man's sole guardian ever since the time
When the old Brazen Age, in sadness saw
Love fly the world !
                        Now, through the harmonious meads,
One glimmering path, or lost in forests, leads,
Or up the winding hill doth labouring climb—
The highway link of lands dissever'd—glide
The quiet rafts adown the placid tide ;
And through the lively fields, heard faintly, goes
The many sheep-bells' music—and the song
Of the lone herdsman, from its vex'd repose,
Rouses the gentle echo !—Calm, along
The stream, gay hamlets crown the pastoral scene,
Or peep through distant glades, or from the hill
Hang dizzy down !   Man and the soil serene
Dwell neighbour-like together—and the still
Meadow sleeps peaceful round the rural door—
And, all-familiar, wreathes and clusters o'er
The lowly casement, the green bough's embrace,
As with a loving arm, clasping the gentle place !

* Demeter.

O happy People of the Fields, not yet
Waken'd to freedom from the gentle will
Of the wild Nature, still content to share
With your own fields earth's elementary law !
Calm harvests to calm hopes the boundary set,
And peaceful as your daily labour, there,
Creep on your careless lives ! *
But ah ! what steals
Between me and the scenes I lately saw—
A stranger spirit a strange world reveals,
A world with method, ranks, and orders rife—
And rends the simple unity of life.
The vista'd Poplars in their long array
The measured pomp of social forms betray.
That stately train proclaims the Ruler nigh ;
And now the bright domes glitter to the sky,
And now from out the rocky kernel flowers
The haughty CITY, with its thousand towers !
Yet though the Fauns † back to their wilds have flown,
Devotion lends them loftier life in stone.
Man with his fellow-man more closely bound—
The world without begirts and cramps him round ;
But in that world within the widening soul,
The unpausing wheels in swifter orbits roll.
See how the iron powers of thoughtful skill
Are shaped and quicken'd by the fire of strife ;
Through contest great—through union greater still.
To thousand hands a single soul gives life—
In thousand breasts a single heart is beating—
Beats for the country of the common cause—
Beats for the old hereditary laws—
The earth itself made dearer by the dead—
And by the gods (whom mortal steps are meeting),
Come from their heaven, large gifts on men to shed.
Ceres, the plough—the anchor, Mercury—
Bacchus, the grape—the Sovereign of the sea,

* Here the Poet (after a slight and passing association of Man's more primitive state with the rural landscape before him) catches sight of the distant city ; and, proceeding to idealise what he thus surveys, brings before the reader, in a series of striking and rapid images, the progressive changes of Civilisation.—See PRELIMINARY REMARKS.
† The Fauns here are meant generally to denote all the early rural gods —the primitive Deities of Italy.

L

The horse ;—the olive brings the Blue-eyed Maid—
While tower'd Cybele yokes her lion-car,
Entering in peace the hospitable gate—
A Goddess-Citizen !
                          All-blest ye are,
Ye Solemn Monuments ! ye men and times
That did from shore to shore, and state to state,
Transplant the beauty of humanity !
Forth send far islands, from the gentler climes,
Their goodly freight—the manners and the arts.
In simple courts the Patriarchal Wise
By social Gates adjudge the unpurchased right.*
To deathless fields the ardent hero flies,
To guard the hearths that sanctify the fight ;
And women from the walls, with anxious hearts
Beating beneath the infants nestled there,
Watch the devoted band, till from their eyes,
In the far space, the steel-clad pageant dies—
Then, falling by the altars, pour the prayer,
Fit for the gods to hear—that worth may earn
The fame which crowns brave souls that conquer, and—
          return !
And fame was yours and conquest !—yet alone
Fame—and not life return'd : your deeds are known
In words that kindle glory from the stone.
" Tell Sparta, we, whose record meets thine eye,
Obey'd the Spartan laws—and here we lie ! " †
Sleep soft !—your blood bedews the Olive's bloom,
Peace sows its harvests in the Patriot's tomb,
And Trade's great intercourse at once is known
Where Freedom guards what Labour makes its own.
The azure River-God his watery fields
Lends to the raft ;—her home the Dryad yields.
Down falls the huge oak with a thunder-groan ;
Wing'd by the lever soars the quickening stone ;
Up from the shaft the diving Miner brings
The metal-mass with which the anvil rings,

---

* Alluding to the ancient custom of administering Law in the open places
near the town gates.
† Herodotus.   The celebrated epitaph on the Spartan tumulus at
Thermopylæ.

Anvil and hammer keeping measured time
As the steel sparkles with each heavy chime :—
The bright web round the dancing spindle gleams ;
Safe guides the Pilot, through the world of streams,
The ships that interchange, where'er they roam,
The wealth of earth—the industry of home ;
High from the mast the garland-banner waves,
The Sail bears life upon the wind it braves ;
Life grows and multiplies where life resorts,
Life crowds the Masts—life bustles through the Ports,
And many a language the broad streets within
Blends on the wondering Ear the Babel and the din.
And all the harvests of all earth, whate'er
Hot Afric nurtures in its lurid air,
Or Araby, the blest one of the Wild,
Or the Sea's lonely and abandoned child
Uttermost Thulè,—to one mart are borne,
And the rich plenty brims starr'd Amalthœa's horn.
  The nobler Genius prospers with the rest:
Art draws its aliment from Freedom's breast ;
Flush'd into life, the pictured Image breaks,
Waked by the chisel, Stone takes soul and speaks !
On slender Shafts a Heaven of Art reposes,
And all Olympus one bright Dome encloses.
Light as aloft we see the Iris spring,
Light as the arrow flying from the string,
O'er the wide river, rushing to the Deep,
The lithe bridge boundeth with its airy leap.

  But all the while, best pleased apart to dwell,
Sits musing Science in its noiseless cell ;
Draws meaning circles, and with patient mind
Steals to the Spirit that the whole design'd,
Gropes through the Realm of Matter for its Laws,
Learns where the Magnet or repels or draws,
Follows the sound along the air, and flies
After the lightning through the pathless skies,
Seeks through dark Chance's wonder-teeming maze
The Guiding Law which regulates and sways,
Seeks through the shifting evanescent shows
The Central Principle's serene repose.

L 2

Now shape and voice—the immaterial Thought
Takes from th' Invented speaking page sublime;
The Ark which Mind has for its refuge wrought,
Its floating Archive down the floods of Time!
Rent from the startled gaze the veil of Night,
O'er old delusions streams the dawning light:—
Man breaks his bonds—ah, blest could he refrain,
Free from the curb, to scorn alike the rein!
" Freedom ! " shouts Reason, " Freedom ! " wild Desire—
And light to Wisdom is to Passion fire.
From Nature's check bursts forth one hurtling swarm—
Ah, snaps the anchor, as descends the storm !
The sea runs mountains—vanishes the shore,
The mastless wreck drifts endless ocean o'er;
Lost,—Faith—man's polar Star !—nought seems to rest,
The Heart's God, Conscience, darkens from the breast—

Yet first the foulness of the slough discern, }
From which to Freedom Nature seeks return * }
Gone Truth from language, and from life, belief;
The oath itself rots blighted to a lie,
On love's most solemn secrets, on the grief
Or joy that knits the Heart's familiar tie—
Intrudes the Sycophant, and glares the spy.
Suspected friendship from the soul is rent,
The hungry treason snares the Innocent—
With rabid slaver, and devouring fangs,
Fast on his prey the foul blasphemer hangs—
Shame from the reason and the heart effac'd,
The thought is abject, and the love debas'd:
Deceit—O Truth, thy holy features steals—
Watches emotion in its candid course—
Betrays what Mirth unconsciously reveals,
And desecrates Man's nature at its source;
And yet the Tribune justice can debate—
And yet the Cot of tranquil Union prate—

* The two lines in brackets are, after much hesitation, interpolated by the
Translator, in order to maintain the sense, otherwise obscured, if not lost,
by the abruptness of the transition. Schiller has already glanced at the
French Revolution, but he now goes back to the time preceding it, and the
following lines portray the corruption of the old régime.

And yet a spectre which they call the Law,
Stands by the Kingly throne, the crowd to awe!
For years—for centuries, may the Mummies there,
Mock the warm life whose lying shape they wear,
Till Nature once more from her sleep awakes—
Till to the dust the hollow fabric shakes
Beneath your hands—Avenging Powers sublime,
Your heavy iron hands, NECESSITY and TIME!

Then, as some Tigress from the grated bar,
Bursts sudden, mindful of her wastes afar,
Deep in Numidian glooms—Humanity,
Fierce in the wrath of wretchedness and crime,
Forth from the City's blazing ashes breaks,
And the lost Nature it has pined for seeks.
Open ye walls and let the prisoner free!—
Safe to forsaken fields, back let the wild one flee!

But where am I—and whither would I stray?
The path is lost—the cloud-capt mountain-dome,
The rent abysses, to the dizzy sense,
Behind, before me! Far and far away,
Garden and hedgerow, the sweet Company
Of Fields, familiar speaking of man's home—
Yea, every trace of man—lie hidden from the eye.
Only the raw eternal MATTER, whence
Life buds, towers round me—the grey basalt-stone,
Virgin of human art, stands motionless and lone.
Roaringly, through the rocky cleft, and under
Gnarl'd roots of trees, the torrent sweeps in thunder—
Savage the scene, and desolate and bare—
Lo! where the eagle, his calm wings unfurl'd,
Lone-halting in the solitary air,
Knits * to the vault of heaven this ball—the world!
No plumèd wind bears o'er the Dœdal soil
One breath of man's desire, and care, and toil.
Am I indeed alone, amidst thy charms,
O Nature—clasped once more within thine arms?—

---

* Knits—*Knüpft.* What a sublime image is conveyed in that single
word!

I dreamed—and wake upon thy heart !—escaped
From the dark phantoms which my Fancy shaped;
And sinks each shape of human strife and woe
Down with the vapours to the vale below !

Purer I take my life from thy pure shrine,
Sweet Nature !—gladlier comes again to me
The heart and hope of my lost youth divine !
Both end and means, eternally our will
Varies and changes, and our acts are still
The repetitions, multiplied and stale,
Of what have been before us.   But with THEE
One ancient law, that will not wane or fail,
Keeps beauty vernal in the bloom of truth !
Ever the same, thou hoardest for the man
What to thy hands the infant or the youth
Trusted familiar; and since Time began,
Thy breasts have nurtured, with impartial love,
The many-changing ages !
                                Look above,
Around, below ;—beneath the self-same blue,
Over the self-same green, eternally,
(Let man's slight changes wither as they will,)
All races which the wide world ever knew,
United, wander brother-like !—Ah ! see,
THE SUN OF HOMER SMILES UPON US STILL !

THE LAY OF THE BELL.

" Vivos voco—Mortuos plango—Fulgura frango." *

I.

FAST, in its prison-walls of earth,
    Awaits the mould of bakèd clay.
Up, comrades, up, and aid the birth—
    THE BELL that shall be born to-day !

---

* "I call the living—I mourn the Dead—I break the Lightning."   These
words are inscribed on the Great Bell of the Minster of Schaffhausen—also
on that of the Church of Art near Lucerne.   There was an old belief in
Switzerland, that the undulation of air, caused by the sound of a Bell, broke
the electric fluid of a thunder-cloud.

Who would honour obtain,
  With the sweat and the pain,
The praise that Man gives to the Master must buy!—
But the blessing withal must descend from on high!

And well an earnest word beseems
  The work the earnest hand prepares;
Its load more light the labour deems,
  When sweet discourse the labour shares.
So let us ponder—nor in vain—
  What strength can work when labour wills;
For who would not the fool disdain
  Who ne'er designs what he fulfils?
And well it stamps our Human Race,
  And hence the gift To UNDERSTAND,
That Man, within the heart should trace
  Whate'er he fashions with the hand.

II.

From the fir the fagot take,
  Keep it, heap it hard and dry,
That the gather'd flame may break
  Through the furnace, wroth and high.
    When the copper within
    Seethes and simmers—the tin,
Pour quick, that the fluid that feeds the Bell
May flow in the right course glib and well.

Deep hid within this nether cell,
  What force with Fire is moulding thus,
In yonder airy tower shall dwell,
  And witness wide and far of us!
It shall, in later days, unfailing,
  Rouse many an ear to rapt emotion;
Its solemn voice with Sorrow wailing,
  Or choral chiming to Devotion.
Whatever Fate to Man may bring,
  Whatever weal or woe befall,
That metal tongue shall backward ring
  The warning moral drawn from all.

III.

See the silvery bubbles spring !
   Good ! the mass is melting now !
Let the salts we duly bring
   Purge the flood, and speed the flow.
     From the dross and the scum,
     Pure, the fusion must come ;
For perfect and pure we the metal must keep,
That its voice may be perfect, and pure, and deep.

   That voice, with merry music rife,
     The cherish'd child shall welcome in ;
   What time the rosy dreams of life,
     In the first slumber's arms begin.
   As yet in Time's dark womb unwarning,
     Repose the days, or foul or fair ;
   And watchful o'er that golden morning,
     The Mother-Love's untiring care !
   And swift the years like arrows fly—
   No more with girls content to play,
   Bounds the proud Boy upon his way,
   Storms through loud life's tumultuous pleasures,
   With pilgrim staff the wide world measures ;
   And, wearied with the wish to roam,
   Again seeks, stranger-like, the Father-Home.
   And, lo, as some sweet vision breaks
     Out from its native morning skies,
   With rosy shame on downcast cheeks,
     The Virgin stands before his eyes.
   A nameless longing seizes him !
     From all his wild companions flown ;
   Tears, strange till then, his eyes bedim ;
     He wanders all alone.
   Blushing, he glides where'er she move ;
     Her greeting can transport him ;
   To every mead to deck his love,
     The happy wild flowers court him !
   Sweet Hope—and tender Longing—ye
     The growth of Life's first Age of Gold
   When the heart, swelling, seems to see
     The gates of heaven unfold !

O Love, the beautiful and brief! O prime,
Glory, and verdure, of life's summer time!

IV.

Browning o'er, the pipes are simmering,
    Dip this wand of clay * within;
If like glass the wand be glimmering,
    Then the casting may begin.
      Brisk, brisk now, and see
      If the fusion flow free;
If—(happy and welcome indeed were the sign!)
If the hard and the ductile united combine.
For still where the strong is betrothed to the weak,
And the stern in sweet marriage is blent with the
    meek,
  Rings the concord harmonious, both tender and strong:
So be it with thee, if for ever united,
The heart to the heart flows in one, love-delighted;
  Illusion is brief, but Repentance is long.

    Lovely, thither are they bringing,
      With her virgin wreath, the Bride!
    To the love-feast clearly ringing,
      Tolls the church-bell far and wide!
    With that sweetest holyday,
      Must the May of Life depart;
    With the cestus loosed—away
    Flies ILLUSION from the heart!
      Yet love lingers lonely,
        When Passion is mute,
      And the blossoms may only
        Give way to the fruit.
    The Husband must enter
      The hostile life,
      With struggle and strife,
      To plant or to watch,
      To snare or to snatch,
      To pray and importune,
    Must wager and venture
      And hunt down his fortune!

* A piece of clay pipe, which becomes vitrified if the metal is sufficiently heated.

Then flows in a current the gear and the gain,
And the garners are fill'd with the gold of the grain,
Now a yard to the court, now a wing to the centre!
      Within sits Another,
        The thrifty Housewife;
      The mild one, the mother—
        Her home is her life.
      In its circle she rules,
      And the daughters she schools,
        And she cautions the boys,
      With a bustling command,
      And a diligent hand
        Employ'd she employs;
      Gives order to store,
      And tho much makes the more;
Locks the chest and the wardrobe, with lavender smelling,
And the hum of the spindle goes quick through the
    dwelling;
And she hoards in the presses, well polish'd and full,
The snow of the linen, the shine of the wool;
Blends the sweet with the good, and from care and en-
    deavour
Rests never!
      Blithe the Master (where the while
      From his roof he sees them smile)
        Eyes the lands, and counts the gain;
      There, the beams projecting far,
      And the laden store-house are,
      And the granaries bow'd beneath
        The blessed golden grain;
      There, in undulating motion,
      Wave the corn-fields like an ocean.
      Proud the boast the proud lips breathe:—
      " My house is built upon a rock,
      And sees unmoved the stormy shock
        Of waves that fret below!"
      What chain so strong, what girth so great,
      To bind the giant form of Fate?—
        Swift are the steps of Woe.

V.

Now tho casting may begin ;
  See tho breach indented there :
Ere we run tho fusion in,
    Halt—and speed tho pious prayer !
      Pull the bung out—
      See around and about
What vapour, what vapour—God help us !—has risen ?—
Ha ! tho flame like a torrent leaps forth from its prison !
  What friend is like the might of fire
  When man can watch and wield tho ire ?
  Whate'er we shape or work, we owe
  Still to that heaven-descended glow.
  But dread tho heaven-descended glow,
  When from their chain its wild wings go,
  When, where it listeth, wide and wild
  Sweeps tho free Nature's free-born Child !
  When the Frantic One fleets,
    While no force can withstand,
  Through the populous streets
    Whirling ghastly the brand ;
  For the Element hates
  What Man's labour creates,
    And the work of his hand !
  Impartially out from tho cloud,
    Or the curse or the blessing may fall !
  Benignantly out from tho cloud,
    Come the dews, tho revivers of all !
  Avengingly out from the cloud
    Come the levin, tho bolt, and tho ball !
  Hark—a wail from tho steeple !—aloud
  Tho bell shrills its voice to the crowd !
    Look—look—red as blood
      All on high !
  It is not tho daylight that fills with its flood
    Tho sky !
  What a clamour awaking
    Roars up through tho street,
  What a hell-vapour breaking
    Rolls on through the street,

And higher and higher
Aloft moves the Column of Fire !
Through the vistas and rows
Like a whirlwind it goes,
And the air like the steam from a furnace glows.
Beams are crackling—posts are shrinking
Walls are sinking—windows clinking—
Children crying—
Mothers flying—
And the beast (the black ruin yet smouldering under)
Yells the howl of its pain and its ghastly wonder !
Hurry and skurry—away—away,
The face of the night is as clear as day !
As the links in a chain,
Again and again
Flies the bucket from hand to hand ;
High in arches up-rushing
The engines are gushing,
And the flood, as a beast on the prey that it hounds,
With a roar on the breast of the element bounds.
To the grain and the fruits,
Through the rafters and beams,
Through the barns and the garners it crackles and
streams !
As if they would rend up the earth from its roots,
Rush the flames to the sky
Giant-high ;
And at length,
Wearied out and despairing, man bows to their strength !
With an idle gaze sees their wrath consume,
And submits to his doom !
Desolate
The place, and dread
For storms the barren bed.
In the blank voids that cheerful casements were,
Comes to and fro the melancholy air,
And sits despair ;
And through the ruin, blackening in its shroud
Peers, as it flits, the melancholy cloud.

One human glance of grief upon the grave
Of all that Fortune gave

The loiterer takes—Then turns him to depart,
And grasps the wanderer's staff and mans his heart:
Whatever else the element bereaves
One blessing more than all it reft—it leaves,
The *faces that he loves !*—He counts them o'er,
See—not one look is missing from *that* store !

VI.

Now clasp'd the bell within the clay—
    The mould the mingled metals fill—
Oh, may it, sparkling into day,
  ' Reward the labour and the skill !
        Alas ! should it fail,
        For the mould may be frail—
And still with our hope must be mingled the fear—
And, ev'n now, while we speak, the mishap may be near !
    To the dark womb of sacred earth
        This labour of our hands is given,
    As seeds that wait the second birth,
        And turn to blessings watch'd by heaven !
Ah seeds, how dearer far than they
    We bury in the dismal tomb,
Where Hope and Sorrow bend to pray
That suns beyond the realm of day
    May warm them into bloom !

            From the steeple
            Tolls the bell,
            Deep and heavy,
            The death-knell !
Guiding with dirge-note—solemn, sad, and slow,
To the last home earth's weary wanderers know.
        It is that worship'd wife—
        It is that faithful mother ! *
Whom the dark Prince of Shadows leads benighted,
From that dear arm where oft she hung delighted.
Far from those blithe companions, born
Of her, and blooming in their morn ;

---

* The translator adheres to the original, in forsaking the rhyme in these
lines and some others.

On whom, when couch'd her heart above,
So often look'd the Mother-Love !

  Ah ! rent the sweet Home's union-band,
    And never, never more to come—
  She dwells within the shadowy land,
    Who was the Mother of that Home !
  How oft they miss that tender guide,
    The care—the watch—the face—the MOTHER—
  And where she sate the babes beside,
    Sits with unloving looks—ANOTHER !

VII.

  While the mass is cooling now,
    Let the labour yield to leisure,
  As the bird upon the bough,
    Loose the travail to the pleasure.
      When the soft stars awaken,
      Each task be forsaken !
And the vesper-bell lulling the earth into peace,
If the master still toil, chimes the workman's release !

  Homeward from the tasks of day,
  Thro' the greenwood's welcome way
  Wends the wanderer, blithe and cheerly,
  To the cottage loved so dearly !
  And the eye and ear are meeting,
  Now, the slow sheep homeward bleating—
  Now, the wonted shelter near,
  Lowing the lusty-fronted steer ;
  Creaking now the heavy wain,
  Reels with the happy harvest grain.
  While, with many-coloured leaves,
  Glitters the garland on the sheaves ;
  For the mower's work is done,
  And the young folks' dance begun !
  Desert street, and quiet mart ;—
  Silence is in the city's heart ;
  And the social taper lighteth
  Each dear face that HOME uniteth ;
  While the gate the town before
  Heavily swings with sullen roar !

Though darkness is spreading
  O'er earth—the Upright
And the Honest, undreading,
  Look safe on the night—
Which the evil man watches in awe,
For the eye of the Night is the Law!
   Bliss-dower'd! O daughter of the skies,
Hail, holy ORDER, whose employ
Blends like to like in light and joy—
Builder of cities, who of old
Call'd the wild man from waste and wold.
And, in his hut thy presence stealing,
Roused each familiar household feeling;
  And, best of all the happy ties,
The centre of the social band,—
The Instinct of the Fatherland!

United thus—each helping each,
  Brisk work the countless hands for ever;
For nought its power to Strength can teach,
  Like Emulation and Endeavour!
Thus link'd the master with the man,
  Each in his rights can each revere,
And while they march in freedom's van,
  Scorn the lewd rout that dogs the rear!
To freemen labour is renown!
  Who works—gives blessings and commands;
Kings glory in the orb and crown—
  Be ours the glory of our hands.
Long in these walls—long may we greet
Your footfalls, Peace and Concord sweet!
Distant the day. Oh! distant far,
When the rude hordes of trampling War
    Shall scare the silent vale;
      And where,
    Now the sweet heaven, when day doth leave
      The air,
    Limns its soft rose-hues on the veil of Eve;
Shall the fierce war-brand tossing in the gale,
From town and hamlet shake the horrent glare!

VIII.

Now, its destin'd task fulfill'd,
 Asunder break the prison-mould ;
Let the goodly Bell we build,
 Eye and heart alike behold.
  The hammer down heave,
  Till the cover it cleave :—
For not till we shatter the wall of its cell
Can we lift from its darkness and bondage the Bell.

To break the mould, the master may,
 If skill'd the hand and ripe the hour ;
But woe, when on its fiery way
 The metal seeks itself to pour.
Frantic and blind, with thunder-knell,
 Exploding from its shattered home,
And glaring forth, as from a hell,
 Behold the red Destruction come !
When rages strength that has no reason,
There breaks the mould before the season ;
When numbers burst what bound before,
Woe to the State that thrives no more !
Yea, woe, when in the City's heart,
 The latent spark to flame is blown ;
And Millions from their silence start,
 To claim, without a guide, their own !
Discordant howls the warning Bell,
 Proclaiming discord wide and far,
And, born but things of peace to tell,
 Becomes the ghastliest voice of war :
" Freedom !   Equality !"—to blood,
 Rush the roused people at the sound !
Through street, hall, palace, roars the flood,
 And banded murder closes round !
The hyæna-shapes, (that women were !)
 Jest with the horrors they survey ;
They hound—they rend—they mangle there—
 As panthers with their prey !
Nought rests to hallow—burst the ties
 Of life's sublime and reverent awe ;
Before the Vice the Virtue flies,
 And Universal Crime is Law !

Man fears the lion's kingly tread ;
  Man fears the tiger's fangs of terror ;
And still the dreadliest of the dread,
  Is Man himself in error !
No torch, though lit from Heaven, illumes
  The Blind !—Why place it in his hand ?
It lights not him—it but consumes
  The City and the Land !

IX.

Rejoice and laud the prospering skies !
  The kernel bursts its husk—behold
From the dull clay the metal rise,
  Pure-shining, as a star of gold !
    Neck and lip, but as one beam,
    It laughs like a sun-beam.
And even the scutcheon, clear-graven, shall tell
That the art of a master has fashion'd the Bell !

Come in—come in
My merry men—we'll form a ring
The new-born labour christening ;
  And " CONCORD " we will name her !—
To union may her heart-felt call
  In brother-love attune us all !
May she the destined glory win
  For which the master sought to frame her—
Aloft—(all earth's existence under,)
  In blue-pavilion'd heaven afar
To dwell—the Neighbour of the Thunder,
  The Borderer of the Star !
Be hers above a voice to raise
  Like those bright hosts in yonder sphere,
Who, while they move, their Maker praise,
  And lead around the wreathèd year !
To solemn and eternal things
  We dedicate her lips sublime !—
As hourly, calmly, on she swings—
  Fann'd by the fleeting wings of Time !—

                                        M

No pulse—no heart—no feeling hers !
　　She lends the warning voice to Fate ;
And still companions, while she stirs,
　　The changes of the Human State !
So may she teach us, as her tone
　　But now so mighty, melts away—
That earth no life which earth has known
　　From the last silence can delay !

*　　　*　　　*　　　*　　　*

Slowly now the cords upheave her !
　　From her earth-grave soars the Bell ;
Mid the airs of Heaven we leave her !
　　In the Music-Realm to dwell !
　　　Up—upwards—yet raise—
　　　She has risen—she sways.
Fair Bell to our city bode joy and increase,
And oh, may thy first sound be hallow'd to—Peace ! *

In "The Walk" we have seen the progress of Society—in "The Bell'
we have the Lay of the Life of Man. This is the crowning Flower of that
garland of Humanity, which, in his Culture-Historic poems, the hand of
Schiller has entwined. In England, "The Lay of the Bell" has been the
best known of the Poet's compositions—out of the Drama. It has been the
favourite subject selected by his translators ; to say nothing of others (more
recent, but with which, we own we are unacquainted), the elegant version
of Lord Francis Egerton has long since familiarised its beauties to the
English public ; and had it been possible to omit from our collection a poem
of such importance, we would willingly have declined the task which
suggests comparisons disadvantageous to ourselves. The idea of this poem
had long been revolved by Schiller.† He went often to a bell-foundry, to
make himself thoroughly master of the mechanical process, which he has
applied to purposes so ideal. Even from the time in which he began the
actual composition of the poem, two years elapsed before it was completed.
The work profited by the delay, and as the Poet is generally clear in proportion to his entire familiarity with his own design, so of all Schiller's moral
poems this is the most intelligible to the ordinary understanding ; perhaps
the more so, because, as one of his Commentators has remarked, the principal ideas and images he has already expressed in his previous writings,
and his mind was thus free to give itself up more to the form than to the
thought. Still we think that the symmetry and *oneness* of the composition
have been indiscriminately panegyrised. As the Lay of Life, it begins
with Birth, and when it arrives at Death, it has reached its legitimate conclusion. The reader will observe, at the seventh strophe, that there is an
abrupt and final break in the individual interest which has hitherto connected the several portions. Till then, he has had before him the pro-
minent figure of a single man—the one representative of human life—whose
baptism the Bell has celebrated, whose youth, wanderings, return to his

---

* Written in the time of the French war.
† See Life of Schiller, by Madame von Wolzogen.

father's house, love, marriage, prosperity, misfortunes, to the death of the wife, have carried on the progress of the Poem ; and this leading figure then recedes altogether from the scene, and the remainder of the Poem, till the ninth stanza, losing sight altogether of *individual* life, merely repeats the purpose of "The Walk," and confounds itself in illustrations of *social* life in general. The picture of the French Revolution, though admirably done, is really not only an episode in the main design, but is merely a copy of that already painted, and set in its proper place, in the Historical Poem of "The Walk."

But whatever weight may be attached, whether to this objection or to others which we have seen elsewhere urged, the "non Ego paucis offendar maculis" may, indeed, be well applied to a Poem so replete with the highest excellences,—so original in conception—so full of pathos, spirit, and variety in its plan—and so complete in its mastery over form and language. . . . Much of its beauty must escape in translation, even if an English Schiller were himself the translator. For that beauty which belongs to form—the "curiosa felicitas verborum"—is always untranslatable. Witness the Odes of Horace, the greater part of Goethe's Lyrics, and the Choruses of Sophocles. Though the life of Man is pourtrayed, it is the life of a *German* man. The wanderings, or apprenticeship, of the youth, are not a familiar feature in our own civilisation; the bustling housewife is peculiarly German ; so is the incident of the fire—a misfortune very common in parts of Germany, and which the sound of the church-bell proclaims. Thus that peculiar charm which belongs to the recognition of familiar and household images, in an ideal and poetic form, must be in a great measure lost to a foreigner. The thought, too, at the end—the prayer for Peace—is of a local and temporary nature. It breathed the wish of all Germany, during the four years' war with France, and was, at the date of publication—like all temporary allusions—a strong and effective close, to become, after the interest of the allusion ceased, comparatively feeble and non-universal. These latter observations are made, not in depreciation of the Poem, but on behalf of it; to show that it has beauties peculiar to the language it was written in, and the people it addressed, of which it must be despoiled in translation.

THE POETRY OF LIFE.

"Who would himself with shadows entertain,
Or gild his life with lights that shine in vain,
Or nurse false hopes that do but cheat the true ?—
Though with my dream my heaven should be resign'd—
Though the free-pinion'd soul that once could dwell
In the large empire of the Possible,
This work-day life with iron chains may bind,
Yet thus the mastery o'er ourselves we find,
And solemn duty to our acts decreed,
Meets us thus tutor'd in the hour of need,
With a more sober and submissive mind!
How front Necessity—yet bid thy youth
Shun the mild rule of life's calm sovereign, Truth."

M 2

So speak'st thou, friend, how stronger far than I;
As from Experience—that sure port serene—
Thou look'st;—and straight, a coldness wraps the sky,
The summer glory withers from the scene,
Scared by the solemn spell; behold them fly,
The godlike images that seem'd so fair!
Silent the playful Muse—the rosy Hours
Halt in their dance; and the May-breathing flowers
Fall from the sister-Graces' waving hair.
Sweet-mouth'd Apollo breaks his golden lyre,
Hermes, the wand with many a marvel rife;—
The veil, rose-woven, by the young Desire
With dreams, drops from the hueless cheeks of Life.
The world seems what it *is*—A Grave! and Love
Casts down the bondage wound his eyes above,
And *sees!*—He sees but images of clay
Where he dream'd gods; and sighs—and glides away.
The youngness of the Beautiful grows old,
And on thy lips the bride's sweet kiss seems cold;
And in the crowd of joys—upon thy throne
Thou sitt'st in state, and hardenest into stone.

THE ANTIQUE AT PARIS.

(FREE TRANSLATION.)

WHAT the Greek wrought, the vaunting Frank may gain,
And waft the pomp of Hellas to the Seine;
His proud museums may with marble groan,
And Gallia gape on Glories not her own;
But ever silent in the ungenial Halls
Shall stand the Statues on their pedestals.
By him alone the Muses are possest,
Who warms them from the marble—at his breast;
Bright, to the Greek, from stone each goddess grew—
Vandals, each goddess is but stone to you!

THE MAID OF ORLEANS.

To flaunt the fair shape of Humanity,
  Lewd Mockery dragg'd thee through the mire it trod.*
Wit wars with Beauty everlastingly—
  Yearns for no Angel—worships to no God—
Views the heart's wealth, to steal it as the thief—
Assails Delusion, but to kill Belief.

Yet the true Poetry—herself, like thee,
  Sprung from the younger race, a shepherd maid,
Gives thee her birthright of Divinity,
  Thy wrongs in life in her star-worlds repaid.
Sweet Virgin-Type of Thought, pure, brave, and high—
The Heart created thee—thou canst not die.

The mean world loves to darken what is bright,
  To see to dust each loftier image brought ;
But fear not—souls there are that can delight
  In the high Memory and the stately Thought ;
To ribald mirth let Momus rouse the mart,
But forms more noble glad the noble heart.

THEKLA.

(A SPIRIT VOICE.)

[It was objected to Schiller's " Wallenstein," that he had suffered Thekla
to disappear from the Play without any clear intimation of her fate. These
stanzas are his answer to the objection.]

WHERE am I ? whither borne ? From thee
  As soars my fleeting shade above ?
Is not all being closed for me,
  And over life and love ?—
Wouldst ask, where wing their flight away
  The Nightbirds that enraptured air
With Music's soul in happy May ?
  But while they loved—they were !

* Voltaire, in " The Pucelle."

And have I found the Lost again?
  Yes, I with him at last am wed;
Where hearts are never rent in twain,
  And tears are never shed.

There, wilt thou find us welcome thee,
  When thy life to our life shall glide:
My father,* too, from sin set free,
  Nor Murther at his side—

Feels there, that no delusion won
  His bright faith to the starry spheres;
Each faith (nor least the boldest one)
  Still towards the Holy nears.

There word is kept with Hope; to wild
  Belief a lovely truth is given!
O dare to err and dream!—the child
  Has instincts of the Heaven!

WILLIAM TELL.

[Lines accompanying the copy of Schiller's Drama of William Tell, presented to the Arch-Chancellor von Dalberg.]

I.

In that fell strife, when force with force engages,
  And Wrath stirs bloodshed—Wrath with blindfold
    eyes—
When, midst the war which raving Faction wages,
  Lost in the roar—the voice of Justice dies,
When but for license, Sin the shameless, rages,
  Against the Holy, when the Wilful rise,
When lost the Anchor which makes Nations strong
  Amidst the storm,—*there* is no theme for song.

---

* Wallenstein:—the next stanza alludes to his belief in Astrology;—
of which such beautiful uses have been made by Schiller in his solemn
tragedy.

II.

But when a Race, tending by vale and hill
  Free flocks, contented with its rude domain—
Bursts the hard bondage with its own great will,
  Lets fall the sword when once it rends the chain,
And, flush'd with Victory, can be human still—
  There blest the strife, and *then* inspired the strain.
Such is my theme—to thee not strange, 'tis true,
Thou in the Great canst never find the New ! *

ARCHIMEDES.

To Archimedes once a scholar came,
"Teach me," he said, " the Art that won thy fame ;—
The godlike Art which gives such boons to toil,
And showers such fruit upon thy native soil ;—
The godlike Art that girt the town when all
Rome's vengeance burst in thunder on the wall ! "
" Thou call'st Art godlike—it is so, in truth,
And was," replied the Master to the youth,
" Ere yet its secrets were applied to use—
Ere yet it served beleaguered Syracuse :—
Ask'st thou from Art, but what the Art is worth ?
The fruit?—for fruit go cultivate the Earth.—
He who the goddess would aspire unto,
Must not the goddess as the woman woo ! "

CARTHAGE.

Thou, of the nobler Mother Child degenerate ;—all the
    while
That with the Roman's Might didst match the Tyrian's
    crafty guile ;
The one thro' strength subdued the earth—that by its
    strength it ruled—
Thro' cunning earth the other stole, and by the cunning
    school'd—

* The concluding point in the original requires some paraphrase in trans
lation.—Schiller's lines are—
      Und solch ein Bild darf ich dir freudig zeigen
      Du kennst's—denn alles Grosse ist dein eigen.

With iron as the Roman, thou (let History speak) didst
    gain
The empire which with gold thou as the Tyrian didst
    maintain.

COLUMBUS.

STEER on, bold Sailor—Wit may mock thy soul that sees
    the land,
And hopeless at the helm may droop the weak and weary
    hand,
YET EVER—EVER TO THE WEST, for there the coast must lie,
And dim it dawns and glimmering dawns before thy reason's
    eye;
Yea, trust the guiding God—and go along the floating
    grave,
Though hid till now—yet now, behold the New World o'er
    the wave !
With Genius Nature ever stands in solemn union still,
And ever what the One foretels the Other shall fulfil.

NÆNIA.*

THE Beautiful, that men and gods alike subdues, must
    perish ;
For pity ne'er the iron breast of Stygian Jove † shall
    cherish !
Once only—Love, by aid of Song, the Shadow-Sovereign
    thrall'd,
And at the dreary threshold he again the boon recall'd.
Not Aphrodite's heavenly tears to love and life restored
Her own adored Adonis, by the grisly monster gored !
Not all the art of Thetis saved her god-like hero son,
When, falling by the Scæan gate, his race of glory run !
But forth she came, with all the nymphs of Nereus, from
    the deep,
Around the silence of the Dead to sorrow and to weep.

* Nænia was the goddess of funerals—and funeral songs were called
Nænia.
† Pluto.

See tears are shed by every god and goddess, to survey
How soon the Beautiful is past, the Perfect dies away!
Yet noble sounds the voice of wail—and woe the Dead can
    grace;
For never wail and woe are heard to mourn above the
    Base!

JOVE TO HERCULES.

'Twas not my nectar made thy strength divine,
But 'twas thy strength which made my nectar thine!

THE IDEAL AND THE ACTUAL LIFE.

In Schiller's Poem of "The Ideal," a translation of which has already
been presented to the reader, but which was composed subsequently to "The
Ideal and the Actual," the prevailing sentiment is of that simple pathos
which can come home to every man who has mourned for Youth, and the
illusions which belong to it—

for the hour
Of glory in the grass, and splendour in the flower.

But "The Ideal and the Actual" is purely philosophical; a poem "in
which," says Hoffmeister, "every object and epithet has a metaphysical
back-ground." Schiller himself was aware of its obscurity to the general
reader; he desires that even the refining Humboldt "should read it in a
kind of holy stillness—and banish, during the meditation it required, all
that was profane." Humboldt proved himself worthy of these instructions,
by the enthusiastic admiration with which the poem inspired him. Previous to its composition, Schiller had been employed upon philosophical
inquiries, especially his "Letters on the Æsthetic Education of Man;" and
of these Letters it is truly observed, that the Poem is the crowning Flower.
To those acquainted with Schiller's philosophical works and views, the poem
is therefore less obscure; in its severe compression such readers behold but
the poetical epitome of thoughts the depth of which they have already
sounded, and the coherence of which they have already ascertained—they
recognise a familiar symbol, where the general reader only perplexes himself
in a riddle.

Without entering into disquisitions, out of place in this translation, and
fatiguing to those who desire in a collection of poems to enjoy the poetical—
not to be bewildered by the abstract—we shall merely preface the poem,
with the help of Schiller's commentators, by a short analysis of the general
design and meaning, so at least as to facilitate the reader's *study* of this remarkable poem—study it will require, and well repay.

The Poem begins, Stanza 1st, with the doctrine which Schiller has often
inculcated, that to Man there rests but the choice between the pleasures of
sense, and the peace of the soul; but both are united in the life of the Immortals, viz., the higher orders of being. Stanza 2nd.—Still it may be ours

to attain, even on earth, to this loftier and holier life—provided we can raise ourselves beyond material objects. Stanza 3rd.—The Fates can only influence the body, and the things of time and matter. But, safe from the changes of matter and of life, the Platonic Archetype, *Form*, hovers in the realm of the Ideal. If we can ascend to this realm—in other words, to the domain of Beauty—we attain (Stanza 4th) to the perfection of Humanity —a perfection only found in the immaterial forms and shadows of that realm —yet in which, as in the Gods, the sensual and the intellectual powers are united. In the Actual Life we strive for a goal we cannot reach; in the Ideal, the goal is attainable, and there effort is victory. With Stanza 5th begins the antithesis, which is a key to the remainder—an antithesis constantly ballancing before us the conditions of the Actual and the privileges of the Ideal. The Ideal is not meant to relax, but to brace us for the Actual Life. From the latter we cannot escape; but when we begin to flag beneath the sense of our narrow limits, and the difficulties of the path, the eye, steadfastly fixed upon the Ideal Beauty aloft, beholds there the goal. Stanza 6th.—In Actual Life, Strength and Courage are the requisites for success, and are doomed to eternal struggle; but (Stanza 7th) in the Ideal Life, struggle exists not; the stream, gliding far from its rocky sources, is smoothed to repose. Stanza 8th.—In the Actual Life, as long as the Artist still has to contend with matter, he must strive and labour. Truth is only elicited by toil—the statue only wakens from the block by the stroke of the chisel; but when (Stanza 9th) he has once achieved the idea of Beauty—when once he has elevated the material marble into form—all trace of his human neediness and frailty is lost, and his work seems the child of the soul. Stanza 9th.—Again, in the Actual world, the man who *strives* for Virtue, finds every sentiment and every action poor compared to the rigid standard of the abstract moral law. But if (Stanza 9th), instead of *striving* for Virtue, merely from the cold sense of duty, we live that life beyond the senses, in which Virtue, becomes as it were natural to us —in which its behests are served, not through duty but inclination—then the gulf between man and the moral law is filled up; we take the Godhead, so to speak, into our will; and Heaven ceases its terrors, when man ceases to resist it. Stanza 10th.—Finally, in Actual Life, sorrows, whether our own, or those with which we sympathise, are terrible and powerful; but (Stanza 11th) in the Ideal World even Sorrow has its pleasures. We contemplate the writhings of the Laocoon in marble, with delight in the greatness of Art—not with anguish for the suffering, but with veneration for the grandeur with which the suffering is idealised by the Artist, or expressed by the subject. Over the pain of Art smiles the Heaven of the Moral world. Stanzas 11th and 12th.—Man thus aspiring to the Ideal, is compared to the Mythical Hercules. In the Actual world he must suffer and must toil; but when once he can cast aside the garb of clay, and through the Ethereal flame separate the Mortal from the Immortal, the material dross sinks downward, the spirit soars aloft, and Hebe (or Eternal Youth) pours out nectar as to the Gods. If the reader will have the patience to compare the above analysis with the subjoined version (in which the Translator has also sought to render the general sense as intelligible as possible), he will probably find little difficulty in clearing up the Author's meaning.

I.

FOR ever fair, for ever calm and bright,
Life flies on plumage, zephyr-light,
For those who on the Olympian hill rejoice—

Moons wane, and races wither to the tomb,
And 'mid the universal ruin, bloom
   The rosy days of Gods—
                    With Man, the choice,
Timid and anxious, hesitates between
   The sense's pleasure and the soul's content;
While on celestial brows, aloft and sheen,
   The beams of both are blent.

II.

Seek'st thou on earth the life of Gods to share,
Safe in the Realm of Death?—beware
   To pluck the fruits that glitter to thine eye;
Content thyself with gazing on their glow—
Short are the joys Possession can bestow,
   And in Possession sweet Desire will die.
'Twas not the ninefold chain of waves that bound
   Thy daughter, Ceres, to the Stygian river—
She pluck'd the fruit of the unholy ground,
   And so—was Hell's for ever!

III.

The Weavers of the Web—the Fates—but sway
The matter and the things of clay;
   Safe from each change that Time to Matter gives,
Nature's blest playmate, free at will to stray
   With Gods a god, amidst the fields of Day,
   The FORM, the ARCHETYPE,* serenely lives.
Would'st thou soar heavenward on its joyous wing?
   Cast from thee, Earth, the bitter and the real,
High from this cramp'd and dungeon being, spring
   Into the Realm of the Ideal!

IV.

Here, bathed, Perfection, in thy purest ray,
Free from the clogs and taints of clay,
   Hovers divine the Archetypal Man!
Dim as those phantom ghosts of life that gleam
And wander voiceless by the Stygian stream,—
   Fair as it stands in fields Elysian,

* "Die Gestalt"—Form, the Platonic Archetype.

Ere down to Flesh the Immortal doth descend :—
  If doubtful ever in the Actual life
Each contest—*here* a victory crowns the end
    Of every nobler strife.

V.

Not from the strife itself to set thee free,
But more to nerve—doth Victory
  Wave her rich garland from the Ideal clime.
Whate'er thy wish, the Earth has no repose—
Life still must drag thee onward as it flows,
  Whirling thee down the dancing surge of Time.
But when the courage sinks beneath the dull
  Sense of its narrow limits—on the soul,
Bright from the hill-tops of the Beautiful,
  Bursts the attainèd goal !

VI.

If worth thy while the glory and the strife
Which fire the lists of Actual Life—
  The ardent rush to fortune or to fame,
In the hot field where Strength and Valour are,
And rolls the whirling thunder of the car,
  And the world, breathless, eyes the glorious game—
Then dare and strive—the prize can but belong
To him whose valour o'er his tribe prevails;
In life the victory only crowns the strong—
  He who is feeble fails.

VII.

But Life, whose source, by crags around it pil'd,
Chafed while confin'd, foams fierce and wild,
  Glides soft and smooth when once its streams expand,
When its waves, glassing in their silver play,
Aurora blent with Hesper's milder ray,
  Gain the still BEAUTIFUL—that Shadow-Land !
Here, contest grows but interchange of Love,
  All curb is but the bondage of the Grace ;
Gone is each foe,—Peace folds her wings above
  Her native dwelling-place.

VIII.

When, through dead stone to breathe a soul of light,
With the dull matter to unite
  The kindling genius, some great sculptor glows;
Behold him straining every nerve intent—
Behold how, o'er the subject element,
  The stately THOUGHT its march laborious goes!
For never, save to Toil untiring, spoke
  The unwilling Truth from her mysterious well—
The statue only to the chisel's stroke
  Wakes from its marble cell.

IX.

But onward to the Sphere of Beauty—go
Onward, O Child of Art! and, lo,
  Out of the matter which thy pains control
The Statue springs!—not as with labour wrung
From the hard block, but as from Nothing sprung—
  Airy and light—the offspring of the soul!
The pangs, the cares, the weary toils it cost
  Leave not a trace when once the work is done—
The Artist's human frailty merged and lost
  In Art's great victory won! *

X.

If human Sin confronts the rigid law
Of perfect Truth and Virtue,† awe
  Seizes and saddens thee to see how far
Beyond thy reach, Perfection;—if we test
By the Ideal of the Good, the best,
  How mean our efforts and our actions are!
This space between the Ideal of man's soul
  And man's achievement, who hath ever past?
An ocean spreads between us and that goal,
  Where anchor ne'er was cast!

* More literally translated thus by the Author of the Article on Schiller
in the *Foreign and Colonial Review,* July, 1843—
    "Thence all witnesses for ever banished
        Of poor Human Nakedness."

† The Law, *i. e.,* the Kantian Ideal of Truth and Virtue. This stanza
and the next embody, perhaps with some exaggeration, the Kantian doctrine
of morality.

XI.

But fly the boundary of the Senses—live
The Ideal life free Thought can give ;
   And, lo, the gulf shall vanish, and the chill
Of the soul's impotent despair be gone !
And with divinity thou sharest the throne,
   Let but divinity become thy will !
Scorn not the Law—permit its iron band
   The sense (it cannot chain the soul) to thrall.
Let man no more the will of Jove withstand,*
   And Jove the bolt lets fall !

XII.

If, in the woes of Actual Human Life—
If thou could'st see the serpent strife
   Which the Greek Art has made divine in stone—
Could'st see the writhing limbs, the livid cheek,
Note every pang, and hearken every shriek
   Of some despairing lost Laocoon,
The human nature would thyself subdue
   To share the human woe before thine eye—
Thy cheek would pale, and all thy soul be true
   To Man's great Sympathy.

XIII.

But in the Ideal Realm, aloof and far,
Where the calm Art's pure dwellers are,
   Lo, the Laocoon writhes, but does not groan.
Here, no sharp grief the high emotion knows—
Here, suffering's self is made divine, and shows
   The brave resolve of the firm soul alone :
Here, lovely as the rainbow on the dew
   Of the spent thunder-cloud, to Art is given,
Gleaming through Grief's dark veil, the peaceful blue
   Of the sweet Moral Heaven.

---

* " But in God's sight submission is command."
" Jonah," by the Rev. F. Hodgson. Quoted in *Foreign and Colonial Review*, July, 1843: Art. Schiller, p. 21.

XIV.

So, in the glorious parable, behold
How, bow'd to mortal bonds, of old
  Life's dreary path divine Alcides trod :
The hydra and the lion were his prey,
And to restore the friend he loved to-day,
  He went undaunted to the black-brow'd God ;
And all the torments and the labours sore
  Wroth Juno sent—the meek majestic One,
With patient spirit and unquailing, bore,
  Until the course was run—

XV.

Until the God cast down his garb of clay,
And rent in hallowing flame away
  The mortal part from the divine—to soar
To the empyreal air !   Behold him spring
Blithe in the pride of the unwonted wing,
  And the dull matter that confined before
Sinks downward, downward, downward as a dream !
  Olympian hymns receive the escaping soul,
And smiling Hebe, from the ambrosial stream,
  Fills for a God the bowl !

THE FAVOUR OF THE MOMENT.

Once more, then, we meet
  In the circles of yore ;
Let our song be as sweet
  In its wreaths as before.
Who claims the first place
  In the tribute of song ?
The God to whose grace
  All our pleasures belong.
Though Ceres may spread
  All her gifts on the shrine,
Though the glass may be red
  With the blush of the vine,

What boots—if the while
  Fall no spark on the hearth ?
If the heart do not smile
  With the instinct of mirth ?—
From the clouds, from God's breast
  Must our happiness fall,
'Mid the blessed, most blest
  Is the MOMENT of all !
Since Creation began
  All that mortals have wrought,
All that's godlike in MAN
  Comes—the flash of a Thought !
For ages the stone
  In the quarry may lurk,
An instant alone
  Can suffice to the work ;
An impulse give birth
  To the child of the soul,
A glance stamp the worth
  And the fame of the whole.*
On the arch that she buildeth
  From sunbeams on high,
As Iris just gildeth,
  And fleets from the sky,
So shineth, so gloometh
  Each gift that is ours ;
The lightning illumeth
  The darkness devours ! †

THE FORTUNE FAVOURED.

[THE first five verses in the original of this Poem are placed as a motto
on Goethe's statue in the Library at Weimar. The Poet does not here
mean to extol what is vulgarly meant by the Gifts of Fortune; he but
develops a favourite idea of his, that, whatever is really sublime and
beautiful, comes freely down from Heaven ; and vindicates the seeming

---

* The idea diffused by the translator through this and the preceding
stanza, is more forcibly condensed by Schiller in four lines.

† " And ere a man hath power to say, ' behold,'
    The jaws of Darkness do devour it up,
    So quick bright things come to confusion."—SHAKESPEARE.

partiality of the Gods, by implying that the Beauty and the Genius given,
without labour, to some, but serve to the delight of those to whom they are
denied.]

Ah! happy He, upon whose birth each God
Looks down in love, whose earliest sleep the bright
Idalia cradles, whose young lips the rod
Of eloquent Hermes kindles—to whose eyes,
Scarce waken'd yet, Apollo steal in light,
While on imperial brows Jove sets the seal of might!
Godlike the lot ordain'd for him to share,
He wins the garland ere he runs the race ;
He learns life's wisdom ere he knows life's care,
And, without labour vanquish'd, smiles the Grace.

    Great is the man, I grant, whose strength of mind,
Self-shapes its objects and subdues the Fates—
Virtue subdues the Fates, but cannot bind
The fickle Happiness, whose smile awaits
Those who scarce seek it ; nor can courage earn
What the Grace showers not from her own free urn !

    From aught *unworthy*, the determined will
Can guard the watchful spirit—there it ends ;—
The all that's *glorious* from the heaven descends ;
As some sweet mistress loves us, freely still
Come the spontaneous gifts of Heaven !—Above
Favour rules Jove, as it below rules Love !
The Immortals have their bias !—Kindly they
See the bright locks of youth enamour'd play,
And where the glad one goes, shed gladness round the way.
It is not they who boast the best to see,
Whose eyes the holy Apparitions bless ;
The stately light of their divinity
Hath oft but shone the brightest on the blind ;—
And their choice spirit found its calm recess
In the pure childhood of a simple mind.
Unask'd they come—delighted to delude   •
The expectation of our baffled Pride ;
No law can call their free steps to our side.
Him whom He loves, the Sire of men and gods,
(Selected from the marvelling multitude,)
Bears on his eagle to his bright abodes ;
And showers, with partial hand and lavish, down,
The minstrel's laurel or the monarch's crown !

Before the fortune-favour'd son of earth,
Apollo walks—and, with his jocund mirth,
The heart-enthralling Smiler of the skies:
For him grey Neptune smooths the pliant wave—
Harmless the waters for the ship that bore
The Cæsar and his fortunes to the shore!
Charm'd at his feet the crouching lion lies,
To him his back the murmuring dolphin gave;
His soul is born a sovereign o'er the strife—
The lord of all the Beautiful of Life;
Where'er his presence in its calm has trod,
It charms—it sways as some diviner God.
   Scorn not the Fortune-favour'd, that to him
The light-won victory by the gods is given,
Or that, as Paris, from the strife severe,
The Venus draws her darling.—Whom the heaven
So prospers, love so watches, I revere!
And not the man upon whose eyes, with dim
And baleful night, sits Fate.   Achaia boasts,
No less the glory of the Dorian Lord *
That Vulcan wrought for him the shield and sword—
That round the mortal hover'd all the hosts
Of all Olympus—that his wrath to grace,
The best and bravest of the Grecian race
Untimely slaughtered, with resentful ghosts
Awed the pale people of the Stygian coasts!
   Scorn not the Darlings of the Beautiful,
If without labour they Life's blossoms cull;
If, like the stately lilies, they have won
A crown for which they neither toil'd nor spun;—
If without merit, theirs be Beauty, still
Thy sense, unenvying, with the Beauty fill.
Alike for thee no merit wins the right,
To share, by simply seeing, their delight.
Heaven breathes the soul into the Minstrel's breast,
But with that soul he animates the rest;
The God inspires the Mortal—but to God,
In turn, the Mortal lifts thee from the sod.
Oh, not in vain to Heaven the Bard is dear;
Holy himself—he hallows those who hear!

* Achilles.

The busy mart let Justice still control,
Weighing the guerdon to the toil!—What then?
A God alone claims joy—all joy is his,
Flushing with unsought light the cheeks of men.
*Where is no miracle, why there no bliss!
Grow, change, and ripen all that mortal be,
Shapen'd from form to form, by toiling time;
The Blissful and the Beautiful are born
Full grown, and ripen'd from Eternity—
No gradual changes to their glorious prime,
No childhood dwarfs them, and no age has worn.—
Like Heaven's, each earthly Venus on the sight
Comes, a dark birth, from out an endless sea;
Like the first Pallas, in maturest might,
Arm'd, from the Thunderer's brow, leaps forth each Thought
    of Light.

THE SOWER.

Sure of the Spring that warms them into birth,
The golden seeds thou trustest to the Earth;
And dost thou doubt the Eternal Spring sublime,
For deeds—the seeds which Wisdom sows in Time?

SENTENCES OF CONFUCIUS.

TIME.

Threefold the stride of Time, from first to last!
    Loitering slow, the Future creepeth—
    Arrow-swift, the Present sweepeth—
And motionless for ever stands the Past.

Impatience, fret howe'er she may,
    Cannot speed the tardy goer;
Fear and Doubt—that crave delay—
    Ne'er can make the Fleet One slower:

* Paraphrased from—
        Aber die Freude ruft nur ein Gott auf sterbliche Wangen.
These lines furnish the key to—
                Nur ein Wunder kann dich tragen
                In das schöne Wunderland.—Schiller, Sehnsucht.
And the same lines, with what follow, explain also the general intention
of the poem on the favour of the moment.

Nor one spell Repentance knows,
To stir the Still One from repose.
If thou would'st, wise and happy, see
Life's solemn journey close for thee,
The Loiterer's counsel thou wilt heed,
Though readier tools must shape the deed;
Not for thy friend the Fleet One know,
Nor make the Motionless thy foe!

SPACE.

A threefold measure dwells in Space—
Restless, with never-pausing pace,
LENGTH, ever stretching ever forth, is found,
And, ever widening, BREADTH extends around,
    And ever DEPTH sinks bottomless below!
In this, a type thou dost possess—
On, ever restless, must thou press,
    No halt allow, no languor know,
    If to the Perfect thou wouldst go;
Must broaden from thyself, until
Creation thy embrace can fill!
Must down the Depth for ever fleeing,
Dive to the spirit and the being.
The distant goal at last to near,
    Still lengthening labour sweeps;
The full mind is alone the clear,
    And Truth dwells in the deeps.

THE ANTIQUE TO THE NORTHERN WANDERER.

AND o'er the river hast thou past, and o'er the mighty sea,
And o'er the Alps, the dizzy bridge hath borne thy steps to
    me;
To look all near upon the bloom my deathless beauty knows,
And, face to face, to front the pomp whose fame through
    ages goes—
Gaze on, and touch my relics now! At last thou standest
    here,
But art thou nearer now to me—or I to thee more near?

GENIUS.

(FREE TRANSLATION.)

[The original and it seems to us the more appropriate, title of this Poem,
was "Nature and the School."]

Do I believe, thou ask'st, the Master's word,
The Schoolman's shibboleth that binds the herd ?
To the soul's haven is there but one chart ?
Its peace a problem to be learned by art ?
On system rest the happy and the good ?
To base the temple must the props be wood ?
Must I distrust the gentle law, imprest,
To guide and warn, by Nature on the breast,
Till, squared to rule the instinct of the soul,—
Till the School's signet stamp the eternal scroll,
Till in one mould, some dogma hath confined
The ebb and flow—the light waves—of the mind?
Say thou, familiar to these depths of gloom,
Thou, safe ascended from the dusty tomb,
Thou, who hast trod these weird Egyptian cells—
Say—if Life's comfort with yon mummies dwells !—
Say—and I grope—with saddened steps indeed—
But on, thro' darkness, if to Truth it lead !

Nay, Friend, thou know'st the golden time—the age
Whose legends live in many a poet's page ?
When heavenlier shapes with Man walked side by side,
And the chaste Feeling was itself a guide ;
Then the great law, alike divine amid
Suns bright in Heaven, or germs in darkness hid,—
That silent law—(call'd whether by the name
Of Nature or Necessity—the same),
To that deep sea, the heart, its movement gave—
Sway'd the full tide, and freshened the free wave.
Then sense unerring—because unreproved—
True as the finger on the dial moved,
Half-guide, half-playmate, of Earth's age of youth,
The sportive instinct of Eternal Truth.

Then, nor Initiate nor Profane were known ;
Where the Heart felt—there Reason found a throne :

Not from the dust below, but life around
Warm Genius shaped what quick Emotion found.
One rule, like light, for every bosom glowed,
Yet hid from all the fountain whence it flowed.

But, gone that blessed Age!—our wilful pride
Has lost, with Nature, the old peaceful Guide.
FEELING, no more to raise us and rejoice,
Is heard and honoured as a Godhead's voice;
And, disenhallowed in its eldest cell
The Human Heart,—lies mute the Oracle; *
Save where the low and mystic whispers thrill
Some listening spirit more divinely still.
There, in the chambers of the inmost heart,
There, must the Sage explore the Magian's art;
There, seek the long-lost Nature's steps to track,
Till, found once more, she gives him Wisdom back!
Hast thou,—(O Blest, if so, whate'er betide!)—
Still kept the Guardian Angel by thy side?
Can thy Heart's guileless childhood yet rejoice
In the sweet instinct with its warning voice?
Does Truth yet limn upon untroubled eyes,
Pure and serene, her world of Iris-dies?
Rings clear the echo which her accent calls
Back from the breast, on which the music falls?
In the calm mind is doubt yet hush'd,—and will
That doubt to-morrow as to-day be still?
†Will all these fine sensations in their play,
No censor need to regulate and sway?
Fear'st thou not in the insidious Heart to find
The source of Trouble to the limpid mind?

No!—then thine Innocence thy Mentor be!
Science can teach thee nought—she learns from thee!

* Schiller seems to allude to the philosophy of Fichté and Schelling then
on the ascendant, which sought to explain the enigma of the universe, and
to reconcile the antithesis between man and nature, by carrying both up
into the unity of an absolute consciousness, *i. e.*, a consciousness anterior to
everything which is *now* known under the name of consciousness—sed de
hâc re satius est silere quàm parvum dicere.

† Will this play of fine sensations (or sensibilities) require no censor to
control it—*i. e.*, will it always work spontaneously for good, and run into no
passionate excess?

Each law that lends lame succour to the Weak—
The cripple's crutch—the vigorous need not seek !
From thine own self thy rule of action draw ;—
That which thou dost—what charms thee—is thy Law,
And founds to every race a code sublime—
What pleases Genius gives a Law to Time !
The Word—the Deed—all Ages shall command,
Pure if thy lip and holy if thy hand !
Thou, thou alone mark'st not within thy heart
The inspiring God whose Minister thou art,
Know'st not the magic of the mighty ring
Which bows the realm of Spirits to their King :
But meek, nor conscious of diviner birth,
Glide thy still footsteps thro' the conquered Earth !

ULYSSES.

To gain his home all oceans he explored—
Here Scylla frown'd—and there Charybdis roar'd ;
Horror on sea—and horror on the land—
In hell's dark boat he sought the spectre land,
Till borne—a slumberer—to his native spot
He woke—and sorrowing, knew his country not !

VOTIVE TABLETS.

[Under this title Schiller arranged that more dignified and philosophical portion of the small Poems published as Epigrams in the "Musen
Almanach;" which rather sought to point a general thought, than a personal satire.—Many of these, however, are either wholly without interest
for the English reader, or express in almost untranslateable laconism
what, in far more poetical shapes Schiller has elsewhere repeated and developed. We, therefore, content ourselves with such a selection as appears
to us best suited to convey a fair notion of the object and spirit of the
class.]

MOTTO TO THE VOTIVE TABLETS.

What the God taught—what has befriended all
Life's ways, I place upon the Votive Wall. ·

THE GOOD AND THE BEAUTIFUL.
(ZWEIERLEI WIRKUNGSARTEN.)

THE Good's the Flower to Earth already given—
The Beautiful—on Earth sows flowers from Heaven !

VALUE AND WORTH.

IF thou *hast* something, bring thy goods—a fair return be
    thine;
If thou *art* something, bring thy soul and interchange with
    mine.

THE DIVISION OF RANKS.

YES, in the moral world, as ours, we see
Divided grades—a Soul's Nobility;
By deeds their titles Commoners create—
The loftier order are by birthright great.*

TO THE MYSTIC.

SPREADS Life's true mystery round us evermore,
Seen by no eye, it lies all eyes before.†

THE KEY.

To know *thyself*—in others self discern;
Wouldst thou know others? read thyself—and learn!

WISDOM AND PRUDENCE.

WOULDST thou the loftiest height of Wisdom gain?
On to the rashness, Prudence would disdain;
The purblind see but the receding shore,
Not that to which the bold wave wafts thee o'er!

* This idea is often repeated, somewhat more clearly, in the haughty
philosophy of Schiller. He himself says, elsewhere—"In a fair soul each
single action is not properly moral, but the whole character is moral.
The fair soul has no other service than the instincts of its own beauty."
"Common Natures," observes Hoffmeister, "can only act as it were by
rule and law; the Noble are of themselves morally good, and humanly
beautiful."
† Query?—the Law of Creation, both physical and moral.

THE UNANIMITY.

TRUTH seek we both—Thou, in the life without thee and
    around;
I in the Heart within—by both can Truth alike be found;
The healthy eye can through the world the great Creator
    track—
The healthy heart is but the glass which gives creation
    back.

THE SCIENCE OF POLITICS.

ALL that thou dost be right—to that alone confine thy
    view,
And halt within the certain rule—the All that's right
    to do!
True zeal *the what already is* would sound and perfect
    see,
False zeal would sound and perfect make the something
    that's to be!

TO ASTRONOMERS.

OF the Nebulæ* and planets do not babble so to me;
What! is Nature only mighty inasmuch as you can
    see?
Inasmuch as you can measure her immeasurable ways?
As she renders world on world, sun and system to your
    gaze?
Though thro' space your object be the Sublimest to
    embrace,
Never the Sublime abideth—where you vainly search—in
    space!

* Nebelflecke; *i. e.*, the nebulous matter which puzzles astronomers. Is Nature, then, only great inasmuch as you can compute her almost incalculable dimensions, or inasmuch as she furnishes almost incalculable subjects for your computations? Your object is, indeed, the sublimest in space; but *the* Sublime does not dwell in space—*i. e.*, the Moral Law is *the* only Sublime, and its Kingdom is where Time and Space are not.

THE BEST GOVERNED STATE.

How the best state to know?—it is found out;
Like the best woman—that least talked about.

MY BELIEF.

WHAT thy religion? those thou namest—none?
None why—because I have religion!

FRIEND AND FOE.

DEAR is my friend—yet from my foe, as from my friend,
  comes good;
My friend shows what I *can* do, and my foe shows what
  I *shou'd.*

LIGHT AND COLOUR.

DWELL, Light, beside the changeless God—God spoke and
  Light began;
Come, thou, the ever-changing one—come, Colour, down
  to Man!

FORUM OF WOMEN.

WOMAN—to judge man rightly—do not scan
Each separate act;—pass judgment on the Man!

GENIUS.

INTELLECT can repeat what's been fulfill'd,
And, aping Nature, as she buildeth—build;
O'er Nature's base can haughty Reason dare
To pile its lofty castle—in the air.
But only thine, O Genius, is the charge,
In Nature's kingdom Nature to enlarge!

THE IMITATOR.

Good out of good—that art is known to all—
But Genius from the bad the good can call;
Then, Mimic, not from leading-strings escaped,
Work'st but the matter that's already shaped:
The already shaped a nobler hand awaits,
All matter asks a Spirit that *creates!*

CORRECTNESS.

(FREE TRANSLATION).

The calm correctness, where no fault we see,
Attests Art's loftiest or its least degree;
Alike the smoothness of the surface shows
The Pool's dull stagner—the great Sea's repose.

THE MASTER.

The herd of scribes, by what they tell us,
Show all in which their wits excel us;
But the True Master we behold,
In what his art leaves—just untold.

EXPECTATION AND FULFILMENT.

O'er Ocean, with a thousand masts, sails forth the stripling
bold—
One boat, hard rescued from the deep, draws into port the
old!

THE EPIC HEXAMETER.

(TRANSLATED BY COLERIDGE.)

Strongly it bears us along in swelling and limitless
billows,
Nothing before and nothing behind but the sky and the
ocean.

THE ELEGIAC METRE.

(TRANSLATED BY COLERIDGE).

In the hexameter rises the fountain's silvery column,
In the pentameter aye falling in melody back.*

OTHER EPIGRAMS, &c.

Give me that which thou know'st — I'll receive and
  attend ;
But thou givest me thyself — prithee, spare me, my
  friend !

THE PROSELYTE MAKER.

"A little earth from out the Earth—and I
The Earth will move : " so spake the Sage divine.
Out of myself one little moment—try
Myself to take :—succeed, and I am thine !

THE CONNECTING MEDIUM.

What to cement the lofty and the mean
Does Nature ?—what ?—place vanity between !

THE MORAL POET.

[This is an Epigram on Lavater's work, called " Pontius Pilatus, oder der
    Mensch in Allen Gestalten," &c.—Hoffmeister.]

"How poor a thing is man !" alas, 'tis true
I'd half forgot it—when I chanced on you !

---

* We have ventured to borrow these two translations from Coleridge's
poems, not only because what Coleridge did well, no living man could have
the presumptuous hope to improve, but because they adhere to the original
metre, which Germany has received from Greece, and show, we venture to
think, that not even Coleridge could have made that more agreeable to the
English ear and taste in poems of *any length*, nor even in small poems *if
often repeated*. It is, however, in their own language the grandest which the
Germans possess, and has been used by Schiller with signal success in his
" Walk," and other poems.

THE SUBLIME THEME.

[Also on Lavater, and alluding to the "Jesus Messias, oder die Evangelien und Apostelgeschichte in Gesängen," &c.]

How God compassionates Mankind, thy muse, my friend, rehearses—
Compassion for the sins of Man !—What comfort for thy verses!

SCIENCE.

To some she is the Goddess great, to some the milch-cow of the field ;
Their care is but to calculate—what butter she will yield.

KANT AND HIS COMMENTATORS.

How many starvelings one rich man can nourish !
When monarchs build, the rubbish-carriers flourish.

TO

THE HEREDITARY PRINCE OF SAXE WEIMAR,

ON HIS JOURNEY TO PARIS, WRITTEN FEBRUARY, 1802.

[Sung in a friendly circle.]

To the Wanderer a bowl to the brim !
    This Vale on his infancy smil'd ;
Let the Vale send a blessing to him,
    Whom it cradled to sleep as a child !

He goes from his Forefathers' halls—
    From the arms that embraced him at birth—
To the City that trophies its walls
    With the spoils it has ravish'd from earth !

The thunder is silent, and now
    The War and the Discord are ended ;
And Man o'er the crater may bow,
    Whence the stream of the lava descended.

O fair be the fate to secure
    Thy way through the perilous track ;
The heart Nature gave thee is pure,
    Bring it pure, as it goes from us, back.

Those lands the wild hoofs of the steeds,
    War yoked for the carnage, have torn ;
But Peace, laughing over the meads,
    Come, strewing the gold of the corn.

Thou the old Father Rhine wilt be greeting,
    By whom *thy* great Father * shall be
Remembered so long as is fleeting
    His stream to the beds of the Sea ;—

There, honour the Heroes of old,
    And pour to our Warden, the Rhine,
Who keeps on our borders his hold,
    A cup from his own merry wine ;

That thou may'st, as a guide to thy youth,
    The soul of the Fatherland find,
When thou passest the bridge where the Truth
    Of the German, thou leavest behind.

TO

A YOUNG FRIEND DEVOTING HIMSELF TO PHILOSOPHY.

SEVERE the proof the Grecian youth was doomed to
    undergo,
Before he might what lurks beneath the Eleusinia
    know—
Art *thou* prepared and ripe, the shrine—that inner shrine
    —to win,
Where Pallas guards from vulgar eyes the mystic prize
    within ?
Know'st thou what bars thy way ? how dear the bargain
    thou dost make,
When but to buy uncertain good, sure good thou dost
    forsake ?

* Duke Bernard of Weimar, one of the great Generals of the Thirty
Years' War.

Feel'st thou sufficient strength to brave the deadliest human
    fray—
When Heart from Reason—Sense from Thought, shall rend
    themselves away ?
Sufficient valour, war with Doubt, the Hydra-shape, to
    wage ;
And that worst Foe within thyself with manly soul
    engage ?
With eyes that keep their heavenly health—the innocence
    of youth
To guard from every falsehood, fair beneath the mask of
    Truth ?
Fly, if thou canst not trust thy heart to guide thee on
    the way—
Oh, fly the charmèd margin ere th' abyss engulf its prey.
Round many a step that seeks the light, the shades of
    midnight close ;
But in the glimmering twilight, see—how safely Child-
    hood goes !

THE PUPPET-SHOW OF LIFE.

(DAS SPIEL DES LEBENS.)

A PARAPHRASE.

[A *literal* version of this Poem, which possibly may have been suggested
by some charming passages in Wilhelm Meister, would be incompatible with
the spirit which constitutes its chief merit. And perhaps, therefore, the
original may be more faithfully rendered (like many of the Odes of Horace)
by paraphrase than translation.—In the general idea, as in all Schiller's
Poems of this kind, something more is implied than expressed. He has
treated, elsewhere, the Ideal or Shadowy life in earnest. He here represents
the Actual as a game; the chief images it brings to view are those of strife
and contest; to see it rightly you must not approach too near; and regard
the Actual Stage only by the lights of Love. True to his chivalry to the
sex, even in sport, as in earnest, Schiller places the prize of life in the hand
of Woman.]

Ho—ho—my puppet-show !
Ladies and gentlemen see my show !
Life and the world—look here, in troth,
Though but *in parvo*, I promise ye both !
The world and life—they shall both appear ;
But both are best seen when you're not too near ;

And every lamp from the stage to the porch,
Must be lighted by Venus, from Cupid's torch;
Never a moment, if rules can tempt ye,
Never a moment my scene is empty!
Here is the babe in his leading-strings—
   Here is the boy at play;
Here is the passionate youth with wings,
   Like a bird's on a stormy day,
To and fro, waving here and there,
Down to the earth and aloft through the air;
Now see the man, as for combat enter—
Where is the peril he fears to adventure?
   See how the puppets speed on to the race,
Each his own fortune pursues in the chase;
How many the rivals, how narrow the space!
But, hurry and scurry, O mettlesome game!
The cars roll in thunder, the wheels rush in flame.
How the brave dart onward, and pant and glow!
How the craven behind them come creeping slow—
Ha! ha! see how Pride gets a terrible fall!
See how Prudence, or Cunning, out-races them all!
See how at the goal, with her smiling eyes,
Ever waits Woman to give the prize!

THE MINSTRELS OF OLD.

WHERE now the minstrel of the large renown,
   Rapturing with living words the heark'ning throng?
Charming the Man to Heaven, and earthward down
   Charming the God!—who wing'd the soul with
     song?
Yet lives the minstrel, not the deeds—the lyre
   Of old demands ears that of old believed it—
Bards of bless'd time—how flew your living fire
   From lip to lip! how race from race received it!
As if a God, men hallow'd with devotion—
   What GENIUS, speaking, shaping, wrought below,
The glow of song inflamed the ear's emotion,
   The ear's emotion gave the song the glow;

Each nurturing each—back on his soul—its tone
    Whole nations echoed with a rapture-peal ;
Then all around the heavenly splendour shone
    Which now the heart, and scarce the heart can feel.

THE

COMMENCEMENT OF THE NEW CENTURY.

WHERE can Peace find a refuge ?—whither, say,
    Can Freedom turn ?—lo, friend, before our view
The CENTURY rends itself in storm away,
    And, red with slaughter, dawns on earth the New.
The girdle of the lands is loosen'd ; *—hurl'd
    To dust the forms old Custom deem'd divine,—
Safe from War's fury not the watery world ;—
    Safe not the Nile-God nor the antique Rhine.
Two mighty nations make the world their field,
    Deeming the world is for their heirloom given—
Against the freedom of all lands they wield
    This—Neptune's trident; that—the Thund'rer's levin.
Gold to their scales each region must afford ;
    And, as fierce Brennus in Gaul's early tale,
The Frank casts in the iron of his sword,
    To poise the balance, where the right may fail—
Like some huge Polypus, with arms that roam
    Outstretch'd for prey—the Briton spreads his reign ;
And, as the Ocean were his household home,
    Locks up the chambers of the liberal main.
On to the Pole where shines, unseen, the Star,
    Onward his restless course unbounded flies ;
Tracks every isle and every coast afar,
    And undiscover'd leaves but—Paradise !
Alas, in vain on earth's wide chart, I ween,
    Thou seek'st that holy realm beneath the sky—
Where Freedom dwells in gardens ever green—
    And blooms the Youth of fair Humanity !
O'er shores where sail ne'er rustled to the wind,
    O'er the vast universe, may rove thy ken ;
But in the universe thou canst not find
    A space sufficing for ten happy men !

    * That is—the settled political question—the balance of power.

O

In the heart's holy stillness only beams
  The shrine of refuge from life's stormy throng ;
Freedom is only in the land of Dreams ;
  And only blooms the Beautiful in Song!

We have now concluded the Poems composed in the third or maturest period
of Schiller's life . . . From this portion, only have been omitted in the
Translation, (besides some of the moral or epigrammatic sentences to which
we have before alluded) a very few pieces, which, whatever their merit in
the original, would be wholly without interest for the general English
reader, viz., the satirical lines on Shakspeare's Translators,—"the Philosopher," "the Rivers," "the Jeremiad," the Remonstrance, addressed to
Goethe on producing Voltaire's "Mahomet" on the Stage, in which the
same ideas have been already expressed by Schiller in poems of more liberal
and general application; and three or four occasional pieces in albums, &c.

The "Farewell to the Reader," which properly belongs to this division of
the Poems, has been transferred, as the fitting conclusion, to the last place
in the entire translation.

SECOND PERIOD.

THE Poems included in the Second Period of Schiller's literary career are
few, but remarkable for their beauty, and deeply interesting from the
struggling and anxious state of mind which some of them depict. It was,
both to his taste and to his thought, a period of visible transition. He had
survived the wild and irregular power which stamps, with fierce and somewhat sensual characters, the productions of his youth; but he had not
attained that serene repose of strength—that calm, bespeaking depth and
fulness, which is found in the best writings of his maturer years. In point
of style, the Poems in this division have more facility and sweetness than
those of his youth, and perhaps more evident vigour, more popular *verve*
and *gusto* than many composed in his riper manhood: in point of thought,
they mark that era through which few men of inquisitive and adventurous
genius—of sanguine and impassioned temperament—and of education chiefly
self-formed, undisciplined, and imperfect, have failed to pass—the era of
doubt and gloom, of self-conflict, and of self-torture.—In the "*Robbers*,"
and much of the poetry written in the same period of Schiller's life, there is
a bold and wild imagination, which attacks rather than questions—innovates
rather than examines—seizes upon subjects of vast social import, that float
on the surface of opinion, and assails them with a blind and half-savage
rudeness, according as they offend the enthusiasm of unreasoning youth.
But now this eager and ardent mind had paused to contemplate; its studies
were turned to philosophy and history—a more practical knowledge of life
(though in this last, Schiller, like most German authors, was ever more or
less deficient in variety and range) had begun to soften the stern and fiery
spirit which had hitherto sported with the dangerous elements of social
revolution. And while this change was working, before its feverish agita-
tion subsided into that Kantism which is the antipodes of scepticism, it was
natural that, to the energy which had asserted, denounced, and dogmatised,
should succeed the reaction of despondency and distrust. Vehement indignation at "the solemn plausibilities" of the world pervades the "*Robbers*."
In "*Don Carlos*," the passion is no longer vehement indignation, but
mournful sorrow—not indignation that hypocrisy reigns, but sorrow that
honesty cannot triumph—not indignation that formal Vice usurps the high
places of the world, but sorrow that, in the world, warm and generous
Virtue glows, and feels, and suffers—without reward. So, in the poems of

this period, are two that made a considerable sensation at their first appearance—" *The Conflict*," published originally under the title of " *The Free-thinking of Passion*," and " *Resignation*." They presented a melancholy view of the moral struggles in the heart of a noble and virtuous man. From the first of these poems, Schiller, happily and wisely, at a later period of his life, struck out the passages most calculated to offend. What hand would dare to restore them? The few stanzas that remain still suggest the outline of dark and painful thoughts, which is filled up in the more elaborate, and, in many respects, most exquisite, poem of " *Resignation*." Virtue exacting all sacrifices, and giving no reward—Belief which denies enjoyment, and has no bliss save its own faith; such is the sombre lesson of the melancholy poet—the more impressive because *so far* it is truth—deep and everlasting truth—but only, to a Christian, a part of truth. Resignation, so sad if not looking beyond the earth, becomes joy, when assured and confident of heaven. Another poem in this intermediate collection was no less subjected to severe animadversion. We mean " *The Gods of Greece*." As the Poem however now stands, though one or two expressions are not free from objection, it can only be regarded as a Poet's lament for the Mythology which was the Fount of poetry, and certainly not as a Reasoner's defence of Paganism in disparagement of Christianity. But the fact is, that Schiller's mind was so essentially religious, that we feel more angry, when he whom we would gladly hail as our light and guide, only darkens us or misleads, than we should with the absolute infidelity of a less grave and reverent genius. Yet a period—a transition state—of doubt and despondency is perhaps common to men in proportion to their natural dispositions to faith and veneration. With them, it comes from keen sympathy with undeserved sufferings—from grief at wickedness triumphant—from too intense a brooding over the mysteries involved in the government of the world. Scepticism of this nature can but little injure the frivolous, and will be charitably regarded by the wise. Schiller's mind soon outgrew the state which, to the mind of a poet, above all men, is most ungenial, but the sadness which the struggle bequeathed seems to have wrought a complete revolution in all his preconceived opinions. The wild creator of the " *Robbers*," drunk with liberty, and audacious against all restraint, becomes the champion of " Holy Order,"—the denouncer of the French Republic—the extoller of an Ideal Life, which should entirely separate Genius the Restless from Society the Settled. And as his impetuous and stormy vigour matured into the lucent and tranquil art of " *Der Spaziergang*," " *Wallenstein*," and " *Die Braut von Messina*," so his philosophy threw itself into calm respect for all that custom sanctioned, and convention hallowed.

But even during the painful transition, of which, in his minor poems, glimpses alone are visible, Scepticism, with Schiller, never insults the devoted, or mocks the earnest mind. It may have sadness—but never scorn. It is the question of a traveller who has lost his way in the great wilderness, but who mourns with his fellow-seekers, and has no bitter laughter for their wanderings from the goal. This Division begins, indeed, with a Hymn which atones for whatever pains us in the two Poems whose strain and spirit so gloomily contrast it, viz., the matchless and immortal " *Hymn to Joy*"—a poem steeped in the very essence of all-loving and all-aiding Christianity—breathing the enthusiasm of devout yet gladsome adoration, and ranking amongst the most glorious bursts of worship which grateful Genius ever rendered to the benign Creator.

And it is peculiarly noticeable, that, whatever Schiller's state of mind upon theological subjects at the time that this Hymn was composed, and though all doctrinal stamp and mark be carefully absent from it, it is yet a poem that never could have been written but in a Christian age, in a Christian land—but by a man whose whole soul and heart had been at one time (nay, *was*, at the *very moment* of composition) inspired and suffused with that firm belief in God's goodness and His justice—that full assurance of rewards beyond the grave—that exulting and seraphic cheerfulness which associates Joy with the Creator—and that animated affection for the Brotherhood of Mankind, which Christianity—and Christianity alone, in its pure, orthodox, gospel form, needing no aid from schoolman or philosopher—taught and teaches.

HYMN TO JOY.

[The origin of the following Hymn is said to be this:—Schiller, when at Leipsic, or its vicinity, saved a poor student of theology, impelled by destitution and the fear of starvation, from drowning himself in the river Pleisse. Schiller gave him what money he had; obtained his promise to relinquish the thought of suicide, at least while the money lasted; and a few days afterwards, amidst the convivialities of a marriage feast, related the circumstance so as to affect all present. A subscription was made, which enabled the student to complete his studies, and ultimately to enter into an official situation. Elated with the success of his humanity, it is to Humanity that Schiller consecrated this Ode.]

SPARK from the fire that Gods have fled—
　　Joy—thou Elysian Child divine,
Fire-drunk, our airy footsteps tread,
　　O Holy One! thy holy shrine.
Strong custom rends us from each other—
　　Thy magic all together brings;
And man in man but hails a brother,
　　Wherever rest thy gentle wings.

Chorus—Embrace ye millions—let this kiss,
　　　　Brothers, embrace the earth below!
　　　　Yon starry worlds that shine on this,
　　　　One common Father know!

He who this lot from fate can grasp—
　　Of one true friend the friend to be—
He who one faithful maid can clasp,
　　Shall hold with us his jubilee;
Yes, each who but one single heart
　　In all the earth can claim his own!—
Let him who cannot, stand apart,
　　And weep beyond the pale, alone!

Chorus—Homage to holy Sympathy,
　　　　Ye dwellers in our mighty ring;
　　　　Up to yon star-pavilions—she
　　　　Leads to the Unknown King!

All being drinks the mother-dew
  Of joy from Nature's holy bosom;
And Vice and Worth alike pursue
  Her steps that strew the blossom.
Joy in each link—to *us* * the treasure
  Of Wine and Love;—beneath the sod,
The Worm has instincts fraught with pleasure;
  In Heaven the Cherub looks on God!

Chorus—† Why bow ye down—why down—ye millions?
    O World, thy Maker's throne to see,
    Look upward—search the Star-pavilions:
    There must His mansion be!

Joy is the mainspring in the whole
  Of endless Nature's calm rotation;
Joy moves the dazzling wheels that roll
  In the great Timepiece of Creation;
Joy breathes on buds, and flowers they are;
  Joy beckons—suns come forth from heaven;
Joy rolls the spheres in realms afar,
  Ne'er to thy glass, dim Wisdom, given!

Chorus—Joyous as suns careering gay
    Along their royal paths on high,
    March, Brothers, march your dauntless way,
    As Chiefs to Victory!

Joy, from Truth's pure and lambent fires,
  Smiles out upon the ardent seeker;
Joy leads to Virtue Man's desires,
  And cheers as Suffering's step grows weaker.
High from the sunny slopes of Faith,
  The gales her waving banners buoy;
And through the shatter'd vaults of Death,
  Lo, mid the choral Angels—Joy!

Chorus—Bear this life, millions, bravely bear—.
    Bear this life for the Better One!
    See ye the Stars?—a life is there,
    Where the reward is won.

* To *us*, emphatically. Schiller means to discriminate the measure of bliss assigned to *us*, to the *worm*, and to the *cherub*.

† The original is obscure here; and the translator is doubtful whether he has seized the meaning, which may simply be—" Have you an innate feeling of Deity—then look for Him above the starry vault!"

Men like the Gods themselves may be,
  Tho' Men may not the Gods requite ;
Go soothe the pangs of Misery—
  Go share the gladness with delight.—
Revenge and hatred both forgot,
  Have nought but pardon for thy foe ;
May sharp repentance grieve him not,
  No curse one tear of ours bestow !

Chorus—Let all the world be peace and love—
      Cancel thy debt-book with thy brother :
    For God shall judge of *us* above,
    As we shall judge each other !

Joy sparkles to us from the bowl—
  Behold the juice whose golden colour
To meekness melts the savage soul,
  And gives Despair a Hero's valour.
Up, brothers !—Lo, we crown the cup !
  Lo, the wine flashes to the brim !
Let the bright Fount spring heavenward !—Up !
  To THE GOOD SPIRIT this glass !—To HIM !

Chorus—Praised by the ever-whirling ring
      Of Stars, and tuneful Seraphim—
    To THE GOOD SPIRIT—the Father-King
    In Heaven !—This glass to Him !

Firm mind to bear what Fate bestows ;
  Comfort to tears in sinless eyes ;
Faith kept alike with Friends and Foes ;
  Man's Oath eternal as the skies ;
Manhood—the thrones of Kings to girth,
  Tho' bought by limb or life, the prize ;
Success to Merit's honest worth ;
  Perdition to the Brood of Lies !

Chorus—Draw closer in the holy ring,
      Swear by the wine-cup's golden river—
    Swear by the Stars, and by their King,
    To keep our vow for ever !

THE INVINCIBLE ARMADA.

SHE comes, she comes—the Burthen of the Deeps!
  Beneath her wails the Universal Sea!
With clanking chains and a new God, she sweeps,
  And with a thousand thunders, unto thee!
The ocean-castles and the floating hosts—
  Ne'er on their like, look'd the wild waters!—Well
May man the monster name "Invincible."
O'er shudd'ring waves she gathers to thy coasts!
    The horror that she spreads can claim
    Just title to her haughty name.
      The trembling Neptune quails
Under the silent and majestic forms;
The Doom of Worlds in those dark sails;—
  Near and more near they sweep! and slumber all the
      Storms!

    Before thee, the array,
Blest island, Empress of the Sea!
The sea-born squadrons threaten thee,
  And thy great heart, BRITANNIA!
Woe to thy people, of their freedom proud—
She rests, a thunder heavy in its cloud!
Who, to thy hand the orb and sceptre gave,
  That thou should'st be the sovereign of the nations?
To tyrant kings thou wert thyself the slave,
  Till Freedom dug from Law its deep foundations;
The mighty CHART thy citizens made kings
  And kings to citizens sublimely bow'd!
And thou thyself, upon thy realm of water,
Hast thou not render'd millions up to slaughter,
  When thy ships brought upon their sailing wings
      The sceptre—and the shroud?
What should'st thou thank?—Blush, Earth, to hear and
      feel:
What should'st thou thank?—Thy genius and thy
      steel!
Behold the hidden and the giant fires!
  Behold thy glory trembling to its fall!
Thy coming doom the round earth shall appal,

And all the hearts of freemen beat for thee,
And all free souls their fate in thine foresee—
　　Theirs is *thy* glory's fall!
One look below the Almighty gave,
Where stream'd the lion-flags of thy proud foe;
And near and wider yawn'd the horrent grave.
"And who," saith HE, "shall lay mine England low—
The stem that blooms with hero-deeds—
The rock when man from wrong a refuge needs—
The stronghold where the tyrant comes in vain?
Who shall bid England vanish from the main?
Ne'er be this only Eden Freedom knew,
Man's stout defence from Power, to Fate consign'd."
God the Almighty blew,
And the Armada went to every wind!

THE CONFLICT.

No! I this conflict longer will not wage,
　　The conflict Duty claims—the giant task;—
Thy spells, O Virtue, never can assuage
　' The heart's wild fire—this offering do not ask!

True, I have sworn—a solemn vow have sworn,
　　That I myself will curb the self within;
Yet take thy wreath, no more it shall be worn—
　　Take back thy wreath, and leave me free to sin.

Rent be the contract I with thee once made;—
　　She loves me, loves me—forfeit be thy crown!
Blest he who, lull'd in rapture's dreamy shade,
　　Glides, as I glide, the deep fall gladly down.

She sees the worm that my youth's bloom decays,
　　She sees my springtime wasted as it flees;
And, marv'ling at the rigour that gainsays
　　The heart's sweet impulse, my reward decrees.

Distrust this angel purity, fair soul!
　　It is to guilt thy pity armeth me;
Could Being lavish its unmeasured whole,
　　It ne'er could give a gift to rival *Thee!*

Thee—the dear guilt I ever seek to shun,
  O tyranny of fate, O wild desires!
My virtue's only crown can but be won
  In that last breath—when virtue's self expires!

RESIGNATION.

AND I, too, was amidst Arcadia born,
  And Nature seem'd to woo me;
And to my cradle such sweet joys were sworn:
And I, too, was amidst Arcadia born,
  Yet the short spring gave only tears unto me!
Life but one blooming holiday can keep—
  For me the bloom is fled;
The silent Genius of the Darker Sleep
Turns down my torch—and weep, my brethren, weep—
  Weep, for the light is dead!
Upon thy bridge the shadows round me press,
  O dread Eternity!
And I have known no moment that can bless;—
Take back this letter meant for Happiness—
  The seal's unbroken—see!
Before thee, Judge, whose eyes the dark-spun veil
  Conceals, my murmur came;
On this our orb a glad belief prevails,
That, thine the earthly sceptre and the scales,
  REQUITER is thy name.

Terrors, they say, thou dost for Vice prepare,
  And joys the good shall know;
Thou canst the crooked heart unmask and bare;
Thou canst the riddle of our fate declare,
  And keep account with Woe.
With thee a home smiles for the exiled one—
  There ends the thorny strife.
Unto my side a godlike vision won,
Called TRUTH, (few know her, and the many shun,)
  And check'd the reins of life.
" I will repay thee in a better land—

Give thou to me thy youth ;
All I can grant thee lies in this command.”
I heard, and, trusting in a holier land,
  Gave my young joys to Truth.

“ Give me thy Laura—give me her whom Love
  To thy heart’s core endears ;
The usurer, Bliss, pays every grief—*above !* ”
I tore the fond shape from the bleeding love,
  And gave—albeit with tears !
“ What bond can bind the Dead to life once more ?
  Poor fool,” (the scoffer cries ;)
“ Gull’d by the despot’s hireling lie, with lore
That gives for Truth a shadow ;—life is o’er
  When the delusion dies ! ”
“ Tremblest thou,” hiss’d the serpent-herd in scorn,
  “ Before the vain deceit ?
Made holy but by custom, stale and worn,
The phantom Gods, of craft and folly born—
  The sick world’s solemn cheat ?
What is this Future underneath the stone ?
  But for the veil that hides, revered alone ;
The giant shadow of our Terror, thrown
  On Conscience’ troubled glass—
Life’s lying likeness—in the dreary shroud
  Of the cold sepulchre—
Embalm’d by Hope—Time’s mummy,—which the proud
Delirium, driv’ling through thy reason’s cloud,
  Calls ‘ *Immortality !* ’
Giv’st thou for hope (corruption proves its lie)
  Sure joy that most delights us ?
Six thousand years has Death reign’d tranquilly !—
Nor one corpse come to whisper those who die
  What *after* death requites us !.”
Along Time’s shores I saw the Season fly ;
  Nature herself, interr’d
Among her blooms, lay dead ; to those who die
There came no corpse to whisper Hope ! Still I
  Clung to the Godlike Word.
Judge !—All my joys to thee did I resign,
  All that did most delight me ;

And now I kneel—man's scorn I scorn'd—thy shrine
Have I adored—Thee only held divine—
   Requiter, now requite me!
" For all my sons an equal love I know
   And equal each condition,"
Answer'd an unseen Genius—"See below,
Two flowers, for all who rightly seek them, blow—
   The HOPE and the FRUITION.
He who has pluck'd the one, resign'd must see
   The sister's forfeit bloom :
Let Unbelief enjoy—Belief must be
All to the chooser ;—the world's history
   Is the world's judgment doom.
Thou hast had HOPE—in thy belief thy prize—
   Thy bliss was centred in it :
Eternity itself—(Go ask the Wise!)
Never to him who forfeits, resupplies
   The sum struck from the Minute!"

THE GODS OF GREECE.

I.

   YE in the age gone by,
Who ruled the world—a world how lovely then!—
And guided still the steps of happy men
   In the light leading-strings of careless joy!
Ah, flourish'd then your service of delight!
   How different, oh, how different, in the day
When thy sweet fanes with many a wreath were bright,
   O Venus Amathusia!

II.

Then, through a veil of dreams
   Woven by Song, Truth's youthful beauty glow'd,
And life's redundant and rejoicing streams
   Gave to the soulless, soul—where'er they flow'd
Man gifted Nature with divinity
   To lift and link her to the breast of Love ;
All things betray'd to the initiate eye
   The track of gods above!

III.

Where lifeless—fix'd afar,
  A flaming ball to our dull sense is given,
Phœbus Apollo, in his golden car,
  In silent glory swept the fields of heaven!
On yonder hill the Oread was adored,
  In yonder tree the Dryad held her home;
And from her Urn the gentle Naiad pour'd
  The wavelet's silver foam.

IV.

Yon bay, chaste Daphnè wreathed,
  Yon stone was mournful Niobe's mute cell,
Low through yon sedges pastoral Syrinx breathed,
  And through those groves wail'd the sweet Philomel,
The tears of Ceres swell'd in yonder rill—
  Tears shed for Proserpine to Hades borne;
And, for her lost Adonis, yonder hill
  Heard Cytherea mourn!—

V.

Heaven's shapes were charm'd unto
  The mortal race of old Deucalion;
Pyrrha's fair daughter, humanly to woo,
  Came down, in shepherd-guise, Latona's son.
Between Men, Heroes, Gods, harmonious then
  Love wove sweet links and sympathies divine;
Blest Amathusia, Heroes, Gods, and Men,
  Equals before thy shrine!

VI.

Not to that culture gay,
  Stern self-denial, or sharp penance wan!
Well might each heart be happy in that day—
  For Gods, the Happy Ones, were kin to Man!
The Beautiful alone the Holy there!
  No pleasure shamed the Gods of that young race;
So that the chaste Camœnæ favouring were,
  And the subduing Grace!

VII.

A palace every shrine :
   Your very sports heroic ;—Yours the crown
Of contests hallow'd to a power divine,
   As rush'd the chariots thund'ring to renown.
Fair round the altar where the incense breathed,
   Moved your melodious dance inspired ; and fair
Above victorious brows, the garland wreathed   ;
   Sweet leaves round odorous hair !

VIII.

The lively Thyrsus-swinger,
   And the wild car the exulting Panthers bore,
Announced the Presence of the Rapture-Bringer—
   Bounded the Satyr and blithe Faun before ;
And Mœnads, as the frenzy stung the soul,
   Hymn'd in the madding dance, the glorious wine—
As ever beckon'd to the lusty bowl
   The ruddy Host divine !

IX.

Before the bed of death
   No ghastly spectre stood—but from the porch
Of life, the lip—one kiss inhaled the breath,
   And the mute graceful Genius lower'd a torch.
The judgment-balance of the Realms below,
   A judge, himself of mortal lineage, held ;
The very Furies at the Thracian's woe,
   Were moved and music-spell'd.

X.

In the Elysian grove
   The shades renew'd the pleasures life held dear :
The faithful spouse rejoin'd remember'd love,
   And rush'd along the meads the charioteer ;
There Linus pour'd the old accustom'd strain ;
   Admetus there Alcestis still could greet ; his
Friend there once more Orestes could regain,
   His arrows—Philoctetes !

XI.

More glorious then the meeds
   That in their strife with labour nerved the brave,
To the great doer of renownèd deeds,
   The Hebe and the Heaven the Thunderer gave.
Before the rescued Rescuer * of the dead,
   Bow'd down the silent and Immortal Host ;
And the Twin Stars † their guiding lustre shed,
   On the bark tempest-tost !

XII.

Art thou, fair world, no more ?
   Return, thou virgin-bloom on Nature's face ;
Ah, only on the Minstrel's magic shore,
   Can we the footstep of sweet Fable trace !
The meadows mourn for the old hallowing life ;
   Vainly we search the earth of gods bereft ;
Where once the warm and living shapes were rife,
   Shadows alone are left !

XIII.

Cold, from the North, has gone
   Over the Flowers the Blast that kill'd their May ;
And, to enrich the worship of the ONE,
   A Universe of Gods must pass away !
Mourning, I search on yonder starry steeps,
   But thee no more, Selene, there I see !
And through the woods I call, and o'er the deeps,
   And—Echo answers me !

XIV.

Deaf to the joys she gives—
   Blind to the pomp of which she is possest—
Unconscious of the spiritual Power that lives
   Around, and rules her—by our bliss unblest—

---

* Hercules, who recovered from the Shades Alcestis, after she had given her own life to save her husband Admetus. Alcestis in the hands of Euripides (that woman-hater as he is called !) becomes the loveliest female creation in the Greek Drama.

† *i. e.* Castor and Pollux are transferred to the Stars, Hercules to Olympus, for their deeds on earth.

Dull to the Art that colours or creates,
  Like the dead timepiece, Godless NATURE creeps
Her plodding round, and, by the leaden weights,
  The slavish motion keeps.

XV.

To-morrow to receive
  New life, she digs her proper grave to-day;
And icy moons with weary sameness weave
  From their own light their fulness and decay.
Home to the Poet's Land the Gods are flown,
  Light use in *them* that later world discerns,
Which, the diviner leading-strings outgrown,
  On its own axle turns.

XVI.

Home! and with them are gone
  The hues they gaz'd on and the tones they heard;
Life's Beauty and life's Melody:—alone
  Broods o'er the desolate void the lifeless Word;
Yet rescued from Time's deluge, still they throng
  Unseen the Pindus they were wont to cherish:
Ah, that which gains immortal life in Song,
  To mortal life must perish!

THE ARTISTS.

THIS justly ranks amongst Schiller's noblest Poems. He confessed "that
he had hitherto written nothing that so much pleased him—nothing to
which he had given so much time." * It forms one of the many Pieces he
has devoted to the progress of Man. "The Eleusinian Festival" records
the social benefits of Agriculture; "The Four Ages" panegyrises the influence of Poetry in all times; "The Walk" traces, in a series of glowing
pictures, the development of general civilisation; the "Lay of the Bell"
commemorates the stages of Life; and "The Artists," by some years the
earliest of the Series, is an elaborate exposition of the effect of Art upon the
Happiness and Dignity of the Human Species—a lofty Hymn in honour of
Intellectual Beauty. Herein are collected into a symmetrical and somewhat
argumentative whole, many favourite ideas of Schiller, which the reader
will recognise as scattered throughout his other effusions. About the time
when this Poem was composed, the narrow notions of a certain School of
miscalled Utilitarians were more prevalent than they deserved; and this
fine composition is perhaps the most eloquent answer ever given to those

---
* Hinrichs.

thinkers, who have denied the Morality of Fiction, and considered Poets rather the Perverters than the Teachers of the World. Perhaps in his just Defence of Art, Schiller has somewhat underrated the dignity of Science; but so many small Philosophers have assailed the divine uses of Poetry, that it may be pardoned to the Poet to vindicate his Art in somewhat too arrogant a tone of retaliation. And it may be fairly contended that Fiction (the several forms of which are comprehended under the name of Art) has exercised an earlier, a more comprehensive, and a more genial influence over the Civilisation and the Happiness of Man, than nine tenths of that investigation of Facts which is the pursuit of Science.

The Poem, in the original, is written in lines of irregular length, the imitation of which—considering the nature and the length of the piece—would probably displease in an English version. Occasionally too (for Schiller in all his philosophical Poems is apt to incur the fault of obscurity, from which his poems of sentiment and narrative are generally free,) it has been judged necessary somewhat to expand and paraphrase the sense—to translate the idea as well as the words. But though, verbally, the Translation may be more free than most others in this collection, yet no less pains have been taken to render the version true to the spirit and intention of the Author. For the clearer exposition of the train of thought which Schiller pursues, the Poem has been divided into sections, and the Argument of the whole prefixed. If any passages in the version should appear obscure to those readers who find the mind of Schiller worth attentive Study, even when deprived of the melodious language which clothed its thoughts, by referring to the Argument the sense will perhaps become sufficiently clear.

ARGUMENT.

SECT. 1.—Man regarded in his present palmy state of civilisation—free through Reason, strong through Law—the Lord of Nature. (2) But let him not forget his gratitude to ART, which found him the Savage, and by which his powers have been developed—his soul refined. Let him not degenerate from serving ART, the Queen—to a preference for her handmaids (the Sciences). The Bee and the Worm excel him in diligence and mechanical craft—the Seraph in knowledge—but Art is Man's alone. (3) It is through the Beautiful that Man gains the Intuition of Law and Knowledge. (4) The supposed discoveries of Philosophy were long before revealed as symbols to Feeling. Virtue charmed and Vice revolted, before the Laws of Solon. (5) That Goddess which in Heaven is Urania—the great Deity whom only pure Spirits can behold, descends to earth as the earthly Venus—viz. the Beautiful. She adapts herself to the childlike understanding. But what we now only adore as Beauty we shall, one day, recognise as Truth. (6) After the Fall of Man, this Goddess—(viz. the Beautiful—(comprehending Poetry and Art) alone deigned to console him, and painted on the walls of his Dungeon the Shapes of Elysium. (7) While Men only worshipped the Beautiful, no Fanaticism hallowed Persecution and Homicide — without formal Law, without compulsion, they obeyed Virtue rather as an instinct than a Duty. (8) Those dedicated to her service (viz. the Poet and the Artist) hold the highest intellectual rank Man can obtain. (9) Before Art introduced its own symmetry and method into the world, all was chaos. (10) You, the Artists, contemplated Nature, and learned to imitate; you observed the light shaft of the cedar, the shadow on the wave. (11) Thus rose the first Column of the Sculptor—the first Design of the Painter—and the wind sighing through the reed suggested the first Music. (12) Art's first attempt was in the first choice of flowers for a posy; its second, the weaving of those flowers into a garland—i. e. Art first observes and selects—next blends and unites—the column is ranged with other columns—the indi-

vidual Hero becomes one of an heroic army—the rude Song becomes an Iliad.
(13) The effect produced by Homeric Song, in noble emulation,—nor in this
alone; Man learns to live in other woes than his own—to feel pleasures
beyond animal enjoyments. (14) And as this diviner intellectual feeling is
developed, are developed also Thought and Civilisation. (15) In the rudest
state of Man, you, the Artists, recognise in his breast the spiritual germ, and
warm it into life—true and holy Love awoke with the first Shepherd's love
song. (16) It is you, the Artists, who generalising, and abstracting, gather
all several excellences into one ideal.—You thus familiarise Man to the
notion of the Unknown Powers, whom you invest with the attributes Man
admires and adores.—He fears the Unknown, but he loves its shadow.—You
suffered the Nature around him to suggest the Prototype of all Beauty.
(17) You make subject to your ends—the passion, the duty, and the instinct
—All that is scattered through creation you gather and concentrate, and
resolve to the Song or to the Stage—Even the murderer who has escaped
justice, conscience-stricken by the Eumenides on the scene, reveals himself—
Long before Philosophy hazarded its dogmas an Iliad solved the riddles of
Fate—And with the wain of Thespis wandered a Providence. (18) Where
your symmetry, your design fail in this world, they extend into the world
beyond the grave—If life be over too soon for the brave and good, Poetry
imagined the Shades below, and placed the hero Castor amongst the Stars.*
(19) Not contented with bestowing immortality on Man—you furnish forth
from Man, the ideal of the Immortals—Virgin Beauty grows into a Pallas—
manly Strength into a Jove. (20) As the world without you is thus enlarged
and the world within you agitated and enriched, your Art extends to Philosophy:—For as the essentials of Art are symmetry and design, so the Artist
extends that symmetry and that design into the system of Creation, the
Laws of Nature, the Government of the World;—Lends to the spheres its
own harmony—to the Universe its own symmetric method. (21) The Artist
thus recognising *Contrivance* everywhere, feels his life surrounded with
Beauty—He has before him in Nature itself an eternal model of the Perfect
and Consummate—Through joy—grief—terror—wherever goes his course—
one stream of harmony murmurs by his side—The Graces are his companions
—his life glides away amidst airy shapes of Beauty—His soul is merged in
the divine ocean that flows around him. Fate itself which is reduced from
Chance and Providence, and which furnishes him with themes of pleasurable
awe, does not daunt him. (22) You, Artists, are the sweet and trusty companions of life—You gave us what life has best—Your reward is your own
immortality and the gratitude of Men's hearts. (23) You are the imitators
of the Divine Artist, who accompanies power with sweetness, terror with
splendour, who adorns himself even in destroying—As a brook that reflects
the evening landscape, so on the niggard stream of life shimmers Poetry.
You lead us on, in marriage garments, to the Unknown Bourne—As your
Urns deck our bones your fair semblances deck our cares.—Through the
history of the world, we find that Humanity smiles in your presence and
mourns in your absence. (24) Humanity came young from your hands, and
when it grew old and decayed, you gave it a second youth—Time has
bloomed twice from seeds sown by Art. (25) When the Barbarians chased
Civilisation from Greece, you transplanted it to Italy—and, with Civilisation,
freedom and gentle manners—Yet you sought not public rewards for your
public benefits—In obscurity you contemplated the blessings you had diffused.
(26) If the Philosopher now pursues his course without obstacles—if he now

---

* To the Poet we are indebted for the *promise* of another life (foreshadow-
ing Divine Revelation) long before the Philosopher bewildered us by *arguing*
for it.

P

would arrogate the crown, and hold Art but as the first Slave to Science—pardon his vain boast.—Completion and Perfection in reality rest with you.—With you dawned the Spring, in you is matured the Harvest, of the Moral World. (27) For although Art sprung first from physical materials, the clay and the stone—it soon also embraced in its scope the spiritual and intellectual—Even what Science discovers only ministers to Art.—The Philosopher obtains his first hints from the Poet or Artist—and when his wisdom flowers, as it were, into beauty—it but returns to the service, and is applied to the uses of its instructor.—When the Philosopher contemplates the Natural World, side by side with the Artist—the more the Latter accumulates images of beauty, and unites the details of the great design, the more the Former enriches the sphere of his observation—the more profound his research—the more bold his speculations—The Imagination always assists the Reason—And Art which teaches Philosophy to see Art (*i. e.* Symmetry and Design) everywhere, may humble the Philosopher's pride, but augments his love.—Thus scattering flowers, Poetry leads on through tones and forms, ever high and higher, pure and purer, till it shall at last attain that point when Poetry becomes but sudden inspiration and the instantaneous intuition of Truth;—when in fact the Art sought by the Poet, the Truth sought by the Philosopher, become one. (28) Then this great Goddess, whom we have hitherto served as the earthly Venus, the Beautiful—shall re-assume her blazing crown—and Man, to whose earlier and initiatory probation she has gently familiarised her splendour, shall behold her without a veil—not as the Venus of Earth, but as the Urania of Heaven—Her beauty comprehended by him in proportion to the beauty his soul took from her—So from the Mentor of his youth shone forth Minerva to Telemachus. (29) To you, O Artists, is committed the dignity of Man—It sinks with you, it revives with you. (30) In those Ages when Truth is persecuted by the Bigotry of her own time, she seeks refuge in Song.—The charm she takes from the Muse but renders her more fearful to her Foes. (31) Aspire then constantly, O Artists, to the Beautiful—covet no meaner rewards.—If Art escape you, search for her in Nature.—Remember that the excellent and the perfect ever must be found in whatsoever fair souls esteem fair.—Do not bound yourselves to your own time—Let your works reflect the shadow of the coming Age—It matters not what paths you select—You have before you the whole labyrinth of being—but all its paths for you unite at one throne—As the white breaks into seven tints, as the seven tints re-dissolve into white—so Truth is the same, whether she dazzles us with the splendour of variegated colours, or pervades the Universe in one Stream of Light.

I.

Upon the century's verge, O Man, how fair
Thou standest, stately as a silent palm
With boughs far-spreading through the solemn air,
In the full growth of mellowest years sublime;
Thro' mildness earnest, thro' achievement calm,
Each sense unfolded, all the soul matured—
The crowning work and ripest born of Time!
Free in the freedom reason has secured,
Strong in the strength that Law bestows, thou art,
Great in thy meekness—rich with countless stores,
Which slept for ages silent in thy heart;
The Lord of Nature, who thy chains adores,

Who in each strife but disciplines thy skill,
And shines from out the desert at thy will!

II.

O not, inebriate with thy victory, scorn—
Scorn not to prize and praise the fostering hand
That found thee weeping—orphan'd and forlorn,
Lone on the verge of Life's most barren strand—
That seized from lawless CHANCE its helpless prey,
And early taught thy young heart the control
Of ART—thy guide upon the upward way—
The softener and the raiser of the soul,—
Cleansing the breast it tutored to aspire,
From the rude passion and the low desire:
The good, the blessed One, who, through sweet play,
To lofty duties lured thy toilless youth;
Who by light parables revealed the ray
That gilds the mystery of each holier Truth;
And but to stranger arms consigned—once more
To clasp her darling, riper for her lore.
O fall not back from that high faith serene,
To serve the Handmaids and forsake the Queen.
In diligent toil thy master is the bee;
In craft mechanical, the worm that creeps
Through earth its dexterous way, may tutor thee;
In knowledge (couldst thou fathom all its deeps),
All to the seraph are already known.
But thine, O MAN, is ART—thine wholly and alone!

III.

But through the Morning-Gate of Beauty goes
Thy pathway to the Land of Knowledge! By
The twilight Charm,—Truth's gradual daylight grows
Familiar to the Mind's unconscious eye;
And what was first—with a sweet tremulous thrill—
Wakened within thee by melodious strings,
Grows to a Power that swells and soars until
Up to the all-pervading God it springs.*

* *i. e.* Poetry prepared the mind for the knowledge of God.

IV.

What first the reason of the Antique Time
Dimly discovered (many a century flown
Lay in the symbol types of the Sublime
And Beautiful—intuitively known:
True, from the seeker as a *lore* concealed,)
But as an *instinct* all to childish sense revealed.
Virtue's fair shape to Virtue love could draw,
From Vice a gentler impulse warned away,
Ere yet a Solon sowed the formal Law,
Whose fruits warmed slowly to the gradual ray;—
Ere the Idea of Space, the Infinite,
Before Philosophy, the Seeker, stole—
Who ever gazed upon the Starry Light,
Nor guess'd the large truth in the silent soul?

V.

She the URANIA, with her wreath of rays,
The glory of Orion round her brow;
On whom pure Spirits only dare to gaze,
As Heaven's bright Habitants before her bow;
And round her splendour the stars wink and fade
So awful, reigning on her sunlit throne—
When she diswreathes her of her fiery crown,
Gliding to Earth (Earth's gentle Venus) down,
Smiles on us but as BEAUTY: *—with the zone
Of the sweet Graces girded, the meek youth
Of Infancy she wears, that she may be
By Infants comprehended, and what we
Here, but as BEAUTY gazed on and obey'd,—
Will, one day, meet us in her name of TRUTH!

VI.

When the Creator from his presence cast
Man to thy dark abyss—Mortality,
Condemn'd the late return to glory past,
To seek and strive for with a weary sigh,

---

* *i.e.* She who, in Heaven, is Urania—the Daughter of Uranus—by
Light, is, on Earth, Venus—the Divinity of Love and Beauty. The Beautiful is to Mortals the revelation of Truth. Truth, in its abstract splendour
too bright for the eyes of Man in his present state, familiarises itself to him
in the shape of the Beautiful.

Amidst the dim paths of the sensual clay,
When every heavenlier Nature from his eye
Veil'd its bright face, and swept in scorn away ;
She only—she, in the low Human cell,
Herself made human, deign'd with him to dwell—
Stoop'd round her darling, wings soft-brooding ; fann'd
With freshening airs, the Sense's barren land ;
And, kind in bright delusions, limn'd with all
The lost Elysium—life's sad dungeon-wall.

VII.

Ah, in that tender Nurse's cradling arms—
While yet reposed the mild Humanity—
War deck'd not Murder with Fame's holy charms,
Reck'd not the innocent blood ;—but guided by
Those gentle leading-strings, the guileless soul
Shunn'd the cold duties, by compulsion taught ;
Virtue was instinct—and without control,
Through ways the lovelier for their winding, sought
The Moral in the Beautiful,—and won ;—
Each path a ray that guided to the Sun !
Ne'er they who tended her chaste service knew
One meaner impulse—and the frown of Fate
Paled not their courage from its healthy hue,
As in some holier realm, their happy state
Regain'd the freedom while it shunn'd the strife,
And won to Earth once more the spiritual, heavenly life.

VIII.

Oh, happy ! and of many millions, they
The purest chosen, whom her service pure
Hallows and claims—whose hearts are made her throne,
Whose lips her oracle—ordain'd secure,
To lead a Priestly life, and feed the ray
Of her eternal shrine,—to them alone
Her glorious Countenance unveil'd is shown :
Ye, the high Brotherhood she links—rejoice
In the great rank allotted by her choice !—
The loftiest rank the spiritual world sublime,
Rich with its starry thrones, gives to the Sons of Time !

IX.

Ere yet unto the early world the Law
Of the harmonious Symmetry, which all
Essence and life now joyously obey,
Your Art divinely gave—wall'd round with Night
And Chaos, gloomier for one sickly ray,
Man struggled with the uncouth shapes of awe,
That through the Dark came giant on the sight,
And chained the senses in a slavish thrall :
Rude as himself press'd round the shadowy throng,
Vast without outline, without substance, strong ;
So gloom'd Creation on the Savage Breast,
While brutal lusts alone allured the eye,
And unenjoy'd, unheeded, and unguest,
The lovely soul of Nature pass'd him by,—

X.

Lo, *as* it pass'd him, with a noiseless hand,
And with a gentle instinct, the fair shade
Ye seiz'd ; and linked in one harmonious band
The airy images your eyes survey'd ;
Ye felt, surveying, how the cedar gave
Its light shaft to the air ;—how sportive, play'd
The form reflected on the crystal wave !
How could ye fail the gentle hints to read
With which free Nature met ye on the way ?
By easy steps did eye observant lead
The hand to mimick the fair forms at play,
Till from the image on the water glass'd
The likeness rose—and Painting grew at last !
Yea, from the substance sever'd, Nature's fair
And phantom shadow—follow'd by the soul,
Cast itself on the silver stream, and there
Rendered its coyness to the hand that stole !
  *So born the craft that imitates and takes
Shape from the shadow ;—so young Art awakes
The earliest genius ;—so in clay and sand
The shade is snatch'd at by the eager hand ;
The sweet enjoyment in the labour grows,
And from your breast the first creation flows.

* See Argument.

XI.

Seized by the power of thoughtful contemplation,
Snared by the eye that steals what it surveys,
Nature, the talisman of each creation
With which her spells enamour you, betrays :
Your quicken'd sense, the wonder-working laws,
The stores in Beauty's treasure-house, conceives—
Your hand from Nature the light outline draws,
And scattered hints in gentle union weaves.
Thus rise—tall Obelisk, and vast Pyramid—
The half-formed Hermes grows—the Column springs ;
Music comes lisping from the Shepherd's reed,
And Song the valour and the victory sings.

XII.

The happier choice of flowers most sweet or fair,
To weave the posy for some Shepherd Maid,
Lo the *first* Art, from nature born, is there !—
The *next*—the flowers the careless tresses braid
In garlands wreath'd :—Thus step by step ascends
The Art that notes, and gathers, shapes and blends !
    But, each once blent with each, its single grace
Each offspring of the Beautiful must lose ;
The artful hand according each its place,
Confounds the separate with the common hues.
Charm'd into method by the harmonious word,
Column with column ranged—proud Fanes aspire,
The Hero melts amidst the Hero herd,
And peals the many-stringed Mœonian Lyre.

XIII.

Soon round this new Creation in great Song
Barbarian wonder gather'd and believed ;
" See," cried the emulous and kindled throng,
" The deeds a Mortal like ourselves achieved ! "
Grouped into social circles near and far,
Listing the wild tales of the Titan war,
Of giants piled beneath the rocks,—and caves
Grim with the lion some stout hero braves,
Still while the Minstrel sung, the listeners grew
Themselves the Heroes his high fancy drew.

Then first did Men the soul's enjoyment find,
First knew the calmer raptures of the mind
Not proved by sense—but from the distance brought;
The joy at deeds themselves had never wrought,—
The thirst for what possession cannot give,—
The power in nobler lives than life to live!

XIV.

Now from the Sensual Slumber's heavy chain,
Breaks the fair soul, which now-born pinions buoy,
And, freed by you, the ancient Slave of Pain
Springs from his travail to the breast of Joy;
Fall the dull Animal-Barriers round him wrought,
On his clear front the HUMAN halo glows,
And forth the high Majestic Stranger—THOUGHT,
Bright from the startled brain, a Pallas, goes!
Now stands sublime THE MAN, and to the star
Lifts his unclouded brow—The Kingly One;
And Contemplation, sweeping to the Far,
Speaks in the eyes commercing with the Sun.
Fair from his cheeks bloom happy smiles, and all
The rich varieties of soulful sound
Unfold in Song—divine emotions call
Sweet tears to feeling eyes;—and, sister-bound,
Kindness and Mirth upon his accents dwell,
Soul, like some happy Nymph, haunting the lips' pure
    well!

XV.

Yea, what though buried in the mire and clay
Grovels the fleshly instinct of the worm;
What though the lusts and ruder passions sway
And clasp him 'round—the intellectual germ
You, Sons of Art, in that dark breast behold,
Warm from its sleep and into bloom unfold:—
Love's spiritual blossom opened to the day,
First—when Man heard the first young Shepherd's lay.
Ennobled by the dignity of Thought,
Passion that blush'd the soft desire to own,
Caught chaster language from the Minstrel's tone;

And Song, the delicate Preacher, while it taught
A love outlasting what the senses sought,
Beyond Possession placed the ethereal goal,
And to the Heart proclaimed and link'd the Soul!

XVI.

The wisdom of the wise, the gentleness
The gentle know—the strength that nerves the strong—
The grace that gathers round the noble—yes
Ye blend them all to limn the Beautiful,
Each ray on Nature's brows commixed and grown
Into one pomp—a halo for your own!
Though from the Unknown Divinity, the awe
Of Man shrinks back—to what he knows no dull,
Yet with what love his young religion saw
The shadow of the Godhead downward thrown; *
Gentle the type—though fearful the Unknown.
The breasts of heroes nobly burn'd to vie
With the bright Gods that rul'd in Homer's sky;
Ye did the Ideal from the Natural call—
Ye bade Man learn how on the Earth is given
The immemorial prototype of all
Glory and Beauty, dream'd of for the Heaven!

XVII.

The wild tumultuous passions of the soul,
The playful gladness of unfetter'd joy,
The duty and the instinct—your control
Grasps at its will—can as its slaves employ
To guide the courses, and appoint the goal;
All that in restless Nature's mighty space
Wander divided—world on world afar—
Ye seize—ye gather, fix them into place,
And show them bright and living as they are,
Link'd into order stately and serene,
Limn'd in the song, or mirror'd on the scene!

* *i. e.* Man shrinks in awe from the notion of a Diviner Power, thoroughly
unknown; but the Greek Mythology familiarised Man to the providence of
the Gods, and elevated him by the contemplation of attributes in which he
recognised whatever he most admired.—Art taught Man to see in the Nature
round him the prototype—the ideal—of Diviner Beauty.

Here, secret Murder, pale and shuddering, sees
Sweep o'er the stage the stern Eumenides ; *
Owns, where Law fails, what powers to Art belong,
And, screen'd from Justice, finds its doom in Song !
Long ere the wise their slow decrees revolved,
A fiery Iliad Fate's dark riddles solved ;
And Art, the Prophetess, Heaven's mystic plan
Of doom and destiny reveal'd to Man,
When the rude goat-song spell'd the early Age,
And Providence,† spoke low from Thespis' wandering
    stage.

XVIII.

Nay, where in *this* world, Reason paus'd perplext,
Ye track'd God onward, and divined the *next*
‡ Full early wont to comprehend and meet
Harmonious systems never incomplete,
What though the vain impatient eye might fail
To pierce the dark Fate through the solemn veil—
Though the brave heart seem'd prematurely still'd,
And life's fair circle halted unfulfilled,
Yet here, ev'n here, your own unaided might
Flung its light Arch across the waves of Night ;
Led the untrembling Spirit on to go
Where dark Avernus, wailing, winds below ;
Bade Hope survive the Urn and Charnel, brave
In the great faith of Life beyond the grave ;

* The Poet here seems to allude to the Story of Ibycus, which at a subsequent period furnished the theme of one of his happiest narratives.
† In the Drama the essentials are Providence and Design.

    ‡ " Doch in den grossen Weltenlauf
      Ward euer Ebenmaass zu früh getragen."

These lines are extremely obscure. Unless we may construe "zu früh,"
"*very* early," or " with bold prematurity." In which case, referring to
the conclusion of the preceding stanza, the sense would be—That the Poet
did not confine the operations of a recompensing Providence to the limited
exhibitions of the Thespian wain ; but, even in the infancy of society, and
with a boldness which might be considered premature, ventured to transfer
them to the greater stage of the actual world, and to claim compensation
beyond the grave for heroic lives inevitably cut short before they had fulfilled their career. The Poet's necessary love of symmetry and system
(of which justice is a part) compels him to carry on the life which fails of
result and completion here, to fulfilment in a life hereafter.

Show'd there—how Love the lov'd once more could win—
How Dorian Castor gained his starry Twin—
The Shadow in the Moon's pale glimmer seen,
Ere yet she fills her horns, and rounds her orb serene !

XIX.

High, and more high, the aspiring Genius goes,
And still creation from creation flows ;
What in the natural world but charms the eyes,
In Art's—to forms which awe the soul must rise ;
The Maiden's majesty, at Art's commands,
Inspires the marble, and—Athenè stands !
The strength that nerves the Wrestler on the sod
Swells the vast beauty which invests a God,
And throned in Elis—wonder of his time—
With brows that sentence worlds—sits Phidian Jove sub-
    lime !

XX.

Without—the World by diligent toil transformed,
Within—by new-born passions roused the heart,
(Strengthened by each successive strife that stormed)
Wider and wider grows your realm of Art.
Still in each step that Man ascends to light
He bears the Art that first inspired the flight ;
And still the teeming Nature to his gaze,
The wealth he gives her with new worlds repays.
Thus the light Victories exercise the mind,
By guess to reach what knowledge fails to find,
Practised—throughout the Universe to trace
An Artist-whole of beauty and of grace,
He sets the Columns Nature's boundary knows,
Tracks her dark course, speeds with her where she goes ;
Weighs with the balance her own hands extend ;
Meets with the gauge her own perfections lend,
Till all her beauty renders to his gaze
The charm that robes it and the law that sways.
In self-delighted Joy the Artist hears
His own rich harmony enchant the spheres,
And in the Universal Scheme beholds
The symmetry that reigns in all he moulds.

XXI.

Yes, in all round him can his ear divine
The voice that tells of method and design;
He sees the life mid which his lot is thrown,
Clasp'd round with beauty as a golden zone;
In all his works, before his emulous eyes,
To lead to victory, fair Perfection flies:
Where'er he hears, or gay Delight rejoice,
Or Care to stillness breathe its whispered voice,
Where starry Contemplation lingers slow,
Or stream from heavy eyes the tears of Woe,
Or Terror in her thousand shapes appal;—
Still one harmonious Sweetness glides through all,
Soft to his ear, and freshening to his look,
And winding on through earth—one haunting music brook!
In the refined and still emotion, glide
With chastened mirth the Graces to his side;
Round him the bright Companions weave their dance;
And as the curving lines of Beauty flow,
Each winding into each, as o'er his glance
The lovely apparitions gleam and go
In delicate outline—so the dreaming day
Of Life, enchanted, breathes itself away.
His soul is mingled with the Harmonious Sea
That flows around his sense delightedly;
And Thought, where'er with those sweet waves it glide,
Bears the all-present Venus on the tide!
At peace with Fate serenely goes his race—
Here guides the Muse, and there supports the Grace;
The stern Necessity, to others dim
With Night and Terror, wears no frown for him:
Calm and serene, he fronts the threatened dart,
Invites the gentle bow, and bares the fearless heart.

XXII.

Darlings of Harmony divine,—all blest
Companions of our Beings!—whatsoe'er
Is of this life, the dearest, noblest, best,
Took life from you! If Man his fetters bear

With a glad heart that chafes not at the chain,
But clings to duty with the thoughts of love;
If now no more he wander in the reign
Of iron Chance, but with the Power above
Link his harmonious being—what can be
Your bright reward?—your Immortality,
And your own heart's high recompense!   If round
The chalice-fountain, whence, to Mortals, streams
The Ideal Freedom, evermore are found
The godlike Joys and pleasure-weaving Dreams;—
For this—for these—be yours the grateful shrine,
Deep in the Human Heart ye hallow and refine.

XXIII.

Ye are the Imitators, ye the great
Disciples of the Mighty Artist—who
Zoned with sweet grace the iron form of Fate—
Gave Heaven its starry lights and tender blue—
Whose terror more ennobles than alarms
(Its awe exalts us, and its grandeur charms)—
Who, ev'n destroying, while he scathes, illumes,
And clothes with pomp the anger that consumes.
   As o'er some brook that glides its lucid way
The dancing shores in various shadow play;
As the smooth wave a faithful mirror yields
To Eve's soft blush, and flower-enamell'd fields;
So, on life's stream, that niggard steals along,
Shimmers the lively Shadow-World of Song.
   Ye, to the Dread Unknown—the dismal goal
Where the stern Fates await the trembling soul—
Ye lead us on, by paths for ever gay,
And robed with joy as for a marriage-day;
And as in graceful urns your genius decks
Our very bones, and beautifies the wrecks:
So with appearances divinely fair,
Ye veil the trouble and adorn the care.
Search where I will the ages that have roll'd,
The unmeasured Past, Earth's immemorial lore,
How smil'd Humanity, where ye consoled,
How smileless mourned Humanity before!

XXIV.

All strong and mighty on the wing, and young
And fresh from your creative hands, It * sprung ;
And when the Time, that conquers all, prevail'd ;
When on its wrinkled cheek the roses fail'd ;
When from its limbs the vigour pass'd away,
And its sad age crept on in dull decay,
And tottered on its crutch ;—within your arms
It sought its shelter and regained its charms :
Out from your fresh and sparkling well, ye pour'd
The living stream that dying strength restored ;
Twice into spring has Time's stern winter glow'd,
Twice Nature blossom'd from the seeds Art sow'd.

XXV.

Ye snatch'd—when chased Barbarian Hosts before—
From sacred hearths the last yet living brand ;
From the dishallow'd Orient Altar bore,
And brought it glimmering to the Western Land.
As from the East the lovely Exile goes,
Fair on the West a young Aurora glows ;
And all the flowers Ionian shores could yield
Blush forth, re-blooming in the Hesperian Field.
Fair Nature glass'd its image on the Soul,
From the long Night the mists began to roll ;
And o'er the world of Mind, adorn'd again,
Light's holy Goddess re-assumed her reign.
Loos'd from the Millions fell the fetters then—
Slaves heard the Voice that told their rights as Men.
And the Young Race in peace to vigour grew,
In that mild brotherhood they learn'd from you !
    And you, averse the loud applause to win,
Still in the joy that overflow'd within,
Sought the mild shade, contented to survey
The World ye brighten'd, basking in the ray.

XXVI.

If on the course of Thought, now barrier-free,
Sweeps the glad search of bold Philosophy ;

* *i. e.* Humanity.

And with self-pæans, and a vain renown,
Would claim the praise and arrogate the crown,
Holding, but as a Soldier in her band,
The nobler Art that did in truth command;
And grants, beneath her visionary throne,
To Art, her Queen—the slave's first rank alone ;—
Pardon the vaunt!—For YOU Perfection all
Her star-gems weaves in one bright coronal!
With you, the first blooms of the Spring, began
Awakening Nature in the Soul of Man !
With you fulfill'd, when Nature seeks repose,
Autumn's exulting harvests ripely close.

XXVII.

If Art rose plastic from the stone and clay,
To Mind from Matter ever sweeps its sway ;
Silent, but conquering in its silence, lo,
How o'er the Spiritual World its triumphs go !
What in the Land of Knowledge, wide and far,
Keen Science teaches—for *you* discovered are :
First in your arms the wise their wisdom learn—
They dig the mine you teach them to discern ;
And when that wisdom ripens to the flower
And crowning time of Beauty—to the Power
From whence it rose, new stores it must impart,
The toils of Science swell the Wealth of Art.
    When to one height the Sage ascends with you,
And spreads the Vale of Matter round his view
In the mild twilight of serene repose ;
The more the Artist charms, the more the Thinker
        knows.
The more the shapes—in intellectual joy,
Link'd by the Genii which your spells employ,
The more the thought with the emotion blends—
The more up-buoy'd by both the Soul ascends
To loftier Harmonies, and heavenlier things ;—
And tracks the stream of Beauty to its springs.
The lovely members of the mighty whole,
Till then confused and shapeless to his soul—
Distinct and glorious grow upon his sight,
The fair enigmas brighten from the Night ;

More rich the Universe his thoughts enclose—
More wide the Ocean with whose wave he flows;
The wrath of Fate grows feebler to his fears,
As from God's Scheme Chance wanes and disappears;
And as each straining impulse soars above—
How his pride lessens—how augments his love!
So scattering blooms—the still Guide—Poetry
Leads him thro' paths, tho' hid, that mount on high—
Thro' forms and tones more pure and more sublime—
Alp upon Alp of Beauty—till the time
When what we long as Poetry have nurst,
Shall as a God's swift inspiration burst,
And flash in glory, on that youngest day—
One with the Truth to which it wings the way!

XXVIII.

She, the soft Venus of the Earth, by Men
Worshipp'd but as the Beautiful till then,
Shall re-assume her blazing coronal,
Let the mock veil that shrouds her splendour fall,
And to her ripen'd Son * divinely rise
In her true shape—the Urania of the skies!
Proportion'd to the Beauty which Man's soul
Took from her culture while in her control,
Shall he, with toilless, lightly-wooing ease,
Truth in the Beautiful embrace and seize.
Thus sweet, thus heavenly, was thy glad surprise,
Son of Ulysses, when before thine eyes,
Bright from the Mentor whom thy youth had known,
Jove's radiant child—Imperial Pallas—shone!

XXIX.

O Sons of Art! into your hands consign'd
(O heed the trust, O heed it and revere!)
The liberal dignity of human kind!
With you to sink, with you to re-appear.
The hallow'd melody of Magian Song
Does to Creation as a link belong,
Blending its music with God's harmony,
As rivers melt into the mighty sea.

* Mündigen,—her Son, who has attained his majority.

XXX.

Truth, when the Age she would reform, expels :
Flies for safe refuge to the Muse's cells.
More fearful for the veil of charms she takes,
From Song the fulness of her splendour breaks,
And o'er the Foe that persecutes and quails
Her vengeance thunders, as the Bard prevails!

XXXI.

Rise, ye free Sons of the Free Mother, rise,
Still on the Light of Beauty, sun your eyes,
Still to the heights that shine afar, aspire,
Nor meaner meeds than those she gives, desire.
If here the Sister Art forsake awhile,
Elude the clasp, and vanish from the toil,
Go seek and find her at the Mother's heart—
Go search for Nature—and arrive at Art!
Ever the Perfect dwells in whatsoe'er
Fair souls conceive and recognise as fair!
Borne on your daring pinions soar sublime
Above the shoal and eddy of the Time.
Far-glimmering on your wizard mirror, see
The silent shadow of the Age to be.
Thro' all Life's thousand-fold entangled maze,
One godlike bourne your gifted sight surveys—
Thro' countless means one solemn end, foreshown,
The labyrinth closes at a single Throne.
    As in seven tints of variegated light
Breaks the lone shimmer of the lucid white;
As the seven tints that paint the Iris bow
Into the lucid white dissolving flow—
So Truth in many-coloured splendour plays,—
Now on the eye enchanted with the rays—
Now in one lustre gathers every beam,
And floods the World with light—a single Stream !

* There is exquisite skill in concluding the Poem (after insisting so eloquently upon the maxim, that whatever Science discovers, only adds to the stores, or serves the purpose of Art) with an image borrowed from Science.

THE CELEBRATED WOMAN.

AN EPISTLE BY A MARRIED MAN—TO A FELLOW-SUFFERER.

[In spite of Mr. Carlyle's assertion of Schiller's "total deficiency in Humour,"* we think that the following Poem suffices to show that he *possessed* the gift in no ordinary degree, and that if the aims of a genius so essentially earnest had allowed him to *indulge* it, he would have justified the opinion of the experienced Iffland as to his capacities for original comedy.]

Can I, my friend, with thee condole ?—
 Can I conceive the woes that try men,
When late Repentance racks the soul
 Ensnared into the toils of Hymen ?
Can *I* take part in such distress ?—
Poor Martyr,—most devoutly, "Yes! "
Thou weep'st because thy Spouse has flown
To arms preferred before thine own ;—
A faithless wife,—I grant the curse,—
And yet, my friend, it might be worse !
Just hear Another's tale of sorrow,
And, in comparing, comfort borrow !

What ! dost thou think thyself undone,
Because thy rights are shared with *One !*
O, Happy Man—be more resign'd,
My wife belongs to all Mankind !
My wife—she's found abroad—at home ;
But cross the Alps and she's at Rome ;
Sail to the Baltic—there you'll find her ;
Lounge on the Boulevards—kind and kinder :
In short, you've only just to drop
 Where'er they sell the last new tale,
And, bound and lettered in the shop,
 You'll find my Lady up for sale !

She must her fair proportions render
To all whose praise can glory lend her ;—
Within the coach, on board the boat,
Let every pedant "take a note ; "
Endure, for public approbation,
Each 'critic's " close investigation,"

* Carlyle's Miscellanies, vol. iii. p. 47.

And brave—nay court it as a flattery—
Each spectacled Philistine's battery.
Just as it suits some scurvy carcase
In which she hails an Aristarchus,
Ready to fly with kindred souls,
O'er blooming flowers or burning coals,
To fame or shame, to shrine or gallows,
Let him but lead—sublimely callous!
A Leipsic man—(confound the wretch!)
Has made her Topographic sketch,
A kind of Map, as of a Town,
Each point minutely dotted down;
Scarce to myself I dare to hint
What this d—d fellow wants to print!
Thy wife—howe'er she slight the vows—
Respects, at least, the *name* of spouse;
But mine to regions far too high
  For that terrestrial Name is carried;
My wife's "THE FAMOUS NINON!"—I
  "The Gentleman that Ninon married!"

It galls you that you scarce are able
To stake a florin at the table—
Confront the Pit, or join the Walk,
But straight all tongues begin to talk!
O that such luck could me befal,
Just to be talked about at all!
Behold me dwindling in my nook,
Edg'd at her left,—and not a look!
A sort of rushlight of a life,
Put out by that great Orb—my Wife!

Scarce is the Morning grey—before
Postman and Porter crowd the door;
No Premier has so dear a levée—
  She finds the Mail-bag half its trade;
My God—the parcels are so heavy!
  And not a parcel carriage-paid!
But then—the truth must be confessed—
They're all so charmingly addressed:
Whate'er they cost, they well requite her—

“ To Madame Blank, The Famous Writer ! ”
Poor thing, she sleeps so soft ! and yet
   ’Twere worth my life to spare her slumber ;
“ Madame—from Jena—the Gazette—
   The Berlin Journal—the last number ! ”
Sudden she wakes ; those eyes of blue
(Sweet eyes !) fall straight—on the Review !
I by her side—all undetected,
While those curs’d columns are inspected ;
Loud squall the children overhead,
Still she reads on, till all is read :
At last she lays *that* darling by,
And asks—“ What makes the Baby cry ? ”

Already now the Toilet’s care
Claims from her couch the restless fair ;
The Toilet’s *care !*—the glass has won
Just half a glance, and all is done !
A snappish—pettish word or so
Warns the poor Maid ’tis time to go :—
Not at *her* toilet wait the Graces,
Uncombed Erynnys takes their places ;
So great a mind expands its scope
Far from the mean details of—soap !

Now roll the coach-wheels to the muster—
Now round my Muse her votaries cluster ;
Spruce Abbé Millefleurs—Baron Herman—
The English Lord, who don’t know German,—
But all uncommonly well read
From matchless A to deathless Z !
Sneaks in the corner, shy and small,
A thing which Men the Husband call !
While every fop with flattery fires her,
Swears with what passion he admires her.—
“ ‘ Passion ! ’ ‘ admire ! ’ and still you’re dumb ? ’
Lord bless your soul, the worst’s to come :—
I’m forced to bow, as I’m a sinner,—
And hope—the rogue will stay to dinner !
But, oh, at dinner !—there’s the sting ;
I see my cellar on the wing !

You know if Burgundy is dear?—
Mine once emerg'd three times a year;—
And now, to wash these learned throttles,
In dozens disappear the bottles;
They well must drink who well do eat,
(I've sunk a capital on meat).
Her immortality, I fear, a
Death-blow will prove to my Madeira;
'T has given, alas! a mortal shock
To that old friend—my Steinberg Hock! *

If Faust had really any hand
In printing, I can understand
The fate which legends more than hint;—
The devil take all hands that print!

And what my thanks for all?—a pout—
Sour looks—deep sighs; but what about?
About! O, *that* I well divine—
That such a pearl should fall to swine—
That such a literary ruby
Should grace the finger of a booby!

Spring comes;—behold, sweet mead and lea
   Nature's green splendour tapestries o'er;
Fresh blooms the flower, and buds the tree;
   Larks sing—the Woodland wakes once more.
The Woodland wakes—but not for her!
   From Nature's self the charm has flown;
No more the Spring of Earth can stir
   The fond remembrance of our own!
The sweetest bird upon the bough
Has not one note of music now;
And, oh! how dull the Grove's soft shade,
Where once—(as lovers *then*)—we stray'd!
The Nightingales have got no learning—
   Dull creatures—how can they inspire her?
The Lilies are so undiscerning,
   They never say—" how they admire her! "

---

* Literally "Nierensteiner,"—a wine not much known in England, and scarcely—according to our experience—worth the regrets of its respectable owner.

In all this Jubilee of being,
Some subject for a point she's seeing—
Some epigram—(to be impartial,
Well turn'd)—there may be worse in Martial!

But, hark! the Goddess stoops to reason :—
" The country now is quite in season,
I'll go! "—" What! to our Country Seat ? "
"No !—Travelling will be such a treat ;
Pyrmont's extremely full, I hear ;
But Carlsbad's quite the rage this year! "
Oh yes, she loves the rural Graces ;
Nature is gay—in Watering-places !
Those pleasant Spas—our reigning passion—
Where learned Dons meet folks of fashion ;
Where—each with each illustrious soul
    Familiar as in Charon's boat,
All sorts of Fame sit cheek-by-jowl,
    Pearls in that string—the Table d'Hôte !
Where dames whom Man has injured—fly,
    To heal their wounds or to efface them ;
While others, with the waters, try
    A course of flirting,—just to brace them !

Well, there (O Man, how light thy woes
    Compared with mine—thou need'st must see !)
My wife, undaunted, greatly goes—
    And leaves the orphans (seven !!!) to me !

O, wherefore art thou flown so soon,
Thou first fair year—Love's Honeymoon !
Ah, Dream too exquisite for life !
Home's Goddess—in the name of Wife !
Reared by each Grace—yet but to be
Man's Household Anadyomenè !
With mind from which the sunbeams fall,
Rejoicing while pervading all ;
Frank in the temper pleased to please—
Soft in the feeling waked with ease.
So broke, as Native of the skies,
The Heart-enthraller on my eyes ;

So saw I, like a Morn of May,
The Playmate given to glad my way;
With eyes that more than lips bespoke,
Eyes whence—sweet words—"I love thee!" broke!
So—Ah, what transports then were mine!
I led the Bride before the shrine!
And saw the future years reveal'd,
Glass'd on my Hope—one blooming field!
More wide, and widening more, were given
The Angel-gates disclosing Heaven;
Round us the lovely, mirthful troop
    Of children came—yet still to me
The loveliest—merriest of the group
    The happy Mother seemed to be!
Mine, by the bonds that bind us more
Than all the oaths the Priest before;
Mine, by the concord of content,
When Heart with Heart is music-blent;
When, as sweet sounds in unison,
    Two lives harmonious melt in one!
When—sudden (O the villain!)—came
    Upon the scene a Mind Profound!—
A Bel Esprit, who whisper'd "Fame,"
    And shook my card-house to the ground.

What have I now instead of all
The Eden lost of hearth and hall?
What comforts for the Heaven bereft?
What of the younger Angel's left?
A sort of intellectual Mule,
    Man's stubborn mind in Woman's shape,
Too hard to love, too frail to rule—
    A sage engrafted on an ape!
To what she calls the Realm of Mind,
    She leaves that throne, *her sex*, to crawl,
The cestus and the charm resign'd—
    A public gaping-show to all!
She blots from Beauty's Golden Book *
    A Name 'mid Nature's choicest Few,
To gain the glory of a nook
    In Doctor Dunderhead's Review.

* The Golden Book.—So was entitled in some Italian States (Venice especially) the Catalogue in which the Noble Families were enrolled.

TO A FEMALE FRIEND.

(WRITTEN IN HER ALBUM.)

[These verses were addressed to Charlotte Von Lengefeld, whom Schiller afterwards married, and were intended to dissuade her from a Court life.]

I.

As some gay child, around whose steps play all
　The laughing Graces, plays the World round thee !
Yet not as on thy soul's clear mirror fall
　The flattered shadows, deem this world to be!
The silent homages thy heart compels
By its own inborn dignity,—the spells
　That thou thyself around thyself art weaving,
The charms with which thy being is so rife,—
'Tis *these* thou countest as the charms of life,
　In Human Nature, as thine own—believing !
Alas! this Beauty but exists, in sooth,
In thine own talisman of holy youth,
　[Who can resist it ?]—mightiest while deceiving ? *

II.

Enjoy the lavish flowers that glad thy way,
　The happy ones whose happiness thou art ;
The souls thou winnest—in these bounds survey
　Thy world !—to *this* world why shouldst thou depart ?
Nay, let yon flowers admonish thee and save !
　Lo, how they bloom while guarded by the fence!
So plant Earth's pleasures—not too near the sense !

* The sense of the original is very shadowy and impalpable, and the difficulty of embodying it in an intelligible translation is great. It may be rendered thus :—"The silent homage which thy nobility of heart compels,— the miracles which thou thyself hast wrought,—the charms with which thy existence has invested life,—these thou lookest on as the substantial attractions of life itself, and as constituting the very staple of human nature. But in this thou art mistaken. What appears to thee to be the grace and beauty of life, is but the reflection of the witchery of thine own undesecrated youth, and the talisman of thine own innocence and virtue, though these certainly are powers which no man can resist. Enjoy the flowers of life, then ; but do not take them for more than they are worth. Theirs is but a surface-beauty; let the glance, therefore, which thou bestowest on them be superficial too. Gaze on them from a distance, and never expect that the core of life will wear the same attractive hues as those which ornament its "exterior." Schiller has repeated this thought in the Poem of the "Actual and Ideal."

Nature to see, but not to pluck them, gave:
  Afar they charm thee—leave them on the stem ;
  Approached by thee, the glory fades from them—
And, in thy touch, their sweetness has a grave !

Here conclude the Poems classed under the Second Period of Schiller's career; we have excepted only his translations from Virgil.

FIRST PERIOD;

OR,

EARLY POEMS.

WE now trace back the stream to its source. We commenced with Schiller's maturest Poems—we close with his earliest. The contrast between the compositions in the first and third period is sufficiently striking. In the former there is more fire and action—more of that lavish and exuberant energy which characterised the earlier tales of Lord Byron, and redeemed, in that wonderful master of animated and nervous style, a certain poverty of conception by a vigour and *gusto* of execution, which no English poet, perhaps, has ever surpassed. In his poems lies the life, and beats the heart, of Schiller. They conduct us through the various stages of his spiritual education, and indicate each step in the progress. In this division, *effort* is no less discernible than power—both in language and thought there is a struggle at something not yet achieved, and not, perhaps, even yet definite and distinct to the poet himself. Here may be traced, though softened by the charm of genius (which softens all things), the splendid errors that belong to a passionate youth, and that give such distorted grandeur to the giant melodrame of "The Robbers." But here are to be traced also, and in far clearer characters, the man's strong heart, essentially human in its sympathies—the thoughtful and earnest intellect giving ample promise of all it was destined to receive. In these earlier poems, extravagance is sufficiently noticeable—yet never the sickly eccentricities of diseased weakness, but the exuberant overflowings of a young Titan's strength. There is a distinction, which our critics do not always notice, between the *extravagance* of a great genius, and the *affectation* of a pretty poet.

HECTOR AND ANDROMACHE.

[This and the following poem are, with some alterations, introduced in the Play of "The Robbers."]

ANDROMACHE.

WILL Hector leave me for the fatal plain,
Where, fierce with vengeance for Patroclus slain,
    Stalks Peleus' ruthless son ?
Who, when thou glid'st amid the dark abodes,
To hurl the spear and to revere the Gods,
    Shall teach thine Orphan One ?

HECTOR.

Woman and wife belovèd—cease thy tears ;
My soul is nerved—the war-clang in my ears !
    Be mine in life to stand
Troy's bulwark !—fighting for our hearths, to go
In death, exulting to the streams below,
    Slain for my father-land !

ANDROMACHE.

No more I hear thy martial footsteps fall—
Thine arms shall hang, dull trophies, on the wall—
  Fallen the stem of Troy!
Thou go'st where slow Cocytus wanders—where
Love sinks in Lethe, and the sunless air
  Is dark to light and joy!

HECTOR.

Longing and thought—yea, all I feel and think
May in the silent sloth of Lethe sink,
  But my love not!
Hark, the wild swarm is at the walls!—I hear!
Gird on my sword—Belov'd one, dry the tear—
  Lethe for love is not!

AMALIA.

Fair as an angel from his blessed hall*—
 Of every fairest youth the fairest he!
Heaven-mild his look, as maybeams when they fall,
 Or shine reflected from a clear blue sea!
His kisses—feelings rife with paradise!
 Ev'n as two flames, one on the other driven—
Ev'n as two harp-tones their melodious sighs
 Blend in some music that seems born of heaven—

So rush'd, mix'd, melted life with life united!
 Lips, cheeks burn'd, trembled—soul to soul was won!
And earth and heaven seem'd chaos, as, delighted,
 Earth—heaven were blent round the belovèd one!
Now, he is gone! vainly and wearily
 Groans the full heart, the yearning sorrow flows—
Gone! and all zest of life, in one long sigh,
 Goes with him where he goes.

   * Literally, Walhalla.

A FUNERAL FANTASIE.

I.

PALE, at its ghastly noon,
Pauses above the death-still wood—the moon;
The night-sprite, sighing, through the dim air stirs;
   The clouds descend in rain;
   Mourning, the wan stars wane,
Flickering like dying lamps in sepulchres!
Haggard as spectres—vision-like and dumb,
   Dark with the pomp of Death, and moving slow,
Towards that sad lair the pale Procession come
   Where the Grave closes on the Night below.

II.

   With dim, deep-sunken eye,
Crutch'd on his staff, who trembles tottering by?
As wrung from out the shatter'd heart, one groan
   Breaks the deep hush alone!
Crush'd by the iron Fate, he seems to gather
   All life's last strength to stagger to the bier,
And hearken—Do those cold lips murmur "Father?"
   The sharp rain, drizzling through that place of fear,
Pierces the bones gnaw'd fleshless by despair,
And the heart's horror stirs the silver hair.

III.

Fresh bleed the fiery wounds
   Through all that agonizing heart undone—
Still on the voiceless lips "my Father" sounds,
   And still the childless Father murmurs "Son!"
Ice-cold—ice-cold, in that white shroud he lies—
   Thy sweet and golden dreams all vanish'd there—
The sweet and golden name of "Father" dies
   Into thy curse,—ice-cold—ice-cold—he lies!
   Dead, what thy life's delight and Eden were!

IV.

Mild, as when, fresh from the arms of Aurora,
  While the air like Elysium is smiling above,
Steep'd in rose-breathing odours, the darling of Flora
  Wantons over the blooms on his winglets of love.—
So gay, o'er the meads, went his footsteps in bliss,
  The silver wave mirror'd the smile of his face;
Delight, like a flame, kindled up at his kiss,
  And the heart of the maid was the prey of his chase.

V.

Boldly he sprang to the strife of the world,
  As a deer to the mountain-top carelessly springs;
As an eagle whose plumes to the sun are unfurl'd,
  Sweet his Hope round the Heaven on its limitless wings.
Proud as a war-horse that chafes at the rein,
  That, kingly, exults in the storm of the brave;
That throws to the wind the wild stream of its mane,
  Strode he forth by the prince and the slave!

VI.

Life, like a spring-day, serene and divine,
  In the star of the morning went by as a trance;
His murmurs he drown'd in the gold of the wine,
  And his sorrows were borne on the wave of the dance.
Worlds lay conceal'd in the hopes of his youth!—
  When once he shall ripen to Manhood and Fame!
Fond Father exult!—In the germs of his youth
  What harvests are destined for Manhood and Fame!

VII.

Not to be was that Manhood!—The death-bell is knelling,
  The hinge of the death-vault creaks harsh on the ears—
How dismal, O Death, is the place of thy dwelling!
  Not to be was that Manhood!—Flow on bitter tears!
Go, belovèd, thy path to the sun,
  Rise, world upon world, with the perfect to rest;
Go—quaff the delight which thy spirit has won,
  And escape from our grief in the Halls of the Blest.

VIII.

Again (in that thought what a healing is found!)
  To meet in the Eden to which thou art fled!—
Hark, the coffin sinks down with a dull, sullen sound,
  And the ropes rattle over the sleep of the dead.
And we cling to each other!—O Grave, he is thine!
  The eye tells the woe that is mute to the ears—
And we dare to resent what we grudge to resign,
  Till the heart's sinful murmur is choked in its tears.
  Pale at its ghastly noon,
Pauses above the death-still wood—the moon!
The night-sprite, sighing, through the dim air stirs:
  The clouds descend in rain;
  Mourning. the wan stars wane,
Flickering like dying lamps in sepulchres.
The dull clods swell into the sullen mound!
  Earth, one look yet upon the prey we gave!
The Grave locks up the treasure it has found;
Higher and higher swells the sullen mound—
  Never gives back the Grave!

FANTASIE TO LAURA.

What, Laura, say, the vortex that can draw
  Body to body in its strong control;
Beloved Laura, what the charmèd law
  That to the soul attracting plucks the soul?
It is the charm that rolls the stars on high,
  For ever round the sun's majestic blaze—
When, gay as children round their parent, fly
  Their circling dances in delighted maze.
Still, every star that glides its gladsome course,
  Thirstily drinks the luminous golden rain;
Drinks the fresh vigour from the fiery source,
  As limbs imbibe life's motion from the brain;
With sunny motes, the sunny motes united
  Harmonious lustre both receive and give,
Love spheres with spheres still interchange delighted,
  Only through love the starry systems live.

Take love from Nature's universe of wonder,
   Each jarring each, rushes the mighty All.
See, back to Chaos shock'd, Creation thunder;
   Weep, starry Newton—weep the giant fall!
Take from the spiritual scheme that Power away,
   And the still'd body shrinks to Death's abode.
Never—love *not* —would blooms revive for May,
   And, love extinct, all life were dead to God.
And what the charm that at my Laura's kiss,
   Pours the diviner brightness to the cheek;
Makes the heart bound more swiftly to its bliss,
   And bids the rushing blood the magnet seek ?—
Out from their bounds swell nerve, and pulse, and sense,
   The veins in tumult would their shores o'erflow;
Body to body rapt—and, charmèd thence,
   Soul drawn to soul with intermingled glow.

Mighty alike to sway the flow and ebb
   Of the inanimate Matter, or to move
The nerves that weave the Arachnèan web
   Of Sentient Life—rules all-pervading Love!
Ev'n in the Moral World, embrace and meet
   Emotions—Gladness clasps the extreme of Care;
And Sorrow, at the worst, upon the sweet
   Breast of young Hope, is thaw'd from its despair.
Of sister-kin to melancholy Woe,
   Voluptuous Pleasure comes, and happy eyes
Delivered of the tears, their children, glow
   Lustrous as sunbeams—and the Darkness flies! *

* Und entbunden von den gold'nen Kindern
Strahlt das Auge Sonnenpracht.

Schiller, in his earlier poems, strives after poetry in expression, as our young imitators of Shelley and Keates do, sanctioned generally by our critics, who quote such expressions in italics with three notes of admiration! He here, for instance, calls tears "the Golden Children of the Eye." In his later poems Schiller had a much better notion of true beauty of diction. The general meaning of this poem is very obscure, but it seems to imply that Love rules all things in the inanimate or animate creation; that, even in the moral world, opposite emotions or principles meet and embrace each other. The idea is pushed into an extravagance natural to the youth, and redeemed by the passion, of the Author. But the connecting links are so slender, nay, so frequently omitted, in the original, that a certain degree of paraphrase in many of the stanzas is absolutely necessary to supply them, and render the general sense and spirit of the poem intelligible to the English reader.

The same great Law of Sympathy is given
    To Evil as to Good, and if we swell
The dark account that life incurs with Heaven,
    'Tis that our Vices are thy Wooers, Hell!
In turn those Vices are embraced by Shame
    And fell Remorse, the twin Eumenides.
Danger still clings in fond embrace to Fame,
    Mounts on her wing, and flies where'er she flees.
Destruction marries its dark self to Pride,
    Envy to Fortune: when Desire most charms,
'Tis that her brother Death is by her side,
    For him she opens those voluptuous arms.
The very Future to the Past but flies
    Upon the wings of Love—as I to thee;
O, long swift Saturn, with unceasing sighs,
    Hath sought his distant bride, Eternity!
When—so I heard the oracle declare—
    When Saturn once shall clasp that bride sublime,
Wide-blazing worlds shall light his nuptials there—
    'Tis thus Eternity shall wed with Time.
In *those* shall be *our* nuptials! ours to share
    That bridenight, waken'd by no jealous sun;
Since Time, Creation, Nature, but declare
    Love,—in our love rejoice, Beloved One!

TO LAURA PLAYING.

WHEN o'er the chords thy fingers steal,
A soulless statue now I feel,
    And now a soul set free!
Sweet Sovereign! ruling over death and life—
Seizes the heart, in a voluptuous strife
    As with a thousand strings—the SORCERY! *

Then the vassal airs that woo thee,
Hush their low breath hearkening to thee.

* "The Sorcery."—In the original, Schiller, with very questionable taste, compares Laura to a conjuror of the name of Philadelphia, who exhibited before Frederick the Great.

In delight and in devotion,
Pausing from her whirling motion,
Nature, in enchanted calm,
Silently drinks the floating balm.
Sorceress, *her* heart with thy tone
Chaining—as thine eyes my own !

O'er the transport-tumult driven,
  Doth the music gliding swim ;
From the strings, as from their heaven,
  Burst the new-born Seraphim.
As when from Chaos' giant arms set free,
'Mid the Creation-storm, exultingly
Sprang sparkling thro' the dark the Orbs of Light—
So streams the rich tone in melodious might.

Soft gliding now, as when o'er pebbles glancing,
  The silver wave goes dancing ;
Now with majestic swell, and strong,
As thunder peals in organ-tones along ;
  And now with stormy gush,
As down the rock, in foam, the whirling torrents rush ;
    To a whisper now
      Melts it amorously,
    Like the breeze through the bough
      Of the aspen tree ;
  Heavily now, and with a mournful breath,
  Like midnight's wind along those wastes of death,
Where Awe the wail of ghosts lamenting hears,
And slow Cocytus trails the stream whose waves are tears.

Speak, maiden, speak !—Oh, art thou one of those
Spirits more lofty than our region knows ?
Should we in *thine* the mother-language seek
  Souls in Elysium speak ?

TO LAURA.

(RAPTURE.)

LAURA—above this world methinks I fly,
And feel the glow of some May-lighted sky,
　　When thy looks beam on mine!
And my soul drinks a more ethereal air,
When mine own shape I see reflected, there,
　　In those blue eyes of thine!
A lyre-sound from the Paradise afar,
A harp-note trembling from some gracious star,
　　Seems the wild ear to fill;
And my muse feels the Golden Shepherd-hours,
When from thy lips the silver music pours
　　Slow, as against its will
I see the young Loves flutter on the wing—
Move the charm'd trees, as when the Thracian's string
　　Wild life to forests gave;
Swifter the globe's swift circle seems to fly,
When in the whirling dance thou glidest by,
　　Light as a happy wave.
Thy looks, when there Love's smiles their gladness wreathe,
Could life itself to lips of marble breathe,
　　Lend rocks a pulse divine;
Reading thine eyes—my veriest life but seems
Made up and fashioned from my wildest dreams,—
　　Laura, sweet Laura, mine!

TO LAURA.

(THE MYSTERY OF REMINISCENCE.)*

WHO, and what gave to me the wish to woo thee—
Still, lip to lip, to cling for aye unto thee?
Who made thy glances to my soul the link—
Who bade me burn thy very breath to drink—
　　My life in thine to sink?

---

* This most exquisite love-poem is founded on the Platonic notion, that
souls were united in a pre-existent state, that love is the yearning of the
spirit to reunite with the spirit with which it formerly made one—and which
it discovers on earth. The idea has often been made subservient to poetry,
but never with so earnest and elaborate a beauty.

As from the conqueror's unresisted glaive,
Flies, without strife subdued, the ready slave—
So, when to life's unguarded fort, I see
Thy gaze draw near and near triumphantly—
    Yields not my soul to thee?
Why from its lord doth thus my soul depart?—
Is it because its native home thou art?
Or were they brothers in the days of yore,
Twin-bound, both souls, and in the links they bore
    Sigh to be bound once more?
Were once our beings blent and intertwining,
And therefore still my heart for thine is pining?
Knew we the light of some extinguished sun—
The joys remote of some bright realm undone,
    Where once our souls were ONE?
Yes, it *is* so!—And thou wert bound to me
In the long-vanish'd Eld eternally!
In the dark troubled tablets which enroll
The Past—my Muse beheld this blessed scroll—
    "One with thy love my soul!"
Oh yes, I learn'd in awe, when gazing there,
How once one bright inseparate life we were,
How once, one glorious essence as a God,
Unmeasured space our chainless footsteps trod—
    All Nature our abode!
Round us, in waters of delight, for ever
Voluptuous flow'd the heavenly Nectar river;
We were the master of the seal of things,
And where the sunshine bathed Truth's mountain-springs
    Quiver'd our glancing wings.
Weep for the godlike life we lost afar—
Weep!—thou and I its scatter'd fragments are;
And still the unconquer'd yearning we retain—
Sigh to restore the rapture and the reign,
    And grow divine again.
And therefore came to me the wish to woo thee—
Still, lip to lip, to cling for aye unto thee;
This made thy glances to my soul the link—
This made me burn thy very breath to drink—
    My life in thine to sink:
And therefore, as before the conqueror's glaive,
Flies, without strife subdued, the ready slave,

So, when to life's unguarded fort, I see
Thy gaze draw near and near triumphantly—
   Yieldeth my soul to thee!
Therefore my soul doth from its lord depart,
Because, beloved, its native home thou art;
Because the twins recall the links they bore,
And soul with soul, in the sweet kiss of yore,
   Meets and unites once more!
Thou too—Ah, there thy gaze upon me dwells,
And thy young blush the tender answer tells;
Yes! with the dear relation still we thrill,
Both lives—tho' exiles from the homeward hill—
   One life—all glowing still!

MELANCHOLY; TO LAURA.

I.

Laura! a sunrise seems to break
  Where'er thy happy looks may glow,
Joy sheds its roses o'er thy cheek,
Thy tears themselves do but bespeak
  The rapture whence they flow:
Blest youth to whom those tears are given—
The tears that change his earth to heaven;
His best reward those melting eyes—
For him new suns are in the skies!

II.

Thy soul—a crystal river passing,
Silver-clear, and sunbeam-glassing,
Mays into bloom sad Autumn by thee;
Night and desert, if they spy thee,
To gardens laugh—with daylight shine,
Lit by those happy smiles of thine!
Dark with cloud the Future far
Goldens itself beneath thy star.

Smil'st thou to see the Harmony
  Of charm the laws of Nature keep ?
Alas ! to me the Harmony
  Brings only cause to weep!

III.

Holds not Hades its domain
  Underneath this earth of ours ?
Under Palace, under Fane,
  Underneath the cloud-capt Towers ?
S'ately cities soar and spread
O'er your mouldering bones, ye Dead !
From corruption, from decay,
  Springs yon clove pink's fragrant bloom ;
Yon gay waters wind their way
  From the hollows of a tomb.

IV.

From the Planets thou may'st know
All the change that shifts below,
Fled—beneath that zone of rays,
Fled to Night a thousand Mays ;
Thrones a thousand—rising—sinking,
Earth from thousand slaughters drinking
Blood profusely pour'd as water ;—
Of the sceptre—of the slaughter—
Wouldst thou know what trace remaineth ?
Seek them where the dark king reigneth !

V.

Scarce thine eye can ope and close
Ere Life's dying sunset glows ;
Sinking sudden from its pride
Into Death—the Lethe tide.
Ask'st thou whence thy beauties rise ?
Boastest thou those radiant eyes ?—
Or that check in roses dy'd ?
All their beauty (thought of sorrow !)
From the brittle mould they borrow.
Heavy interest in the tomb
For the brief loan of the bloom,

For the beauty of the Day,
Death, the Usurer, thou must pay,
  In the long to-morrow!

VI.

Maiden!—Death's too strong for scorn;
  In the cheek the fairest, He
  But the fairest throne doth see;
Though the roses of the morn
Weave the veil by Beauty worn—
Aye, beneath that broidered curtain,
Stands the Archer stern and certain!
Maid—thy Visionary hear—
Trust the wild one as the seer,
When he tells thee that thine eye,
  While it beckons to the wooer,
Only lureth yet more nigh
  Death, the dark undoer!

VII.

Every ray shed from thy beauty
  Wastes the life-lamp while it beams,
And the pulse's playful duty,
  And the blue veins' merry streams,
Sport and run unto the pall—
Creatures of the Tyrant, all!
As the wind the rainbow shatters,
Death thy bright smiles rends and scatters,
Smile and rainbow leave no traces;—
From the spring-time's laughing graces,
From all life, as from its germ,
Grows the revel of the worm!

VIII.

Woe, I see the wild wind wreak
  Its wrath upon thy rosy bloom,
Winter plough thy rounded cheek,
  Cloud and darkness close in gloom;
Blackening over, and for ever,
Youth's serene and silver river!
Love alike and Beauty o'er,
Lovely and belov'd no more!

IX.

Maiden, an oak that soars on high,
    And scorns the whirlwind's breath,
Behold thy Poet's youth defy
    The blunted dart of Death !
His gaze as ardent as the light
    That shoots athwart the Heaven,
His soul yet fiercer than the light
    In the Eternal Heaven
Of Him, in whom as in an ocean-surge
Creation ebbs and flows—and worlds arise and merge !
Thro' Nature steers the Poet's thought to find
No fear but this—one barrier to the Mind ?

X.

And dost thou glory so to think ?
    And heaves thy bosom ?—Woe !
This Cup, which lures him to the brink,
As if Divinity to drink—
    Has poison in its flow !
Wretched, oh, wretched, they who trust
To strike the God-spark from the dust !
The mightiest tone the Music knows,
    But breaks the harp-string with the sound ;
And Genius, still the more it glows,
But wastes the lamp whose life bestows
    The light it sheds around.
Soon from existence dragg'd away,
The watchful gaoler grasps his prey ;
Vowed on the altar of the abusèd fire,
The spirits I raised against myself conspire !
Let—yes, I feel it—two short springs away
    Pass on their rapid flight ;
And life's faint spark shall, fleeting from the clay,
    Merge in the Fount of Light !

XI.

And weep'st thou, Laura ?—be thy tears forbid ;
Wouldst thou my lot, life's dreariest years amid,
    Protract and doom ?—No ; sinner, dry thy tears !

Wouldst thou, whose eyes beheld the eagle wing
Of my bold youth through air's dominion spring,
Mark my sad age (life's tale of glory done)—
Crawl on the sod and tremble in the sun?
Hear the dull frozen heart condemn the flame
That as from Heaven to youth's blithe bosom came;
And see the blind eyes loathing turn from all
The lovely sins Age curses to recall?
    Let me die young!—sweet sinner, dry thy tears!
Yes, let the flower be gathered in its bloom!
And thou, young Genius, with the brows of gloom,
    Quench thou Life's torch, while yet the flame is
      strong!
Ev'n as the curtain falls; while still the scene
Most thrills the hearts which have its audience been;
As fleet the shadows from the stage—and long
When all is o'er, lingers the breathless throng!

THE INFANTICIDE.

I.

Hark where the bells toll, chiming, dull and steady,
    The clock's slow hand hath reach'd the appointed
      time.
Well, be it so—prepare, my soul is ready,
    Companions of the Grave—the rest for crime!
Now take, O world! my last farewell—receiving
    My parting kisses—in these tears they dwell!
Sweet are thy poisons while we taste believing,
    Now we are quits—heart-poisoner, fare-thee-well!

II.

Farewell, ye suns that once to joy invited,
    Changed for the mould beneath the funeral shade;
Farewell, farewell, thou rosy Time delighted,
    Luring to soft desire the careless maid.
Pale gossamers of gold, farewell, sweet-dreaming
    Fancies—the children that an Eden bore!
Blossoms that died while Dawn itself was gleaming,
    Opening in happy sunlight never more.

III.

Swanlike the robe which Innocence bestowing,
  Deck'd with the virgin favours, rosy fair,
In the gay time when many a young rose glowing,
  Blush'd through the loose train of the amber hair.
Woe, woe! as white the robe that decks me now—
  The shroud-like robe Hell's destin'd victim wears;
Still shall the fillet bind this burning brow—
  That sable braid the Doomsman's hand prepares!

IV.

Weep ye, *who never fell*—for whom, unerring,
  The soul's white lilies keep their virgin hue,
Ye who when thoughts so danger-sweet are stirring,
  Take the stern strength that Nature gives the few .
Woe, for too human was this fond heart's feeling—
  Feeling!—my sin's avenger * doom'd to be;
Woe—for the false man's arm around me stealing,
  Stole the lull'd Virtue, charm'd to sleep, from me.

V.

Ah, he perhaps shall, round another sighing,
  (Forgot the serpents stinging at my breast,)
Gaily, when I in the dumb grave am lying,
  Pour the warm wish or speed the wanton jest,
Or play, perchance with his new maiden's tresses,
  Answer the kiss her lip enamour'd brings,
When the dread block the head he cradled presses,
  And high the blood his kiss once fever'd springs.

VI.

Thee, Francis, Francis,† league on league, shall follow
  The death-dirge of the Lucy once so dear;
From yonder steeple, dismal, dull, and hollow,
  Shall knell the warning horror on thy ear.

---

  * "Und Empfindung soll mein Richtschwert seyn."
  A line of great vigour in the original, but which, if literally translated,
would seem extravagant in English.
    † Joseph, in the original.

On thy fresh leman's lips when Love is dawning,
   And the lisp'd music glides from that sweet well—
Lo, in that breast a red wound shall be yawning,
   And, in the midst of rapture, warn of hell!

VII.

Betrayer, what! thy soul relentless closing
   To grief—the woman-shame no art can heal—
To that small life beneath my heart reposing!
   Man, man, the wild beast for its young can feel!
Proud flew the sails—receding from the land,
   I watch'd them wanning from the wistful eye,
Round the gay maids on Seine's voluptuous strand,
   Breathes the false incense of his fatal sigh.

VIII.

And there the Babe! there, on the mother's bosom,
   Lull'd in its sweet and golden rest it lay,
Fresh in life's morning as a rosy blossom,
   It smiled, poor harmless one, my tears away.
Deathlike yet lovely, every feature speaking
   In such dear calm and beauty to my sadness,
And cradled still the mother's heart, in breaking,
   The soft'ning love and the despairing madness.

IX.

"Woman, where is my father?"—freezing through me,
   Lisp'd the mute Innocence with thunder-sound;
"Woman, where is thy husband?"—call'd unto me,
   In every look, word, whisper, busying round!
Alas, for thee, there is no father's kiss;—
   He fondleth *other* children on his knee.
How thou wilt curse our momentary bliss,
   When Bastard on thy name shall branded be!

X.

Thy mother—oh, a hell her heart concealeth,
   Lone-sitting, lone in social Nature's All!
Thirsting for that glad fount thy love revealeth,
   While still thy look the glad fount turns to gall.

In every infant cry my soul is heark'ning,
  The haunting happiness for ever o'er,
And all the bitterness of death is dark'ning
  The heavenly looks that smiled mine eyes before.

XI.

Hell, if my sight those looks a moment misses—
  Hell, when my sight upon those looks is turn'd—
The avenging furies madden in *thy* kisses,
  That slept in *his* what time my lips they burn'd.
Out from their graves his oaths spoke back in thunder!
  The perjury stalk'd like murder in the sun—
For ever—God!—sense, reason, soul, sunk under—
  The deed was done!

XII.

Francis, O Francis! league on league, shall chase thee
  The shadows hurrying grimly on thy flight—
Still with their icy arms they shall embrace thee,
  And mutter thunder in thy dream's delight!
Down from the soft stars, in their tranquil glory,
  Shall look thy dead child with a ghastly stare;
That shape shall haunt thee in its cerements gory,
  And scourge thee back from heaven—its home is
    there!

XIII.

Lifeless—how lifeless!—see, oh see, before me
  It lies cold—stiff!—O God!—and with that blood
I feel, as swoops the dizzy darkness o'er me,
  Mine own life mingled—ebbing in the flood—
Hark, at the door they knock—more loud within me—
  More awful still—its sound the dread heart gave!
Gladly I welcome the cold arms that win me—
  Fire, quench thy tortures in the icy grave!

XIV.

Francis—a God that pardons dwells in heaven—
  Francis, the sinner—yes—she pardons thee—
So let my wrongs unto the earth be given:
  Flame seize the wood!—it burns—it kindles—see '

There—there his letters cast—behold are ashes—
His vows—the conquering fire consumes them here:
His kisses—see—see all—all are only ashes—
All, all—the all that once on earth were dear!

XV.

Trust not the roses which your youth enjoyeth,
Sisters, to man's faith, changeful as the moon!
Beauty to me brought guilt—its bloom destroyeth:
Lo, in the judgment court I curse the boon:
Tears in the headsman's gaze—what tears?—'tis spoken!
Quick, bind mine eyes—all soon shall be forgot—
Doomsman—the lily hast thou never broken?
Pale Doomsman—tremble not!

The poem we have just concluded was greatly admired at the time of its
first publication, and it so far excels in art most of the earlier efforts by the
author, that it attains one of the highest secrets in true pathos;—it produces
interest for the *criminal* while creating terror for the *crime*. This, indeed,
is a triumph in art never achieved but by the highest genius. The inferior
writer, when venturing upon the grandest stage of passion (which unquestionably exists in the delineation of great guilt as of heroic virtue), falls
into the error either of gilding the crime, in order to produce sympathy for
the criminal, or, in the spirit of a spurious morality, of involving both crime
and criminal in a common odium. It is to discrimination between the doer
and the deed, that we owe the sublimest revelations of the human heart:
in this discrimination lies the key to the emotions produced by the Œdipus
and Macbeth. In the brief poem before us a whole drama is comprehended.
Marvellous is the completeness of the pictures it presents—its mastery over
emotions the most opposite—its fidelity to nature in its exposition of the
disordered and despairing mind in which tenderness becomes cruelty, and
remorse for error tortures itself into scarce conscious crime.
But the art employed, though admirable of its kind, still falls short of the
perfection which, in his later works, Schiller aspired to achieve, viz. the
point at which *Pain* ceases. The tears which Tragic Pathos, when purest
and most elevated, calls forth, ought not to be tears of pain. In the ideal
world, as Schiller has inculcated, even sorrow should have its charm—all
that harrows, all that revolts, belongs but to that inferior school in which
Schiller's fiery youth formed itself for nobler grades—the school of " Storm
and Pressure " (Sturm und Drang, as the Germans have expressively
described it). If the reader will compare Schiller's poem of the " In-
fanticide," with the passages which represent a similar crime in the Medea
(and the author of " Wallenstein " deserves comparison even with the
Euripides), he will see the distinction between the art that seeks an *elevated*
emotion, and the art which is satisfied with creating an *intense* one. In
Euripides, the detail—the reality—all that can degrade terror into pain—
are loftily dismissed. The Titan grandeur of the Sorceress removes us from
too close an approach to the crime of the unnatural Mother—the emotion of
pity changes into awe—just at the pitch before the coarse sympathy of
actual pain can be effected. And it is the avoidance of reality—it is the
all-purifying Presence of the Ideal, which make the vast distinction in our

emotions between following, with shocked and displeasing pity, the crushed, broken-hearted, mortal criminal to the scaffold, and gazing with an awe which has pleasure of its own upon the mighty Murderess—soaring out of the reach of humanity, upon her Dragon-Car!

THE GREATNESS OF CREATION.

Upon the winged winds, among the rolling worlds I
    flew,
Which, by the breathing spirit, erst from ancient Chaos
    grew;
        Seeking to land
        On the farthest strand,
Where life lives no longer to anchor alone,
And gaze on Creation's last boundary-stone.

Star after star around me now its shining youth uprears,
To wander through the Firmament its day of thousand
    years—
        Sportive they roll
        Round the charmèd goal:
Till, as I look'd on the deeps afar,
The space waned—void of a single star.

On to the Realm of Nothingness—on still in dauntless
    flight,
Along the splendours swiftly steer my sailing wings of
    light;
        Heaven at the rear,
        Paleth, mist-like and drear;
Yet still as I wander, the worlds in their glee
Sparkle up like the bubbles that glance on a Sea!

And towards me now, the selfsame path I see a Pilgrim
    steer!
"Halt, Wanderer, halt—and answer me—What, Pilgrim,
    seek'st thou here?"
        "To the World's last shore
        I am sailing o'er,
Where life lives no longer to anchor alone,
And gaze on Creation's last boundary-stone."

"Thou sail'st in vain—Return! Before thy path, IN-
  FINITY!"
"And thou in vain!—Behind me spreads INFINITY to
  thee!
      Fold thy wings drooping,
      O Thought, eagle-swooping!—
O Fantasie, anchor!—The Voyage is o'er:
Creation, wild sailor, flows on to no shore!"

♂ ELEGY ON THE DEATH OF A YOUTH.*

[Said to be the Poet Rudolf Weckherlin.]

HEAVY moans, as when Nature the storm is foretelling,
  From the Dark House of Mourning come sad on the ear;
The Death-note on high from the steeple is knelling,
  And slowly comes hither a youth on the Bier;—
A youth not yet ripe for that garner—the tomb,
  A blossom pluck'd off from the sweet stem of May,
Each leaf in its verdure, each bud in its bloom:
  A youth—with the eyes yet enchanted by day:
A Son—to the Mother, O word of delight!
  A Son—to the Mother, O thought of despair!
My Brother, my friend!—To the grave and the night
  Follow, ye that are human, the treasure we bear.

Ye Pines, do ye boast that unshattered your boughs
  Brave the storm when it rushes, the bolt when it falls?
Ye Hills, that the Heavens rest their pomp on your brows?
  Ye Heavens, that the Suns have their home in your
    halls?
Does the Aged exult in the works he has done—
  The Ladders by which he has climb'd to Renown?
Or the Hero, in deeds by which valour has won
  To the heights where the Temple of Glory looks down?

---

* Of this Poem, as of Gray's divine and unequalled Elegy, it may be truly
said that it abounds in thoughts so natural, that the reader at first believes
they have been often expressed before, but his memory will not enable him
to trace a previous owner. The whole Poem has the rare beauty of being
at once familiar and original.

When the canker the bud doth already decay,
  Who can deem that *his* ripeness is free from the worm ;
Who can hope to endure, when the young fade away,
  Who can count on life's harvest—the blight at the germ ?

How lovely with youth,—and with youth how delighted,
  His days, in the hues of the Rose glided by !
How sweet was the world and how fondly invited
  The Future, that Fairy enchanting his eye !
All life like a Paradise smil'd on his way,
  And, lo ! see the Mother weep over his bed,
See the gulf of the Hades yawn wide for its prey,
  See the shears of the Parcæ gleam over the thread !
Earth and Heaven which such joy to the living one gave,
  From his gaze darkened dimly !—and sadly and sighing
The dying one shrunk from the Thought of the grave,—
  The World, oh ! the World is so sweet to the Dying !

Dumb and deaf is all sense in the Narrow House !—deep
  Is the slumber the Grave's heavy curtains unfold !
How silent a Sabbath eternally keep,
  O Brother—the Hopes ever Busy of old !
Oft the Sun shall shine down on thy green native hill,
  But the glow of his smile thou shalt feel never more !
Oft the west wind shall rock the young blossoms, but still
  Is the breeze for the heart that can hear never more !
Love gilds not for thee all the world with its glow,
  Never Bride in the clasp of thine arms shall repose ;
Thou canst see not our tears, though in torrents they flow,
  Those eyes in the calm of eternity close !
Yet happy—oh, happy, at least in thy slumber—
  Serene is the rest, where all trouble must cease ;
For the sorrows must die with the joys they outnumber,
  And the pains of the flesh with its dust—are at peace !
The tooth of sharp slander thou never canst feel,
  The poison of Vice cannot pierce to thy cell ;
Over thee may the Pharisee thunder his zeal,
  And the rage of the Bigot devote thee to Hell !
Though the mask of the saint may the swindler disguise ;
  Though Earth's Justice, that Bastard of Right, we may see
At play with mankind as the cheat with his dice,
  As now so for ever—what matters to thee ?

Over thee too may Fortune (her changes unknown)
 Blindly give to her minions the goods they desire;
Now raising her darling aloft to the throne,
 Now hurling the wretch whom she raised—to the mire!
Happy thou, happy thou—in the still narrow cell!
 To this strange tragi-comedy acted on earth,
To these waters where Bliss is defil'd at the well,
 To this lottery of chances in sorrow and mirth,
To this rot and this ferment—this sloth and this strife,
 To the day and the night of this toilsome repose,
To this Heaven full of Devils—O, Brother!—TO LIFE—
 Thine eyes in the calm of Eternity close!

Fare-thee-well, fare-thee-well, O Belov'd of the soul!
 Our yearnings shall hallow the loss we deplore;
Slumber soft in the Grave till we win to thy goal—
 Slumber soft, slumber soft, till we see thee once more!
Till the Trumpet that heralds God's coming in thunder,
 From the hill-tops of light shall ring over thy bed—
Till the portals of Death shall be riven asunder,
 And the storm-wind of God whirl the dust of the Dead;
Till the breath of Jehovah shall pass o'er the Tombs,
 Till their seeds spring to bloom at the life of the Breath,
Till the pomp of the Stars into vapour consumes,
 And the spoils he hath captured are ravished from Death.
If not in the worlds dream'd by sages, nor given
 In the Eden the Multitude hope to attain,
If not where the Poet hath painted his Heaven,
 Still, Brother, we know we shall meet thee again!
Is there truth in the hopes which the Pilgrim beguile?
 Does the thought still exist when Life's journey is o'er?
Does Virtue conduct o'er the dreary defile?
 Is the faith we have cherish'd a dream and no more?
Already the riddle is bared to thy sight,
 Already thy soul quaffs the Truth it has won,
The Truth that streams forth in its waters of light
 From the chalice the Father vouchsafes to the Son!
Draw near, then, O silent and dark gliding Train,
 Let the feast for the Mighty Destroyer be spread;
Cease the groans which so loudly, so idly complain,
 Heap the mould o'er the mould—heap the dust o'er the
   Dead!

Who can solve the decrees of God's Senate?—the heart
 Of the groundless abyss, what the eye that explores?
Holy!—holy!—all holy in darkness thou art,
 O God of the Grave, whom our shudder adores!
Earth to Earth may return, the material to matter,
 But high from the coil soars the spirit above;
His ashes the winds of the tempest may scatter—
 The life of Eternity lives in his love!

THE BATTLE.

  Heavy and solemn,
  A cloudy column,
   Thro' the green plain they marching came!
Measureless spread, like a table dread,
For the wild grim dice of the iron game.
The looks are bent on the shaking ground,
And the heart beats loud with a knelling sound;
Swift by the breasts that must bear the brunt,
Gallops the Major along the front—
   "Halt!"
And fetter'd they stand at the stark command,
And the warriors, silent, halt!

 Proud in the blush of morning glowing,
What on the hill-top shines in flowing!
"See you the Foeman's banners waving?"
"We see the Foeman's banners waving!"
"God be with ye—children and wife!"
Hark to the Music—the trump and the fife,
How they ring thro' the ranks which they rouse to the
  strife!
Thrilling they sound with their glorious tone,
Thrilling they go through the marrow and bone!
Brothers, God grant when this life is o'er,
In the life to come that we meet once more!
 See the smoke how the lightning is cleaving asunder!
Hark the guns, peal on peal, how they boom in their
  thunder!
From host to host, with kindling sound,
The shouting signal circles round,

Ay, shout it forth to life or death—
Freer already breathes the breath!
The war is waging, slaughter raging,
And heavy through the reeking pall,
  The iron Death-dice fall!
Nearer they close—foes upon foes
" Ready! "—From square to square it goes,
  Down on the knee they sank,
And the fire comes sharp from the foremost rank.
Many a man to the earth it sent,
Many a gap by the balls is rent—
O'er the corpse before springs the hinder-man,
That the line may not fail to the fearless van.
To the right, to the left, and around and around,
Death whirls in its dance on the bloody ground.
God's sunlight is quench'd in the fiery fight,
Over the host falls a brooding Night!
Brothers, God grant when this life is o'er,
In the life to come that we meet once more!
  The dead men lie bathed in the weltering blood,
And the living are blent in the slippery flood,
And the feet, as they reeling and sliding go,
Stumble still on the corpses that sleep below.
"What, Francis!"   "Give Charlotte my last farewell."
As the dying man murmurs, the thunders swell—
"I'll give—Oh God! are their guns so near?
Ho! comrades!—yon volley!—look sharp to the rear!—
I'll give thy Charlotte thy last farewell,
Sleep soft! where Death thickest descendeth in rain,
The friend thou forsakest thy side shall regain!"
Hitherward—thitherward reels the fight,
Dark and more darkly Day glooms into night—
Brothers, God grant when this life is o'er,
In the life to come that we meet once more!
Hark to the hoofs that galloping go!
  The Adjutants flying,—
The horsemen press hard on the panting foe,
  Their thunder booms in dying—
      Victory!
The terror has seized on the dastards all,
  And their colours fall!
      Victory!

Closed is the brunt of the glorious fight :
And the day, like a conqueror, bursts on the night.
Trumpet and fife swelling choral along,
The triumph already sweeps marching in song.
Farewell, fallen brothers, tho' this life be o'er,
There's another, in which we shall meet you once more !

ROUSSEAU.

(FREE TRANSLATION.)

O MONUMENT of Shame to this our time !
Dishonouring record to thy mother clime ;
Hail Grave of Rousseau !—here thy troubles cease !
Thy life one search for Freedom and for Peace :
Thee, Peace and Freedom life did ne'er allow,
Thy search is ended, and thou find'st them now !
When will the old wounds scar !—In the dark age
Perish'd the wise ;—Light comes—How fares the sage ?
The same in darkness or in light his fate,
Time brings no mercy to the Bigot's hate !
Socrates charmed Philosophy to dwell
On Earth—by false philosophers he fell ;
In Rousseau, Christians mark'd their victim—when
Rousseau enlisted Christians into Men !

FRIENDSHIP.

[From "*Letters of Julius to Raphael*," an unpublished Novel.]

FRIEND !—the Great Ruler, easily content,
  Needs not the laws it has laborious been
The task of small Professors to invent ;
  A single wheel impels the whole machine
Matter and spirit ;—yea that simple law,
Pervading Nature, which our Newton saw.

s 2

This taught the spheres, slaves to one golden rein,
   Their radiant labyrinths to weave around
Creation's mighty heart; this made the chain,
   Which into interwoven systems bound
All spirits streaming to the spiritual Sun,
As brooks that ever into ocean run !

Did not the same strong mainspring urge and guide
   Our Hearts to meet in Love's eternal bond ?
Link'd to thine arm, O Raphael, by thy side
   Might I aspire to reach to souls beyond
Our earth, and bid the bright Ambition go
To that Perfection which the Angels know !

Happy, O happy—I have found thee—I
   Have out of millions found thee, and embraced ;
Thou, out of millions, mine !—Let earth and sky
   Return to darkness, and the antique waste—
To chaos shock'd, let warring atoms be,
Still shall each heart unto the other flee !

Do I not find within thy radiant eyes
   Fairer reflections of all joys most fair ?
In thee I marvel at myself—the dyes
   Of lovely earth seem lovelier painted there,
And in the bright looks of the Friend is given
A heavenlier mirror even of the Heaven !

Sadness casts off its load, and gaily goes
   From the intolerant storm to rest awhile,
In Love's true heart, sure haven of repose ;
   Does not Pain's veriest transports learn to smile
From that bright eloquence Affection gave
To friendly looks ?—there, finds not Pain a grave ?

In all Creation did I stand alone,
   Still to the rocks my dreams a soul should find,
Mine arms should wreathe themselves around the stone,
   My grief should feel a listener in the wind ;
My joy—its echo in the caves should be !
Fool, if ye will—Fool, for sweet Sympathy !

We are dead groups of matter when we hate;
  But when we love we are as Gods !—Unto
The gentle fetters yearning, through each state
  And shade of being multiform, and thro'
All countless spirits (save of all the sire)—
Moves, breathes, and blends the one divine Desire.

Lo ! arm in arm, thro' every upward grade,
  From the rude Mongol to the starry Greek,
Who the fine link between the Mortal made,
  And Heaven's last Seraph—everywhere we seek
Union and bond—till in one sea sublime
Of Love be merg'd all measure and all time !

Friendless ruled God His solitary sky;
  He felt the want, and therefore Souls were made,
The blessed mirrors of His bliss !—His Eye
  No equal in His loftiest works surveyed;
And from the source whence souls are quickened—He
Called His Companion forth—ETERNITY !

A GROUP IN TARTARUS.

HARK, as hoarse murmurs of a gathering sea—
  As brooks that howling through black gorges go,
Groans sullen, hollow, and eternally,
  One wailing Woe !
Sharp Anguish shrinks the shadows there;
And blasphemous Despair
Yells its wild curse from jaws that never close;
  And ghastly eyes for ever
  Stare on the bridge of the relentless River,
Or watch the mournful wave as year on year it flows,
  And ask each other, with parch'd lips that writhe
Into a whisper, " When the end shall be ? "
  The *end* ?—Lo, broken in Time's hand the scythe,
And round and round revolves Eternity !

ELYSIUM.

PAST the despairing wail—
And the bright banquets of the Elysian Vale
  Melt every care away!
Delight, that breathes and moves for ever,
Glides through sweet fields like some sweet river!
  Elysian life survey!
There, fresh with youth, o'er jocund meads,
His merry west-winds blithely leads
  The ever-blooming May!
Through gold-woven dreams goes the dance of the Hours,
In space without bounds swell the soul and its powers,
  And Truth, with no veil, gives her face to the day.
And joy to-day and joy to-morrow,
  But wafts the airy soul aloft;
The very name is lost to Sorrow,
  And Pain is Rapture tuned more exquisitely soft.
Here the Pilgrim reposes the world-weary limb,
And forgets in the shadow, cool-breathing and dim,
  The load he shall bear never more;
Here the Mower, his sickle at rest, by the streams,
Lull'd with harp-strings, reviews, in the calm of his dreams,
  The fields, when the harvest is o'er.
Here, He, whose ears drank in the battle roar,
Whose banners stream'd upon the startled wind
  A thunder-storm,—before whose thunder tread
The mountains trembled,—in soft sleep reclined,
  By the sweet brook that o'er its pebbly bed
In silver plays, and murmurs to the shore,
Hears the stern clangour of wild spears no more!
Here the true Spouse the lost-beloved regains,
And on the enamell'd couch of summer-plains
  Mingles sweet kisses with the zephyr's breath.
Here, crown'd at last, Love never knows decay,
Living through ages its one BRIDAL DAY,
  Safe from the stroke of Death!

THE REFUGEE.

FRESH breathes the living air of dawning Day,
The young Light reddens thro' the dusky pines,
Ogling the tremulous leaves with wanton ray :
The cloud-capt hill-tops shine,
With golden-flame divine;
And all melodious thrills the lusty song
Of sky-larks, greeting the delighted Sun;
As to Aurora's arms he steals along—
And now in bright embrace she clasps the glowing one !
O Light, hail to thee !
How the mead and the lea
The warmth and the wave of thy splendour suffuse !
How silver-clear, shimmer
The fields, and how glimmer
The thousand suns glass'd in the pearl of the dews !
How frolic and gay
Is young Nature at play,
Where the cool-breathing shade with low whispers is sweet;
Sighing soft round the rose,
The Zephyr, its lover, caressingly goes,
And over the Meadow the light vapours fleet !
How, high o'er the city the smoke-cloud is reeking,
What snorting, and rattling, and trampling, and creaking;
Neighs the horse—the bull lows,
And the heavy wain goes
To the valley that groans with the tumult of Day ;
The life of the Woodlands leaps up to the eye—
The Eagle, the Falcon, the Hawk, wheel on high,
On the wings that exult in the ray !
Where shall I roam,
O Peace, for thy home ?
With the staff of the Pilgrim, where wander to Thee ?
The face of the Earth
With the smile of its mirth
Has only a grave for me !
Rise up, O rosy Morn, whose lips of love
Kiss into blushing splendour grove and field ;
Sink down, O rosy Eve, that float'st above
The weary world, in happy slumbers seal'd.

Morn, in the joyous world thou reddenest over
　　But one dark Burial-place the Pilgrim knows !
O Eve, the sleep thy rosy veil shall cover
　　Is—but my long repose !

THE FLOWERS.

CHILDREN of Suns restored to youth,
　　In purfled Fields ye dwell,
Reared to delight and joy—in sooth,
　　Kind Nature loves ye well ;
Broidered with light the robes ye wear,
And liberal Flora decks ye fair,
　　In gorgeous-coloured pride :
Yet woo—Spring's harmless Infants—Woe,
Mourn, for ye wither while ye glow—
　　Mourn for the soul denied !

The Skylark and the Nightbird sing
　　To you their Hymns of Love,
And Sylphs that wanton on the wing
　　Embrace your blooms above ;
Woven for Love's soft pillow, were
The Chalice crowns ye blushing bear,
　　By the Idalian Queen :
Yet weep, soft Children of the Spring,
The feelings Love alone can bring
　　To you denied have been !

But me in vain my Laura's * eyes,
　　Her Mother hath forbidden ;
For in the buds I gather, lies
　　Love's symbol-language hidden—
Mute Heralds of voluptuous pain
I touch ye—life, speech, heart, ye gain,
　　And soul, denied before :
And silently your leaves enclose
The mightiest God in arch repose,
　　Soft cradled in the core !

* *Nanny*, in the Editions of Schiller's collected Works; but Laura, when
the Poem was first printed in the Anthology. In the earlier form of the
poem, it was not, however, the Poet who sent the flowers to Laura, but
Laura who sent the flowers to him.

TO MINNA.

I.

Do I dream? can I trust to my eye?
  My sight sure some vapour must cover?
Or, there, did my Minna pass by—
  My Minna—and knew not her lover?
On the arm of the coxcomb she crost,
  Well the fan might its zephyr bestow;
Herself in her vanity lost,
  That wanton my Minna?—Ah, no!

II.

In the gifts of my love she was drest,
  My plumes o'er her summer-hat quiver;
The ribbons that flaunt in her breast
  Might bid her—remember the giver!
And still do they bloom on thy bosom,
  The flowerets I gathered for thee!
Still as fresh is the leaf of each blossom,
  'Tis the Heart that has faded from me!

III.

Go and take, then, the incense they tender;
  Go, the one that adored thee forget!
Go, thy charms to the Feigner surrender,
  In my scorn is my comforter yet!
Go, for thee with what trust and belief
  There beat not ignobly a heart,
That has strength yet to strive with the grief
  To have worshipp'd the trifler thou art!

IV.

Thy beauty *thy* heart hath betray'd—
  Thy beauty—shame, Minna, to thee!
To-morrow its glory will fade,
  And its roses all withered will be!
The swallows that swarm in the sun
  Will fly when the north winds awaken,
The false ones thine Autumn will shun,
  For whom thou the true hast forsaken!

V.

'Mid the wrecks of thy charms in December,
  I see thee alone in decay,
And each Spring shall but bid thee remember
  How brief for thyself was the May!
Then they who so wantonly flock
  To the rapture thy kiss can impart,
Shall scoff at thy winter, and mock
  Thy beauty as wreck'd as thy heart;

VI.

Thy beauty thy heart hath betray'd—
  Thy beauty—shame, Minna, to thee!
To-morrow its glory will fade—
  And its roses all withered will be!
O, what scorn for thy desolate years
  Shall I feel!—God forbid it in me!
How bitter will then be the tears
  Shed, Minna, O, Minna, for thee!

TO THE SPRING.

Welcome, gentle Stripling
  Nature's darling, thou!
With thy basket full of blossoms,
  A happy welcome now!
Aha!—and thou returnest,
  Heartily we greet thee—
The loving and the fair one,
  Merrily we meet thee!
Think'st thou of my Maiden
  In thy heart of glee?

I love her yet, the Maiden—
  And the Maiden yet loves me!
For the Maiden, many a blossom
  I begg'd—and not in vain!
I came again, a-begging,
  And thou—thou giv'st again:

Welcome, gentle Stripling,
　Nature's darling thou—
With thy basket full of blossoms,
　A happy welcome, now!

THE TRIUMPH OF LOVE.

A HYMN.

Blessed through love are the Gods above—
　Through love like the Gods may man be;
Heavenlier through love is the heaven above,
　Through love like a heaven earth can be!
Once, as the poet sung,
　In Pyrrha's time 'tis known,
From rocks Creation sprung,
　And Men leapt up from stone;
Rock and stone, in night
　The souls of men were seal'd,
Heaven's diviner light
　Not as yet reveal'd;
As yet the Loves around them
Had never shone—nor bound them
　With their rosy rings;
As yet their bosoms knew not
Soft song—and music grew not
　Out of the silver strings:
No gladsome garlands cheerily
　Were love-y-woven then;
And o'er Elysium drearily
　The May-time flew for men,*
The morning rose ungreeted
　From ocean's joyless breast;
Unhail'd the evening fleeted
　To ocean's joyless breast—
Wild through the tangled shade,
By clouded moons they stray'd,

' "The World was sad, the garden was a wild,
　And Man, the Hermit, sigh'd—till Woman smiled."—
Campbell.

The iron race of Men !
Sources of mystic tears,
Yearnings for starry spheres,
  No God awaken'd then !

*   *   *   *   *

Lo, mildly from the dark-blue water,
Comes forth the Heaven's divinest Daughter,
  Borne by the Nymphs fair-floating o'er
  To the intoxicated shore !
Like the light-scattering wings of morning
Soars universal May, adorning
As from the glory of that birth
Air and the ocean, heaven and earth !
Day's eye looks laughing, where the grim
Midnight lay coil'd in forests dim ;
And gay narcissuses are sweet
Wherever glide those holy feet—
  Now, pours the bird that haunts the eve
The earliest song of love,
  Now in the heart—their fountain—heave
The waves that murmur love !
O blest Pygmalion—blest art thou—
It melts, it glows, thy marble now !
  O Love, the God, thy world is won !
  Embrace thy children, Mighty One.

*   *   *   *   *

Blessed through love are the Gods above—
  Through love like the Gods may man be ;
Heavenlier through love is the heaven above,
  Through love like a heaven earth can be.

*   *   *   *   *

Where the nectar bright-streams,
Like the dawn's happy dreams,
Eternally one holiday,
The life of the Gods glides away.
Throned on his seat sublime,
Looks He whose years know not time ;
At his nod, if his anger awaken,
At the wave of his hair all Olympus is shaken.
Yet He from the throne of his birth,
Bow'd down to the sons of the earth,

Through dim Arcadian glades to wander sighing,
  Lull'd into dreams of bliss—
  Lull'd by his Leda's kiss—
Lo, at his feet the harmless thunders lying!

The Sun's majestic coursers go
  Along the Light's transparent plain,
  Curb'd by the Day-god's golden rein;
The nations perish at his bended bow;
  Steeds that majestic go,
  Shafts from the bended bow,
  Gladly he leaves above—
  For Melody and Love!
Low bend the dwellers of the sky,
When sweeps the stately Juno by;
Proud in her car, the Uncontroll'd
  Curbs the bright birds that breast the air,
As flames the sovereign crown of gold
  Amidst the ambrosial waves of hair—
Ev'n thou, fair Queen of Heaven's high throne,
Hast Love's subduing sweetness known;
From all her state, the Great One bends
  To charm the Olympian's bright embraces,
The Heart-Enthraller only lends
  The rapture-cestus of the Graces!
   o   *   o   o   o

Blessed through love are the Gods above—
  Through love like a God may man be;
Heavenlier through love is the heaven above,
  Through love like a heaven earth can be!
   o   *   o   o   *

Love can sun the Realms of Night—
Orcus owns the magic might—
Peaceful where She sits beside,
Smiles the swart King on his Bride;
Hell feels the smile in sudden light—
Love can sun the Realms of Night!
Heavenly o'er the startled Hell,
Holy, where the Accursed dwell,
  O Thracian, went thy silver song!
Grim Minos, with unconscious tears,
Melts into Mercy as he hears—

The serpents in Megara's hair,
Kiss, as they wreathe enamour'd there;
  All harmless rests the madding thong;—
From the torn breast the Vulture mute
Flies, scared before the charmèd lute—
Lull'd into sighing from their roar
The dark waves woo the listening shore—
Listening the Thracian's silver song!—
Love was the Thracian's silver song!

    o   o   o   o   o

Blessed through love are the Gods above—
  Through love like a God may man be;
Heavenlier through love is the heaven above,
  Through love like a heaven earth can be!

    o   o   *   o   o

Through Nature, blossom-strewing,
One footstep we are viewing,
  One flash from golden pinions!—
If from Heaven's starry sea,
  If from the moonlit sky;
If from the Sun's dominions,
  Look'd not Love's laughing eye;
Then Sun and Moon and Stars would be
Alike, without one smile for me!
    But, oh, wherever Nature lives
      Below, around, above—
    Her happy eye the mirror gives
      To thy glad beauty, Love!
Love sighs through brooklets silver-clear,
  Love bids their murmur woo the vale;
Listen, O list!   Love's soul ye hear
  In his own earnest nightingale.
No sound from Nature ever stirs,
But Love's sweet voice is heard with hers!
Bold Wisdom, with her sunlit eye,
Retreats when Love comes whispering by—
  For Wisdom's weak to Love!
To victor stern or monarch proud,
Imperial Wisdom never bow'd
  The knee she bows to Love!
Who through the steep and starry sky,
Goes onward to the Gods on high,

Before thee, hero-brave?
Who halves for thee the land of Heaven;
Who shows thy heart, Elysium, given
   Through the flame-rended Grave?
Below, if we were blind to Love,
Say, should we soar o'er Death, above?
Would the weak soul, did Love forsake her,
E'er gain the wing to seek the Maker?
Love, only Love, can guide the creature
Up to the Father-fount of Nature;
What were the soul did Love forsake her?
Love guides the Mortal to the Maker!

  o   o   o   o   o

Blessed through love are the Gods above—
   Through love like a God may man be;
Heavenlier through love is the heaven above,
   Through love like a heaven earth can be!

TO A MORALIST.

ARE the sports of our youth so displeasing?
   Is love but the folly you say?
Benumb'd with the Winter, and freezing,
   You scold at the revels of May.

For you once a nymph had her charms,
   And oh! when the waltz you were wreathing,
All Olympus embraced in your arms—
   All its nectar in Julia's breathing.

If Jove at that moment had hurl'd
   The earth in some other rotation,
Along with your Julia whirl'd,
   You had felt not the shock of creation.

Learn this—that Philosophy beats
   Sure time with the pulse,—quick or slow
As the blood from the heyday retreats,—
   But it cannot make gods of us—No!

It is well, icy Reason should thaw
  In the warm blood of Mirth now and then,
The Gods for themselves have a law
  Which they never intended for men.

The Spirit is bound by the ties
  Of its Gaoler the Flesh;—if I can
Not reach as an Angel the skies,
  Let me feel on the earth as a Man!

FORTUNE AND WISDOM.

In a quarrel with her lover
  To Wisdom Fortune flew;
" I'll all my hoards discover—
  Be but my friend—to you.
Like a mother I presented
  To one each fairest gift,
Who still is discontented,
  And murmurs at my thrift.
Come, let's be friends.   What say you ?
  Give up that weary plough,
My treasures shall repay you,
  For both I have enow! "
" Nay, see thy Friend betake him
  To death from grief for thee—
He dies if thou forsake him—
  Thy gifts are nought to *me* !"

COUNT EBERHARD, THE QUARRELLER (DER GREINER) OF WURTEMBERG.

[Count Eberhard reigned from 1344–92. His son Ulrick was defeated
before Reutling in 1377, and fell the next year in battle, at Doffingen, near
Stuttgard, in a battle in which Eberhard was victorious. There is something of national feeling in this fine war-song, composed in honour of the
old Suabian hero, by a poet himself a Suabian.]

HA, ha!—take heed,—ha, ha! take heed—*
  Ye knaves both South and North!
For many a man both bold in deed,
And wise in peace the land to lead,
  Old Suabia has brought forth.

Proud boasts your Edward and your Charles,
  Your Ludwig, Frederick—are!
Yet Eberhard's worth, ye bragging carles!
Your Ludwig, Frederick, Edward, Charles—
  A thunder-storm in war!

And Ulrick, too, his noble son,
  Ha, ha! his might ye know;
Old Eberhard's boast, his noble son,
Not he the boy, ye rogues, to run,
  How stout soe'er the foe!

The Reutling lads with envy saw
  Our glories, day by day;
The Reutling lads shall give the law—
The Reutling lads the sword shall draw—
  O Lord—how hot were they!

Out Ulrick went, and beat them not—
  To Eberhard back he came—
A lowering look young Ulrick got—
Poor lad, his eyes with tears were hot—
  He hung his head for shame.

" Ho—ho "—thought he—" ye rogues beware;
  Nor you nor I forget—
For by my father's beard † I swear
Your blood shall wash the blot I bear,
  And Ulrick pay you yet! "

---

* " Don't bear the head too high."
   Ihr, ihr dort aussen in der Welt,
    Die Nasen eingespannt!—

† Count Eberhard had the nickname of Rush-Beard, from the rustling of that appendage, with which he was favoured to no ordinary extent.

T

Soon came the hour! with steeds and men
　The battle-field was gay;
Steel closed on steel at Doffingen—
And joyous was our stripling then,
　And joyous the hurra!

"The battle lost" our battle-cry;
　The foe once more advances:
As some fierce whirlwind cleaves the sky,
We skirr, through blood and slaughter, by,
　Amidst a night of lances!

On, lion-like, grim Ulrick sweeps—
　Bright shines his hero-glaive—
Her chase before him Fury keeps,
Far-heard behind him, Anguish weeps,
　And round him—is the Grave!

Woe—woe! it gleams—the sabre-blow—
　Swift-sheering down it sped—
Around, brave hearts the buckler throw—
Alas! our boast in dust is low!
　Count Eberhard's boy is dead!

Grief checks the rushing Victor-van—
　Fierce eyes strange moisture know—
On rides old Eberhard, stern and wan,
"My son is like another man—
　March, children, on the Foe!"

And fiery lances whirr'd around,
　Revenge, at least, undying—
Above the blood-red clay we bound—
Hurra! the burghers break their ground,
　Through vale and woodland flying!

Back to the camp, behold us throng,
　Flags stream, and bugles play—
Woman and child with choral song,
And men, with dance and wine, prolong
　The warrior's holyday.

And our old Count—and what doth he?
    Before him lies his son,
Within his lone tent, lonelily,
·The old man sits with eyes that see
    Through one dim tear—his son!

So heart and soul, a loyal band,
    Count Eberhard's band, we are !
His front the tower that guards the land,
A thunderbolt his red right hand—
    His eye a guiding star !

Then take ye heed —Aha ! take heed,
    Ye knaves both South and North !
For many a man, both bold in deed
And wise in peace, the land to lead,
    Old Suabia has brought forth !

With this ballad conclude all in the First Period, or early Poems which Schiller himself thought worth preserving, and which are retained in the editions of his collected works ;—except the sketch of "Semele," which ought to be classed amongst his dramatic compositions.

FAREWELL TO THE READER.

(TRANSFERRED FROM THE THIRD PERIOD.)

The Muse is silent; with a virgin cheek,
    Bow'd with the blush of shame, she ventures near –
She waits the judgment that thy lips may speak,
    And feels the deference, but disowns the fear.
Such praise as Virtue gives, 'tis hers to seek—
    Bright Truth, not tinsel Folly to revere ;
He only for her wreath the flowers should cull
Whose heart, with hers, beats for the Beautiful.

Nor longer yet these lays of mine would live,
    Than to one genial heart, not idly stealing,
There some sweet dreams and fancies fair to give,
    Some hallowing whispers of a loftier feeling.

T 2

Not for the far posterity they strive,
   Doom'd with the time, its impulse but revealing,
Born to record the Moment's smile or sigh,
And with the light dance of the Hours to fly.

Spring wakes—and life, in all its youngest hues,
   Shoots through the mellowing meads delightedly ;
Air the fresh herbage scents with nectar-dews ;
   Livelier the choral music fills the sky ;
Youth grows more young, and age its youth renews,
   In that field-banquet of the ear and eye ;
Spring flies—and with it all the train it leads,
And flowers in fading leave us but their seeds.

THE ODES AND EPODES OF
HORACE.

TO THE

REV. F. W. FARRAR, B.D.,

MASTER OF MARLBOROUGH COLLEGE,

IN admiration of an intellect enriched by the variety of culture which gives renown to the Scholar, ennobled by the unity of purpose which blends the vocation of the Scholar with the mission of the Divine,

IS INSCRIBED

This attempt to facilitate among English readers the study of an Author so humane, whether in his weakness or his strength, that his sympathies with mankind have obtained for him the indulgence which man accords to a friend. That indulgence is necessarily the greatest among those most indulgent as to man's weakness, if most exacting as to man's strength, 'THE SEEKERS AFTER GOD.'

TORQUAY, *April* 3, 1872.

PREFACE

TO THE EDITION OF 1872.

—·—

THE first impression of this work having become somewhat rapidly exhausted, this new Edition would have appeared long since, but for my desire to consider whether any fresh pains on my part could make the book more worthy of the favour with which it has been received by the general reader, and the courtesy with which it has been noticed by the critical press, wherever the review of it has been written by a scholar.

Of course no pains of mine can meet the objection of those who dissent to the whole framework of the translation, viz., the adoption of rhymeless metres—just as no reasonings, and certainly no examples, in favour of rhymed verse can alter my opinion, formed after long and careful deliberation, that while for the purposes of imitation or paraphrase rhyme may be advantageously employed in selected specimens of the Odes, it is utterly antagonistic to a faithful translation of them, taken as a whole, whether in substance or in spirit.

Leaving, however, the question of rhythm one of those disputes of taste which admit of no arbiter but time, I may perhaps be pardoned for saying that I find many readers, failing, in the first instance, to accommodate the ear to the metres I have invented, who have contrived, on reperusal, to do so, and come round, more or less, to my side of the question.

Necessarily, therefore, whatever care I could take in revision is confined to details, and my main object has been to attend to every suggestion by competent authorities that might guide me towards closer approximation to the intention and sense of the original. In one or two instances of rhythm apart from interpretation, where it has seemed to me that this could be best effected by varying the type or form of the metre first selected, the Ode has been rewritten.

My task after all is one of those very humble ones, which are frequent enough among labours of love, and my ambition is not disproportioned to the humility of the task. Whatever the differences of taste and opinion as to the value of my translation, I venture to hope that neither that nor the book of which it is a portion can fail to obtain a place lowly indeed, but not unenduring, among those elucidations of one of the most popular, and in some respects one of the most difficult, poets of antiquity, to which every conscientious student of Horace will find it worth his while to refer.

THE ODES AND EPODES

OF

HORACE.

BOOK I.—ODE I.

DEDICATORY ODE TO MÆCENAS.

It is doubtful whether this ode was composed as a dedicatory preface to the first three books, or only to Book I.: the former supposition is more generally favoured. The poet condenses a rapid survey of the various objects of desire and ambition, commencing with the competition of the Olympic games, and passing from that reference to the Greeks, to the pursuits of his own countrymen in the emulation for power, the acquisition of riches, and so on, through the occupations and tastes of mankind in that busy world from which, at the close, he intimates that he himself is set apart.

The punctuation and construction of the fifth and sixth lines of the ode have been a matter of much dispute. Macleane, sanctioned by Mr. George Long—and Munro, supported "by the emphatic advocacy of Dr. Kennedy"—adopt the reading which puts an end to the sentence at "nobilis," and joins on "Terrarum dominos evehit ad Deos" to what follows. By this reading, the lords of earth, or masters of the world, are neither (according to Orelli and most modern commentators) taken in apposition with "Deos," as in Ovid, Ep. ex Ponto, i. 9, 35, sq.—

> "Nam tua non alio coluit penetralia ritu
> Terrarum dominos quam colis ipse Deos;"

nor, according to elder commentators, approved by Ritter, is the term applied to regal or lordly competitors in the Greek games, such as Gelo, Hiero, &c. "Terrarum dominos" Macleane understands to signify, with a tinge of irony, the Romans, styled by Virgil, Æn. i. 282, and Martial, xiv. 123, "Romanos rerum dominos." Fortified in my own judgment by authorities of such eminence, I accept this interpretation. From these lords of earth Horace immediately passes on to select representatives of the two great orders of proprietors—the senatorial and the equestrian: a member of the first placing his happiness in the pursuit of the highest honours; a member of the second, which comprised in its ranks the chiefs of commercial enterprise, in the success of gigantic speculations.

"According to the usual punctuation," says Munro, "verses 7—10 appear to me to have no construction at all; with mine, all is plain. . . In ancient Rome, too, as in modern England, high office and vast wealth, more than aught else, raised men to the sky."—MUNRO, Introduction, xxv.

For the three odes in this measure I have employed in translation a metre consisting of our ordinary form of blank verse converted into a couplet by alternate terminations in a dissyllable and monosyllable ; and though that is a very simple, and may seem at first a very slight, modification of a familiar rhythm, it will be found to constitute, in the regular recurrence of alternated terminals, a marked difference from the chime of our epic line, and is yet equally in unison with the laws of our prosody. I have adopted the same metre in my version of the more inportant epodes, and in a few of the other odes.

Sprung from a race which mounts to kings, Mæcenas,
    Shield and sweet ornament of life to me ;
There are whose sovereign joy is dust Olympic
    Gathered in whirlwind* by the car ; the goal
Shunned by hot wheels ; and the palm's noble trophy.—
    Up to the gods it bears the lords of earth,
One—if the mob of Rome's electors fickle
    Through triple honours to exalt him vie ;
One—if he harvest, stored in his own garner,
    Whate'er from Libyan threshing-floors is fanned.
Treasures Attalic † could not tempt the rustic,
    Delving with ready hoe paternal glebes,
To cut, poor timorous mariner, a furrow
    On seas Myrtoan with the Cyprian keel.
Seized by dismay, when with Icarian billows
    Wrestle the blasts of stormy Africus,
The merchant sighs for ease and modest homestead
    Nestled in fields beside his native town ;
Schooled not to bear the pinch of straitened fortunes,‡
    Soon he refits his shattered argosies.

* "Collegisse juvat." To have gathered together or collected the scattered atoms of dust into a whirlwind—"pulvis collectus turbine," Sat. I. iv. 31.

† A proverbial phrase for great riches. The rustic here meant is the small peasant proprietor, like those cultivators by spade-labour now so common in France. The "sarculum" was a lighter tool than a spade or mattock (with which Forcellini observes that Horace here confounds it by synecdoche), and was used as a hoe for digging up weeds. The author of the article on "Agriculture" in Smith's "Dictionary of Greek and Roman Antiquities" says that "it was an implement by which, after covering up the seed, the husbandman loosened the roots of the young blades in order that air and moisture might gain free access."

‡ "Indocilis pauperiem pati." "Pauperies" does not here mean what is commonly understood by poverty, but, as Macleane expresses it, "a humble estate." Macleane, indeed, states "that 'pauperies,' 'paupertas,' 'pauper,' are *never* by Horace taken to signify privation, or anything beyond a humble estate." This assertion is, however, too sweeping. In the lines (Epod. xvii. 47, 48),

    " Neque in sepulcris pauperum prudens anus
    Novendiales dissipare pulveres,"

Lo, one who scorns not beakers of old Massic,
  Nor lazy hours cut from the solid day,
Now with limbs stretched beneath the verdant arbute,
  Now by soft well-head of nymph-hallowed streams.
Camps delight many ; clarion shrill, deep trumpet
  Commingling stormy melodies ; and war,
Hateful to mothers.   His young bride forgetting,
  In wintry air the hunter stands at watch,
If start the deer in sight of his stanch beagles,
  Or burst through close-knit toils the Marsian boar.
Me, prize of learnëd brows, the wreathen ivy,
  Associates with the gods ; me woodlands cool
And the light dance of nymphs with choral satyrs,
  Set from the many and their world apart ;
If with no checked and hesitating utterance
  Euterpe lend her breath unto her flutes ;
And for my touch the harp-strings heard in Lesbos
  If Polyhymnia scorn not to retune.
But amid lyric bards if thou enrol me,
  With crest uplifted I shall strike the stars.

EXCURSUS.

"Me doctarum hederæ præmia frontium."

Wolff, Hare, Tate, and some other commentators, would substitute "Te"
for "Me"—applying the line to Mæcenas, "*Thee* the ivy—the prize of
learned brows—associates with gods above ; *Me* the cool woods, &c., set
apart from the common crowd."   This reading is rejected by the highest
critical authorities, including Orelli and Macleane ; but it appears in itself
entitled to more respect than is shown by the latter.   For there is some
force in the remark, that in referring to the various tastes and characteristics
of men, Horace would scarcely avoid all complimentary reference to Mæcenas
himself ; and there is yet more force in another remark that, if Horace says
that the ivy wreath associates him with the higher or celestial gods, there is
a certain bathos, if not contradiction, in immediately afterwards saying that
his tastes associate him with the inferior or terrestrial deities—*i. e.*, nymphs
and satyrs.   It is said, in vindication of "Me" instead of "Te," that "doctus"
is a word very appropriate to poets ; that the ivy, sacred to Bacchus, was the

---

"pauper" clearly means a person of the very poorest class.   May not the same
be said of "Pauperum tabernas" in contradistinction to "Regum turres" ?
Lib I. Od. iv. 13, 14.   The words "pauper," "pauperies," "paupertas,"
have, indeed, some of the elastic sense of our own Poor Man, or Poverty,
which may imply only comparatively restricted means, or sometimes absolute want.   The English language has expressions denoting the gradations
of stinted circumstances correspondent to those in the Latin.   The English
has poverty, penury, destitution : the Latin has paupertas, inopia, egestas.   So
also the Greek language has πενία, honourable poverty ; πτωχεία, discredit-
able poverty ; ἔνδεια, destitution.

fit and usual garland for a lyric poet; and that Horace could never stoop to
the absurd flattery of insinuating that Mæcenas was a greater poet than
himself. But, in answer to all this, it may be urged that Horace elsewhere
especially applies the word "doctus" to Mæcenas; in Lib. III. Od. viii.
line 4,—

> "Docte sermones utriusque linguæ;"

and again, more emphatically, Epist. xix. line 1,—

> "Prisco si credis, Mæcenas docte, Cratino."

And though the ivy was appropriate to poets, it was not appropriate to poets
alone. Horace (Lib. I. Epist. iii., addressed to Julius Florus) speaks of it
as the reward of excellence in forensic eloquence or jurisprudence as well as
of song :—

> "Seu linguam causis acuis seu civica jura,
> Respondere paras seu condis amabile carmen,
> Prima feres *hederæ* victricis *præmia.*"

And if the ivy crown may be won by pleading causes or giving advice to
clients, it can be no inappropriate reward to the brows of a statesman so accomplished as Mæcenas. Thus, I think, there is much to be said in favour
of the construction—"Thee, Mæcenas, the ivy wreath—prize of learned or
skilled brows—associates with the higher gods (*i. e.*, with those who watch
over states and empires) ; me, the love of rural leisure and the dreams that
it begets set apart from the crowd." On the other side, Ritter has the best
vindication I have seen of the alleged contradiction or bathos in the Poet's
boasted association, first, with the higher gods, and, next, with the inferior
deities. According to him, Horace is speaking of two kinds of lyric poetry
—the lofty and the sportive. The first, symbolised by the ivy, associates
him with gods in heaven ; the second, connecting him with the pastimes of
nymphs and satyrs, separates him from the popular pursuits of men. For
the first, he trusts to the aid of Polyhymnia, presiding over the Lesbian
lyre (of Alcæus) ; for the second, to the livelier inspiration of Euterpe.

ODE II.

TO CÆSAR.

The exact date of this ode has been matter of controversy, but most
recent authorities concur in assigning it to about A.U.C. 725, after the taking
of Alexandria, and at the height of Augustus's popularity on his return to
Rome. Ritter argues strongly in favour of the later date, A.U.C. 732. The
prodigies described in the earlier verses are those which followed the death
of Julius Cæsar, A.U.C. 710, and Horace therefore, at the opening of the
poem, transports himself in imagination to that time—See Orelli's excursus,
Macleane's introduction, and Ritter's procœmium. On the merit of the ode
itself opinion differs. By some it is highly praised for its imagery, the
delicacy with which it flatters Augustus, and the humane art with which
it insinuates that his noblest revenge for his uncle's murder is in becoming
the protector and father of his people. Against this praise it may be said,
not without reason, that the poem has blemishes of a kind from which
Horace is free in odes of similar importance ; that there is something forced
and artificial in the kind of humour admitted into the description of
Pyrrha's flood ; that the idea of the uxorious River bursting his banks out
of complaisance to the complaints of his wife is little better than a frigid

conceit; and that the "extravanga2a" contained in the transfiguration of Mercury into the earthly form of Augustus, fails in that manliness of genuine enthusiasm with which Horace celebrates Augustus in Odes B. III. and IV. Whatever weight may be attached to these objections, they suffice to render the ode one of the most difficult to translate so as to impress an English reader with some sense of the beauties ascribed to it by its admirers.

Now of dire hail and snow enough the Sire
Has launched on earth, and with a red right hand
Smiting the sacred Capitolian heights *
    Startled the City,

Startled the nations, lest the awful age
Of Pyrrha, wailing portents new, return,
When Proteus up to visit mountain-peaks
    Drove his whole sea-flock,

When fishes meshed in topmost boughs of elms
Floundered amidst the doves' familiar haunts,
And deer, through plains † above the old plains heapen,
    Swam panic-stricken.

We have seen the tawny Tiber, with fierce waves
Wrenched violent back from vents in Tuscan seas,
March on to Numa's hall and Vesta's shrine,‡
    Menacing downfall;

Vaunting himself the avenger of the wrong
By Ilia too importunately urged,
The uxorious River leftward burst his banks,
    Braving Jove's anger.§

* "Sacras—arces," the sacred buildings on the Capitoline Hill.
  † 'Et superjecto pavidæ natarunt
      Æquore damæ."
"Æquor" is a plain or level surface, whether of land or sea. The former appears to have been its original and simple meaning, though the poets applied it afterwards to the latter (Cicero, Acad. 2). Though the word here implies "water," the point would be lost in so translating it. There would be no prodigy in deer swimming through water—the prodigy is in their swimming through plains cast over those on which they had been accustomed to range.
  ‡ The palace of Numa adjoined the temple of Vesta at the foot of Mount Palatine. Fea says that the Church of Sta Maria Liberatrice occupies this site.
  § Ilia, mother of Romulus, was, according to legend, thrown into the Tiber by Amulius—hence the fable that she became wife to the god of that river. She complains to her husband of the murder of Julius Cæsar, to whom she

Thinned by parental crime, the younger race
Shall hear how citizens made sharp the steel
By which should rather have been slain the Mede :
         Hear—of what battles !

Who is the god this people shall invoke
To save a realm that rushes to its fall ?
By what new prayer shall sacred virgins tire
         Vesta to hearken ?

To whom shall Jove assign the part of guilt's
Blest expiator ?   Come, at last, we pray,
With shoulder brightening through the stole of cloud,
         Augur Apollo !

Or com'st thou rather, Venus, laughing queen,
Ringed by the hovering play of Mirth and Love ;
Or satiate with, alas, too lengthened sport,
         Thou, Parent War-god,

Joying in battle-clang and glancing helms
And the grim aspect of the unhorsed Moor,*
Fixing his death-scowl on the gory foe,
         Come, if regarding

Thine own neglected race, thine offspring, come !
Or thou, mild Maia's wingèd son, transformed
To mortal youth,† submitting to be called
         Cæsar's avenger ;

claims affinity. The special reason for Jove's displeasure at the river-god's
incursion on the left bank is variously conjectured : it may be either that
on that side he threatened the temple of Jove himself, or that Jove, as
supreme guardian of all temples and of Rome itself, resented the outbreak
as an offence to himself, or, as Macleane interprets it, " He disapproved the
presumption of the river-god, because he had reserved the task of expiation
for other hands and happier means.'
    * All recent editors have " Mauri peditis."   Munro, though retaining that
reading in his text, is " not convinced that ' Marsi peditis ' is not far finer
and more appropriate."   The Moors fighting habitually on horseback, the
interpretation of " peditis " most favoured by the commentators is that in
the translation ; the rider being unhorsed is rendered more fierce and stubborn by despair.
    † Mercury in the form of Augustus. Orelli dryly observes that Augustus
was forty years old at the date when he is here called " juvenem." No doubt
" juvenis " and " adolescens " were words descriptive of any age between
" pueritia " and " senectus," and Cicero called himself " adolescens " at the

Stay thy return to heaven : long tarry here
Well pleased to be this Roman people's guest,
Nor with our vices wroth, untimely soar,
    Rapt by the whirlwind.

Here rather in grand triumphs take glad rites,
Here love the name of Father and of Prince,
No more unpunished let the Parthian ride,
    Thou our chief—Cæsar.*

ODE III.

ON VIRGIL'S VOYAGE TO ATHENS.

There is a well-known dispute as to the date, and the occasion of this ode, and it has been even called in question whether the Virgil addressed were the poet. It is, no doubt, difficult to reconcile the received chronology of the publication of the first three books of Odes with the supposition that this ode was addressed to Virgil the poet, on the occasion of the voyage to Athens, from which he only returned to die : but there is no reason why Virgil should not have made or contemplated such a voyage before the last one ; and Macleane, here agreeing with Dillenburger, is "inclined to think such must have been the case."—See his introduction to this ode.

So may the goddess who rules over Cyprus,
    So may the brothers of Helen, bright stars,
So may the Father of Winds, while he fetters
    All, save Iapyx, the Breeze of the West,

age of forty-four, when he crushed the conspiracy of Catiline ; but still a "juvenis" of forty, or even of thirty years old, would have little resemblance to the popular effigies of the smooth-faced son of Maia (Mercury) ; and considering the whole space of time which this poem reviews and condenses, starting from the death of Julius Cæsar, is it not probable that Horace here applies the word "juvenis" to Augustus in reference to the age in which he first announced himself as "Cæsaris ultor" (Cæsar's avenger), and in order to achieve that name and fulfil that object descended from his celestial rank as Mercury, or (to define more clearly the mythical functions of Mercury) as the direct messenger from Jove to man ? Augustus, then, was a youth in every sense of the word. In fact he was barely twenty when he declared it to be his resolve and his mission to avenge the death of his uncle. At that age, judging by his effigies in gems, the resemblance of the young Octavius to the face of Mercury in the statues is sufficiently striking to have created general remark, and to save from extravagant flattery the lines in the ode. For of the two faces that of the young Octavius is of a higher and more godlike type of beauty than appears in any extant statue of Mercury.

* "The way in which he introduces the name of Cæsar unexpectedly at the end, has always appeared to me an instance of consummate art."—MACLEANE.

Speed thee, O Ship, as I pray thee to render *
   Virgil, a debt duly lent to thy charge,
Whole and intact on the Attican borders,
   Faithfully guarding the half of my soul.

Oak and brass triple encircled his bosom,
   Who first to fierce ocean consigned a frail bark,
Fearing not Africus, when, in wild battle,
   Headlong he charges the blasts of the North;

Fearing no gloom in the face of the Hyads;
   Fearing no rage of mad Notus, than whom,
Never a despot more absolute wieldeth
   Hadria, to rouse her or lull at his will.

What the approach by which Death could have daunted
   Him who with eyelids unmoistened beheld
Monster forms gliding and mountain waves swelling,
   And the grim Thunder-Crags dismally famed?

Vainly by wastes of an ocean estranging
   God, in his providence, severed the lands,
Vainly if nathless, the ways interdicted
   Be by our vessels profane traversed o'er.

Rushes man's race through the evils forbidden,
   Lawlessly bold to brave all things and bear:
Lawlessly bold did the son of the Titan
   Bring to the nations fire won through a fraud.

Fire stolen thus from the Dome Empyrèan,
   Meagre Decay swooped at once on the earth,
Leagued with a new-levied army of Fevers—
   Death, until then the slow-comer, far off,

---

* I side with Dillenburger, Ritter, Munro, and Macleane in rejecting the punctuation of Orelli, who places a comma before "precor," putting the word in parenthesis, for the reason thus ably stated in the following note, for which I am indebted to a friend, than whom there is no higher authority in critical scholarship: "It is not commonly observed, but certainly true, that the 2d pers. pres. subj. (reddas) is never used as a mere imperative, = 'redde.' It may be used *precatively* in addressing a deity, a superior (or in politeness), as 'serves' in Ode xxxv. l. 29. Where it is used with 'precor,' the verb is not in parenthesis, but distinctly governs 'reddas,' 'I pray you to render.' There should therefore be no comma between them; and this view shows 'precor' to be the true apodosis of the passage."

Hurried his stride, and stood facing his victim ;
　　Dædalus sounded the void realms of air,
Borne upon wings that to man are not given :
　　Hercules burst through the portals of hell.

Nought is too high for the daring of mortals ;
　　Heav'n's very self in our folly we storm.
Never is Jove, through our guilty aspiring,
　　Suffered to lay down the bolt we provoke.

ODE IV.

TO LUCIUS SESTIUS.

The Lucius Sestius here addressed was the son of the Sestius or Sextius
defended by Cicero in an oration still extant.　Lucius served under Brutus
in Macedonia, and after his chieftain's death continued to honour his
memory and preserve his images.　He did not on that account incur the
displeasure of Augustus, who made him Consul Suffectus in his own place,
B.C. 23.
　There is no other ode in this metre, which has its name (Archilochian)
from Archilochus of Paros.　The difference in rhythm between the first and
second verse of the strophe is remarkable, and suggests the idea of being
chanted by two voices in alternate lines.

Keen winter melts in glad return of spring and soft Fa-
　　　　vonius ;
　　And the dry keels the rollers seaward draw ;
No more the pens allure the flock, no more the hearth the
　　　　ploughman ;
　　Nor glint the meadows white with rime-frost hoar—

Beneath the overhanging moon, now Venus leads her
　　　　dances,
　　And comely Graces, linked with jocund Nymphs,
Shake with alternate foot the earth, while ardent Vulcan
　　　　kindles
　　The awful forge in which the Cyclops toils,*

* Venus dances—Vulcan toils : *i. e.* in spring man reawakens both to
pleasure and labour.　"*Urit*"—"Though I have retained the ordinary
reading of editions here, I believe that MS. authority, properly interpreted,
indicates *uissit* (*i. e. visit*, as Bentley and, before him, Rutgersius read) . .
Venus dancing in the moonshine, while her husband is away visiting the
stithies of the Cyclops, is a beautiful picture."—MUNRO, Introduction,
xxix. xxx.　See there the elaborate argument by which this eminent
scholar supports the reading he would prefer.

Now well becomes anointed brows to wreathe with verdant
    myrtle,
  Or such rath flowers as swards, relaxing, free ;
And well becomes the votive lamb, or kid if more it please
    him,
  Offered to Faunus amid shadowy groves.

Pale Death with foot impartial knocks alike at each man's
    dwelling,
  The huts of beggars and the towers of kings.
Blest Sestius, life's brief sum forbids commencing hope too
    lengthened ;
  Ev'n now press on thee Night and storied ghosts,

And Pluto's meagre hall, which gained, the wine-king's
    reign is over—
  No more the die allots the frolic crown.*
     *   *   *   *   *

ODE V.

TO PYRRHA.

I cannot presume to attempt any rhymeless version of this ode in juxta-
position with Milton's famous translation, which I therefore annex. "Any
resemblance between the metre he selects and that of the original depends,"
as Mr. Conington observes, " rather on the length of the respective lines
than on any similarity in the cadences," and his rhythm is perhaps somewhat
too cramped to convey the lyrical spirit in lighter and livelier odes of the
same measure in the original ;—even in this translation such contractions as

    "T' whom thou untried seem'st fair ! Me, in my vowed
      Picture, the sacred wall declares t' have hung "—

are not without a certain harshness. But all minor defects are amply com-
pensated by the masterly closeness and elegance of the general version.
The metre is ranked with the Asclepiadeans, and is repeated, Book I. 14, 21,
23 ; III. 7, 13 ; IV. 13.

---

  * The Romans chose by cast of the die the symposiarch or king of the
feast.

What slender youth, bedewed with liquid odours,*
Courts thee on roses in some pleasant cave,†
  Pyrrha? for whom bind'st thou
    In wreaths thy golden hair,

Plain in thy neatness? O, how oft shall he
On faith and changèd gods complain, and seas
  Rough with black winds, and storms
    Unwonted shall admire!

Who now enjoys thee credulous, all gold,
Who always vacant, always amiable
  Hopes thee, of flattering gales
    Unmindful. Hapless they

T'whom thou untried seem'st fair! Me, in my vowed
Picture, the sacred wall declares t'have hung
  My dank and dropping weeds
    To the stern god of sea.‡

ODE VI.

TO M. VIPSANIUS AGRIPPA.

No public man among the partisans of Augustus is more remarkable for the union of extraordinary talents with extraordinary fortune than the Vipsanius Agrippa to whom this ode is addressed. Sprung from a very obscure family, he might have failed in obtaining a fair career for his powers but for the accident of being a fellow-student with the young Octavius at Apollonia. He thus, at the age of twenty, became one of the most intimate associates, and one of the most influential advisers, of the

---

* The reader will observe that the first line is the only one in the translation which ends with a dissyllable. Whether Milton makes this variation of the rhythm he selects through oversight or intention, the reader can conjecture for himself. Probably Milton regarded the two first lines of each strophe simply as heroic blank verse, in which the termination of a monosyllable or dissyllable is optional.

† "Grato, Pyrrha, sub antro." "Some pleasant cave" appears scarcely to give the sense of the original. "Antrum" means the grotto attached to the houses of the luxurious, and in which was placed a statue of Venus. Grottoes are still in use among the richer Italians, and it is not *some* cave to which Horace alludes, but with a certain tenderness of reproach to *the* grotto in which Pyrrha had been accustomed to receive him.

‡ "Potenti—maris deo" Milton translates "the stern god of sea," not observing that "potens" governs "maris," as "potens Cypri."—MACLEANE.

future emperor of the world. While he was yet in youth he had achieved
the highest distinctions, and secured the most eminent station. He had
passed through the office of prætor and consul, and established, by a series
of brilliant successes, the fame of a great general. As a naval commander
he became yet more illustriously distinguished. He constructed the Roman
navy; defeated Sextus Pompeius, then master of the sea; commanded the
fleet against M. Antony; and the victory at Actium was mainly owing to
his skill. It was soon after that last victory that this ode is supposed to
have been written. All the honours Augustus could confer were heaped on
him; the emperor united him to his own family, first by a marriage with his
niece Marcella, subsequently, yet more closely, by marriage with his
daughter Julia. Fortune never deserted Agrippa to the close of his life at
the age of fifty-one. His character seems to have been a union of qualities
rarely found together,—sagacity of design, rapidity of action, a brilliant
genius in construction, devoted to practical purposes. When he was forming
a fleet he turned the Lucrine Lake into a harbour for a school to the
mariners by whom he afterwards defeated the tried sailors of Sextus
Pompeius. As ædile his first care was to supply Rome with water, restoring
the Appian, Marcian, and Anienian aqueducts, and building a new one
fifteen miles long from the Tepula to Rome. With this utility of purpose
he combined great magnificence in taste, adorning the city with public
buildings and statues by the ablest artists he could find. All these daring
and splendid qualities were accompanied by a modesty or a prudence which
preserved the affection of the people and avoided all chance of exciting the
jealousy of Augustus. He twice refused a triumph.

The reader will observe with what ease Horace avoids all servility in the
brief homage he delicately renders to Agrippa, and the playfulness of the
concluding stanza would seem to intimate a certain familiarity of intercourse, or at all events that there was nothing in the temper of Agrippa,
two years younger than himself, so austere as to be shocked by the poet's
favourite subjects for song. Of the poems of Varius, to whose muse Horace
refers the due celebration of Agrippa's deeds, only a few fragmentary lines
have been preserved. Among these is the description of a hound, which is
vigorous and striking. The fragment has been imitated by Virgil, whom he
preceded as an epic poet. His tragedy of "Thyestes" seems to have survived in repute his epics, since Quintilian does not mention those, while he
accords to "Thyestes" the high praise of saying "that it might have stood
comparison with any of the Greek dramatic master-pieces."

'Tis by Varius that Song, borne on pinions Homeric,
Shall exalt thy renown as the valiant and victor,
Whatsoe'er the bold soldier by land or by ocean
       With thee for his leader achieved.

Themes so lofty we slight ones attempt not, Agrippa,
Not the terrible wrath of Pelides unyielding,
Not the course through strange seas of the crafty * Ulysses,
       Not the fell House of Pelops, we sing.

* "*Duplicis*—Ulixei." Horace very naturally, in speaking of Ulysses,
adopts the characteristic epithet employed from the Greek. In Latin
"duplex" is very rarely used in the sense of crafty or deceitful. I know
not of any other instance in which it is so used by the Latin poets except in
Catullus, lxviii. 51, "duplex Amathusia."

While the Muse that presides over lute-strings unwarlike,
And my own sense of shame would forbid me to lessen,
By the inborn defect of a genius unequal,
    The glories of Cæsar and thee.

Who can worthily sing Mars in adamant tunic,
Or Merion all grim with the dust-cloud of Ilion,
Or Tydides, when, thanks to the favour of Pallas,
    He stood forth a match for the gods?

We of feasts, we of battles, on youths rashly daring
Waged by maids armed with nails too well pared for much
    slaughter,
Sing, devoid of love's flame; or, if somewhat it scorch us,
    Still wont to make light of the pain.

ODE VII.

TO PLANCUS.

This ode is generally supposed to be addressed to L. Munatius Plancus,
than whom those versatile times did not engender a more selfish renegade
or a more ungrateful traitor. Estré, loath to grant that Horace condescended
to immortalise this person (who, however, contrived to make himself important to all parties, and died safe, wealthy, and honoured at least by
Augustus, who even conferred upon him the censorship, B.C. 27), thinks
that it was some other Plancus, possibly his son, designated as Munatius,
Lib. I. Ep. iii. v. 31. Horace, however, in this ode does not ascribe any
virtues to the person addressed at variance with the general character of the
successful renegade, and only bids him not take grief much to heart, but
enjoy himself as much as he could, whether in the camp or at his villa—an
admonition which he was not likely to disregard. The measure of the ode
takes its name from Alcman. It consists of a complete hexameter alternated with a verse made up of the last four feet of a hexameter. Horace
only employs this metre twice again, Book I. Ode xxviii., and Epode xii.

Other bards shall extol brilliant Rhodes, Ephesus, or
    Mytilene,
  Or, queen of two seas, stately Corinth,
Embattled Thebes, famous through Bacchus, Delphi as
    famed through Apollo,
  Or Thessaly's beautiful Tempè.

Some are whose sole task is to laud the city of Pallas
    the spotless,
Prolonging the hymn into Epic,*
On every side plucking a leaf to garland their brows with
    the olive ;
And many, in honour of Juno,

Tell of Argos, the breeder of steeds, and the rich stores of
    Mycenæ ;
But me more have stricken with rapture
Than patient Laconia's defiles, than fertile Larissa's ex-
    panses
The grot of Albunea † resounding,

The Anio's precipitous rush, the woodlands and orchards of
    Tibur,
All dewy with quick-winding waters.
As the white southern wind often clears clouds from a sky
    at its darkest,
Nor teems with a rain that is lasting,

So, Plancus, let those weary hours, when life seems but
    labour and sorrow,
Be lulled to their end in the wine-cup ;
Whether camps with banners ablaze hold thee now, or
    shall hold thee hereafter
The thick-leavëd shades of thy Tibur,

When from Salamis and from his sire, Teucer was passing
    to exile,
'Tis said that he crowned with the poplar ‡
Brows first besprinkled with drops from the strength-giving
    boon of Lyæus,
To friends as they sorrowed thus speaking :

* " Carmine perpetuo celebrare." I adopt the interpretation of Orelli,
Macleane, and Yonge—a continuous poem, like an epic, culling all the asso-
ciations and myths connected with Athens, and formed into a whole like
Ovid's Metamorphoses.
† Albunea, the Sibyl, who gave her name to a grove and fountain, and
apparently to a grotto at Tibur.
‡ Emblematic of courage and adventure. The poplar was consecrated
to Hercules.

"Go WE wheresoever a fate more kind than the heart of a
    parent
May bear us, associates and comrades;
Despair of nought, Teucer your chief—of nought under
    auspice of Teucer,
Unerring Apollo predicts us

"A Salamis built on new soil, which Fame shall confound
    with the lost one; *
Brave friends who have borne with me often
Worse things as men, let the wine chase to-day every care
    from the bosom,
To-morrow—again the great Waters."

ODE VIII.

TO LYDIA.

This ode has been paraphrased by Henry Luttrell into that elegant and
playful satire upon the manners of his own day, called "Advice to Julia."
The names are clearly fictitious. Whether the persons designated by the
names existed is another matter—probably enough: their types are always
existing. There is no reason for supposing the various Lydias whom
Horace addresses were the same person; every reason, judging by the
internal evidence of the several poems, to suppose they were not. There is
no other ode in this metre.

By all gods, Lydia, say
Why haste to ruin Sybaris thro' loving?
    Why has the Campus grown
To him, of dust and sun so patient,—hateful?

'Mid comates why no more
Parades that martial rider, with sharp wolf-bit
    Breaking in Gallic † mouths?
Why shuns that athlete oil

* "Ambiguam tellure nova Salamina futuram"—a new Salamis, which
might in future be confounded with the old one. The new Salamis was
in Cyprus.
    † "Gallica nec lupatis
    Temperat orat frenis."

Gallic mouths—horses from Gaul. These were considered very high
mettled, but, when well broken-in, so serviceable in war that they were
in great request in the Roman cavalry. "Lupatis," a bit, jagged liked
wolves' teeth.

More than the froth of vipers ; why no longer
  Baring arms nobly bruised ;
He, for so many a feat of dart and discus
  Hurled beyond mark—renowned ?

Where lurks he, as the son of ocean-Thetis
  From funeral fates in Troy
Lurked,—they say—hidden, lest to Lycian squadrons
  And carnage, rapt away
If once detected in the guise of manhood ?

ODE IX.

TO THALIARCHUS.

Thaliarchus signifies in Greek "arbiter bibendi"—commonly translated "feastmaster." Some editors, as Dillenburger and Macleane, refusing to consider it meant to be a proper name, print, "thaliarche," "O feast-master." Orelli and Yonge, however, retain the capital T, and it is perhaps more agreeable to Horace's habit of individualising generals, and is certainly more animated in itself, to consider, with Buttmann, that the word is meant for a proper name, though of course a fictitious one, and invented to signify the official character of the person addressed. I may also add that there is no instance, I believe, in Latin authors, in which the word thaliarchus is used as a feastmaster ; and that, therefore, if Horace did not mean it to be considered a proper name, it would have been unintelligible to those of his readers who did not understand Greek ; and to those who did, would have appeared a pedantic affectation, which was precisely the reproach that a man of Horace's good taste and keen sense of the ridiculous would not voluntarily have incurred. The references to the manner in which Thaliarchus may spend his day, all belong to the life of a town ; and there is no reason to suppose the scene otherwise than at Rome. Walckenaer says that the isolated and singular form of Soracte strikes the eye on quitting the city by one of the two gates to the north.

Though, to judge by a fragment preserved in Athenæus, the poem is more or less imitated from an ode by Alcæus, the scene and manners are altogether Roman ; in fact, the more the fragments left of Greek poets are fairly compared with the verses in which they are imitated by Horace, the more Horace's originality in imitating becomes conspicuous.

See how white in the deep-fallen snow stands Soracte !
Labouring forests no longer can bear up their burden ;
  And the rush of the rivers is locked,
    Halting mute in the gripe of the frost.

Thaw the cold; more and more on the hearth heap the
    fagots—
More and more bringing bounteously out, Thaliarchus,
    The good wine that has mellowed four years
      In the great Sabine two-handled jar.

Leave the rest to the gods, who can strike into quiet
Angry winds in their war with the turbulent waters,
    Till the cypress stand calm in the sky—
      Till there stir not a leaf on the ash.

Shun to seek what is hid in the womb of the morrow;
Count the lot of each day as clear gain in life's ledger;
    Spurn not thou, who art young, dulcet loves;
      Spurn not, thou, choral dances and song,

While the hoar-frost morose keeps aloof from thy verdure.
Thine the sports of the Campus,* the gay public gardens;
    Thine at twilight the words whispered low;
      Each in turn has its own happy hour:

Now for thee the sweet laugh of the girl—which betrays
    her
Hiding slyly within the dim nook of the threshold,
    And the love-token snatched from the wrist,
      Or the finger's not obstinate hold.

ODE X.

TO· MERCURY.

The scholiast Porphyrion says this ode was taken from Alcæus, who, he
asserts, and Pausanias confirms it, invented the story about Apollo's cows or

---

* "Campus et arcæ"—the Campus Martius, in which, in the forenoon,
athletic sports were practised, and the public promenades (areæ) in different
parts of the city, and especially round the temples, which were the resort of
loungers in the afternoon. Orelli thus gracefully elucidates the concluding
verse. "The scene," he says, "is this: the lover goes at the appointed
hour to the door of his mistress, which stands ajar; he calls upon her with
low whispers: the girl keeps silence, having playfully hid herself behind
the threshold, until at last she betrays herself by her laugh. The lover
then rushes in, and carries off as a love-pledge her bracelet or ring, after a
struggle on her part not too pertinaciously coy."

oxen. The story is celebrated in the Homeric hymn to Hermes, as well as
the invention of the lyre by stringing a tortoise-shell, at whatever date that
hymn was written. Horace always ascribes to Mercury the characteristics
of the Greek Hermes, with whom the Mercurius of the Latins had little in
common.

Mercury, thou eloquent grandson of Atlas,
Who didst the rude manners of earth's early races
First mould into form, both by graceful Palæstra,*
    And by skilled language—

Of thee will I sing, to great Jove and Olympus
Light herald ;—sing thee of wreathed lute the inventor,
So cunning to hide whatsoe'er the whim took thee
    Gaily to pilfer.

When Phœbus in wrath sought to frighten thy childhood
If thou didst not restore the kine tricksomely stolen,
While threatening his shafts he was robbed of his
    quiver;
    Laughed out Apollo !

So too, led by thee, Priam bearing his treasures
From Ilion, eluded the vaunting Atridæ,†
The watchlights of Thessaly and the remorseless
    Tents of the Argive.

Thou placest pure souls in the calm of blest dwellings,
With golden staff shepherding ghost-flocks of shadow
To gods, whether throned in Olympus or Hades,
    Equally welcome.

* No English paraphrase can adequately render Palæstra, which was
especially attributed to the invention of Hermes. It appears to have been
originally distinct from the gymnasia, and appropriated chiefly to the
training of the athletæ in wrestling and the Pancratium. When towards
the decline of the Republic the Romans imitated the Greeks in these and
other less manly customs, they attached to their villas places for exercise
called indiscriminately Gymnasia or Palæstræ. The meaning of the stanza
is that Mercury taught the early races how to discipline body by skilled
exercise, and express thought by cultivated language; and I agree with
Orelli in construing "voce" thus, and not as song or music, which is rather
the gift of Apollo.
† "Quin et Atridas." Here Horace abruptly elevates the astuteness of
Mercury from the playful thefts of infancy to the wise caution with which
he leads the innocent and helpless through the severest dangers ; and then
naturally, and with all his inimitable terseness, the poet represents him as
conducting no less safely the souls of the dead. Throughout all these stanzas,

ODE XI.

TO LEUCONOË.

The desire to solve the doubts by which man is beset in the present, will, perhaps, so long as the world lasts, give an audience to those who pretend to divine the future; and of all modes of divination, astrology has been, from time immemorial, the most imposing, because it arrogates the rank of a science, and asserts that it bases its predictions upon deductions from a vast accumulation of facts. Rome, of course, abounded in astrologers, who called themselves Chaldæans, as Cicero calls them; and were probably as much Chaldæans as the Gipsies of Norwood are Bohemians or Indians. Horace gives his fair friend a brief admonition, which, in proof of the common-sense that keeps him always modern, might be equally given to ladies, and even to the ruder sex, in our own day. For wherever we travel in England or Europe, it is rare to find a town, however deficient in books, in which a prophetic astrological almanac may not be seen in the shop-windows.

Nay, Leuconoë, seek not to fathom what death unto me
    —unto thee
(Lore forbidden) the gods may assign; nor the schemes
    of the Chaldee consult.*
How much better it is whatsoever the future shall bring
    to endure!
Whether Jove may vouchsafe our existence more winters,
    or this be the last,

Which now breaks Tuscan ocean in spray on the time-
    eaten rocks that oppose,
Be thou wise; strain thy wine from the lees; and to
    space which thine eye can survey
Cut the length thou allottest to hope. While we talk—
    grudging Time will be gone;
Seize the present; as little as may, confide in a morrow
    beyond.

from the theft of oxen, when Mercury was an infant in his cradle, to his crowning mission as the conductor of souls departed, the same ruling idea of *stealth* is preserved and deified. Mercury steals the kine from Apollo, he steals Priam through the Grecian camp, he steals souls through the passage between earth and Hades,—all with a union of guarded secrecy and imperturbable serenity which, throughout the more playful attributes of Hermes, imply the grandeur and inspire the awe that characterise a supernatural being. No deity can be more exclusively Greek in this combination of open joyousness and mystic power. It was a type of divinity as impossible to be conceived by the Latins as by the Germanic and Scandinavian races, though they all worshipped a Mercurius.

    * "Nec Babylonios tentaris numeros,"—*i. e.* the astrological calculations, or, in technical phrase, "schemes," for which the Chaldees were so famous.

ODE XII.

IN CELEBRATION OF THE DEITIES AND THE WORTHIES OF ROME.

This poem is commonly inscribed very inappropriately "De Augusto," and sometimes more accurately "De laudibus Deorum vel hominum." It was certainly composed before the death of the young Marcellus, A.U.C. 731; and Orelli and Macleane agree in accepting Franke's date, A.U.C. 729.

What man, what hero, or what god select'st thou,
Theme for sweet lyre or fife sonorous, Clio?
Whose honoured name shall that gay sprite-voice, Echo,
          Hymn back rebounding,

Whether on Helicon's umbrageous margent,
Whether on heights of Pindus or cold Hæmus,
Whence woods, at random, vocal Orpheus followed?
          He who stayed rivers

In their swift course, and winds in their wild hurry
By art maternal;* and with bland enchantment
Led the huge oaks at his melodious pleasure
          List'ning his harp-strings.

Whom should I place for wonted rites of homage
Before the Father-King of gods and mortals,
Who earth, and ocean, and heaven's varying seasons †
          Orders and tempers,

From whom not greater than Himself proceedeth—
To whom exists no semblance and no second?
Yet where he hath a nearest, be its honours
          Sacred to Pallas.

Left not unsung be Liber, bold in battle;
Nor she, the brute-world's foe—virgin Diana;
Nor thou, dread Lord of the unerring arrow,
          Phœbus Apollo.

* "Arte materna"—the Muse Calliope, mother of Orpheus.
          † "Qui mare ac terras variisque mundum
                    Temperat horis."
"Mundum" here means "cœlum," "sky"—i. e. the whole framework of nature, in sea, earth, and heaven, is under the dominion of Jove.

Sing let me, too, the demigod Alcides,
And Leda's twins, the rider and the athlete—
At whose joint star, what time on storm-beat seamen
    Dawns its white splendour,

Back from the rocks recedes the rush of waters,
Winds fall, clouds fly, and every threatening billow,
Lulled at their will, upon the breast of ocean
    Sinks into slumber.

Should, after these, be Romulus first honoured,
Numa's calm reign, or Tarquin's haughty fasces?
I pause in doubt; or is it rather Cato's
    Noble self-slaughter?

Regulus, and the Scauri,* and Æmilius
Lavish of his great life when Carthage triumphed,
Grateful I name for song's most signal honours;—
    Thee, too, Fabricius;

He and rude unkempt Curius and Camillus,—
These were the men whom hardy thrift, rude nurture,
The ancestral farm, and unluxurious homestead
    Fitted for warfare.

Tree-like grows up through unperceived increases
Marcellus' † fame. As the moon throned in heaven
'Mid lesser lights, the Julian constellation
    Shines out resplendent.

Father and Guardian of all human races,
Saturnian Jove, to thee the Fates have given
Charge o'er great Cæsar; mayst thou reign supremely,
    Next to thee Cæsar.

* Either the Scauri enjoyed at that time a higher reputation than they have retained in history, or Horace had some special reason, personal or political, now inexplicable, for placing them in the rank of Rome's foremost worthies. Æmilius Paulus, having advised the disastrous battle of Cannæ, refused the horse offered to him by a tribune of the soldiers, and remained to perish on the field.

† "As the name of Marcellus, whom I understand, with Orelli, to be the Marcellus who took Syracuse, stands for all his family, and particularly the young Marcellus, so the star of Julius Cæsar, and the lesser lights of that family, are meant by what follows."—MACLEANE.

Whether the Parthians over Rome impending
Grace his full* triumph, or the farthest dwellers,
Indian and Seric, upon Orient margins
    Under the sunrise,†

Wide earth with justice he shall rule, thy viceroy;
With awful chariot Thou shalt shake Olympus;
Thou through the sacred groves profaned impurely
    Launch angry lightnings.‡

ODE XIII.

TO LYDIA.

    In this ode is expressed naturally enough the sort of jealousy which a Lydia would be likely to inspire in a general lover, such as Horace represents himself in his poems—"sive quid urimur non præter solitum leves." The ode in itself, whether borrowed or not from a Greek original, is replete with the elegance which characterises Horace's love-poems, and there is a tenderness which seems genuine and heartfelt in the concluding stanza.

    The metre in Horace is the same as in Ode iii., but no English measure seems to me so well to express the sense and spirit of the ode as the graver and more elegiac form in which the translation is cast.

When thou the rosy neck of Telephus,
    The waxen arms of Telephus, art praising,
Woe is me, Lydia, how my jealous heart
    Swells with the anguish I would vainly smother.

---

* "Justo triompho." "'Justo,' 'regular, full, complete,' in which sense this adjective is attached to such nouns as exercitus, legio, acies, prælium, victoria."—YONGE.

† "Sive subjectos Orientis oræ
    Seras et Indos."

The Seres, whom some conjecture to be the Chinese, represent the nations at the farthest east known to the Romans. "Subjectos oræ," " unde the edge or extremity of the East."—YONGE.

‡ "Tu gravi curru quaties Olympum,
    Tu parum castis inimica mittes
    Fulmina lucis."

The general meaning seems to be, that Jove left the political government of earth to Augustus, his vicegerent; but he reserved to himself alone the dominion of heaven, and the task of avenging such crimes as offended the gods, or polluted the sanctity of the temples.

Then in my mind thought has no settled base.
   To and fro shifts upon my cheek the colour,
And tears that glide adown in stealth reveal
   By what slow fires mine inmost self consumeth.

I burn, or whether quarrel o'er his wine,
   Stain with a bruise dishonouring thy white shoulders,
Or whether my boy-rival on thy lips
   Leave by a scar the mark of his rude kisses.

Hope not, if thou wouldst hearken unto me,
   That one so little kind prove always constant ;
Barbarous indeed to wound sweet lips imbued
   By Venus with a fifth part of her nectar.*

Thrice happy, ay more than thrice happy, they
   Whom one soft bond unbroken binds together,
Whose love, serene from bickering and reproach,
   Ends not before the day when life is ended.

ODE XIV.

THE SHIP—AN ALLEGORY.

I know not what safer title for this poem can be selected from the many assigned to it in the MSS. All or most critics nowadays are agreed that it is a political allegory, and not, as Grævius, Bentley, and others contended, an address to the actual ship that brought Horace from Philippi, and in which his friends were about to re-embark. Quinctilian illustrates the meaning of the word "allegory" by a reference to the ode, and the ode itself is an imitation of an allegorical poem by Alcæus on the political troubles of Mitylene, of which a fragment is extant. Quinctilian's interpretation of the allegory, though still popularly received—viz., that the ship means the Commonwealth or Republic—is not without eminent disputants ; and unless there were more assured data as to the time in which the poem was written, and under what political circumstances, the dispute is not likely to be settled. The opinion advanced by Acron and supported with

---

* "Quinta parte sui nectaris." It has been disputed whether Horace means by this expression the Pythagorean quintessence, which is ether. Most modern translators so take it—"an interpretation," says Macleane, "which I am surprised to find Orelli adopts with others, that does not commend itself to my mind at all." Neither does it to mine. I think the interpretation rendered by Dillenburger much less pedantic and much more poetical. The ancients supposed that honey contained a ninth or tenth part of nectar, and therefore the lips of Lydia were imbued with double the nectar bestowed on honey.

x

much force by Buttmann is, that the poem is addressed, not to the Commonwealth, but to a remnant of the political party with which Horace had
fought under Brutus, and in remonstrance against their launching once
more into civil war under Sextus Pompeius. This view has been somewhat
rudely assailed, and the generality of critics remain loyal to the good old
simile of Ship and State. But of late the argument of a critic at once so
acute and so profound as Buttmann has been silently gaining ground with
reflective scholars, and has much in its favour. Nothing in itself is more
probable than that Horace should have sought to express to his old comrades
in an allegorical poem his dissuasion from the hazardous junction with
S. Pompeius, and place on record his own vindication for refusing to put
forth in so shattered a vessel, and resting in port—*i. e.* with the government
established under Augustus.

The other supposition most favoured as to the date of the poem is that
which places it in the year before the battle of Actium, when M. Antony
and Augustus were making their preparations for war. This does not seem
so probable a date as the other. The images of the poem would ill accord
with it. Horace could scarcely have said then that the ship under Augustus
was disabled, destitute of rowers and chiefs, and could not last through a
storm; and as in that war Cæsar went forth against Antony rather than
Antony against Cæsar, the expostulation to keep in port would have been
very ill received by Augustus, and very contrary to the spirit with which
Horace always speaks of that war and its results, and to the willingness
expressed in Epode i. to have taken a share in the enterprise, had Mæcenas
been appointed to command in it. At the outbreak of the war with Antony,
Horace was a decided partisan of the established government, and this poem
is evidently written by a man who has affection and fear for those about to
hazard some new enterprise against the existent order of things. He certainly would not have addressed that warning to Antony's supporters.
Whether the poem allegorises the entire Republic, or that party belonging
to it with which Horace had been so intimately connected, and with whose
renewed hazards he declined to associate himself, does not, however, very
materially signify; for a writer who has been a strong party-man generally
has his party in his mind whenever he proposes to address the State. But
if Horace really designed the allegory for his old comrades under Brutus,
about to cast their fortunes with Sextus Pompeius, he could not more
affectionately part from them, nor more delicately imply his own rational
excuses for doing so.

O ship, shall new waves drift thee back into ocean ?
What wouldst thou ? Make fast, O, make fast for the
        haven !
     Ah! dost thou not see how thy sides
        Are all naked of even the rowers ? *

Thy mast by the south wind in fury is shattered,
And loud groan thy mainyards, and scarce,† without
        cables
     Undergirding the keel, couldst thou strive
        With the sway of the tyrannous waters.

* *I. e.*, whether the lines apply to the State or to a party in it, men and
appliances are wanting to the cause.
† "Sine funibus vix durare carinæ." The usual interpretation of

Thy sails are not whole, and the gods thou wouldst
call on
Once more, in the stress of thy peril have left thee,
   August Pontic pine,* though thou art
    Of a forest illustrious the daughter,

All useless the race, and the name that thou vauntest;
Scared sailors trust nought to the stern's painted colours.
   Beware, O beware, lest thou owe
    But a mock to the winds thou wouldst hazard.

Thou, lately the cause of my wearisome trouble,
And now of deep care and regretful affection,
   Mark well where the Cyclades shine,
    And avoid the waves flowing between them.

ODE XV.

THE PROPHECY OF NEREUS.

This ode is considered by critics to bear the stamp of an early composition.
It has certainly the vigour and fire of youth, but it is seldom that the poetry
of youth is equally terse and condensed.

"funibus," "girding-ropes," is here adopted. Macleane construes "deprived of her rigging."—See his note.

  * In translating these lines I feel very strongly how much they favour Acron's opinion and Buttmann's argument for the application of the allegory to the old Brutus party about to share the fortunes of the great Pompey's son, Sextus. The old gods, or the statues of the tutelary deities niched in the stern, were indeed gone; the cry for Republican liberty or Senatorial rights was hushed in the graves of Brutus and Cassius. Assuming with Acron and Buttmann that by the Pontic pine is symbolised Pompey, whose chief successes were achieved in Pontus as the conqueror of Mithridates, his name and race were indeed idly vaunted by Sextus. Recruits distrusted the colours painted on the battered ship to which they were invited. Applying the lines to the cause of the old Brutus party, well might Horace exclaim, "Nuper sollicitum quæ mihi tædium," in reference to the anxieties and to the disgusts with which his share in that cause had subjected him, the loss of friends and hopes and fortune; and well and tenderly might he add, in affection for former comrades and deprecation of the perils they were about to risk, "Nunc desiderium curaque non levis." "Desiderium" is a word that implies affection, and "a missing of something—a regret." The whole of the poem thus construed seems to me in complete harmony with all the poems in which Horace takes a retrospective view of his connection with Brutus's party, and the attachment he retained for his old friends, so strongly evinced in his welcome to Pompeius Varus, Lib. ii. Ode vii.

When the false Shepherd bore through the waters
In Idæan ships, Helen his hostess,
Nereus buried swift winds in loathed slumber
      That Fate's fell decrees he might sing.

" Woe the day that thou lead'st to thy dwelling
Her whom Greece shall ask back by great armies,
Sworn in league to dissolve, with thy nuptials,
      The ancient dominion of Troy.

" Ah ! what death-sweat to war-horse and warrior !
Ah ! what funerals that move with thy rowers
Bring'st thou home to the race of the Dardan !
      Already stern Pallas prepares

" Helm, and ægis, and chariot, and fury ;
Vainly, bold in the safeguard of Venus,
Shalt thou trim thy sleek locks and charm women
      With songs set to chords—not of war ; *

" Vainly shun in thy paramour's chamber †
Pond'rous spears and the darts of the Cretan,
And the roar of the battle ;—and Ajax
      So swift when he follows a foe ;

" Late, alas ! dust shall yet smear thy love-locks.
Lo behind thee, thy race's destroyer,
Lo Ulysses !—lo Nestor !—Thee, Teucer,
      Thee, Sthenelus, skill'd in the fight

" Or the chariot-chase, fearlessly follow :
Merion, too, thou shalt know,—but look yonder,
Through the battle comes raging to find thee
      Tydides, more dread than his sire ! '

" Ah ! from him, as a hart in the valley
Sees the wolf and forgetteth its pasture,
All unnerved and deep-panting thou fliest ;
      Not such was the pledge to thy love.

* " Carmina divides "—i.e., accompany your harp with singing.—YONGE.
† Hom. Il. iii. 381.

"Though the wrath in the fleet of Achilles
Bring a respite to Troy and Troy's mothers;
Ilion's domes, after winters predestined,
        Shall sink in the flames of the Greek!"

ODE XVI.

RECANTATION.

There is no ground for safe conjecture as to the person here addressed.
The old inscriptions applying it to Tyndaris, the daughter of Gratidia, celebrated as Canidia in the Epodes, or the assertion in Cruquius that it is
Gratidia herself, are now generally considered to be purely fictitious.
Horace, no doubt, in his youth wrote a great many satirical or vituperative
poems which he had too good taste to republish, and which, happily for his
fame, have perished altogether. To some lady so libelled we may well
suppose this ode to have been addressed, for it has an air of reality about it.
It may have been suggested by the poem in which Stesichorus recanted his
slanders on Helen, but to what extent Horace here imitates that poem, there
are no means of judging.

O, of mother so fair thou the yet fairer daughter,
To such end as thou wilt put my guilty iambics,
        Fling them into the flames to consume,
            Or the Ocean of Hadria to drown.

Phrygian Cybele, no, nor the Pythian Apollo
In the innermost shrines soul-convulsing his priesthood,
        No, nor Liber, nor Corybants mad
            When their cymbals redouble the clash,

Craze the mind like the woeful disorders of anger,
Which are scared from their vent, nor by Norican falchion,
        Wreckful oceans—untameable fires,
            Nor ev'n Jove though himself thunder down.

It is said that Prometheus to man's primal matter
Was compelled to add something from each living creature,
        And thus from the wild lion he took
            Rabid virus to place in our gall.

Anger shattered in ruins the House of Thyestes;
Anger stands forth the cause by which cities have perished,
        And the ploughshare of insolent hosts
            Has passed over the site of their walls.

Be appeased then : that vehement heat of the bosom
In the sensitive heyday of youth tempted me too,
    And it whirled me all frantic away
      Down the torrent of scurrilous song.

Now I seek to exchange rude emotions for soft ones
Provided my penitence move thee to pardon,
    And my full recantation thus made,
      O be friends, and restore me thy heart.

ODE XVII.

INVITATION TO TYNDARIS.

It is impossible to do more than conjecture whether the person addressed
under the feigned name of Tyndaris actually existed or not.   There are one
tr two touches in the poem which seem to individualise her as a creature of
he earth—such as the selection of one particular song about the rivalry of
Penelope and Circe, which is not a theme especially appropriate to the place
of invitation, and may well have been the favourite song of some fair lute-
player ; and the reference to the jealous violence of Cyrus looks like an
allusion to some incident that had previously occurred.   On the one hand,
nothing is more likely than that Horace should have known, and invited to
his villa, some such accomplished freed-woman as is here addressed.   On the
other hand, nothing is more consonant to his exquisite art than the invention of attributes and incidents for the purpose of giving the interest of
reality to a purely imaginary creation.   A compliment to the beauty of the
person addressed is insinuated by the name of Tyndaris, "as if," says Orelli,
"she were another Helen."

For Lucretilis oft nimble Faunus exchanges,
So delightful its slopes, his Arcadian Lycæus—
    From my she-goats still turning aside
      Rainy winds and the scorch of the sun.

All in safety the waves of the strong-scented husband
Rove where arbute and thyme lurk in woodlands secreted :
    Never green adder daunts them, nor there
      Martial wolf from Hædilia descends,

Whilesoever, my Tyndaris, round and about us
Ring the smooth sheeny lime-rocks of sloping Ustica,
    And the valleys embosomed below,
      With the sweet haunting pipe of the god.

Over me watch the gods with an aspect of favour,
To the gods dear at heart are the muse and my worship.
    Here our rich rural honours shall flow
      From a brimmed cornucopia to thee.

Here, within the deep vale, thou shalt shun the red dog-
    star,
And shalt sing us that tale on the lute strings of Teos,
    How Penelope vied with the Sea's
      Crystal Circe, for one human heart;

Safely here shalt thou quaff, under cool leafy shadows,
Sober cups from the innocent vineyards of Lesbos;
    'Tis not here that gay Semele's son *
      Shall with Mars his encounters confound;

Dread not here lest pert Cyrus, suspecting thee vilely,
Lay rash hands on that form not a match for rude anger,
    Rend the garland which clings to thy hair,
      Or the robe—which deserves no such wrong.

ODE XVIII.

TO VARUS.

Varus was no uncommon name, and it has been a dispute with commentators what Varus is here addressed. It is generally believed to be the Quinctilius Varus for whose death Horace seeks to console Virgil, Ode xxiv. of this Book.

By the way in which Bacchus and Venus are here addressed, Horace implies a temperate and elegant conviviality; Bacchus is hailed as "father," benignant, not cruel; and Venus as "decens"—that is, accompanied with the Graces, "ipsa decens est, cum comites sint decentes Gratiæ" (Carm. I. 4, 6; Dillenburger); and the poet proceeds to contrast a Bacchus and a Venus so characterised with the brawl and lust of the Centaurs, who, invited to the marriage-feast of Peirithous, King of the Lapithæ, attempted in their drunkenness to carry off the bride and the other women, which of course led to a fight with the Lapithæ and with the Sithonians, a people in Thrace, who were afflicted by Bacchus with the curse of never drinking without fighting.

---

* Bacchus.

Of all trees that thou plantest, O Varus, the vine, holy vine
    be the first,
On the soil that surrounds genial Tibur and Catilus' ram-
    parted walls
To the lips of the dry does the godhead taint all with a
    taste of the sour,
And only by wine are the troubles gnawing into the bosom
    dispersed.
Fresh from wine who complains of the hardships he bears
    or in want or in war ?
Who not more hails thee, Bacchus, as father ; thee, Venus,
    as linked with the Grace ?
But Evius himself has forewarned us by his curse on the
    Thracians of old,
And the battle o'er riotous wine-cups which the Centaurs
    with Lapithæ fought,
How the drunkard divides right from wrong by the vanish-
    ing line of his lust,
And not to pass over the limit the Unbinder of Care has
    imposed.
'Tis not I who will shake, comely Bacchus, the thyrsus
    against thy consent,*
Or drag forth to daylight thy symbols covered over with
    manifold leaves.
Silence! hush, savage horn Berecynthian! let the clash of
    the timbrel be hushed,
Making music which Self-conceit follows, dull egotist
    reeling stone blind,
Idle Vainglory over-exalting her empty and arrogant head,
And a Faith which is lavish of secrets,—with bosom more
    seen through than glass.

---

* " Non ego te, candide Bassareu,
    Invitum quatiam, nec variis obsita frondibus
    Sub divum rapiam."

"Quatiam," poetically applied to the god himself, refers to the shaking
of the thyrsus, cymbals, or images in the wild dance of the Orgies.
"Variis obsita frondibus" means the vessels in which the mystical symbols
of Bacchus were concealed, covered over with various leaves, chiefly of vine
and ivy.

ODE XIX.

TO GLYCERA.

Whether Glycera and Cinara be the same person—whether the Glycera here addressed be the same Glycera as is elsewhere mentioned—whether she existed anywhere or under any name except in Horace's fancy—are questions that have been as fiercely debated as if they could be decided, or were of the slightest consequence if they could. The poem itself is charmingly pretty, and has much more the air of complimentary gallantry than of real affection.

Methought I had finished with love
When the mother herself of the Cupids, a merciless mother
    she is,
And the Theban boy, Semele's son,
And the goddess called Wantonness bade me to love again
    render my soul.

Me the beauty of Glycera burns,
Shining out with a delicate light than the marble of Paros
    more pure;
It burns me that dear saucy charm,
And that face in its dazzle too sheen for the eye without
    danger to rest.*

All Venus, in rushing on me
Has deserted her temples in Cyprus. She will not permit
    me to sing
Of Scythian, or Parth who exults
In the feints of the swift-wheeling steeds, or of aught which
    belongs not to love.

Quick, slaves, here! an altar in haste—
Pile it up with the green living sod; hither vervain and
    frankincense bring,
And wine winters two have matured:
Thus appeased by the blood of a victim, more gently the
    goddess may come.

* "Voltus nimium lubricus adspici." This bold expression, which will not bear a translation too literal, is, according to some recent commentators, taken from the glitter and smoothness of ice; as ice is too slippery for the foot, so Glycera's face is too slippery for the gaze. Earlier critics, coupling the previous reference to the Parian marble, suggest that the allusion is

ODE XX.

TO MÆCÊNAS.

Nothing can be more simple in form and spirit than this ode, in which Horace invites Mæcenas to a homely entertainment in language equally unostentatious. In this, as in other of Horace's purely occasional odes, one feels the presence of the genuine poet by his abstemious avoidance of the would-be poetical. The date of the poem has been variously conjectured. Judging by the reference to the Sabine wine which Mæcenas is invited to drink, and which came into use in its second year, reaching its prime in its fourth, the poem would have been written between two and four years after the reception that the audience at the theatre gave to Mæcenas on his recovery from his illness. But the date of that event is not determined. Franke and Lübker refer the composition of the ode to A.U.C. 729–730. Macleane favours the latter year. Orelli inclines to Weber's date, from A.U.C. 726–727.

Sabine wine poor thou'lt drink in modest goblets,
Into Greek cask I myself racked and sealed it,
Knightly and dear Mæcenas, when the applausive
    Theatre hailed thee ;

So that the banks of thine ancestral river,
So that in choral symphony the Sprite-voice
Haunting the Vatican mountain—sportive Echo—
    Rang back the plaudits.

Elsewhere the costly Cæcuban thou quaffest,
Or of the grape tamed in Calenian presses :
No Formian hill-side, no Falernian cluster,
    Flavour my wine-cups.

ODE XXI.

IN PRAISE OF DIANA AND APOLLO.

It was supposed by Franke that this hymn was composed for the first celebration of the quinquennial games—Ludi Actiaci—instituted by Augustus in honour of Apollo and Diana, when he dedicated a temple to Apollo on the Palatine after his return from the taking of Alexandria, A.U.C. 728.

---

rather to a statue like that of Hecate, in the temple of Diana at Ephesus, which Pliny tells us the spectators were warned by the priests not to suffer the eye to rest upon too intently, so blindingly bright was the shine of the marble.

There are two objections to this supposition :—the one, observed by Macleane, is in the word "principe," for Augustus did not get that title till the ides of January, A.U.C. 727, and therefore after the first celebration of the Actian games. The other objection is in the nature of the poem itself, which, as Orelli remarks, is of too light a quill for the ceremonial pomp of solemn games or earnest supplication. The reference to the Persians and Britons at the close would seem to intimate the same date as the 29th Ode of this Book, when Augustus was preparing a military expedition against Britain and the East, viz. A.U.C. 727. The notion of Sanadon, that the ode was an introduction to the Secular Hymn, has long been exploded.

> Hymn ye the praise of Diana, young maidens,
> Hymn ye, O striplings, the unshorn Apollo.
>   And hymn ye Latona, so dear
>   To the Father Supreme in Olympus.
>
> Maidens, sing her who delights in the rivers,
> And the glad locks on the brow of the forests
>   That nod over Algidus cold,
>   Verdant Cragus and dark Erymanthus ; *
>
> Youths, sing of Tempè with emulous praises,
> Delos, the fair native isle of Apollo,
>   And sing of the shoulder adorned
>   With the quiver, and shell of the Brother.†
>
> Moved by your prayer, may the god in his mercy
> Save, from war and from pest and from famine,
>   Our people, and Cæsar our prince,
>   And direct them on Persia and Britain.

ODE XXII.

TO ARISTIUS FUSCUS.

Of Aristius Fuscus Horace speaks (Epp. i. 10) with particular affection. He says "they were almost twins in their tastes and sentiments." Fuscus appears to have been an author, but there is some doubt as to what he

---

* "Nigris aut Erymanthi
    Silvis, aut viridis Cragi."

The epithet "viridis" applied to Cragus is in opposition to "nigris" applied to Erymanthus, from the different kinds of foliage on either mountain, Cragus being covered with oak and beech, Erymanthus with pine and fir.

† "Fraternaque humerum lyra"—the shell invented by his brother Mercury.

wrote,—Acron says "Tragedies"—Porphyrian, "Comedies;" which last supposition seems more in keeping with the humorous joke he plays upon Horace, Sat. i. 9. Cruquius says he was a grammarian.

He of life without flaw, pure from sin, need not borrow
Or the bow or the darts of the Moor, O my Fuscus!
He relies for defence on no quiver that teems with
      Poison-steept arrows;

Though his path be along sultry African Syrtes,
Or Caucasian ravines, where no guest finds a shelter,
Or the banks which Hydaspes, the River of Story,
      Licks languid-flowing.

For as lately I strayed beyond pathways accustomed,
And with heart free from care was of Lalage singing,
A wolf in the thick of the deep Sabine forest
      Met, and straight fled me,

All unarmed though I was; yet so deadly a monster
Warlike Daunia ne'er bred in her wide acorned forests,
Nor the thirst-raging nurse of the lion—swart Juba's
      African sand-realm.

Place me lone in the sterile wastes, where not a leaflet
Ever bursts into bloom in the breezes of summer;
Sunless side of the world, which the grim air oppresses,
      Mist-clad and ice-bound;

Place me lone where the earth is denied to man's dwelling
All so near to its breast glows the car of the day-god;
And I still should love Lalage—her the sweet-smiling,
      Her the sweet-talking.*

* "Dulce ridentem Lalagen amabo,
    Dulce loquentem."

If I might have allowed myself to expand the literal words of the original into what seems to me the sense implied by the poet, I should have proposed to translate the lines thus:—

"I still should love Lalage—*see her*, sweet smiling;
    Hear her, sweet talking."

For I take it that Horace does not merely mean that he would still love Lalage "sweetly smiling" and "sweetly talking"—an assurance which seems in itself to belong to a school of poetry vulgarly called namby-pamby —but rather that, however solitary, still, and lifeless be the place to which he might be transported, he would still be so true to her image, that in the

ODE XXIII.

TO CHLOË.

This ode has the appearance of being imitated, though but slightly, from a fragment in Anacreon preserved in "Athenæus," ix. p. 396. But it is not the less an illustration of the native grace with which Horace invests his more trivial compositions.

Like a fawn dost thou fly from me, Chloë,
Like a fawn that, astray on the hill-tops,
   Her shy mother misses and seeks,
     Vaguely scared by the breeze and the forest.

Shudders Spring,* newly born, thro' quick leaflets ?
Slips the green lizard stirring a bramble !
   She is seized with a panic of fear,
     And her knees and her heart are one tremble.

Nay, but not as a merciless tiger,
Or an African lion I chase thee ;
   Ah ! cling to a mother no more,
     When thy girlhood is ripe for a lover.

solitude he would see her sweetly smiling, and amidst the silence hear her sweetly talking. So Constance, in Shakespeare, says :—

> "Grief fills the room up of my absent child,
> Lies in her bed, walks up and down with me,
> *Puts on her pretty looks, repeats her words.*"

* Munro, though preserving "veris" in the text, argues (Introduction, p. xxi.) in favour of the reading *vepris*, commended by Bentley and some earlier commentators. The main reason for his preference is, "that the advent of Spring must mean when the *genitabilis aura Favoni* begins to blow freshly and steadily ; that is, on some day in the month of February : but in the Italian forests the lightly moving leaves come almost, or quite, as late as in the English, and the zephyr blowing steadily for days together would be the last thing to startle a fawn."

This criticism is founded on nice observation of details in external nature, but I do not think such nicety of observation is a characteristic of Horace. The simile itself of the fawn is rather a proof of the contrary ; for the fawn just missing her dam is by no means of an age to be wooed, nor does she attract the courtship of the male till she has parted company with the mother altogether, and is mingling with the other does.

ODE XXIV.

TO VIRGIL ON THE DEATH OF QUINCTILIUS VARUS.

Quinctilius died A.U.C. /30. Little is known of him beyond the mention
with which he is immortalised by Horace. In the Ars Poetica he is spoken
of as dead, and as having been a frank and judiciously severe critic, who, if
you trusted your verses to him, would bid you correct this and that. If
you replied you could not do better—that you had tried twice or thrice in
vain—he would tell you to strike the lines out altogether, and put them
anew on the forge. This character as critic is in harmony with the
character here assigned to him as man (verses 7, 8).

What shame or what restraint unto the yearning
For one so loved ?   Music attuned to sorrow
Lead * thou, Melpomene, to whom the Father
   ʼ Gave liquid voice and lyre.

So, the eternal slumber clasps Quinctilius,
Whose equal when shall shame-faced sense of Honour,
Incorrupt Faith, of Justice the twin sister,
   Or Truth disguiseless, find ?

By many a good man wept, he died ;—no mourner
Wept with tears sadder than thine own, O Virgil !
Pious, alas, in vain ! thou redemandest
   Quinctilius from the gods ;'

Not on such terms they lent him !—Were thy harp-strings
Blander than those by which the Thracian Orpheus
Charmed listening forests, never flows the life-blood
   Back to the phantom form.

Which Hermes, not reopening Fate's closed portal
At human prayer, amid the dark flock shepherds
With ghastly rod. Hard ! yet still Patience lightens
   That which admits no cure.

* " Præcipe "—" lead."—YONGE.

ODE XXV.

TO LYDIA.

Little need be said about this poem. The reader has been already warned against the assumption that in the application of names, evidently fictitious, to poems of this kind, the same person is designated by the same name. It is obviously too absurd to suppose that the blooming Lydia of the 13th Ode in this very book is identical with the faded hag lampooned in the following ode. The poem itself is, with others of the same kind, only valuable as illustrative of Horace's character on its urban or town-bred side—its combination of the man of a fashionable world when at Rome, and of the solitary poet wrapped in his fancies, and meditating his art amidst Sabine woods or in the watered valleys of Tibur. In the translation, the third and fourth stanzas of the original are omitted. In these omitted stanzas the taste is sufficiently bad to vitiate the poetry. Horace never writes worse than when he is cynical. Cynicism was in him a spurious affectation, contrary to his genuine nature, which was singularly susceptible to amiable, graceful, generous, and noble impressions of man and of life.

More rarely now shake thy closed windows
With quick knocks of petulant gallants,—
They break not thy sleep; to thy threshold
    Fondly the door clings

Once turning so glib on its hinges.
Thou hear'st less and less, " Lydia, sleep'st thou ?
'Tis I—all night long for thee dying—
    I thine own lover ! "

    *   *   *   *   *

Now thou whin'st that this new generation
Likes but young shoots of ivy and myrtle,
And dedicates dry leaves to Hebrus *
    Winter's cold comrade ?

ODE XXVI.

TO L. ÆLIUS LAMIA.

Horace addresses this same Lamia again, Lib. III. Ode xviii. Lamia must have been very young when this ode was written, the date of which is to be guessed from the reference to Tiridates and the Parthian disturbances.

---

* " Hebro "—a river in Thrace : as we should say, " to the north pole.'

Assuming with Orelli, Macleane, and others, that it was composed A.U.C. 729, just before Tiridates fled from his kingdom, Lamia survived fifty-seven years, dying A. U. c. 786 (Tac. Ann. vi. 27).

I, the friend of the Muses, all fear and all sorrow
Will consign to wild winds as a freight for Crete's ocean ;
    I, the one man who feels himself safe,
      Whatever king reigns at the Pole—

Whatever the cause that appals Tiridates.
Muse, thou sweetener of Life, haunting hill-tops Pimpleian,
    Whose delight is in founts ever pure,
      Weave the blooms opened most to the sun—

O weave for the brows of my Lamia the garland :
Nought my praise without thee. Let thyself and thy sisters
    Make him sacred from Time by the harp
      Heard at Lesbos ; but new be its strings.

ODE XXVII.

TO BOON COMPANIONS.

In this poem, as in others of a convivial nature, Horace transports himself as it were into the midst of the company, and imparts an air of reality to an imaginary scene, so that it seems as if actually an impromptu.

Brawl and fight over cups which were born but for plea-
    sure*
Is the custom in Thrace.   Out on manners barbaric,
    'Do not put modest Bacchus to shame
      By the scandal of bloody affrays.

In what strange want of keeping with wine-cups and lustres
Are the dirks of the Mede.   Hush that infamous clamour,
    Be quiet ! Companions ! seats—seats !
      Lean in peace on prest elbows again !

Do you wish me to share a Falernian so doughty ?
Well then, let the young brother of Locrian Megilla
    Reveal by what wound, by what shaft
      He is smitten and dies—happy boy.

---

* " Natis in usum lætitiæ scyphis."   "Natis "—" born," as if made by nature, and destined exclusively for that purpose.—ORELLI.

What, refuse? tut! I drink on no other condition,
Come, no matter what Venus may conquer thee—blush not,
    For we know that thy sins in that way
      Must be always high-bred and refined.

Nay, thy secret is safe in these faithful ears whispered,
Ha! indeed luckless wretch! whirled in what a Charybdis!
    How I pity thy struggles, O youth,
      Thou, so worthy less dismal a flame!

O what witch or, with potions Thessalian, what wizard—
Nay, what God could avail from such coils to release thee?
    From that triple Chimæra's embrace
      Scarce could Pegasus carry thee off.

ODE XXVIII.

ARCHYTAS.

No ode in Horace has been more subjected than this one to the erudite ingenuity of conflicting commentators; nor are the questions at issue ever likely to find a solution in which all critics will be contented to agree.

The earlier commentators took for granted that the ode was composed as a dialogue between the ghost of Archytas and a voyager. The voyager, landing on the shore of Matinus, finds there the unburied bones of Archytas, and indulges in a sarcastic soliloquy, which ends either at verse 6, verse 16, verse 20, or, as Macleane was once of opinion, in the middle of verse 15—

    "Sed omnes una manet nox."

Two other theories have been started, by both of which Archytas is got rid of altogether. According to the first theory, the moralising voyager continues his reflections over the grave of the great geometrician, till (whether at verse 15, 16, or 20) the ghost, not of Archytas, but of another, whose bones are bleaching on the sand, rises up, accosts him, and prays to be sprinkled with the dust that may serve for burial and fit him for the Styx.

The second theory, favoured by Macleane, and supported by Mr. Long, dispenses not only with Archytas, but with the notion of dialogue. According to this conjecture, the whole poem is assigned to the ghost of a shipwrecked and unburied man, who moralises over Archytas and the certainty of death, &c., till, seeing a living sailor approach, he asks for burial. This supposition, the simplest in itself, and sanctioned by great critical authorities, appears to be gaining a more general, if recent, assent with scholars than any other hypothesis—and, after much consideration, I have adopted it in my version. If the poem is, however, to be considered a dialogue, I should not agree with Macleane in placing the division at verse 15,* but at

---

   * I believe that most critics are now agreed that if the poem be a

Y

verse 20—"Me quoque devexi," &c. The very abruptness of the interposition of the ghost at that line, which has been considered by many critics
objectionably harsh, appears to me a special merit. The ghost, commencing
his appeal at that verse, goes at once to the purpose. He, being dead, has
no need to say that all must die; but, contenting himself with briefly
informing the voyager that he has been drowned, hastens to implore the
handfuls of dust which suffice for burial. That it is not Archytas himself
who speaks, whether in monologue or dialogue, is, I think, made perfectly
apparent by the second and third verses of the ode—

> "Mensorem cohibent, Archyta,
> Pulveris exigui prope litus parva Matinum
> Munera,"

which I agree with Macleane in considering clearly to intimate that the
body of Archytas has already received that which he is supposed so earnestly
to pray for. "For," thus continues this judicious scholar, "though many,
I am aware, get over this difficulty by supposing "cohibent munera" to
mean that the *want* of the scanty gift of a little earth was keeping him
back from his rest, I do not see how the words will bear that sense; nor can
I translate "cohibent" with Dillenburger and others as if it was meant
that his body occupied only a small space on the surface of the ground.
The words can only mean that he was under the sand, whether partially or
otherwise, and in either case he could not require dust to be cast three times
on him."—MACLEANE, "Introduction to Ode xxviii. Lib. I."

The conjecture of Lübker and others that Horace is supposing himself to
be a ghost drowned off Palinurus, is too far-fetched and fantastic for serious
refutation. For these and other points in controversy the reader is referred
to Orelli's Excursus and Macleane's Introduction to this ode.

The poem itself is singularly striking. Though abounding in those
observations of the brevity of life and the certainty of death in which
Horace so frequently indulges, with the half-sportive melancholy of a nature
eminently sensuous, the poem has, on the whole, something almost of a
Gothic character. The humour takes the sombre colour of the mediæval
Dance of Death, and is not without a touch of the genius which speaks in
the grave-diggers of Hamlet. It is impossible to fix a date for its composition; but I incline to rank it among Horace's earlier odes, from a certain
likeness in its tone and treatment to the 5th Epode, which has also somewhat of the Gothic character in its gloomy earnestness of description, and
its employment of the grotesque as an agency of terror.

I concur in the general opinion that the scene is laid at the promontory
of Matinus, where Archytas is said to have had his tomb. Macleane sees
no occasion for that supposition, and thinks the subject of the ode is more
likely to have been suggested at Tarentum than elsewhere. He deems

---

dialogue the first speaker cannot be interrupted at verse 6, or before verse
15. The lines 14, 15—

> "Judice te non sordidus auctor
> Naturæ verique,"

seem to settle that question. Archytas, if commencing at line 16, could
scarcely appeal to the sailor as a judge of the learning of Pythagoras, while
the first speaker would very appropriately say that Archytas was a judge of
it. The attempt to get over this difficulty by corrupting a text sanctioned
by all the MSS., and substituting "me judice" for "te judice," is nowadays rejected by rational commentators, who rightly oppose unauthorised
amendments of texts supported by the concurrence of MSS.

" that the words 'Neptuno custode Tarenti' seem to fix the scene, and that it does not appear why a person speaking at Matinus should talk of Neptune particularly as the 'custos Tarenti.'"

I do not see the force of this objection. Neptune was particularly honoured at Tarentum, where he is said to have had a temple, and of which his son Tarus was the mythical founder. On the coins of Tarentum Neptune is represented as the tutelary deity. It would appear, therefore, quite natural that Neptune should be mentioned as the guardian of Tarentum, as Fortune is elsewhere mentioned as the guardian of Antium, without supposing that the person so referring to the deity was in the neighbourhood of the place specially protected; while the length at which Archytas is addressed at the commencement seems to indicate the scene as that in which the philosopher so emphatically selected was buried. Archytas himself was a Greek of Tarentum, which would render yet more appropriate a reference to that city whoever may be supposed to be speaking —the poem having commenced with the address to the shade of the great Tarentian.

Archytas was amongst the most illustrious of the ancient worthies—a general, a statesman, a philosopher, and especially a mathematician. He belonged to the Pythagorean school, but is supposed to have founded a new sect. The alleged inventor of analytical geometry, he is said to have originated the application of mathematics to mechanics, and constructed a flying dove of wood, which was to the myths of the ancients what Roger Bacon's brazen head is to those of the moderns. He is considered to have been a contemporary of Plato, and Aristotle wrote a life of him which is lost.

The metre is the same as in Ode vii., but I have not employed the same measure in the translation, thinking that the spirit of it requires the more elegiac rhythm which I have appropriated to some of the Epodes, and, indeed, to some other of the Odes.

Thee, arch-surveyor of the earth and ocean
    And the innumerous sands, Archytas, thee,
Pent in a creeklet margined by Matinus,
    The scanty boon of trivial dust keeps close.

What boots it now into the halls of Heaven
    To have presumed, and drawn empyreal air,
Ranged through the spheres and with thy mind of mortal
    Swept through creation to arrive at death?

The sire of Pelops with the gods did banquet,
    And yet he died;—remote into thin air
Vanished, if lingering long, at last Tithonus;
    Minos shared Jove's high secrets,—yet he died.

The son of Panthous, though he called to witness *
    His ancient buckler and the times of Troy,
That to grim Death he gave but skin and sinew,
    Tartarus regains,—and, this time, holds him fast;

* The shield of Euphorbus, son of Panthous (the valiant Trojan who

Y 2

Yet he of Truth and Nature, in thy judgment,
    Was an authority of no mean rank.
But one Night waits for all, and one sure pathway
    Trodden by all, and only trodden once.

Some do the Furies to stern Mars exhibit
    On the red stage in which disports his eye ;
The greedy ocean swallows up the sailors ;
    Old and young huddled swell the funeral throng :

And not a head* escapes the ruthless hell-queen,
    Me also, Notus,† hurrying on to join
His comrade setting amidst storm, Orion,
    Plunged into death amid Illyrian waves.

But thou, O sailor, churlishly begrudge not
    A sand-grain to my graveless bones and skull ;
So may whatever the east wind shall threaten
    To waves Hesperian, pass thee harmless by

And waste its wrath upon Venusian forests :
    So from all-righteous Jove and him who guards
Tarentum's consecrated haven, Neptune,
    Be every profit they can send thee showered.

Think'st thou 'tis nought to doom thy guiltless children
    To dread atonement for their father's wrong ?
Nay, on thyself may fall dire retribution
    And the just laws that give back scorn for scorn.

I'll not be left, with prayers disdained, revengeless,
    No expiation could atone such crime ;
Whate'er thy haste, this task not long delays thee—
    A little dust thrice sprinkled—then away.

wounded Patroclus), was preserved with other trophies in the temple of
Juno at or near Mycenæ ; and, according to a well-known legend, Pythagoras recognised this shield as that which he had borne when he lived in the
person of Euphorbus. The son of Panthous, therefore, means Pythagoras,
whom the speaker sarcastically compliments as no mean judge of truth and
nature in the opinion of Archytas, who belonged to his school.

    * "Nullum sæva caput Proserpina fugit"—in allusion to the lock of
hair which, according to the popular superstition, Proserpine cut off from
the head of the dying.

    † "Me also, Notus," &c. If the poem be supposed a dialogue, it
seems to me that this is the place at which the second speaker, as the
ghost of an unburied man, suddenly starts up and interposes.—See Introduction.

ODE XXIX.

TO ICCIUS.

In the 12th Ode of this Book Horace referred to the expedition into Arabia Felix meditated by Augustus, and which was sent from Egypt, A.U.C. 730, under the command of the Governor of Egypt, Ælius Gallus. Many Roman youths were attracted to this expedition by love of adventure and hope of spoil; among others, the Iccius here addressed, who survived to become the peaceful steward to Vispanius Agrippa's estates in Sicily. The good-natured banter on the warlike ardour conceived by a student of philosophy, was probably quite as much enjoyed by Iccius himself as by any one. They who suppose that so well-bred a man of the world as Horace is always insinuating moral reproofs to the friends he publicly addresses, are the only persons likely to agree with the scholiasts that he means gravely to rebuke Iccius for avarice in coveting the wealth of the Arabs.

So, Iccius, thou grudgest their wealth to the Arabs,
Wouldst war on kings Sheban, as yet never conquered,
    And art sternly preparing the chains
      For the limbs of the terrible Mede?

What virgin barbaric shall serve thee as handmaid,
Her betrothed being laid in the dust by thy falchion?
    And what page, born and bred in a court,
      Nor untaught Seric arrows to launch

From a bow-string paternal, with locks sleek and perfumed,
Shall attend at thy feasts, and replenish thy goblets?
    Who that rivers can flow to their founts,
      And the Tiber runs back, will deny,

If the sage of a promise so rare can surrender
All that priceless collection, the works of Panœtius,
    And the school in which Socrates taught,
      In exchange for a Spanish coat-mail?

ODE XXX.

VENUS INVOKED TO GLYCERA'S FANE.

This ode has the air of a complimentary copy of verses to some fair freed-woman who had fitted up a pretty fane to Venus, probably in the grotto, or antrum, attached to her residence.

Venus, O queen of Cnidos and of Paphos,
Spurn thy loved Cyprus—here transfer thy presence:
Decked is the fane to which, with incense lavish,
    Glycera calls thee.

Bring with thee, glowing rosy red, the Boy-god,
Nymphs and loose-girdled Graces, and—if wanting
Thee, wanting charm—bring Youth, nor let persuasive *
    Mercury fail us.

ODE XXXI.

PRAYER TO APOLLO.

After the battle of Actium, Augustus, in commencing the task of social
reformer, restored the ancient temples and built new ones. Amongst the
latter, A.U.C. 726, he dedicated to Apollo a temple, with a library attached
to it, on the Palatine. This charming poem expresses the poet's private
supplication to the god thus newly installed.

What demands at Apollo's new temple the poet ?
For what prays he outpouring new wine in libation ?
    Not fertile Sardinia's rich sheaves,
      Not sunny Calabria's fair herds;

Neither prays he for gold, nor the ivory of Indus,
Nor the meadows whose margin the calm-flowing Liris
    Eats into with murmurless wave.
      Let those on whom Fortune bestows

So luxurious a grape, prune the vine-trees of Cales,
And let trade's wealthy magnate exchange for the vintage
    Spiced cargoes of Syria, and drain
      Cups † sculptured for pontiffs in gold ;

Dear, indeed, to the gods must be he who revisits
Twice and thrice every year the Atlantic, unpunished :
    To me for a feast, mallows light,
      And endives and olives suffice.

* For the addition of this explanatory epithet, see the notes of Orelli and
Dillenburger.
† "Culullis," sculptured cups used by the pontiffs and Vestal virgins in
the sacred festivals.

Give me health in myself to enjoy the things granted,
O thou son of Latona; sound mind in sound body;
  Keep mine age free from all that degrades,
    And let it not fail of the lyre.

ODE XXXII.

TO HIS LYRE.

This short invocation to his lyre has the air of a prelude to some meditated poem of greater importance. Several of the Manuscripts commence
" Poscimus," which reading Bentley adopts. The modern editors agree in
preferring " Poscimur," which has more of the outburst of song, and
renders the poem more directly an address to the lyre.

We are summoned. If e'er, under shadow sequestered,
Has sweet dalliance with thee in light moments of leisure
  Given birth to a something which lives, and may, haply,
    Live in years later,

Rouse thee now, and discourse in the strains of the Roman,
Vocal shell, first attuned by the patriot of Lesbos,
  Who, in war though so fierce, yet in battle, or mooring
    On the wet sea-sand

His bark, tempest-tossed, chaunted Liber, the Muses,
Smiling Venus, the Boy ever clinging beside her,
  And, adorned by dark locks and by eyes of dark lustre,
    Beautiful Lycus.

O thou grace of Apollo, O charm in Jove's banquets,
Holy shell, dulcet solace of labour and sorrow,
  O respond to my greeting, when I, with rite solemn,
    Duly invoke thee.

ODE XXXIII.

TO ALBIUS TIBULLUS.

This poem is addressed to the most touching of all the Latin elegiac poets,
Tibullus. Various but not satisfactory attempts have been made to identify
Glycera with one of the two mistresses, Nemesis and Delia, celebrated in
Tibullus's extant elegies.

Nay, Albius, my friend, set some bounds to thy sorrow,
Let not this ruthless Glycera haunt thee for ever,
Nor, if in her false eyes a younger outshine thee,
    Such heart-broken elegies dole.

With passion for Cyrus glows low-browed Lycoris,*
Cyrus swerving to Pholoë meets with rough usage:
When with wolves of Apulia the roe has her consort,
    With that sinner Pholoë shall sin.

'Tis ever the way thus with Venus—it charms her
To mate those that match not in mind nor in person;
In jest to her yoke she compels the wrong couples;
    Alas! cruel jest, brazen yoke!

Myself, when a far better love came to woo me,
Myrtale the slave-born detained in fond fetters;
And Hadria can fret not the bay of Tarentum
    So sorely as she fretted me.

ODE XXXIV.

TO HIMSELF.

In this poem Horace appears to recant the Epicurean doctrine, which referred to secondary causes, and not to the providential agency of Divine power, the government of the universe, and which he professed, Sat. I. v. 101, and Epp. I. iv. 16. But, in fact, he candidly acknowledges his own inconsistency in all such matters, and is Stoic or Epicurean by fits and starts. In this ode he evidently connects the phenomenon of thunder in a serene sky with the sudden revolutions of fortune. The concluding verses are generally held to refer to the Parthian revolution, in which power was

---

* "Insignem tenui fronte Lycorida." So again, "Nigros angusta fronte capillos."—Epp. I. vii. 26: a low forehead seems to have long remained in fashion. Petronius, c. 126, in describing a beautiful woman, says, "Frons minima et quæ apices capillorum retro flexerat." Low foreheads came into fashion again at the close of the last century with the French Republic. Both with men and women the hair was then brought down to the very eyebrow, as may be seen in the portraits of that time. Yet the Greek sculptors in the purer age of art did not give low foreheads to their ideal images of beauty, and it is difficult to guess why an intellectual people like the Romans should have admired a peculiarity fatal to all frank and noble expression of the human countenance. The Roman ladies were accustomed to hide their foreheads by a bandage, elegantly called "nimbus"—i.e., the cloud which accompanied the appearance of the celestials.

transferred now from Phraates to Tiridates, and again from Tiridates back to Phraates. In the last stanza—

> "Hinc apicem rapax
> Fortuna cum stridore acuto
> Sustulit, hic posuisse gaudet"—

it was suggested in the "Cambridge Philological Museum," May, 1832, that Horace had in his mind the legend of the eagle taking off the cap of Tarquinius. For the convenience of the general reader the story may be briefly thus told. Demaratus, one of the Bacchiadæ of Corinth, flying from his native city when Cypselus destroyed the power of that aristocratic order, settled at Tarquinii, in Etruria, and married an Etruscan wife. His son Lucumo succeeded to his wealth, and married Tanaquil, of one of the noblest families in Tarquinii, but being, as a stranger, excluded from state offices, Lucumo, urged by his wife, resolved to remove to Rome. Just as he and his procession reached the Janiculum, within sight of Rome, an eagle seized his cap, soared with it to a great height—"cum magno clangore"—and then replaced it on his head. Tanaquil predicted to him the highest honours from this omen, and Lucumo, who assumed the name of Tarquinius Priscus, ultimately obtained the Roman throne. Macleane, in referring to the legend, and to the reference to Phraates, thinks it not probable that Horace meant to allude to both these historical facts together, and is therefore inclined to suppose that he intended neither one nor the other. His objection does not impress me. Nothing is more probable than that Horace should exemplify the sudden act of fortune in the Parthian revolution and render his allusion more lively by a metaphor borrowed from a familiar Roman myth.

Worshipper rare and niggard of the gods,
While led astray, in the Fool's wisdom versed,
   Now back I shift the sail,
     Forced in the courses left behind to steer:

For not, as wont, disparting serried cloud
With fiery flash, but through pure azure, drove
   Of late Diespiter
     His thundering coursers and his wingèd car;

Wherewith the fixed earth and the vagrant streams—
Wherewith the Styx and horror-breathing realms
   Of rayless Tænarus, shook—
     Shook the world's end on Atlas. A god reigns,

Potent the high with low to interchange,
Bid bright orbs wane, and those obscure come forth:
   Shrill-sounding,* Fortune swoops—
     Here snatches, there exultant drops, a crown.

---

* "Cum stridore acuto." These words (if Horace really had, here, the Tarquinian legend in his mind) are very suitable to the swoop of the eagle, descriptive alike of the noise of its scream and the shrilly whirr of its wings.

ODE XXXV.

TO FORTUNE.

Macleane places the date of this ode A.U.C. 728, when Augustus was medi-
tating an expedition against the Britons and another against the Arabs.
Fortune is here distinguished from Necessity, and recognised as a Divine
Intelligence, rather with the attributes of Providence than those of Fate.
As Fortune had her oldest temples in Rome, so she seems to have been the
last goddess whose worship was deserted by the Roman emperors.   ·

Goddess, who o'er thine own loved* Antium reignest
Potent alike to raise aloft the mortal
    From life's last mean degree,
      Or change his haughtiest triumphs into graves ;—

To thee the earth's poor tiller prays imploring—
To thee, Queen-lady of the deeps, whoever
    Cuts with Bithynian keel
      A passing furrow in Carpathian seas.†

Thee Dacian rude—thee Scythia's vagrant nomad‡—
Thee states and races—thee Rome's haughty children—
    Thee purple tyrants dread,
      And the pale mothers of Barbarian kings,

Lest thou spurn down with scornful foot the pillar
Whereon rest States ;§ lest all, from arms yet ling'ring,
    To arms some madding crowd
      Rouse with the shout to which an empire falls.

   * " Gratum—Antium." Orelli prefers interpreting " gratum" as
" dilectum," " dear to the goddess," rather than as " amœnum," or
" pleasant."
   † i. e., whether man ploughs earth or sea he equally prays to Fortune.
   ‡ " Profugi Scythiæ." The epithet "profugi" applies to the nomad
character of the Scyth, not to simulated flights as those of the Parthian
cavalry.
   § " Stantem columnam." The standing column was the emblem of fixity
and firmness. " In ancient monuments," says Dillenburger, "the column
is thus assigned to images of Peace, Security, Felicity." Horace naturally
writes in the spirit of his land and age in deprecating civil tumult as the
most formidable agency for the overthrow of the column and the destruction
of government and order.

Theo doth untamed Necessity for ever
Stalk fierce before ;—the ship nails and the wedges
    Bearing in grasp of bronze,
      Which lacks nor molten lead nor stedfast clamp.*

But thee Hope follows, and rare Faith, the white-robed,
True to thee, ev'n when thou thyself art altered,
    And from the homes of Power
      Passest away, in mourning weeds, a foe ;

While the false herd, the parasite, the harlot,
Shrink back : their love is dried up with the wine-cask,
    Their lips reject its lees ;
      Their necks will halve no yoke that Sorrow draws.

Guard Cæsar, seeking on earth's verge the Briton,—
Guard Rome's young swarm of warriors on the wing,
    Where they alight, to awe
      The rebel East and Araby's red sea.

Shame for the scars, the guilt, the blood of brothers !
What have we shunned—we, the hard Age of Iron ?
    What left undared of crime ?
      What youthful hand has fear of heaven restrained,

Where stands an altar sacred from its rapine ?
Dread goddess,—steel made blunt in impious battles
    On anvils new reforge ;
      And turn its edge on Arab and on Scyth !

* Most recent commentators of authority agree in rejecting the notion of the commentator in Cruquius, adopted by earlier editors, that " uncus " and " plumbum " are used here as emblems of punishment and crime, and consider them as emblems of tenacity and fixity of purpose. Maclcane observes that the metaphor of molten lead for strengthening buildings is employed by Euripides, " Androm.," 267. Herder suggests that the whole picture of Necessity and her attributes is taken from some picture in the temple of Fortune at Antium.

ODE XXXVI.

ON NUMIDA'S RETURN FROM SPAIN.

Horace congratulates Numida on his return from Spain—probably from the army with Augustus, A.U.C. 730. Who Numida was can be only matter of conjecture.

Repay both with incense and harp-string,
  Repay with the heifer's blood due, Numida's guardians
      divine;
Safe back from Hesperia the farthest,
  Now among loving friends shares he many a brotherly
      kiss,

But the portion of Lamia is largest;
  Mindful of childhood subjected to the same monarch's*
      control,
And how they both, donning the toga,
  Leapt into manhood together. Let not this happy day
      lack

Its record of white by the Crete stone:
  Be there no stint to the wine-cask, be there no pause
      to the feet,
Blithe in the bound of such measure
  Salii on holidays dance to! Bassus shall gallantly vie

With Damalis, queen of she-topers,
  Toss off his cup with a swallow like the grand drinkers
      of Thrace; †
And banquets shall want not the roses,
  Garlands of parsley the long-lived, garlands of lilies the
      brief.

All eyes shall for Damalis languish;
  But yet more encircling than ivy, climbing its way as
      it winds,
Shall Damalis, proof to their glances,
  Turning aside from the old loves, cling root and branch
      to the new.

---

* "Memor actæ non alio rege puertiæ."   Most modern scholars by "rege" understand schoolmaster.
† "Threïcia amystide."   "Amystis" was a deep draught taken without drawing breath.

ODE XXXVII.

ON THE FALL OF CLEOPATRA.

In this ode Horace conspicuously manifests his unrivalled art of combining terseness and completeness. The animated rapidity with which the images succeed each other does not render them less distinct. The three pictures of Cleopatra constitute the action of a drama; her insolent power with its Oriental surroundings,—her flight and fall,—her undaunted death. And while, with his inherent manliness of sentiment, Horace compels admiration for the foe who defrauds the victor of his triumph, and dies a queen, that very generosity of his serves more to justify the joyous exultation with which the poem commences, since it implies the determined nature of the great enemy from whom Rome is delivered. The date of the poem is sufficiently clear. M. Tullius Cicero, son of the orator, brought to Rome the news of the taking of Alexandria, and the deaths of Antony and Cleopatra, Sept. A.U.C. 724, suggesting this exhortation to private and public rejoicings. It will be observed here, as elsewhere, how Horace avoids naming Mark Antony. Two lines from a fragment of Alcæus are cited by commentators to show that the commencement of this ode is imitated from them. They rather serve to show with what sedulous avoidance of servility Horace does imitate, and how thoroughly Roman the whole treatment of his poem is, whatever be the lines to which a Greek poem may furnish hint and suggestion.

Now is the time, companions, for carousal,
Free now the foot to strike the earth in dances,
　　For Salian banquets * now
　　Deckt be the couches on which gods repose.

Sinful before were Cæcuban wines time-mellowed,
While for the Capitol the crash of ruin—
　　While for the life of Rome—
　　Funereal fates, the madding Queen prepared,

Girt with a herd obscene of tainted outcasts,
Fooled by false hope and drunken with sweet Fortune ;
　　Tamer her frenzy grew
　　　When from the flames slunk, scarcely slunk, one
　　　ship !

* The Salii were the priests of Mars Gradivus, twelve in number. Their habitual festival was in March, when they paraded the city in their official robes, carrying with them the twelve sacred shields of Mars, which they struck with rods, keeping time to the stroke by song and dance. At the conclusion of the festival the Salii partook of a banquet, proverbial for its magnificence, in the temple of Mars. "Pulvinaria" are the couches on which the statues were placed, as if the gods themselves were banqueters.

Speeding to change to real forms of terror
Vain dreams by Marcotic fumes * engendered,
    Fast on her hurrying flight
       From Latian coasts press Cæsar's rapid oars.

As on the cowering dove descends the falcon,
As the keen hunter thro' the snows of Hæmus
    Chases the hare, he comes
       To bind in chains this fatal Prodigy.

For chains too nobly born, she dies and spurns them,—
She from no sword recoils with woman shudder,—
    She crowds no sail to shores
       Where life might save itself and lurk obscure.

Brave to face fallen grandeur and void palace
With look serene ; brave to provoke the serpents
    That, where they fixed, their fangs
       Her form might readiest drink the poison in ;

Sterner thro' death deliberate, she defranded
The fierce Liburnians† of the victor's triumph ;
    She, forsooth, captive, She !
       No, the grand woman to the last was Queen !

ODE XXXVIII.

TO HIS WINE-SERVER.

Boy, I detest the pomp of Persic fashions—
Coronals wreathed with linden rind‡ displease me ;
Cease to explore each nook for some belated
    Rose of the autumn.

* "Mentemque lymphatam Marcotico." "Lymphatam" denotes panic or visionary terrors ("lymphata somnia"). "Lympha" and "nympha," as Macleane observes, are the same word. Nympholepsy was the madness occasioned by the sight of the nymph flashing up from the fountain, scaring the traveller out of his senses; and "lymphatus" literally means "driven mad by the glare of water." Horace ascribes this effect to the fumes, or perhaps rather the sparkle, of the Marcotic wine, produced on the banks of Lake Marcotis, in the neighbourhood of Alexandria.

† "Liburnians," light swift-sailing vessels, which constituted a chief portion of Augustus's fleet at Actium.

‡ "Philyra," the rind of the lime-tree used in elaborate garlands.

Weave with plain myrtle nothing else, I bid thee ;
Thee not, in serving, misbecomes the myrtle,
Me not, in drinking, underneath the trellised
        Bowery vine-leaves.*

---

* "Sub arta vite "—" arta," " close," " embowering ; " as in the trellised
vine-arbours still common in Italy and parts of Germany.

BOOK II.—ODE I.

TO ASINIUS POLLIO.

Pollio was among Cæsar's generals when he crossed the Rubicon, and at the battle of Pharsalia. After Cæsar's death he joined M. Antony, and sided with him in the Perusian war. He remained neutral after the battle of Actium. Indeed he retired from an active share in public life after his victorious expedition against the Parthini, an Illyrian people bordering on Dalmatia, and it is to that victory which Horace refers as the "Dalmatian triumph." He then gave himself up to literature. His tragedies, of which there are no remains, are highly praised by Virgil, who says they were worthy of Sophocles. Porphyrion says he was the only one of his time who could write tragedy well. But the author of the " Dialog. de Oratoribus" asserts that both as a tragic writer and an orator his style was hard and dry. His History appears to have been in seventeen books; and it is after having heard him read a part of it (he is said to have introduced at Rome the custom of such readings to assemblies, more or less familiar, before publication) that we may suppose Horace to have written the ode, of which the date is uncertain. Pollio appears to have been one of the most truly illustrious, and certainly one of the most accomplished, personages of the Augustan era.

The civil feuds which from Metellus date,
The causes, errors, conduct of the war,
 Fortune's capricious sport,
  The fatal friendships of august allies,

And arms yet crusted with inexpiate blood ;—
Such work is risked upon a perilous die ;
 Thou tread'st on smouldering fires,
  By the false lava heaped on them concealed.

Let for awhile the tragic Muse forsake
Her stage, till thou set forth the tale of Rome,
 Then the grand gift of song,
  With the Cecropian buskin, reassume,

Pollio, in forum and in senate famed,
Grief's bold defender, counsel's thoughtful guide,
 For whom the laurel, won
  In fields Dalmatian, blooms forth ever green.

Now, now, thou strik'st the ear with murmurous threat
From choral horns—now the loud clarions blare;
    Lightnings from armour flashed,
      Daunt charging war-steeds * and the looks of men!

Now, now, I seem to hear the mighty chiefs,
Soiled with the grime of no dishonouring dust,
    And see all earth subdued,
      Save the intrepid soul of Cato.   Foiled

Of her revenge, Juno, with all the gods,
Quitting the Afric they had loved in vain,
    Back to Jugurtha's shade
      Brought funeral victims in his conqueror's sons.

What field, made fertile by the Roman's gore,
Attests not impious wars by ghastly mounds,
    And by the crash, borne far
      To Median ears, or falling Italy?

What gulf, what stream, has boomed not with the wail
Of dismal battle-storms?   What sea has hues
    From Daunian carnage pure,
      What land has lacked the tribute of our blood?

Hush, wayward Muse, nor, playful strains laid by,
Strive to recast the Cean's † dirge-like hymn;
    In Dionæan grot,
      With me, seek measures tuned to lighter quill.

ODE II.

TO C. SALLUSTIUS CRISPUS, GRAND-NEPHEW OF THE HISTORIAN.

Many years before this ode, which is assigned to A.U.C. 730, Horace
satirises the frailties of this personage, who was then a young man (Sat. I.

-----

* "Fugaces terret equos." "Fugaces" here does not mean steeds in
flight, but rather in charge—it applies to their swiftness.—PORPHYRION.
Orelli adopts that interpretation.
  † "Ceæ—neniæ." Horace does not confine this word to the usual sense
of a dirge; but it suits the quality of Simonides's poetry, which was of a
severe and melancholy cast.—MACLEANE.

z

ii. 48).   He was now second only to Mœcenas in the favour of Augustus, to
whom he subsequently became the chief adviser.   Tacitus gives a vigorous
sketch of his character.   He died A.D. 20.

Yes, Sallust, scorn the mere inactive metal;
There is no lustre of itself in silver,
While niggard earth conceals; from temperate usage
      Comes its smooth polish.

Known by the heart of father for his brethren,
Time's latest age shall hear of Proculeius.*
Him shall uplift, and on no waxen pinion,
      Fame, the survivor.

Wider thy realm, a greedy soul subjected,
Than if to Libya joined the farthest Gades,
And either Carthage † to thy single service
      Ministered riches.

The direful dropsy feeds itself, increasing;
To expel the thirst we must expel the causes,
And healthier blood must chase the watery languor
      From the wan body.

Virtue, dissentient from the vulgar judgment,
Strikes from the list of happy men Phraates,
Ev'n when restored to the great throne of Cyrus;
      Virtue unteaches

Faith in false doctrines mouthed out by the many,
Holding safe only *his* realm, crown, and laurel,
Whose sight nor blinks, nor swerves, though, heaped
      before it,
      Shine the world's treasures.

---

* Proculeius, a friend and near connection of Mœcenas, with whom he is
coupled by Juvenal (S. vii. 94) as a patron of letters, is said by the
scholiasts to have divided his fortune with his brothers Licinius Murena,
and Fannius Cœpio, whose property had been despoiled in the civil wars.
It is doubted, however, whether Licinius was his brother or cousin, and
whether Cœpio was related to him.   Proculeius was among the Roman
knights on whom Augustus thought of bestowing Julia in marriage.
† "Either Carthage"—viz., the African Carthage and her colonies in
Spain.

ODE III.

TO Q. DELLIUS.

The commentator in Cruquius has Gellius for Dellius, assuming the person addressed to be L. Gellius Poplicola, brother of Messalla, the famous orator. But the common supposition is that the poem is addressed to Q. Dellius, to whose changeful and adventurous life its admonitions would be very appropriate. Dellius sided first with Dolabella, then went over to Cassius, then to M. Antony and Cleopatra. To Cleopatra he is said to have dictated the advice that she should rather subjugate M. Antony than be subjugated by him. Not long before the battle of Actium, he gave some offence to Cleopatra, probably more serious than that which has been assigned—viz., a sarcasm on the meagreness of her entertainments—and deserted Antony for Augustus, by whom he was cordially received. Like so many other public men of his time he cultivated literature, and wrote a history (now lost) of the war against the Parthians, in which he served under Antony. A terse sketch of his versatile career will be found in Estré, "Pros. Horat.," 314.

With a mind undisturbed take life's good and life's evil,
Temper grief from despair, temper joy from vainglory;
For, through each mortal change, equal mind,
O my Dellius, befits mortal-born,

Whether all that is left thee of life be but trouble,
Or, reclined at thine ease amid grassy recesses,
Thy Falernian, the choicest, records
How serenely the holidays glide.

Say, for what do vast pine and pale poplar commingle
Friendly boughs that invite to their welcoming shadow? *
Wherefore struggles and murmurs the rill
Stayed from flight by a curve in the shore? †

* "The oldest and best MSS. have 'quo,' which signifies 'to what purpose;' as, 'Quo mihi fortunam, si non conceditur uti?' (Epp. I. v. 12). He seems to mean, 'What were the stream and the cool shade given for? Bring out the wine and let us drink.'"—MACLEANE. Yonge, in his notes, cites parallels. from English poets with the elegance of taste which characterises his edition.
† "Laborat—trepidare." The stream struggles or labours to hurry on (trepidare), being obstructed by the curve in the bank (obliquo rivo), from which delay comes its pleasant murmur."—ORELLI.

Thither, lo, bid them bring thee the wine and the per-
   fumes,
And the blooms of the pleasant rose dying too swiftly ;
   While thy fortune, and youth,* and the woof
      Of the Three Fatal Sisters allow.

Woodlands dearly amassed † round the home proudly
   builded,
Stately villa with walls laved by Tiber's dun waters,
   Thou must quit ; and the wealth piled on high
      Shall become the delight of thine heir.

For no victim has Death either preference or pity,
Be thy race from the king who first reigned o'er the
   Argive,
   Or thy father a beggar, thy roof
      Yonder sky,—'tis the same to the Grave.

Driven all to that fold ; ‡ in one fatal urn shaken,
Soon or late must leap forth the sure lot for an exile
   In the dark passage-boat which comes back
      To the sweet native land never more.

ODE IV.

TO XANTHIAS PHOCEUS.

Xanthias Phoceus is evidently a fictitious designation. Xanthias is a
Greek name, and given by Aristophanes to slaves ; and Phoceus characterises the person named as a Phocian. The date of the ode is clearly A.U.C.
729, or the beginning of 730, when Horace, born A.U.C. 689, was just concluding his eighth lustre.

---

* " Ætas," which Acron translates "youth," an interpretation approved
by Estré and Macleane. It more accurately, however, means "the time of
life," including every period before that in which old age deadens the sense
of such holiday enjoyments. Dellius was not young at the date of this
poem ; but, at years more advanced, M. Antony was young enough to enjoy
the present hour rather too much.
† " Coëmptis saltibus." "Bought up," "extensive properties added
together."—YONGE.
‡ " Cogimur." "Gregis instar compellimur"—"we are driven like
sheep."—ORELLI.

Love for thy handmaid, Xanthias, need not shame thee :
Long since the slave Briseïs, with white beauty,
O'ermastering him who ne'er before had yielded,[*]
          Conquered Achilles ;

So, too, the captive form of fair Tecmessa
Conquered her captor Telamonian Ajax ;
And a wronged maiden, in the midst of triumph,
          Fired Agamemnon,

What time had fallen the barbarian forces
Before the might of the Thessalian victor,
And Hector's loss made easy to worn Hellas
          Troy's mighty ruin.

How dost thou know but what thy fair-hair'd Phyllis
May make thee son-in-law to splendid parents ?
Doubtless she mourns the wrong to race and hearth-gods
          Injured, but regal.

Believe not thy beloved of birth plebeian;
A girl so faithful, so averse from lucre,
Could not be born of an ignoble mother
          Whom thou wouldst blush for.

That lovely face, those arms, those tapering ankles—
Nay, in my praises never doubt mine honour :
The virtuous man, who rounds the age of forty,
          Hold unsuspected.

ODE V.

TO GABINIUS.

This poem is designated variously in the MSS. as "Lalage," "To the Lover of Lalage," &c. According to one early MS. (the Zurich), it is inscribed to Gabinius. But even Estré cannot tell us who Gabinius was, though Orelli conjectures him to have been son or grandson to A. Gabinius, Cicero's enemy. The poem is of very general application, and the leading idea is expressed with great elegance and spirit.

---

[*] " Insolentem—Achillem." I agree with Yonge in his suggestion that "insolentem" means "not wont to be moved."

Not yet can she bear, with neck supple, the yoke,
Not yet with another submit to be paired;
    Immature for the duties of mate,
      And the fiery embrace of the bull,

Thine heifer confines all her heart to green fields;
Now pausing to slake summer heats in the stream,
    Now with steerlings yet younger at play
      Midst the sallows that drip on the shore.

Till ripe, do not long for the fruit of the grape;
Anon varied Autumn shall deepen its hues,
    And empurple the clusters that now
      Do but pallidly peep from the leaf:

Anon, 'tis thyself she will seek; fervent Time
Speeds on, adding quick to her youth's crowning flower
    Blooming seasons subtracted from thine;
      Then shall Lalage glow for a spouse:

And then not so lovely the coy Pholoë,
Nor Chloris resplendent with shoulders of snow,
    As a moon in the stillness of night
      Shining pure on the calm of a sea;

Nor even Cnidian Gyges, whom, placed amid girls,
No guest the most shrewd could distinguish from them,
    So redundant the flow of his locks,
      And his face so ambiguously fair.

ODE VI.

TO SEPTIMIUS.

It is a reasonable conjecture, though nothing more, that this is the same
Septimius whom Horace introduces to Tiberius, Ep. I. ix., and whom
Augustus mentions in a letter to Horace, preserved in the life attributed to
Suetonius. The scholiast in Cruquius says that he was a Roman knight,
and had been fellow-soldier with Horace; that a Titius Septimius wrote
lyrics and tragedies in the time of Augustus; and there are those who make
the Septimius of the ode identical with the Titius of whom Horace speaks
in his Epistle to Julius Florus, lib. i. 3, v. 9, *et seq.* All this is uncertain;
not less uncertain is the date at which the ode was composed.

To the world's end thou'dst go with me, Septimius,
View tribes Cantabrian, for our yoke too savage;
And barbarous Syrtes, where the Moorish billow
      Whirls, ever-seething;

No, my Septimius, may mine age close calmly
In that mild Tibur by the Argive founded;
There, tired of ranging lands and seas, and warfare,
      Reach my last limit.

Or if such haven the hard Fates deny me,
Thee will I seek, Galæsus, gentle river,
Dear to flocks skin-clad;* and thy rural kingdom,
      Spartan Phalanthus.†

Out of all earth most smiles to me that corner,
Where the balmed honey yields not to Hymettus,
Where olives vie with those whose silvery verdure
      Gladdens Venafrum;

Where Jove bestows long springs and genial winters,
And Aulon's mount, friend to a fertile Bacchus,
Never has cause the purple of Falernian
      Clusters to envy.

Both thee and me that place, those blessed hill-tops,
Invite; thy tear shall there bedew the relics
Of thy lost poet-friend, while yet there lingers
      Warmth in the ashes.

ODE VII.

TO POMPEIUS VARUS.

The person addressed in this charming ode must not be confounded with
the rich Pompeius Grosphus, to whom the 16th Ode, Book II., is inscribed.

---

* "Pellitis ovibus." "Pellitis" is supposed by Orelli and others to refer
to the hides with which the fleeces of the sheep were protected from thorns
and brambles and atmospheric changes.
  † Tarentum, of which Phalanthus, the leader of the emigrant Partheniæ,
after the first Messenian war, got possession.

Oh, oft with me, in last extremes of peril,[*]
Brother in arms, what time our chief was Brutus,—
    Who to thy native gods,
To skies Italian and the Roman rights,

Hath thee restored,—chief of my friends, Pompeius?
With whom how oft has loitering day been broken
    O'er brimmëd cups, our locks
Flower-crowned, and glistening with Arabian balms!

With thee I shared, in field and flight, Philippi;—
Where, not too bravely, left behind my buckler,[†]
    When Valour's self gave way,
And tongues that threatened loudest licked the dust.

But me swift Mercury [‡] rapt thro' lines of foemen,
And bore aloft in cloud, secure but trembling;
    Thee did the stormy surge
Into the whirl of battle drag once more.

To Jove, then, give the feast thou ow'st his mercy,
And rest the limbs with lengthened warfare wearied
    Under my laurel. Come,
Nor spare yon casks :—they were reserved for thee.

---

[*] " Tempus in ultimum "—" in summum vitæ discrimen " (in extremest danger of life). See Catullus, 64, 151—" Supremo in tempore ; " et v. 169 —" Extremo tempore sæva fors," &c.—ORELLI.

[†] " Relicta non bene parmula ;
    Cum fracta virtus, et minaces
    Turpe solum tetigere mento."

Horace's modest confession of having left his shield behind him at Philippi has been very harshly perverted into a proof of cowardice—probably the last accusation to which a soldier who had shared with his friend the extremest dangers of Brutus would be fairly subjected. The accusation derived from his own playful reference is confuted by the lines that immediately follow :—When valour was broken, and those who had most menaced touched ground with their chins—i. e., as Orelli construes it, begged for quarter, than which flight itself was more honourable. In fact, Brutus himself advised flight. We much prefer this interpretation to that which would make Horace sneer at those haughty boasters for *being slain.* Horace was the last man to sneer at the soldier who fell bravely in battle, while he has specially singled for contempt the soldier who asks for quarter —(Lib. III. Ode v. 1. 36.)

[‡] Mercury was the tutelary god of poets, whom, according to astrologers, his planet still favours. In C. iii. 4, 26, Horace ascribes his preservation, not to Mercury, but to the Muses.

Boys, fill the cups—smooth-wide-lipp'd cups of Egypt *—
With lulling Massic that makes Care forgetful ;
    Shed balms from amplest shells.
Who parsley fresh and myrtle first will wreathe ?

Ah! whom will Venus † single for our wine-king ?
As for myself, I will out-drink a Thracian :
    Sweet to go mad with joy—
Joy for the friend whom I regain once more !

ODE VIII.

TO BARINE.

Some of the MSS., upon what authority is unknown, prefix Julia to Barine. Bentley objects to the name as being neither Greek nor Latin. Orelli shrewdly suggests that there were plenty of gay ladies at Rome who were of other nations besides Greece and Rome. The name, however, is very likely invented by Horace himself—as no doubt Cinara was—and may possibly be an adaptation from Βαρίνος, a kind of fish. There is not a line in the poem to justify the wild assumption of some commentators that Horace himself was in love with Barine, whoever she was. Judging by internal evidence, it seems to me that a real person was certainly thus addressed, and in a tone which to such a person would have been the most exquisite flattery; and as certainly that the person is not so addressed by a lover.

If for thy vows forsworn the least infliction
Came from the gods ; were one white tooth less pearl-
    like,
One very nail less rosy, then, Barine,
    I might believe thee.

But in proportion as that head perfidious
Thou doom'st to Orcus, brighter shines thy beauty,
And grows still more the universal theme of
    Youthful adorers.

Clearly with thee it prospers to be perjured :
Oaths "by a mother's urn," "night's starry silence,"
"All heaven," "the deathless gods," obtain thee bless-
    ings
    Only when broken.

* "Ciboria," cups shaped like the pod of the Egyptian bean. "Ore superius lato, inferius angusto."—ORELLI.
† "Quem Venus arbitrum dicet bibendi." Venus was the highest throw on the dice, Canis the lowest.

At all this treason Venus laughs, then ? laugh out
The very nymphs,* so truthful, and fierce Cupid,
Sharpening his fiery arrows on a whetstone,
  Red with men's heart-blood.

Meanwhile, new youths grow up beneath thy thraldom;
Grow up new slaveries; and the earlier lovers
Threaten each day to quit thy faithless threshold—
  Threaten, and throng there.

For their raw striplings tremble all the mothers,
And all the fathers of a thrifty temper;
And, as a gale retarding home-bound husbands,†
  Weeping brides fear thee.

ODE IX.

TO C. VALGIUS RUFUS.

(In Consolation.)

This Valgius, of consular rank, appears to have been much esteemed in
his time as a poet. He wrote elegies and epigrams, and had even a high
claim to the pretensions of an epic poet, according to the author of the
"Panegyric on Messala"—

> "Est tibi, qui posset magnis se accingere rebus,
> Valgius, æterno propior non alter Homero."

Horace might therefore well call upon him to lay aside his elegiac complaints and sing the triumphs of Augustus. He is said also to have written
in prose on the nature of plants, &c. Torrentius endeavours, "nullo argu-
mento," to distinguish between C. Valgius Rufus the consul and prose
writer, and T. Valgius Rufus the poet. The Mystes whose loss Valgius
deplores must have been a slave, or of servile origin, as the name denotes
—not, as Dacier and Sanadon suppose, the son of Valgius.—See Estré,
p. 457.

'Tis not always the fields are made rough by the rains,
'Tis not always the Caspian is harried by storm;
 Neither is it each month in the year
  That the ice stands inert on the shores of Armenia;

* "Simplices Nymphæ"—"ab omni fraude alienæ."—ORELLI.

† "Tua ne retardet
Aura maritos."

There are many conjectures as to the sense of the word "aura" in this passage, for which see Orelli's note. Yonge interprets it "a metaphor for
influence."

Nor on lofty Garganus the loud-groaning oaks
Wrestle, rocked to and fro with the blasts of the
    north,
  Nor the ash-trees droop widowed of leaves.
    O my friend, O my Valgius, shall grief last for
      ever ?

Yet for ever, in strains which we weep at, thy love
Mourns its Mystes bereaved ; not for thee doth the star
  Which rises at Eve, not for thee when it flies
    From the rush of the Sun, respite love from its
      sorrow.

But the old man, who three generations lived through,
For Antilochus lost did not mourn all his years;
  Nor for Troilus, nipped in his bloom,
    Flowed for ever the tears of his parents and sisters.

Wean thy heart then at last from such softening laments,
Chant we rather fresh trophies our Cæsar has won,
  Linking on, to the nations subdued,
    Bleak Niphates * all ice-locked, the Mede's haughty
      river,

Now submissively humbling the crest of its waves;
While the edict of Rome has imprisoned the Scyths
  In the narrow domain of their steppes,
    And the steed of each rider halts reined at the
      borders.

* "Rigidum Niphaten,
Medumque flumen."

That Niphates was the name of a mountain-range east of the Tigris is
certain; whether there was also a river of that name is much disputed,
though Lucan and Juvenal take it for granted. Possibly the Tigris, which,
according to Strabo, rises on the mountain-range of Niphates, may be the
river here meant. There was a small river called Medus which flowed into
the Araxes, but this was too insignificant for the mention Horace makes
of the "Medum flumen," even if he knew of its existence; and most of the
later commentators concur in thinking the river thus designated was the
Euphrates.

ODE X.

TO LICINIUS.

Licinius Murena was the son of the Murena whom Cicero defended, subsequently adopted by A. Terentius Varro. He was then called A. Terentius Varro Murena. Mæcenas married his sister; and Horace speaks of him subsequently (C. iii. 19) as one of the College of Augurs. The caution to discretion and moderation contained in this ode has a melancholy interest as that of a foreboding. He was put to death despite the intercession of Mæcenas and Proculeius, on the charge, whether true or false, of having entered with Fannius Cæpio and others into a conspiracy against Augustus. As his death occurred A.U.C. 732, this ode must have been composed before that date. Dio speaks of the unrestrained license he allowed to his tongue, and his words may have incriminated him more than his actions, the guilt of which Dio leaves doubtful.

Licinius, wouldst thou steer life's wiser voyage,
Neither launch always into deep mid-waters,
Nor hug the shores, and, shrinking from the tempest,
    Hazard the quicksand.

He who elects the golden mean of fortune,
Housing life safely, not in sordid hovels
Nor in proud halls, shuns with an equal prudence
    Pen'ry and Envy.

Winds rock most oft the pine that tops the forest,
The heaviest crash is that of falling towers,
The spots on earth most stricken by the lightning
    Are its high places.

The mind well trained to cope with either fortune,
Fears when Fate favours, hopes when Fate is adverse.
Jove, at his will, brings back deforming winters,
    Jove, when he wills it,

Scatters them. Sad days may have happy morrows.
His deadly bow not always bends Apollo,
His hand at times the silent muse awakens
    With the sweet harpstring.

In life's sore straits brace and display thy courage.*
Boldness is wisdom then: as wisely timid
When thy sails swell with winds too strongly fav'ring,
    Heed, and contract them.

* "Animosus atque fortis apparo"—not only *be*, but *show thyself*, courageous.

ODE XI.

TO QUINTIUS HIRPINUS.

Who this Hirpinus was we do not know. Orelli considers it probable
that he is the Quintius to whom Ep. I. xvi. is addressed. But Maclcane
observes "that the latter appears to have been younger than the former,
whom Horace addresses (v. 15) as if he were a contemporary." But the .
question is immaterial; for we know no more about the Quintius of the
Epistle than the Hirpinus of the Ode.

What the warlike Cantabrian or Scythian,
From ourselves by an ocean disparted,
    Take it into their heads to devise,
        Do not class with the questions that press.

Be not over-much anxious, Hirpinus,
For the things of a life that needs little ;
    See how Beauty recedes from our side
        With her beardless * twin playfellow Youth.

Grizzled Age, dry and sapless, comes chasing
Frolic Loves and the balm of light Slumbers ;
    Not the same glory lasts to the flower,
        Not the same glowing face to the moon:

Why to fathom the counsels eternal
Strain the mind without strength for such labour ?
    Why not rather, yon plane-tree beneath,
        Or this pine, fling us carelessly down,

While we may ; letting locks whiten under
Syrian nard and the fragrance of roses ?
    Drink ! Evius dispels eating cares.
        Ho ! which of you, boys, will assuage

This Falernian in yon running waters ?
Which entice that sequestered jade, Lydè,†
    With her iv'ry lute, and with her locks,
        Like a Spartan maid's, simply knit back ?

---

* "Levis" here means "beardless," as in "Levis Agyieu," Book IV.
Ode vi. 28.
        † " Quis devium scortum eliciet domo
          Lyden ? "
It need scarcely be said the word " scortum " is not used here in its most

ODE XII.

The Licymnia (or, as the scholiasts spell it, Licinia) celebrated in this ode was most probably Terentia, the wife of Mæcenas; and if so, the poem was evidently written within a few years after their marriage. It is not pleasant to think that the wedded happiness so charmingly described was of brief duration, and that the faults laid to the charge of the lady embittered the life of Mæcenas at its close. Some of the commentators have, however, doubted whether Horace could have ventured to speak so freely, as in the concluding lines, of a Roman matron of rank so illustrious as Terentia, and would therefore assume Licymnia to have been rather the mistress than the wife of Mæcenas. This supposition is incompatible with the description of Licymnia joining in the festivals of Diana; and probably Horace sufficiently preserved such respect to the wife of his patron as the manners of the time required by substituting a feigned name for her own.

Ask not thou to attune to this lute's relaxed numbers
Tales of long wars Numantian, or Hannibal direful,
Or the hues which, bestowed by the life-blood of Carthage,
  Incarnadined Sicily's seas ;

Or of Lapithæ fell, and the great drunken Centaur ;
Or of Earth's giant sons, overborne by Alcides,
Threat'ning perils that shook to its starry foundations
  Old Saturn's refulgent abode.

And far better thy prose than my verse, O Mæcenas,
Shall record, in grave story, the battles of Cæsar,
And the necks of the kings who have loftily threatened
  His Rome, to pass under her yoke.

Me the Muse has enjoined for the theme of my praises,
The Lady Licymnia—her dulcet-voiced singings,
And the sunshine of eyes that illumine her beauty,
  And the loving heart true to thine own.

Graced alike, whether joining at home in the dances,
Or contesting the palm in gay wit's playful skirmish,
Or amid holy sports on the feast-day of Dian,
  With virgins entwining the arm.

uncomplimentary sense. "Devium "—" one who lives out of the way," as Ovid, Heroid. ii. 118, " Et cecinit mæstum devia carmen avis."—ORELLI, MACLEANE.

Say, for all that Achœmenes boasted of treasure,
All the wealth which Mygdonia gave Phrygia in tribute,
    All the stores of all Araby—say, wouldst thou barter
        One lock of Licymnia's bright hair ?—

When at moments she bends down her neck to thy kisses,
Or declines them with coy but not cruel denial ;
    Rather pleased if the prize be snatched off by the spoiler,
        Nor slow in reprisal sometimes.

ODE XIII.

TO A TREE.

Few of the odes are more remarkable than this for the wonderful ease with which Horace rises from humorous pleasantry into the higher regions of poetic imagination. His escape from the falling tree seems to have made a deep and lasting impression on him. The more probable date of the poem is A.U.C. 728, or perhaps, 729.

Evil-omened the day whosoever first planted,
Sacrilegious his hand whosoever first raised thee,
    To become the perdition of races unborn,
        And a stain on the country, thou infamous tree.

Ah ! I well may believe that the man was a monster,
Had at night stabbed his hearth-guest, and strangled his
    father,
    Dealt in poisons of Colchis—committed, in short,
        Every crime the most fell which the thought can con-
        ceive ;—

He, the villain who, bent upon treason and murder,
Stationed thee, dismal log, stationed thee in my meadow,
    With remorseless design coming down unawares
        On the head of a lord who had done thee no wrong.

Who can hope to be safe ? who sufficiently cautious ?
Guard himself as he may, every moment's an ambush.
    Thus the sailor of * Carthage, alarmed at a squall
        In the Euxine, beyond it no danger foresees.

      * " Navita Bosporum
      Pœnus perhorrescit."
See Munro, Introduction, xxii. 111, for accepting Lachmann's Thynus or

Thus the soldier of Rome mails his breast to the Parthian,
And believes himself safe if secure from an arrow;
  And the Parthian, in flying Rome's dungeon * and chains,
    Fondly thinks that in flight he escapes from the grave!

Death has seized, and shall seize, when least looked for, its
    victims.
Ah! how near was I seeing dark Proserpine's kingdom,
  And the Judge of the Dead and the seats of the Blest,
    Sappho wailing melodious of loves unreturned; †

Ay, and thee, too, with strains sounding larger, Alcæus,
To thy golden shell chanting of hardships in shipwreck,
  And of hardships in exile, and hardships in war,
    While the Shadows admiringly hearken to both;

Due to either is silence as hushed as in temples,
But more presses the phantom mob, shoulder on shoulder,
  Drinking into rapt ears the grand song, as it swells
    With the burthen of battles and tyrants o'erthrown.

No wonder, when spelled by the voice of the charmer,
The dark hell-dog his hundred heads fawningly crouches,
  And the serpents that writhe interweaved in the locks
    Of the Furies, repose upon terrible brows;

And Prometheus himself and the Father of Pelops,
By the dulcet delight are beguiled from their torture,
  While the hand of Orion the arrow lets fall,
    And the spectres of lions unheeded flit on.

Thœnus for Pœnus—"Horace says that men only guard against dangers
near at hand and expected. The Punic skipper has no special business in
the straits of the Bosporus, all along the shore of which lived the Thyni,
Thuni, or Thœni."
  * "Italum robur." Orelli gives the weight of his authority in favour of
interpreting "robur" as the Roman prison ("Tullianum"), an inner cell in
which malefactors were placed, and in which the State captives, as
Jugurtha, were also sometimes immured. Yonge adopts the same interpretation. Dillenburger translates it in the simple sense of the strength or
power of Italy, which Macleane also favours.

† "Querentem
Sappho puellis de popularibus."

"Incertum autem est quid quereretur."—Estré, Horat. Prosop. 26. Estré

ODE XIV.

TO POSTUMUS.

Who this Postumus may have been is, in spite of the various conjectures
of various commentators, as uncertain as, happily, it is immaterial.   It is,
at all events, an agreeable supposition that he may be identical with the
Postumus whom Propertius (Lib. iii. Eleg. 10) reproached for leaving his
wife Galba to join a military expedition, possibly that of Ælius Gallus
against the Arabians.   This supposition would give a more pathetic significance to the "placens uxor" of the ode.

Postumus, Postumus, the years glide by us,
Alas! no piety delays the wrinkles,
    Nor old age imminent,
      Nor the indomitable hand of Death.

Though thrice each day a hecatomb were offered,
Friend, thou couldst soften not the tearless Pluto,
    Encoiling Tityus vast,
      And Geryon, triple giant, with sad waves—

Waves over which we all of us must voyage,
All whosoe'er the fruits of earth have tasted;
    Whether that earth we ruled
      As kings, or served as drudges of its soil.

Vainly we shun Mars and the gory battle,
Vainly the Hadrian hoarse with stormy breakers,
    Vainly, each autumn's fall,
      The sicklied airs through which the south wind sails.*

Still the dull-winding ooze of slow Cocytus,
The ill-famed Danaids, and, to task that ends not,
    Sentenced, Æolides;
      These are the sights on which we all must gaze.

cites the various interpretations, and inclines to that of the commentators
in Cruquius—viz., Sappho complained of the girls of her country that they
loved Phaon whom she loved.   This is, at all events, the most agreeable
conjecture.   Welcker has written with ingenious eloquence in vindication
of Sappho's memory from the scandal, "quod nimis diu ei adhæsit."
  * "Auster," "the sirocco."

Lands, home, and wife in whom thy soul delighteth,
Left; and one tree alone of all thy woodlands,
    Loathed cypress, faithful found,
      Shall follow to the last the brief-lived lord.

The worthier heir thy Cæcuban shall squander,
Bursting the hundred locks that guard its treasure,
    And wines more rare than those
      Sipped at high feast by pontiffs,* dye thy floors.

ODE XV.

ON THE IMMODERATE LUXURY OF THE AGE.

This ode is generally considered to be among those written to assist
Augustus in his social reforms, and, as Macleane observes, it should be read
in connection with the earlier odes of Book III. Dillenburger assigns the
date to A.U.C. 726, in which year Octavius, then Censor, restored and
adorned the public temples fallen into decay. Macleane favours that date.
But the poem alludes also to the sumptuary laws passed by Augustus at
various periods;—practically inoperative, as sumptuary laws always must
be in rich communities.

Lo, those regal piles rising! methinks, to the harrow
They will leave but few acres; on every side round us
    Vasty stewponds for fishes extend
      Wider bounds than the Lake of Lucrinus.

Yield the vine-wedded elms † to that Cælebs the planc-
        tree;
Then the violet, the myrtle, the whole host of odours
    Scatter sweets where the owner of old
      Placed his pride and his wealth in the olive;

---

* As the English say, "A dinner fit for an alderman," so the Romans
said, "A banquet fit for a pontiff." "Pontificum dapes, Saliares cœnæ."

        † "Platanusque cælebs,
    Evincet ulmos."

I have added to ulmos the explanatory epithet "vine-wedded," without
which the general reader could not understand the author's intention. The
elm, as supporting the vine, was useful and remunerative, the plane-tree
not.—Horace intimates that the growth of luxury was hostile to the "resources of industry,"—that garden flowers and plants appropriated the soil
in which the vine and the olive had sufficed for the income of other and
simpler owners—Poets and Communists sometimes agree in contempt for
the rudiments of Political Economy.

Serried laurel must, next, screen each stroke of a sun-
  beam.
Ah! not such the decrees left by Rome's hardy
  Founder,
  Nor the auspice of Cato unshorn,
  Nor the customs bequeathed by our fathers.

Petty then was to each man the selfish possession,
Mighty then was all to men the Commonwealth's trea-
  sure;
  No one sought the cool shade of the North
  Under peristyles planned out for temples; *

The chance turf next at hand roofed the citizen's
  dwelling,
But the State, at its charge, rarest marble devoted
  To the State's sacred heirlooms;—the shrines
  Of the gods, and the courts of a people.

ODE XVI.

TO POMPEIUS GROSPHUS.

According to the scholiast in Cruquius, this Pompeius Grosphus, a Sicilian
by origin, was of the Equestrian order. Cicero (in Cic. *Verr.* II. iii. 23)
speaks of Eubulides Grosphus Centuripinus, as a man of eminent worth,
noble birth, and princely wealth. Estré conjectures that this Grosphus was
made a Roman citizen by Pompey, and took his name, which descended to
the Grosphus of the ode as son or grandson. In Epist. i. 12, Horace com-
mends him to Iccius, then acting as superintendent or steward to Vipsanius
Agrippa's estates in Sicily, as one whom Iccius might willingly oblige, for
he would never ask anything not honest and just.

For ease prays he who in the wide Ægæan
Storm-seized, looks up on clouds that heap their dark-
  ness
O'er the lost moon, while dim the constellations
  Fade from the sailor.

* " Nulla decempedis
 Metata privatis opacam
  Porticus excipiebat Arcton."

No private man had porticoes measured by a ten-feet rule, which appears to
have been a measurement for temples and public buildings. The peristyles
at Pompeii, which form an inner court to the house, give sufficient idea of
these corridors, opening to the north for coolness in summer, and to the
south for sunshine in winter.

Ease, still for ease, sighs Thracia fierce in battle,
Still for ease sighs the quivered Mede.   Ah, Grosphus !
Nor gems nor purple, no, nor gold can buy it ;
   Ease is not venal.

Bribed by no king,* dispersed before no lictor,
Throng the wild tumults of a soul in trouble,
And the cares circling round a sleepless pillow,
   Under ceil'd fretwork.†

He lives on little well who, for all splendour,
Decks his plain board with some prized silver heirloom.‡
From him no greed of gain, of loss no terror,
   Snatch the light slumbers.

Why, briefly strong, with space in time thus bounded,
Launch we so many arrows into distance ?
Why crave new suns ?   What exile from his country
   Flies himself also ?

Diseasëd Care § ascends the brazen galley,
And rides amidst the armed men to the battle, ‖
Fleeter than stag, and fleeter than, when driving
   Rain-clouds, the east wind.

The mind, which now is glad, should hate to carry
Its care beyond the Present ; what is bitter
With easy smile should sweeten : nought was ever
   Happy on all sides.

* "Non enim gazæ."   "Gazæ," from a Persian word, means "the king's treasury," "the royal coffers."
† "Laqueata tecta," "non totius domus sed cubiculorum et tricliniarum."—DILLENBURGER.
‡ "Paternum salinum" — "the paternal or hereditary salt-cellar." Horace here, as elsewhere, distinguishes the comparative poverty of a small independence from absolute neediness and squalor.   The poverty he praises is not without its own modest refinements.   The board may be simple, but still it can display the old family salt-cellar, kept with religious care.   If the owner has not increased the paternal fortune, he has not diminished it.
§ "Vitiosa cura."   In the translation, Orelli's interpretation of "vitiosa," "morbosa"—i. e. morbid or diseased, from the vice of the mind whence it springs—is adopted.   But this hardly gives the full force of the word. Horace means that Care, which *spoils or infects* everything, ascends the galley, &c.
‖ "Turmas equitum."   "This properly refers to the horsemen riding to battle made anxious by the hope of booty or the fear of death."—ORELLI.

Untimely death snatched off renowned Achilles ;
Tithonus lived to dwindle into shadow ;
And haply what the Hour to thee shall grant not
     Me it will profer.*

. Around thine home a hundred flocks are bleating,
Low the Sicilian heifers, neighs the courser
Trained to the race-car ; woofs in Afric purple
     Twice-tinged array thee :

To me the Fate, that cannot err,† hath given
Some roods of land, some breathings, lowly murmured,
Of Grecian Muse, and power to scorn the malice
     Of the mean vulgar.

ODE XVII.

TO MÆCENAS.

This ode is addressed to Mæcenas in illness, but the date of the illness is necessarily uncertain in the life of a valetudinarian like Mæcenas. Though, as Macleane observes, the last two lines of this ode, showing that Horace had not yet paid the sacrifice he had vowed to Faunus for his preservation from death, make it most probable that it was written not long after C. 13 of this book, the composition of which has been assigned, with some hesita-

---

"With 'turmas equitum' is usually compared 'post equitem sedet atra cura,' but the sense there is a little different. Here he speaks of care following a man to the field of battle; there he refers to the rich man ambling on his horse."—MACLEANE.

    * "Et mihi forsan, tibi quod negarit,
      Porriget Hora."

I think, with Orelli, that this simply means, "Fortune, or the Hour, will perhaps give something of good to me which she denies to you; and I dissent altogether from the usual interpretation—viz., "Time may perhaps give me a longer life than it concedes to you." That interpretation would be very little in keeping with Horace's general politeness in addressing a friend. Nothing can well be worse-bred than telling a man that perhaps you will live longer than he will. Besides, Horace immediately proceeds to define that which is granted peculiarly to himself in opposition to the riches bestowed upon Grosphus.

† "Parca non mendax"—"sure," "unfailing in the fulfilment of their decrees." Compare "veraces," C. Sæcul, 25, and Persius, v. 42, "Parca tenax veri."—So ORELLI. "Genius is represented as the gift of Fate in Pind. Od. ix. 26, 28 ; also in Nem. iv. 41-43, where the poet infers from it his own eventual triumph over detraction; as Horace may be said to do here."—YONGE.

tion, to A.U.C. 728. Mæcenas was subject to what appears to have been a low nervous fever, attended with loss of sleep. According to the verses attributed to him, and censured with a stoic's lofty disdain by Seneca (Epp. 101), Mæcenas had a passionate and clinging desire for life, very uncommon in a Roman, deeming that, under any suffering or infirmity, life was still dear—

> " Vita dum superest bene est:
>   Hanc mihi vel acuta
>   Si sedeam cruce sustine." *

If this sentiment was sincerely expressed, the pathos of the poem is increased. A man so dreading death may well desire a companion in the last journey. And it is not unlikely that the melancholy view which Horace habitually takes of the next world, and his exhortations to make the best of this one, may have been coloured, perhaps insensibly to himself, by his conversations and intercourse with Mæcenas.

Why destroyest thou me with the groan of thy sufferings ?
Neither I nor the gods will let thee die before me,
    O Mæcenas, the glory and grace,
    And the column itself, of my life.

Ah ! if some fatal force, prematurely bereaving,
Wrenched from me the one half of my soul, could the other
    Linger on, with its dearer part lost,
    And the fragment of what was a whole ?

No ! in thy life is mine ; both, the same day shall shatter.
I have made no false vow ; where thou lead'st me I follow ;
    Fellow-travellers, the same solemn road
    We will take, we will take, side by side.

Me, no flames bursting forth from the jaws of Chimæra,
Me, no Gyas once more rising up hundred-handed,
    Could dispart from thyself,—such the will
    Of omnipotent Justice and Fate.

* The fragment is thus very happily rendered into English by Mr. Farrar in the biographical essay on Seneca, which forms the larger portion of his impressive and eloquent work, " The Seekers after God " :—

> " Numb my hands with palsy,
>   Rack my feet with gout,
>   Hunch my back and shoulder,
>   Let my teeth fall out;
>   Still, if *life* be granted,
>   I prefer the loss—
>   Save my life and give me
>   Anguish on the cross."

Whether Libra, or Scorpio with aspect * malignant,
In mine horoscope, ruled o'er the Houses of Danger,
    Or moist Capricorn, lord of the west;
        It is strange how our stars have agreed.

Thee, thine own native Jupiter snatched from fell
        Saturn,
And outshining his beam, stayed the wings of the Parcæ,
    When the theatre hailed thee restored,
        And the multitude thrice shouted joy.

Me the fall of the tree would have brained, had not
        Faunus,
To men born under Mercury, guardian benignant,
    O'er my head stretched the saving right hand,
        And made lighter the death-dealing blow.

Then forget not to render to Jove, the Preserver
Of a life so august, votive chapel and victims,
    While I, to mine own sylvan god,
        Offer grateful mine own humble lamb.

ODE XVIII.

AGAINST THE GRASPING AMBITION OF THE COVETOUS.

This ode is in a metre of which there is no other example in Horace. It
is said to have been invented by Hipponax of Ephesus, and is called generally

---

* "Adspicit," "aspected," is still the technical term in use among astrologers,
according to whom the native star may be evilly aspected in various ways.
But "pars violentior" would apply to the hostile influences affecting "the
Lord of life," chiefly found in the significations of the 8th and 12th House.
By his allusion to Capricorn, Horace clearly refers to his dangers by sea—
"Sicula unda." To astrology (a science then so much in fashion) Horace
often refers—sometimes with scorn, sometimes with a seeming credulity—
always as a man who knew very little about it. But where he speaks of it
with scorn, as in addressing Leuconoë, Book I. Ode xi., it is less to denounce
astrology itself as an imposture, than to dissuade from all attempts to divine
the future—"better that the future should remain unknown and uncon-
jectured." On the other hand, where, as in this ode, he seems to affect
credulity, it is only for a playful purpose. He regarded "the Science of the
Chaldee," as he did most of the popular beliefs affecting the future, without
serious examination of its truth or falsehood, as a question of speculative
philosophy, but to be freely used, whether in sport or in earnest, for the
purposes of poetic art.

by his name; though sometimes Euripidian, because often used by Euripides. It abounds in trochees. I can only attempt to give a general idea of its trippingness and brevity of sound. It treats, with more than usual beauty, Horace's favourite thesis of declamation against the grasping nature of avarice; and, as Dillenburger observes, it takes up and expands the senti- ment with which he had closed Ode xvi.

> To me nor gold nor ivory lends
>   Its shine to fret my ceiling;
> Nor shafts, in farthest Afric hewn,
>   Prop architraves Hymettian.*
>
> I do not claim, an unknown heir,
>   The spoils of Orient kingdoms,†
> No wives ‡ of honest clients weave
>   For me Laconian purples.
>
> Yet mine is truth and mine some vein
>   Of inborn genius kindly;
> Though poor, I do not court the rich,
>   But by the rich am courted.
>
> I do not weary heaven for more;
>   I tax no kindly patron;
> Content with all I own on earth.
>   Some rural acres Sabine.
>
> Day treads upon the heels of day,
>   New moons wane on to perish;
> Thou on the brink of death dost make
>   Vain contracts for new marble;

* The Numidian or Libyan marble, known to us as the Giallo antico. The " architraves Hymettian " (" trabes Hymettiæ ") are the white marble of Hymettus.

        † "Neque Attali
    Ignotus heres regiam occupavi."

Attalus the third made by will the Romans his heirs; the older commentators suppose that the lines satirically imply the will to have been fraudulently obtained. But the word "ignotus" does not necessarily bear that signfica- tion. As Orelli observes, the irony consists in the fact that Attalus did not know the persons he enriched. Torrentius supposes the lines to refer to Aristonicus, who, after the death of Attalus, seized on the throne by false pretences, defeated Licinius Crassus, was afterwards conquered by Perpenna, carried to Rome, and strangled in prison by orders of the Senate. The former interpretation is preferable.

‡ " ' Honestæ clientæ.' I have seen no satisfactory explanation of the words 'honestæ clientæ.' Mr. Long has suggested to me that they may refer to the rustic women on a man's farms—the wives of the Coloni."— MACLEANE.

Building proud homes, and of thy last—
   The sepulchre—forgetful;
As if the earth itself too small
   Thou robb'st new earth from ocean,

And, urging on a length of shore
   Upon the deep's foundation,
Thou thrustest back the angry wave
   That wars in vain on Baiæ.*

What, must thou also, greeding still,
   Remove thy neighbour's landmark—
Must ruthless avarice overleap
   Each fence of humble clients ?

And man and wailing wife, expelled
   The dear paternal dwelling,
Clasp ragged babes and exiled gods
   To wandering homeless bosoms ?

And yet no surer hall awaits
   The wealthy tyrant-master,
Than that which yields yet ampler room
   In yet more greedy Orcus.

Where farther tend?   Impartial earth
   Opes both for prince and peasant;
No gold bribed Charon to row back
   The crafty-souled Prometheus.

Death holds the haughty Tantalus;
   Death holds his children haughty:
Invoked or not, Death hears the poor,
   And *He* gives rest to labour.

* In allusion to the practice of the wealthy Romans in building villas out into the sea, on artificial foundations—as, long afterwards, rose the whole city of Venice,

ODE XIX.

IN HONOUR OF BACCHUS.

Macleane appears to me greatly to underrate the beauty of this poem, in which he says the Greek fire is wanting. This is not the opinion of the earlier critics, nor of readers in general. It has as much of the character of the dithyramb as the taste of a Roman audience would sanction and the character of the Latin language allow. The date of the poem is uncertain. Macleane suggests that it was perhaps composed at the time of the Liberalia, though in what year there are no means of determining. From its dithyrambic character, Orelli conjectures it to have been a copy from some Greek poem. The metre in this and the translation immediately following has some slight deviations from the preceding versions of the Alcaic, but not such as to affect the general character and form of the rhythm.

Amid sequestered rocky glens,—ye future times believe
    it !—
Bacchus I saw, in mystic verse his pupil nymphs in-
    structing—
        Instructing prickëd ears intent
        Of circling goat-hoofed Satyrs.

Œvoë, with the recent awe is trembling yet my spirit,
Filled with the god, my breast still heaves beneath the
    stormy rapture.
        Œvoë ! spare me ; Liber, spare,
        Dread with the solemn thyrsus !

Vouchsafed to me the glorious right to chant the head-
    strong Thyads,
The wine that from the fountain welled, the rills with
    milk o'erflowing,
        And, from the trunks of charmëd trees,
        The lapse of golden honey.

Vouchsafed to sing thy consort's crown which adds a
    star to heaven,*
Or that just wrath which overwhelmed the house of
    Theban Pentheus,
        And doomed to so disastrous end
        The frantic king Lycurgus.†

---

* Ariadne.

† Lycurgus, the King of the Edones, persecuted Bacchus on his passage through Thrace, and imprisoned his train of Satyrs. The mythologists vary as to the details of his punishment for this offence, but he was first afflicted with madness, and finally torn to pieces by horses.

Thou bow'st the rivers to thy will, barbarian ocean
    rulest ; *
Bedewed with wine in secret hills, thy charm compels
    the serpents
        To interweave, in guileless coil,
        The locks of Thracian Mœnads.

Thou, when aloft through arduous heaven the impious
    host of giants
Scaled to the Father's realm, didst hurl again to earth
    huge Rhœtus—
        Fronting his might with lion-fangs,
        And jaws of yawning horror ;

Albeit thou wert deemed a god more fit for choral
    dances,
For jest and sport the readiest Power, of slenderer use
    in battle ;
        Yet peace and war found thee the same,
        Of both the soul and centre.

When flashed the golden horn that decks thy front through
    Stygian shadows,
Harmless the Hell-dog wagged his tail to greet thy glorious
    coming,
        And gently licked with triple tongue
        Thine hallowed feet receding.†

* "Tu flectis amnes, tu mare barbarum." "Flectis amnes" does not
mean, as it is usually translated, "thou turnest aside the course of the
rivers;" the reference is to the Hydaspes and Orontes, over which Bacchus
is said to have walked dryshod; and "flecto" here must be taken either in
the sense of "to bow" or "direct," or, in its more metaphorical sense, "to
appease." By "mare barbarum" is meant the Indian Ocean.

† Orelli observes that in this stanza there are two images,—one at the
entrance of Liber into Hades, when Cerberus gently wags his tail to greet
him—the other when Liber is leaving and the Hell-dog licks his feet. The
poet thus expresses the security with which the god passes through the
terrors of the nether world.

ODE XX.

OF HIS FUTURE FAME.

Horace has no ode more remarkable than this for liveliness of fancy and fervour of animal spirits. It is composed half in sport, half in earnest, though I cannot agree with Macleane that it has in its style anything of "the mock heroic," properly so called, still less that it was written impromptu. Its rapid vivacity is no proof of want of artistic care. Dillenburger (in his Qu. Hor.) conjectures the ode to have been written in youth, and on the occasion of Mæcenas's first invitation (recorded Sat. I. vi.), so interpreting "quem vocas, dilecte Mæcenas." But, as Macleane observes, "the epithet 'dilecte,' implying a familiarity of some standing, is opposed to this view;" to which I may add the remark, that it is scarcely probable that Horace would have spoken with such confidence of his future fame till his claims as a lyrical poet were acknowledged by competent judges, to whom most of the odes in the first two, or perhaps the first three, books, if not yet collected into one publication, were familiarly known. It was probably enough written in some moment of joyous excitement occasioned by a success more signal than any private invitation from Mæcenas could confer; but we know too little of the various stepping-stones in Horace's poetical career to form any reasonable conjecture as to its date and occasion. It is enough that the poem itself so wonderfully vindicates the pretension of the poet to be also the prophet.

I shall soar through the liquid air buoyed on a pinion
Not familiar, not slight ; I will tarry no longer
    On this earth ; but victorious o'er envy, two-
      formed,
    Bard and bird, I abandon the cities of men.

Born of parents obscure though I be, O Mæcenas,
I who still from thy mouth hear the title "Belovëd," *
    I shall pass not away through the portals of death,
      I shall not be hemmed round by the waters of
      Styx.

* "Quem vocas dilecte." I agree with Mr. Conington in accepting Ritter's interpretation that "dilecte" is Mæcenas's address to Horace. Upon this disputed point a very illustrious scholar, to whom, indeed, I am indebted for line 6 in the translation, writes to me thus:—"I rather doubt the naked use of 'vocas' in the sense of 'invite to your society' ('revocas' is used Sat. I. vi. 61, but then of a particular repeated invitation, not of a general one); I therefore incline to prefer the interpretation 'Quem, Mæcenas, vocas "dilecte,"' though I admit the boldness of this construction." Munro prints "dilecte."

Now, now on my nether limbs rougher skin settles ;
Now above to the form of white bird I am changing ; *
 Swiftly now from the hands and the shoulders
  behold
  Smooth and smoother the down of the plumes
   springing forth !

Than the swift son of Dædalus swifter † I travel.
I shall visit shores loud with the boom of the Euxine,
 And fields Hyperborèan and African sands,
  And wherever I wander shall sing as a bird.

Me the Colchians shall know, me the Dacian ‡ dis-
  sembling
His dismay at the might of his victor the Roman ;
 Me Scythia's far son ;—learned students in me
  Shall be Spain's rugged child and the drinker of
   Rhone.§

* "Album mutor in alitem superne." The white bird is, of course, the
swan—" Multa Dircœum levat aura cycnum.'"—Lib. IV. Od. ii. 25.
 † " Horace did not write ' Dœdaleo ocior.' The old Bernese and other
high authorities have ' notior,' which, if a gloss, suits the sense and context
admirably, far better than ' tutior,' ' audacior,' or any other conjecture."—
MUNRO, Introd. xxvi. Bentley has " tutior."

   ‡ " Et qui dissimulat metum
  Marsæ cohortis Dacus."

The Marsian infantry was the flower of the Roman armies, and the Marsian
here represents the might of Rome. Either the interruption to the rapidity
of the verse by the allusion to the Dacian's haughty dissimulation of the
terror with which he regards the Roman arms must be considered, as it has
been considered by critics, one of those " impertinences," for the sake of a
popular hit, which is noticed in the preliminary essay as a defect in Horace ;
or it may possibly escape that reproach, and, pertinently to the purpose of
the poem, mean that whatever the disguised terror in which the Dacian
holds the Roman soldier, he will welcome the Roman poet.

   § " Me peritus
  Discet Hiber, Rhodanique potor."

" Peritus Hiber " does not mean " the learned Spaniard," as it is commonly
translated. The adjective applies, as in similar cases is habitual with
Horace, both to " Hiber " and " Rhodani potor ;" and as Dillenburger,
Orelli, and Macleane agree, the meaning is, " that these barbaric nations
will *become* versed in me." Macleane thinks that by " Hiber " is probably
meant the Caucasian people of that name ; I follow, however, the interpretation popularly accepted—and sanctioned by Orelli—that " Hiber " means
" the Spaniard." The " Drinker of Rhone " is the Gaul.

Not for me raise the death-dirge, mine urn shall be
　　empty; *
Hush the vain ceremonial of groans that degrade me,
　　And waste not the honours ye pay to the dead
　　　On a tomb in whose silence I shall not repose.

* "Absint inani funere neniæ." "Inani funere," because the body is
not there.—ORELLI.

BOOK III.—ODE I.

ON THE WISDOM OF CONTENT.

This ode opens with a stanza which modern critics generally consider to be an introduction not only to the ode itself, but also to the five following—all six constituting, as it were, serial parts of one varied poem, written about the same time and for the same object—viz. to aid in the reformation of manners which Augustus undertook at the close of the civil wars. The date of these and other odes conceived in the same spirit (as Lib. II. Od. xv. and xviii.) would therefore be referable to the period from A.U.C. 725 to A.U.C. 728. The first line of the introductory stanza to this ode imitates the formal exhortation of the priest at the Mysteries, warning away the profane. The conclusion of the stanza, " Virginibus puerisque canto," if, as recent interpreters assume, addressed to the chorus of boys and girls surrounding the priests and singing the praises of the gods, has also, according to the scholiasts, a much wider significance, and is a special address to the rising generation. "Horace," says Macleane, " speaks as if he despaired of impressing his precepts on any but the young, and bids the rest stand aside, as incapable of being initiated in the true wisdom of life." It is not easy to assign an appropriate heading to this ode. That which I select appears, on the whole, better than any other in use, though not quite satisfactory. The whole ode, which ranks high among the noblest attempts of a poet to embody didactic purpose in lyrical form, consists in a succession of brilliant images or pictures, seemingly detached, but constituting a moral whole: 1stly, The solemn recognition of the supreme God triumphant over brute force (" Clari Giganteo triumpho"), and governing the universe; 2ndly, The impartiality of Fate, and the certainty of death; 3rdly, The misery of the guilty conscience not to be soothed by sensual or artistic enjoyments. At line 25, " Desiderantem quod satis est," the main object of the poem—viz. in the inculcation of that wisdom of contentment by which Horace contrives to unite Epicurean with Stoic philosophy—develops itself, and is continued to the close.

I hate the uninitiate crowd—I drive it hence away;
Silence, while I, the Muses' priest, chant hymns unheard
      before;
    I chant to virgins and to youths,
    I chant to listeners pure.

Dread kings control their subject flocks; o'er kings them-
      selves reigns Jove,
Glorious for triumph won in war when giants stormed
    . his heaven,
    And moving, with almighty brow,*
    The universe of things.

* " Cuncta supercilio moventis." With his usual felicity of wording, Horace avoids the commonplace expression of " the Olympian nod," though

Man vies with man—'tis so ordained ; this, wider sets his
     vines,*
That, nobler-born, the Campus † seeks, competitor for
     power
    With one who boasts of purer life,
    And one of clients more :

Necessity with equal law assorts the varying lots ;
Though this may bear the lofty name and that may bear
     the low,
    Each in her ample urn she shakes,
    And casts the die for all.‡

To him above whose guilty neck hangs down the naked
     sword,
Sicilian feasts shall furnish not the sweets that flavour
    food,
    Nor song of bird nor chord of lute
    Charm back the truant sleep.§

the line implies that and something more; it implies the Deity's intellectual
government of all things, and explains the connection with the stanzas that
immediately follow,—the nod of Jove confirms the law of Fate to which all
men are subjected.

       * " Est ut viro vir latius ordinet
           Arbusta sulcis."

  " Est ut," " it is the case, it is ordained that men should vary in wealth
and condition."—YONGE. "Latius ordinet arbusta sulcis "—viz., one man
may compete with another man in extent of possessions : literally, that he
may marshal trees—chiefly, but not exclusively, vines—in parallel lines, or
in the shape of the quincunx, to a greater extent than another.
  † " Descendat in Campum." It was on the Campus Martius that the
Comitia Centuriata, at which the election of magistrates took place, were
held. The Campus was on low ground; but Yonge observes that "descendat"
is the exact word to express a contest, to descend into the arena.
  ‡ " Omne capax movet urna nomen." The image is taken from the use
of the dice, so familiar to the Romans. Fate is represented as holding the
urn which contains the lots of all men. This she keeps shaking (as we
shake or rattle the dice-box), and casts out the lots indifferently.
  § " Non avium citharæque cantus." It must not be supposed that the
natural song of the wild bird out of doors is here meant. Horace is speaking
of artificial luxuries in contradistinction to the banks and vales of the
following stanza, to which the song of the wild bird would apply. Here
he means the singing-birds which the Romans kept in aviaries within their
houses. Their notes, and the sound of distant music, and the trickling of
water, were among the artificial means for soothing the nerves and inducing
sleep, practised by the luxurious. Mæcenas, who suffered from insomnia
during that kind of nervous depression which saddened his later years, is
said by Seneca to have endeavoured to lull himself to sleep by the aid of

Sleep does not scorn the lowly cots that shelter rural
      toil,
Nor banks that find their pall of state in shadowy summer
      boughs,
    Nor vales in Tempö never vexed
    Save by the Zephyr's wing.

To him who curbs desire within the bounds of " The
      Enough,"
The wildest blasts that heave the sea awake no fear of
      wreck :
    He quails not though Arcturus set,
    Or Hædus rise, in storm ;

Though reel the vines beneath the hail, though crops belie
      the hope,
Though trees despoiled of fruit accuse now spring's corrod‧
      ing showers,
    Now summer's scorch and fiery stars,
    Now winter's crowning wrongs.

Lo, where the mighty moles extend new lands into the
      deep,
The scalëd races feel their sea shrink round the invading
      piles ;
    As many a builder's burly gang
    Heaves the huge rubble down,*

Obedient to a lord who scorns so small a bound as
      earth,
Yet Conscience, whispering fears and threats, ascends with
      him the tower,
    Black Care sits by him in the bark,
    Behind him, on the steed.†

distant music. It is not to Mæcenas, however, that Horace here alludes, for
such an allusion in this place would have been an unfeeling affront.
         * " Huc frequens
      Cæmenta demittit redemptor
      Cum famulis."
" Cæmenta," the rough mixture of large and small stones, mortar, &c.
(rubble), which served for foundations. " Redemptor," literally the " con‧
tractor" or " architect."
        † " Sed Timor et Minæ
    Scandunt eodem, quo dominus; neque
      Decedit ærata triremi, et
    Post equitem sedet atra Cura."

Since Phrygian marble* nought avails to soothe a mind
  diseased,
And nought the pomp of purple robes albeit outshining
  stars,
  And nought the Achœmenian balm,
   Nought the Falernian vine;

Why should I rear some hall sublime to Rome's last taste
  refined,
With pillared doors † which never ope but envy enters
  in ?—
  Oh, why for riches, wearier far,
   Exchange my Sabine vale ?

ODE II.

THE DISCIPLINE OF YOUTH.

As in the preceding ode the virtue of contentment is enforced, so this commences with enjoining that early training in simple and hardy habits which engenders the spirit of content, because it forms the mind betimes to disdain luxury. Discipline of this kind is the foundation of courage, love of country, the independence of character which loves virtue for its own sake, and the self-restraint which is essential to social good faith and honour.

To bear privation ‡ as a friend—to love its wholesome
  stint,
Train the youth nerved by hardy sports which form the
  school of war,
  A rider dread, with practised spear,
   To harry Parthian foes,

"Minœ internœ propter facinora commissa." — ORELLI. "Threats of conscience." "Scandunt," ascend the lofty tower or belvidere, which was then the fashionable appendage to the villas of the wealthy. "The 'œrata triremis' was the rich man's private yacht."—MACLEANE. The distinction between "Post equitem sedet atra Cura," and "Cura nec turmas equitum relinquit," Lib. II. Od. xvi. 22, has been noticed in the note to the line last mentioned.
 * "Phrygius lapis," a costly marble from Synnada in Phrygia, white, with red spots, in great esteem for columns, &c.
 † "Postibus invidendis." "Postes" were the jambs, columns, or pilasters that flanked the entrance door, and the word is often used for the door itself. I do not know of any authority for interpreting "postes" as the rows of pillars *within* the "atrium" itself, which some commentators are inclined to do. I ask indulgence for my paraphrase of *invidendis*.
 ‡ "Pauperiem." It is difficult here, as elsewhere, to find an English

Inured to danger and to days beneath unsheltered skies.
On him from high embattled walls of kings at war with
      Rome,
    Matron and ripening maid shall gaze
      And inly sigh, " Alas !

" O never may our princely lord in arms unskilled,
      provoke
Yon lion whom 'twere death to touch ; by the fell rage for
      blood,
    Where most the slaughters thicken round,
      Hurried, in rapture, on ! "

Glorious and sweet it is to die—when for our native
      land ; *
Ev'n him who runs away from Death, Death follows fast
      behind—
    Death does not spare the recreant back,
      And hamstrings limbs that flee.

Virtue ne'er knows of a defeat which brings with it dis-
      grace ; †
The blazon of her honours ne'er the breath of men can stain;
    Her fasces she nor takes nor quits
      As veers the popular gale.

word that correctly renders the sense of "pauperies." In this passage I
can think of no better word than "privation," interpreted as the privation
of luxuries. Poverty would be here wholly inapplicable, this ode being
addressed, with the one that precedes and the three that follow it, to youths
quite as much of the richer classes as of the poorer. "Robustus acri militia
puer :" I take "robustus" with "militia"—the boy made robust by
martial exercise and discipline. Among the Romans, the age for military
exercise began at seventeen.
    * "Dulce et decorum est pro patria mori." "In Horace's mind there
was a close connection between the virtue of frugal contentment and devotion to one's country."--MACLEANE.
               † " Virtus, repulsæ nescia sordidæ,
                    Intaminatis fulget honoribus."
The meaning of these lines has been much disputed, but seems to me
sufficiently clear. The point is in the epithets, "sordidæ," "intaminatis."
It cannot be truly said that Virtue is ignorant or unconscious of a defeat or
rejection ("repulsæ" applies to the defeat at a popular election (a)), but it is

    (a) Thus, in the Epistles, I. i. 42, Horace says,—
                 " Vides, quæ maxima credis
        Esse mala, exiguum censum turpemque repulsam ; "
which Macleane, referring to "repulsæ—sordidæ" of this ode, interprets
quaintly, "He who would secure an election must have a command of
money."

Virtue essays her flight through ways to all but her
    denied;
To those who do not merit death she opes the gates of
    heaven,
    And, spurning vulgar mobs and mire,
      Soars with escaping wing.

There is a silence unto which a safe reward is due.
With him whose tongue the sacred rites of Ceres blabs
    abroad,
    May I ne'er sit beneath a roof,
      Nor launch a shallop frail!

For Jove neglected oft confounds the good man with the
    bad;
And though avenging Punishment is lame indeed of foot,
    Yet rarely lags she long behind
      The swiftest flight of Crime.

ODE III.

ON STEADFASTNESS OF PURPOSE.

The two preceding odes, addressed to youth, inculcate the formation of
private character; this ode and the two that follow have a political intention and bearing. In this ode Horace commences with his famous picture
of the steadfast man not turned aside from that which his reason and
conscience hold to be right, either by the excitement of a populace or the
threat of a tyrant. Among the mortals which the exercise of this virtue
has raised to the gods he places Augustus, who certainly did not want
firmness of purpose in founding and cementing his authority, and to whom
the Senate had already decreed the honours habitually paid only to the
Divine Powers. The poet's mention of Romulus among those thus promoted
to the rank of immortals, leads on to what in itself appears, at first sight, a
somewhat prolix and irrelevant digression—viz., the speech of Juno pre-
dicting the glories of Rome, and prohibiting the restoration of Troy. Closely

---

said truly that Virtue knows not any such defeat as can disgrace her
(sordidæ). The honours that Virtue seeks are distinguished from civil
honours, insomuch as the latter, being conceded by the people or the state,
are by the people or the state to be reversed or sullied; but the honours
which Virtue seeks, being acquired by herself alone, cannot by others be
stained or touched (intaminatis). Cicero has exactly the same sentiment
(Pro Sestio, 28, 60), and Horace almost literally versifies the passage,
"Virtus lucet in tenebris—splendetque per sese semper, neque alienis
unquam sordibus obsolescit."—See Orelli's note, vol. i. p. 315.

examined, the digression is not purely episodical, but in harmony with the preceding verses, and a development of the purpose of the whole poem; for it is in the nature of the steadfast man, unswayed by the fickle passions of the time, to adhere firmly to the interests of his country, and cherish the memory of its glories and heroes. We are told by Suetonius ("Life of Julius Cæsar," c. 79), that it was a current report that Julius Cæsar meditated a design of transferring the seat of empire from Rome to Alexandria, or to Ilium. Lucan, ix. 997, ascribes to him the same intention. But we are not to suppose, with some, that Augustus entertained any such notion: this ode in itself is a proof to the contrary; for Horace would certainly not have volunteered a direct opposition to the wish of Augustus in poems intended to praise and support his policy, and, no doubt, composed with his entire approval. But it is possible enough that, when Augustus commenced his work of reformation, there were many among the broken remains of the old political parties who, whether from the dilapidation of their fortune, the distaste for Roman institutions, the supremacy of Augustus himself and aversion to his reforms, the animosities of faction—which, if crushed down, were still sore and rankling—or the restless love of change and adventure, might have entertained and proclaimed a desire for establishing a settlement in the East, for which the ancestral site of Troy would have been a popular selection. If Julius Cæsar really did entertain, or was commonly supposed to have entertained, the design imputed to him by Suetonius and Lucan, many of his followers and disbanded soldiers may have shared in this project, and rendered it a troublesome subject for Augustus to deal with. The idea is not likely to have gone to the extent of a transfer of the seat of empire from Rome to Troy (nor does Horace intimate *that* notion in this ode). More probably it was confined to establishing at Troy, or in its neighbourhood, a colonial or branch government, with special privileges and powers. Nor would there have been wanting plausible political reasons for thus planting a military Roman settlement to guard the empire acquired in the East. Upon the assumption that such an idea had favourers sufficiently numerous to raise it to importance, and that Augustus wished to discourage it, the intention of Horace, in the speech he ascribes to Juno, becomes clear.

Not the rage of the million commanding things evil,
Not the doom frowning near in the brows of the tyrant,
    Shakes the upright and resolute man
       In his solid completeness of soul;

No, not Auster, the Storm-King of Hadria's wild waters,
No, not Jove's mighty hand when it launches the
    thunder;
    If in fragments were shattered the world,
       Him its ruins would strike undismayed.

By this virtue * did Pollux and wandering Alcides
Scale, with toil, starry ramparts, and enter on heaven,

* "Hac arte," "ἀρετῇ," "by the virtue of this constancy, unwearied by labours, unswerving in purpose, men, becoming the heroes and benefactors of the human race, attain to the glory of immortals."—See Orelli, note 9 to this ode.

Whom between, now Augustus reclined,
  Quaffs the nectar that purples his lip; *

By this virtue deservedly, thee, Father Bacchus
Did the fierce tigers draw † with necks tamed by no
      mortal;
  By this virtue Quirinus escaped,
    Rapt on coursers of Mars—Acheron:

Juno having thus spoken words heard with approval
By the gods met in council,‡ "Troy, Troy lies in ruins—
  By a fatal and criminal judge §
    And the false foreign woman o'erthrown;

"Condemned from the day when Laomedon ‖ cheated
Vengeful gods of the guerdon agreed;—forfeit debtor
  With its people and fraudulent king
    Unto me and Minerva the pure.

"But now the vile guest of the Spartan adult'ress
Glitters forth nevermore;—the forsworn race of Priam
  By the aid of its Hector, no more
    Breaks in fragments the force of the Greek;

"Sunk to rest is the war so prolonged by our discords,
Ever henceforth to Mars I give up my resentment,
  And my grudge to the grandson ¶ who springs
    From the womb of a priestess of Troy.

* "Purpureo bibit ore nectar." Horace speaks in the present tense, and
no doubt with reference to the decree of the Senate after the battle of Actium—
viz., that libations should be offered to Octavian in private as well as in
public tables, and his name should be inserted in the hymns of praise equally
with those of the gods.—DIO. 51, 19. Compare Lib. IV. Od. v. 33 et seq.,
and Lib. II. Ep. i. 15.
  † "Vexere tigres," i. e. to the seats of the gods, to Olympus. The tigers
are the symbols of the savage ferocity tamed by Bacchus.—ORELLI. Bacchus
is here represented as the civiliser of life.
  ‡ Met in council to deliberate whether Romulus should be admitted
among the gods.
  § Paris adjudging the golden apple to Venus.
        ‖ "Ex quo destituit deos
      Mercede pacta Laomedon."
Troy is here represented as doomed by the crime of its founder Laomedon,
who, according to legend, defrauded Neptune and Apollo of the reward
promised them for building the walls of the city. It is Laomedon who is
meant by "the fraudulent king," "duce fraudulento"—not Priam, on
whom, innocent himself, the fraud of his ancestor is visited.
  ¶ Romulus being Juno's grandson, born of Mars her son, and Ilia the
Trojan priestess.

"I admit him to enter the luminous dwellings;
I admit him to sip * of the juices of nectar,
  And, enrolled in the order serene
    Of the gods, to partake of their calm.

"While between Rome and Ilion there rage the wide
      ocean,
May the exiles be blest wheresoe'er their dominion;
  So long as the wild herd shall range,
    And the wild beast shall litter her cubs

"Undisturbed, 'mid the barrows of Priam and Paris,
May the Capitol stand, brightening earth with its
      glory,
  And dauntless Rome issue her laws
    To the Mede she subdues by her arms.

"Wide and far may the awe of her name be extended
To the uttermost shores, where the girdle of ocean
  Doth from Africa Europe divide,
    And where Nile floods the lands with his swell.

"Be she stronger in leaving disdainfully buried
In the caverns of earth the gold—better so hidden,
  Than in wringing its uses to men,
    With a hand that would plunder the gods.†

"What limit soe'er may obstruct her in nature
Let her reach by her arms; and exultingly visit
  Either pole, where the mist or the sun
    Holds the orgies of water or fire.

---

* "Ducere noctaris succos." "Ducere," *i.e.* "sorbillere," to sip.—ORELLI.
Several MSS. have "discere," which reading is favoured by Dillenburger.
Orelli, Munro, and Macleane prefer "ducere," "which," "as the last observes,
"is in very common use in the sense of 'quaffing.'"

  † "Quam cogere humanos in usus
      Omne sacrum rapiente dextra."

The point here, as Orelli observes, is in the antithesis between "humanos"
and "sacrum." Macleane paraphrases the general meaning of the passage
thus,—"Let Rome extend her arms as she will, only let her not, as her
possessions increase, learn to prize gold above virtue." The more literal
meaning, according to Dillenburger and Orelli, is, that in the lust of gold
the hand of rapine sacrilegiously despoils the sacred vessels dedicated to
gods in their shrines and temples.

"I to Rome's warlike race speak such fates, on con-
          dition
That they never, too pious to antique forefathers,
     Nor confiding too far in their power,
          Even wish Trojan roofs to restore.

"What though Troy could revive under auspices fatal—
All her fortunes should be repetition of carnage ;
     I myself leading hosts to her doom—
          I the consort and sister of Jove !

" Rose her brazen wall thrice, with Apollo for founder,*
Still her brazen wall thrice should be razed by my
          Argives ;
     Thrice the captive wife mourn for her lord,
          Thrice the mother her children deplore."

Ah, this strain does not chime to my lute's lively
          measures !
Whither tendest thou, Muse ?   Cease, presumptuous, to
          mimic
     The discourses of gods ; nor let down
          To a music low-pitched, lofty themes.

ODE IV.

INVOCATION TO CALLIOPE.

It is observable that in this ode as well as in the last, and in Odes v.
and vi., composed for political purposes, Horace indulges much more in the
flights and fancies and seeming digressions proper to poetry purely lyrical
than in Odes i. and ii., in which, inculcating moral or noble sentiments
applicable to men of all parties, he is earnestly didactic. But treating
political subjects, on which men's minds were divided, he shows wonderful
delicacy of art in conveying his purpose through forms of poetry least likely
to offend. In Ode iii., dissuading from the project of a settlement in Troy,
it is not he that speaks, it is Juno. In Ode iv., desiring to imply that the
ascendancy of Augustus is the intellectual and godlike mastery over irrational
force, he begins by an invocation to Calliope, intimating his ambition to
accomplish a majestic or sustained poem without revealing its purport;
passes on to the lovely stanzas descriptive of his own devotion to poetry
from childhood ; links this description with inimitable subtlety of touch to
Augustus's culture of the humanising arts (v. 37, "Vos Cæsarem," &c.) ;
implies the union of such literary tastes with the policy of peace ("militia

---

* "Auctore Phœbo," the founder of the first Troy.

simul Fessas cohortes addidit oppidis," &c.), and with conciliatory and clement dispositions ("lene consilium," &c.); and then, with a lyrical suddenness, bursts into the theme for which he had invoked the muse at the commencement,—"Scimus ut impios;" insinuating, in the myth of the victory obtained over brute force by the gods that represent wisdom (Pallas), industry (Vulcan), social and domestic order (Juno), the ennobling arts (Apollo), not only the victory of Augustus, but the social and civilising influences to which the victory is ascribed, and by which it is lastingly maintained.

Descend, O Queen Calliope, from heaven,
And on thy fife discourse in lengthened music ; *
    Or lov'st thou more the lyre
        By Phœbus strung ; or thrill of vocal song ?

Hear ye, or doth the sweet delirium fool me ?
I seem to hear her, and with her to wander
    Where gentle winds and waves
        Steal their soft entrance into hallowed groves.

Me, when a child, upon the slopes of Vultur
Strayed, truant, from my nurse Apulia's threshold,†
    And tired with play and sleep,
        Did mythic doves with budding leaves bestrew ;

A miracle to all who hold their eyrie
In beetling Acherontia, or whom forests
    Embower in Bantian glens,
        Or rich Forentum's lowland glebes enclose,

That, safe from prowling bear and baleful adder—
That, heaped with myrtle and the hallowing laurel,
    Calm I should slumber on,
        Infant courageous under ward divine.

Yours, yours am I, O Muses, whether lifted
To Sabine hills—or whether cool Præneste,
    Or Tibur's sunny slopes,
        Or limpid Baiæ ‡ more my steps allure.

* "Longum—melos."
           "In notes, with many a winding bout
            Of linked sweetness, long drawn out."—MILTON.
Macleane says "longum" means a sustained and stately song. Yonge observes, that though it may be so translated, it is enough to understand it, with Orelli, as a mode of saying "Come, and leave me not hastily or soon."
  † See Excursus at the end of the ode.
  ‡ "Liquidæ Baiæ." The epithet applies either to the salubrity and

The lines arrayed and routed at Philippi,
The accursèd tree, the rock of Palinurus,*
    Stormed by Sicilian waves,
        Spared me, the lover of your choirs and founts.

Where ye be with me I would go undaunted;
Tempt, a glad mariner, the madding Euxine;
    Or, a blithe traveller, brave
        The sands that burn upon Assyrian shores;

Visit the Briton, terrible to strangers,
Concanian hordes, drunk with the blood of horses,
    And, safe from every harm,
        Quivered Geloni and the Scythian stream.

High Cæsar, seeking to conclude his labours,
Settling in peaceful towns war-wearied cohorts,†
    Ye solace and refresh
        In the Pierian grotto's placid shade.

---

purity of the waters, or to the clearness of the air at Baiæ.—Schol. Cruq.
Orelli prefers the latter interpretation. "Limpid" appears the best translation of "liquidæ," being applicable equally to either air or water, which
"liquid," in our sense of the word, would not be.

   * "Nec Sicula Palinurus unda." Cape Palinurus, a promontory on the
western coast of Lucania. All attempts to ascertain at what period of his
life, or on what occasion, Horace escaped shipwreck off Palinurus, are but
mere conjectures.

           † "Militia simul
       Fessas cohortes addidit oppidis."

The MSS. vary in the reading—"addidit," "abdidit," and "reddidit."
Dillenburger prefers "abdidit," which the scholiasts explain as being sent
to winter quarters. Orelli powerfully contends for "addidit," as significant
of new towns or colonies, in favour of which he cites Tacitus, Ann. xiii. 31,
"Coloniæ Capua atque Nuceria additis veteranis firmatæ sunt." After the
conquest of the Salassi, a people of the Gaulish Alps (A.U.C. 729), Augustus
assigned their territory to the Prætorian troops, who built Augusta Prætoria
(Aosta). To other troops were assigned lands in Lusitania, Augusta Emerita
(Merida). Macleane agrees with Orelli. Munro, a higher authority on such
questions than Macleane, prefers and adopts "abdidit." The true reading
being, however, uncertain, I have left it equally vague in the translation.
I may observe, however, that as Macleane, in common with other eminent
commentators, considers this ode written between A.U.C. 725 and 728, the
line cannot refer to the new towns in the territory taken from the Salassi,
A.U.C. 729.

Ye are the natural givers of mild counsel,
Your joy to give it, ye yourselves so gentle ! *
   † We know how He, whose law
      Tempers the sluggish earth and windy sea,

He who, the Sole One, rules with tranquil justice
The 'stablished states—the varying crowd of mortals,
   Gods, and the Ghastly Realms—
      · Smote with prone bolt the Titan's impious crew,

And banded giants towering into battle :
That horrid youth in strength of arm confiding—
   Brethren who sought to pile
      Pelion on dun Olympus, and to Jove

Himself sent fear.   But what availed Typhoëus,
What Mimas or Porphyrion's stand of menace,‡
   What Rhœtus, or the bold
      Hurler of trees uptorn, Enceladus,

Rushing against Minerva's sounding ægis ?
Here, keen, stood Vulcan—here the matron Juno,
   And he, who never more
      Will from his shoulders lay aside the bow,

---

   * "Vos lene consilium et datis, et dato
      Gaudetis, almæ."

"Ye give peaceful counsel, and rejoice in giving it because ye are gentle."
—MACLEANE.

  † Here Horace, starting from the picture of Augustus cultivating the Muses, and taking from them humane counsels, proceeds with poetic abruptness to symbolise the victory of Augustus over the violent and irrational forces hostile to the great social interests of man. The reader must not suppose (as some critics have inconsiderately done) that Horace signifies Augustus himself in the attributes he assigns to Jove. He would very imperfectly understand Horace who could conceive him thus to abase to the level of an earthly vicegerent that supreme divinity, to whom there is no likeness and no second. Horace does but imply that the same Divine Powers who defeated the brute forces of the Titans and giants were on the side of Augustus in the civil wars.

  ‡ "Aut quid minaci Porphyrion statu." As more poetic and expressive, I have adopted the literal translation of "status"—i. e. "a standing still," as opposed to motion—rather than that of "attitude," in which sense Forcellini interprets the word in these lines,—an interpretation commended by Yonge.

Who, in the pure dew of Castalia's fountain,
Laves loosened hair,* who holds the Lycian thicket
    And his own native wood,
        Apollo, Delian, and Patarćan king.

By its own weight sinks force, when void of counsel:
Let force be tempered and the gods increase it:
    But force which urges on
        To each unhallowed deed—the gods abhor.

Witness this truth, the hundred-handed Gyas—
Witness the doom of Dian's vast assailer,
    Lustful Orion, quelled
        By the chaste conqueror with the virgin shaft.

Earth heaped above them mourns her buried monsters,
And wails her offspring, into lurid Orcus
    Hurled by the heavenly bolt;
        The swiftest fires consume not Ætna, piled

Over the struggling giant; † the wing'd jailer ‡
Of lustful Tityus never quits its captive;
    Three hundred fetters hold
        The ravisher Pirithous fast in hell.

---

* Every reader of taste will be struck by the exquisite grace with which Horace lingers on this lovely picture of Apollo (Augustus's favourite deity), in contrast, as Orelli observes, to the monstrous images to which he is opposed. "Delius et Patareus:" Apollo is mythically said to have resided (or given oracles) at Patara, in Lycia, for six months in the year—the other six at Delos, his native isle. Macleane remarks that, "In enumerating the principal gods who assisted Zeus in the battle, Horace means to say, that although they were present, it was Pallas to whom the victory is mainly owing, otherwise the force of his argument is lost." But, as is said in the introduction, Horace appears to me to have desired emphatically, though symbolically, to intimate the nature of the Powers that were ranged on the side of Pallas, *i. e.* in the cause of Augustus—Vulcan, the representative of industry—Juno, of social order and marriage—Apollo, of arts and letters. This supposition is in accordance with the social or political objects to which these odes are devoted, and with the special benefits which Horace elsewhere ascribes to the reign of Augustus.

† "Nec perdit
Impositam celer ignis Ætnam."

The fires of Ætna, however swiftly they burst forth, cannot consume the heap piled above Enceladus, so as ever to free him.—ORELLI. Horace does not say who was the giant crushed under Ætna. Callimachus says it was Enceladus, and also Briareus; Pindar and Æschylus say it was Typhoëus. I have left this question in the translation as vague as Horace leaves it, though I have been compelled to take the licence of adding the words, "the

Excursus.

> "Me fabulosæ Volture in Apulo⁻
> Altricis extra limen Apuliæ
> Ludo fatigatumque somno."

I omit in the translation the adjective Apulian‾(Apulo) applied to Vultur, because, as between Apulo in one line and Apuliæ in the next, the text is generally supposed to be corrupt. Apu(lo) in the first line, is Apu(liæ) in the second; and though there are sufficient instances of variation of quantity in proper names—such as Prïamus, Prïamides, Sicanus, Sicania, Italus, &c. —yet it is thought improbable that in so elaborate a poem Horace would have varied the quantity in two consecutive lines, and, says Munro, "to shorten an essentially long Italian syllable like Apulia or Appenninus would be portentous in classical times." Passing by the prosodiacal objection, a graver difficulty has been found in the construction, "Me in Apulian Vultur beyond the threshold of my nurse Apulia." The Appennine range, still called "Monte Vulture," was partly in Apulia, partly in Lucania. And Horace, Satire ii. 1, says it is doubtful whether he was a Lucanian or an Apulian, for the farmers of Venusia (his birthplace) ploughed the boundaries of both these provinces. Had he said "Lucanian Vultur," "beyond the threshold of Apulia," the passage, therefore, would have been clear; but "in Apulian Vultur, out of Apulia," is a puzzle for commentators. It is not to be wondered at that Bentley, ever ready upon slighter ground to disturb a text and hazard an invention, should vehemently repudiate this reading; and getting rid of Apulia and poetry altogether, boldly propose to read, "Nutricis (or Altricis) extra limina sedulæ," "beyond the threshold of my careful nurse." Another critic, still more ingenious, not contented with taking "altrix" or "nutrix" literally as Horace's nurse in flesh and blood, has discovered her name to be Pulia, "extra limina Puliæ;" in which case the lines may be imitated thus:—

> "Me on the slope of Brighton Downs,
> Beyond the threshold of nurse Downie."

The most recent and the most plausible conjecture will be found in the preface to Mr. Yonge's edition, p. vi., "Altricis extra limina villulæ," "beyond the precincts of my native homestead." To this Munro objects "that diminutives used to such excess in the language of the people, in the comic poets, in Catullus and others, almost disappeared from the higher poetry of the Augustan and later ages." Mr. Yonge suggests, p. vii., a yet bolder, but a less acceptable emendation, "Nutricis extra limina villicæ," observing, that the "villica" was an important person in a plain country-house—the responsible manager for every part of the household arrangements. The construction would then be, "beyond the threshold of my nurse the bailiff's wife." As the obscurity of this passage has tasked the subtlest critics, I feel that I shall gratify all Horatian scholars by subjecting the following communication from a very high authority:—"I cannot see any difficulty about the Apuliæ and Apulo; the adjective and substantive often differ in accent, as gallánt and gallànt. Horace claims Vultur as an Apulian mountain, but says that he has strayed beyond its Apulian side; just as a child at Macugnaga might say that he had strayed on the 'Piedmontese Monte Moro' beyond the limits of Piedmont."

---

struggling giant," in order to prevent a misconception of the meaning,— such as occurs, for instance, in Smart, "Nor does the active fire consume Ætna, that is placed *over it.*"

‡ The vulture.

ODE V.

THE SOLDIER FORFEITS HIS COUNTRY WHO SURRENDERS HIMSELF
TO THE ENEMY IN BATTLE.

In this ode the political object of Horace is to stigmatise the Roman soldiers, who, being made prisoners—or, to use an appropriate French word, *détenus*—after the defeat of Crassus, had accustomed themselves to the country in which they were detained, married into barbarian families, and accepted military service under the conqueror; and in thus energetically representing the moral disgrace of these men, Horace is very evidently opposing some proposition then afloat for demanding their restoration from the Parthians. Such demand, which would no doubt be urged by the relatives of the *détenus*, and perhaps by many old fellow-soldiers in the Roman army, might easily have acquired the importance of what we call a party question. And if Horace here opposes it, it is pretty certain that Augustus opposed it also at that time. Hence the ode would have been written before Augustus redemanded (A.U.C. 731) the Roman captives and standards from Phraates. And the date A.U.C. 728 or 729, assigned to the ode by Orelli, is probably the true one. A demand which circumstances rendered reasonable and politic in 731, might have been very inopportune and unwise two or three years before. In aiming at his political object, Horace skilfully eludes its exact definition. He begins by saying, that as it is by his thunder we believe in Jove, so the power of Augustus will be recognised when he shall have added the Britons and Parthians to his empire. Thus, agreeably with the oratorical character of his poetry, on which I have observed in the preliminary essay, his exordium propitiates the ear of the party he is about to oppose, viz. those clamorous for the restoration of the Parthian prisoners. He follows this exordium with a rapid outburst on the ignominy of these very prisoners, and then, with admirable boldness, places the argument against their restoration in the mouth of the national hero Regulus. It is in these and similar passages that Horace not only soars immeasurably above the level of didactic poetry properly so called, but justifies his claim to a far higher rank even in lyrical poetry than many of his modern critics are disposed to accord to him. He attains to that region of the sublime which belongs to heroic sentiment, and which is the rarest variety of the sublime even in the tragic drama.

'Tis by his thunder we believe Jove reigns
In heaven: on earth,* as a presiding god,
    When to his realm annexed
      Briton and Persian,† Cæsar shall be held!

What! hath the soldier who with Crassus served,
Lived the vile spouse of a barbarian wife?
    Shame to Rome's Senate! ‡ shame
      On manners that invert the Rome of old!

* "'Præsens divus' is obviously 'præsens in terris,' as opposed to 'cælo.'" —MACLEANE.
† Persian for Parthian, as Lib. I. Od. ii. 22.
‡ "Pro Curia," &c.—viz., "Shame to the Senate for the scandal to its dignity in having so long endured a disgrace so ignominious."—ORELLI.

Marsian, Apulian, sons-in-law to foes
Of their own sires! grown grey in hireling mail
　　Beneath a Median king!
　　　　Oblivious of the sacred shields of Mars,

Oblivious both of toga and of name,
And Vesta's unextinguishable fire,*
　　While yet live Jove and Rome! †
　　　　Ah! this the provident mind of Regulus

Foresaw, when arguing that to buy from Death
Captives unworthy pity, on vile terms,
　　Would serve in after days,
　　　　As the sure precedent of doom to Rome.

"I," thus he said, "have with these eyes beheld
The Roman standards nailed to Punic shrines;
　　From Roman soldiers seen
　　　　The bloodless weapons wrenched without a blow;

"Seen the stout arms of Roman citizens
Twisted, all slave-like, behind free-born backs,
　　While foes retilled safe fields,
　　　　And left expanded portals sentryless.

"The soldier, ransomed by your gold, forsooth,
Comes back the braver! you add loss to shame.‡
　　Never the wool regains
　　　　Gone hues, when once drugg'd with the sea-weed's
　　　　dye;

"Never true valour, when it once departs,
Deigns to resettle in degenerate souls.
　　If, when from toils set free,
　　　　The hind will fight, the captive will be brave

* "Horace collects the most distinguished objects of a Roman's reverence
—his name, his citizenship (togæ), the shield of Mars only to be lost, and
the fire of Vesta only to be extinguished, when Rome should perish."—
MACLEANE.
† Incolumi Jove." "Salvo Capitolio," Schol.—viz., the Capitol in
which stood the temple of Capitoline Jove.
‡ "Flagitio additis Damnum." Orelli, Dillenburger, and Macleane agree
in considering that "damnum" does not refer, as some suppose, to the loss
of the ransom, but to the damage done by the example of ransoming
captives who had evinced so little courage.

"Who hath consigned himself to faithless foes,
He will crush Carthage in fresh battle-fields,
    He—who hath felt the thong
        On passive wrists,—and owned the fear of death.

" How to hold life ignoring,—he hath made
Peace for himself amidst his country's war,*
    O shame ! great Carthage hail,
        Throned on the ruins of a Rome disgraced ! "

Then it is said, he turned from the embrace
Of his chaste wife and babes, as one to whom
    All the old rights are lost ; †
        Stern, and with manly face bent earthward
        down.

Until the unexampled counsel fixed
The wavering senate on its author's side,
    And, pauseless, through the ranks
        Of mournful friends, the glorious exile passed.

Albeit he knew what the barbarian skill
Of the tormentor for himself prepared,
    He motioned from his path
        The opposing kindred, the retarding crowd,

Calmly as if, some client's tedious suit
Closed by his judgment,‡ to Venafrian fields
    Or mild Tarentum, built
        By antique Spartans, went his quiet way.

* " Hic, unde vitam sumeret inscius,
    Pacem duello miscuit."

That is, such a man, not comprehending that it is only by his own unyielding valour that he should save his life, confounds peace and war by
making peace for himself on the field of battle. Conditions of peace
belong to the state, not to the individual soldier, upon whom the state
imposes the duty to fight at any hazard of life.—See Orelli's note.
  † " Capitis minor." The expression signifies the man who has lost his
civil rights, as did the Roman citizen taken prisoner by the enemy.
  ‡ The patrons were accustomed to settle the dispute between their
clients.

ODE VI.

ON THE SOCIAL CORRUPTION OF THE TIME.

Macleane observes that, "As the former (five) odes are addressed more to qualities of young men, this refers more especially to the vices of young women, and so Horace discharges the promise with which this series of odes begins." To me, on the contrary, it is precisely because of the lines which so freely describe the vices of young women, single and married, that I hesitate to class this ode among those to which the introductory verse of the first ode applies. Let any man consider if a poet, as the Muse's priest, could have addressed, in the original, lines from 21 to 32, not to freed-women and singing-girls, but to the well-born maidens and brides of Rome. That the poem was written about the same time as the others is a reasonable conjecture, and probably with the same intention of assisting the reforms of Augustus, among which Horace subsequently celebrates the stricter laws regulating and affecting marriage. But I do not think the poem was or could be one of those specially addressed to the young; and, independently of the lines I have referred to, the concluding stanza, in fierce condemnation of themselves and their immediate parents, would be very unlike the skilful way in which Horace "admissus circum præcordia ludit."

Roman, the sins thy fathers have committed,
From thee, though guiltless, shall exact atonement,
  Till tottering fanes * and temples be restored,
   And smoke-grimed † statues of neglected gods.

Thou rul'st by being to the gods subjected,
To this each deed's conception and completion
  Refer; full many an ill, the gods contemned
   Have showered upon this sorrowing Italy.

Twice have Monæses ‡ and the Parthian riders
Of Pacorus crushed our evil-omened onslaught,
  And to their puny torques smiled to add
   The spoils of armour stripped from Roman breasts,

---

* The restoration of the temples and fanes decayed by time, or burned down in the civil wars, was among the chief reforms of Augustus.—Suet., Oct. xxx.

† "Smoke-grimed,"—partly by conflagrations commemorated by Tacitus and Suetonius, partly by the fumes from the sacrifices. Stated times for the washing of the statues, with solemn rites, were appointed.

‡ Pacorus, son of the Parthian king Arsaces XIV., defeated Decidius Saxa, legate to M. Antony. Four years later, when Pacorus was dead, the Parthians defeated Antony commanding in person. It is not known who is meant by Monæses. Plutarch mentions a Parthian of that name who fled to Antony, but it nowhere appears that he bore arms against the Romans. Orelli and Macleane favour the conjecture that by Monæses is meant Surenas, who defeated Crassus, A.U.C. 701—supposing Surenas to be merely an Oriental title of dignity, and Monæses to have been the proper name of Crassus's conqueror.

Dacian and Æthiopian,* dread-inspiring—
One with his archers, with his fleets the other—
   Well-nigh destroyed this very Rome herself,
     While all her thought was on her own fierce brawls.

This age, crime-bearing, first polluted wedlock,
Hence race adulterate, and hence homes dishallowed ; †
   And from this fountain flowed a poisoned stream,
     Pest-spreading through the people and the land.

The ripening virgin, blushes, learns delighted
Ionic dances ; in the art of wantons
   Studiously fashioned ; even in the bud,
     Tingles, within her, meditated sin.‡

Later, a wife—her consort in his cups,
She courts some younger gallant, whom, no matter,
   Snatching the moment from the board to slip,
     And hide the lover from the tell-tale lights.§

* This is an allusion to the threats of Antony and Cleopatra against Rome—

     "Dum Capitolio
    Regina dementes ruinas,
     Funus et imperio parabat."
       —Lib. I. Od. xxxvii.

The Dacian archers were auxiliaries in Antony's army at Actium. By the Æthiopians is meant the Egyptian fleet. The ode must therefore have been written after the battle of Actium.

  † Here Horace, tracing the corruption of the times to the contempt of the marriage-tie, whether by adultery or the excess to which the licence of divorce was carried, aids Augustus in the reforms he effected in the law of marriage.

    ‡ "Jam nunc et incestos amores.
     De tenero meditatur ungui."

I have adhered to the received and simplest interpretation of "de tenero ungui," "from earliest youth or tender years." But another interpretation, which Orelli considers very ingenious and appears to approve, will be found in his note to the passage, "penitus ex intimis nervis"—as we say in English, "tingling to the finger-ends;" or, as the French say, clever or wicked, "au bout des ongles."

    § "Impermissa raptim
    Gaudia, luminibus remotis."

"Raptim non est 'furtim' sed 'celeriter,' ita est statim post venerem in triclinium redeat," &c.—ORELLI.

Prompt at the beck (her venal spouse conniving)
Of some man-milliner * or rude sea-captain
    Of trade-ship fresh from marts of pilfered Spain,
      Buying full dearly the disgrace she sells.

Not from such parents sprang that race undaunted,
Who reddened ocean with the gore of Carthage,
    Beat down stout Pyrrhus, great Antiochus,
      And broke the might of direful Hannibal.

That manly race was born of warriors rustic,
Tutored to cleave with Sabine spades the furrow,
    And, at some rigid mother's bluff command,
      Shouldering the logs their lusty right hands hewed,

What time the sun reversed the mountain shadows,
And from the yoke released the wearied oxen,
    As his own chariot slowly passed away,
      Leaving on earth the friendly hour of rest.

What does time dwarf not and deform, corrupting!
Our father's age ignobler than our grandsires'
    Bore us yet more depraved; and we in turn
      Shall leave a race more vicious than ourselves.

ODE VII.

TO ASTERIA.

This poem tells its own tale. It has that peculiar grace in which Horace is inimitable. Orelli says, "On account of its elegant pleasantry, and the mode in which the action is brought out into evidence—although the whole scene, and the three persons who play their part in it, are pure poetic inventions—it may be classed among Horace's happiest poems." It is indeed a miniature lyrical comedy, and, slight though it be in substance, may be cited as an example of the skill with which Horace can give to a few stanzas the lively effect of a drama. The date is unknown, but is referred by some to A.U.C. 729.

---

* "'Institor,' 'an agent, a trader in articles of dress or for the toilet.'"
—YONGE. I have translated this "man-milliner," for there seems some kind of antithesis intended between the effeminate occupations of the "institor" and the rough manners of the shipmaster.

Nay, Asteria, why weep'st thou for Gyges,
Whom, enriched with Bithynia's rich cargoes,
   The first sparkling zephyrs of spring
     Shall waft back to thee, constant as ever ?

By the south wind on Oricus driven,
At the rise of the turbulent goat-star,
   Unsleeping, he weeps, through the night,
     The dull chill of his partnerless pillow,

But the agent of Chloë, his hostess,
Tells the youth that in her he has kindled
   A flame no less ardent than thine,
     In a thousand ways craftily tempting :

Warns him how the false consort of Prœtus
Duped her credulous lord, by feigned charges,
   Into plotting Bellerophon's death,
     For too chastely regarding his hostess.*

Tells how Peleus Hippolyte † slighted,
And was all but consigned to dark Hades ;
   Then seeks to allure him by tales
     Teaching lessons for sinning in safety :

All in vain !   To his words is thy true-love
Deaf as rocks to the breakers Icarian ;
   But keep sharp look-out on thyself,
     Lest too charmed with thy neighbour Enipeus ;

---

* Prœtus, believing the story of his wife Anteia, that Bellerophon had attempted to seduce her, but unwilling himself to slay his guest, sent him to his father-in-law Iobates, king in Lycia, with sealed letters, in which Iobates was requested to destroy the bearer.

† This lady, otherwise called Astydamia, made the same charge against Peleus to her husband Acastor that Anteia did to Prœtus against Bellerophon, and for the same reason. Acastor, like Prœtus, having scruples of conscience which forbade him to slay his guest with his own hand, invited Peleus to hunt wild beasts in Mount Pelion ; and when Peleus, overcome with fatigue, fell asleep on the mountain, Acastor concealed his sword, and left him alone and unarmed to be devoured by the beasts. Peleus on waking and searching for his sword was attacked by Centaurs, but saved by Chiron.

Though no rider so skilled and so noticed
Wheels a steed on the turf of the Campus ;*
   No swimmer so lustily cleaves
      Rapid way down the stream of the Tuscan.

Make thy door fast at eve, never looking
Down the street if shrill fifes serenade thee ;
   And be but more rigidly cold
      Whensoe'er he complains of thy coldness.

ODE VIII.

TO MÆCENAS, ON THE ANNIVERSARY OF HORACE'S ESCAPE FROM THE FALLING TREE.

According to Franke, Horace's escape from the tree was in A.U.C. 728. Ritter places it in 724. This poem commemorates the anniversary of that accident.

Learn'd as thou art in lore of either language,†
Thou marvellest why these hymeneal Kalends
Of March ‡ I keep—I, solitary Cœlebs,
      Wherefore these flow'rets ?

This censer full of incense ? this heaped fuel
On the live sod ?   Know that, escaped the death-blow
Of the dire tree, I a white goat to Bacchus
      Vowed, and feast off'rings.

The day, thus sacred, with the year returning,
Shall free from pitch-seal'd cork-bonds which confine it,
That jar § which first imbibed the smoke-reek under
      Tullus the Consul.

* "Flectere equum." This was to wheel the horse round in a small circle.—MACLEANE.

† Viz., Greek and Latin, which, as the commentators observe, comprehended all the learning a Roman could well acquire.

‡ The Matronalia, in honour of Juno Lucina, were held in the March Kalends.

§ "Amphorae fumum." The jar, or amphora, was kept in the apotheca, and ripened by the smoke from the bath below it. The pitch and cork which fastened it protected the wine itself from being smoked. The wine in the amphora now to be broached, dating back to Tullus the Consul, A.U.C. 683, would have been a year older than Horace himself.

In honour of thy friend thus saved, Mæcenas,
Quaff brimming cups—a hundred be the number;
Let the gay lights watch with us for the morning,
    Noise and broil banished.

Give to thy provident cares for Rome a respite,
Routed are Cotiso's fierce Dacian armies,
Mede wroth with Mede, upon fraternal slaughter,
    Wastes his wild fury.*

Subject to Rome, and curbed in tardy fetters,
The old Cantabrian foe on shores Hispanian;
Lo! the grim Scythians meditate retreating—
    Lax are their bow-strings.

As one who takes in private life his leisure,
A while forego the over-care for nations;
Leave things severe; life offers one glad moment—
    Seize it with gladness.

ODE IX.

THE RECONCILIATION.

"One of Buttmann's remarks with reference to this Ode is well worth quoting: 'The ancients had the skill to construct such poems so that each speech tells us by whom it is spoken; but we let the editors treat us all our lives as schoolboys, and interline such dialogues after the fashion of our plays with the names. To their sedulity we are indebted for the alternation of the lyrical name Lydia with the name Horatius in this exquisite work of art; and yet even in an English poem we should be offended by seeing Collins at the side of Phyllis.' "—MACLEANE.

The poem itself is, perhaps, an imitation from the Greek. Macleane observes, "It is just such a subject as one might expect to find among the erotic poetry of the Greeks."

HE.

"While I yet to thee was pleasing,
  While no dearer youth entwined lavish arms round thy
    white neck,

* The precise dates of these historical allusions are matters of controversy, and not possible to determine. By the Mede is meant the Parthian, distracted by the civil feuds between Phraates and Tiridates.

Happy then, indeed, I flourished,
  Never Persian king * was blest with such riches as were
    mine."†

She.

" While no other more inflamed thee, ˛
  And below no Chloë's rank Lydia in thy heart was
    placed,
Glorious then did Lydia flourish,
  Roman Ilia's lofty name not so honoured as was mine."†

He.

" O'er me now reigns Thracian Chloë,
  Skilled in notes of dulcet song and the science of the
    lute ;
If my death her life could lengthen,
  So that Fate my darling spared, I without a fear could
    die."‡

She.

" From a mutual torchlight kindled
  Is my flame for Calaïs, son of Thurian Ornytus,§
If my death his life could lengthen,
  So that Fate would spare the boy, I a double death
    would die !"

He.

" What if Venus fled—returning,
  Forced us two, dissevered now, back into her brazen
    yoke;
If I shook off auburn Chloë,
  And to Lydia, now shut out, opened once again the
    door ? "

* " Persarum vigui rege beatior." The opposition between the lover's comparison in this stanza and the girl's in the next (" Romana vigui clarior Ilia ") is this : The lover means that he was richer in her love than the wealthiest king ; the girl that she (the humble freed-woman) was more honoured in his love than the most illustrious matron.

† Ilia, as the mother of Romulus, queen and priestess, stands here as the noblest type of Roman matrons, " Romanorum nobilissima."

‡ " Si parcent animæ fata superstiti." " Animæ meæ " denotes a familiar expression of endearment, as in Cicero, ad. Fam. xiv. 14; and as the Italians still call their mistress, " Anima mia."

§ " Thurini Calaïs—Thressa Chloë." The alliteration between the names here selected seems studied. In making Chloë a Thracian and

SHE.

" Than a star though he be fairer,
  Lighter thou than drifted, cork—rougher thou than
        Hadrian wave,*
Yet how willingly-I answer,
  'Tis with thee that I would live—gladly I with thee
      would die."

ODE X.

TO LYCE.

This humorous ode belongs to a kind of serenade common enough with the Greeks, and is probably imitated from a Greek original. There is no reason for supposing the Lyce whose cruelty is here complained of, to be identical with the Lyce who is lampooned in Book IV. Ode xiii.

Didst thou drink at the uttermost waters of Don,
To some savage barbarian, O Lyce, the spouse,
Still, thy heart with compassion might think of me stretched
    Where the north winds are quartered outside of thy door.

Hark! the hinge of thy gate; hark! the plants in thy
        hall,†
With what dissonant howl they re-echo the blasts,
And with what icy clearness the frost-air above
    Renders crisper the snows that are heapen below!

Calaïs the son of a Sybarite (Thurium, a town of Lucania, near the site of the ancient Sybaris), the poet perhaps insinuates that the lady who had replaced Lydia was somewhat too rude or masculine—the gentleman who had replaced the lover of the dialogue somewhat too soft and effeminate.

  * "Improbo — Hadria." Orelli interprets "improbo" by "töbent," "raging." The poets use the word "improbus" to imply anything in violent excess. Ritter, with perhaps over-subtlety, considers that the comparison to a cork refers, not to levity of temperament, but to the insignificant stature of the poet in contrast to the beauty of Calaïs.

  † "Nemus Inter pulchra satum tecta." Small trees were sometimes planted round the impluvium of a Roman house. This is the interpretation adopted by Orelli. Ritter contends that the line refers to one of the two sacred groves situated between the two heights of the Capitoline.

Lay the haughtiness hateful to Venus aside,
Lest the wheel should run back and the rope should be
    snapped,*
Thy gay parent Tyrrhenian ne'er meant to produce
A Penelope cruel to suitors in thee.

Ah! although thou art proof against presents and prayers,
And the pale-blue complexion of lovers disdained;
Nor ev'n bowed to revenge on the spouse led astray
    By a roving Pierian † less chaste than a Muse;

Yet, while granting thy heart is not softer than oak,
And as mild as the snakes in the land of the Moor,
Spare the life of a suppliant! I am of flesh,
    And can bear not for ever this porch and that sleet.‡

ODE XI.

TO THE LYRE.

"The common inscription, 'Ad Mercurium' (to Mercury), adopted by
Bentley and others, is plainly wrong, and calculated to mislead. The in-
scription should be 'Ad testudinem' (to the lyre or shell) if anything, for
Mercury disappears after the first two verses. The miracles alluded to,
except Amphion's, were those of Orpheus, and of the lyre in his hands, not
Mercury's—which Orelli not perceiving, contradicts himself."—MACLEANE.

Mercury (for, tutored in thy lore, Amphion
Charmed into motion rocks by his sweet singing),
And thou, my lyre, with sevenfold chord resounding
    Measures not skill-less,

* "Ne currente retro funis eat rota." This line has been tortured to
many interpretations. "Lest the wheel turn back and the rope with it," is
Orelli's, accepted by Macleane, who observes, the metaphor in that case is
taken from a rope wound round a cylinder, which, being allowed to run
back, the rope runs down, and the weight or thing attached goes with it.
"The rope may break and the wheel run back," is the construction
Macleane gives in his argument to the ode.
† "Pieria pellice," Macedonian lady of pleasure.—ORELLI, RITTER.
There is some humour as well as wit in coupling "pellico" with an epithet
so suggestive of an opposite idea.
‡ "Aquæ Cœlestis patiens." The expression can scarcely apply to rain,
since the night has been described as one of wind and frost:—
                "Glaciet nives
        Puro numine Juppiter;"
"puro" being, as Macleane observes, "an epithet well suited to a clear,

Albeit once, unmusical, unheeded,*
Now welcome both in banquet-halls and temples,
Teach me some strain resistlessly beguiling
       Lyde to listen.

Wild as the filly in its third year, frisking
Through the wide meadows, the least touch dismays her;
Never yet won, she views as saucy freedom
       Even the wooing.

But thou† hast power to lead away the tigers,
And in their train the forests; stay swift rivers;
Cerberus himself, dread jailer of dark thresholds,
       Soothed into meekness,

Yielded to thy bland voice his hundred strongholds
Of fury-heads, each garrisoned with serpents,
And hushed the triple tongue in jaws whose breath-reek
       Tainted the hell-gloom;

The tortured lips of Tityos and Ixion
Reluctant smiled; awhile their urn stood thirsty
As paused the Danaids, to the charmer's music
       Dreamily list'ning.

Let Lyde hear the guilt of those stern virgins,
Hear, too, their well-known penance; doomed for ever
To toil at filling up a sieve-like vessel;
       Tell her how surely

frosty night." The wind would keep off the snow, but there might be
gusty showers of sleety hail. Horace, however, no doubt, uses the expression in a general sense, such as the "floods of heaven," whether they be
snow, rain, or sleet.

* "Nec loquax," *i. e.,* "canora,"—DILLENBURGER, ORELLI. Horace,
though a born poet, if ever there was one—and telling us that even as an
infant, when the doves covered him with bay and myrtle, he was marked
out for the service of the Muses—does not disdain, here and elsewhere, to
intimate that, if a born poet, he had taken very great pains to make himself
a good one.

† "Thou" refers not to Mercury, but to the lyre—*i. e.,* symbolically to
the power of song and music, as exercised by Orpheus.

Slow fates await such crimes,—though under Orcus;
Impious—for can impiety be greater?
Impious in giving to the sword their bridegrooms,
    Ruthlessly murdered.*

Amidst the many, One alone was worthy
The nuptial torch;—a maid, through all the ages,
By glorious falsehood to her perjured father,
    Nobly immortal.

" Rise," to her youthful bridegroom, thus she whispered;
" Rise, lest there come, and whence thou dost suspect not,
Into thy lids the everlasting slumber!
    Baffle my father;

" Elude my blood-stained sisters—lionesses;
Each—woe is me!—her separate victim rending:
Softer than they, I can nor strike nor hold thee
    Pent in these shambles!

" Let my sire load me with his barbarous fetters,
Wroth with the pitying love that spares a husband,
Or ship me outlawed to Numidian deserts!
    Be it so! Hasten!

" Go wheresoe'er swift foot or sail can bear thee;
Blest be the auspice! Night and Venus favour!
Go; be some word that mourns me and remembers
    Carved on my tombstone! " †

* The old mythologists differ among themselves as to the fable of Danaus and the fate of his daughters. Horace here adopts the common story that Danaus, having reason to think that the fifty sons of his brother Ægyptus were plotting against him, fled with his fifty daughters from Libya (the domain assigned him by his father Belus, Ægyptus having Arabia), and ultimately became King of Argos. His nephews came to his new realm and demanded his daughters in marriage. Danaus consented, but, in distrust or revenge, enjoined his daughters to murder their bridegrooms with the swords he gave them for that amiable purpose. On alone, Hypermnestra, spared her husband, Lynceus. According to the earlier writers, the Danaïdes were purified of their crime, and even married again. Later poets, deeming it perhaps more prudent to make a severe example of such dangerous bed-fellows, sent them to Orcus.

† It is pleasant to think that the modern law of what is called "poetic justice," has a precedent in the final restoration of this young lady to the arms of the husband she had so mercifully spared. Ovid's Epistle of Hypermnestra to Lynceus, supposed to be written while imprisoned by her father, is much indebted to Horace's lines. But perhaps both poets borrowed from a common source which is lost to modern discoverers.

ODE XII.

NEOBULE'S SOLILOQUY.

Most of the earlier commentators took it for granted that the poet is here addressing Neobule. Dillenburger, Orelli, and Macleane prefer to consider that Neobule is throughout the ode addressing herself. The poem is, perhaps, more or less imitated from one by Alcæus, of which only a single verse is preserved. The metre of the ode has given much trouble to commentators, especially to those who insist upon the theory that all Horace's odes are reducible to quatrain stanzas, while this ode is in a stanza of three lines, according to the authority of MSS. (with the exception of the Turinese one). An attempt to remodel it into quatrain will be found in Orelli's excursus to the ode, and is adopted by Yonge in his edition.

How unhappy the lot of poor girls; neither play to their
    fancies in love,
Neither balm for their sorrows in wine! frightened out of
    their souls by the lash
      In the tongue of some testy relation.*

Neobùle, wing'd Love has flown off with thy spindles and
    basket of wools!
And thy studious delight in the toils of Minerva is chased
    from thy heart
      By young Hebrus, the bright Liparæan.

Hardy swimmer in Tiber to plunge gleaming shoulders
    anointed with oil!
Sure, Bellerophon rode not so well; as a boxer no arm is
    so strong;
      And no foot is so fleet as a runner.

Skilful marksman, when over the champaign the hounds
    drive and scatter the deer,
To select the right stag for his dart; and as nimble to start
    the wild boar,
      Lurking grim in the dense forest-thicket.

* Literally "uncle." "Uncles," Torrentius observes, "had considerable power over their nephews and nieces by the Roman law, and, being less indulgent than fathers, their severity passed into a proverb."

ODE XIII.

TO THE BANDUSIAN FOUNTAIN.

The site of this fountain has been a matter of controversy, interesting to those who seek to ascertain the localities of places endeared to them by the poets. Acron and others assumed it to be in the neighbourhood of Horace's Sabine home, and identify it with the rivulet of Digentia (Licenza). It is, however, generally now agreed, upon what appears sufficiently competent authority, that Bandusia was in Horace's native soil, about six miles from the site of Venusia (Dillenburger, Orelli, Macleane). If so, it is conjectured that the poem would have been written in earlier life, when Horace revisited his native spot—perhaps A.U.C. 717—since it is held scarcely probable that he would have thought of consecrating the fountain in Venusia, when he was settled in the remote district of his Sabine farm. It may, however, be likely enough, as Tate contends (Horat. Restit. p. 88), that Horace transferred the name, endeared to him by early association, to the spring near his later home. Yonge suggests the query, " Was Bandusia the name of the place, or of the presiding nymph of the fountain?"—See Orelli's full and very elegant note on this subject.

Fount of Bandusia, more lucid than crystal,
Worthy of honeyed wine, not without flowers,
　　I will give thee to-morrow a kid,
　　　　Whose front, with the budded horn swelling,

Predicts to his future life Venus and battles;
Vainly!　The lymph of thy cold running waters
　　He shall tinge with the red of his blood,
　　　　Fated child of the frolicsome people!

The scorch of the Dog-star's fell season forbears thee;
Ever friendly to grant the sweet boon of thy coolness
　　To the wild flocks that wander around,
　　　　And the oxen that reek from the harrow.

I will give thee high rank and renown among fountains,
When I sing of the ilex o'erspreading the hollows
　　Of rocks, whence, in musical fall,*
　　　　Leap thy garrulous silvery waters.

* " Me dicente cavis impositam ilicem Saxis"—the cavern overshadowed with the ilex from which the fountain gushes.—ORELLI.

ODE XIV.

"Composed at the close of the Cantabrian war, A.U.C. 729, when Augustus's return was expected, or on his return the following year."—MACLEANE.

In noticing the critical animadversions on this ode "as unequal to the occasion," Macleane observes justly that "it was evidently only a private affair." The familiar lightness of the concluding stanzas would indicate a merry-making kept with a few personal friends.

Joy, O ye people! it was said that Cæsar
Went forth like Hercules, in quest of laurels
Bought but by death; now home from shores Hispanian
    Comes he back victor.

Let her whose joy in her sole lord is centred*
Join, in thanksgivings due, the glad procession—
Join with the sister of our glorious chieftain—
    Join with the mothers,

Chastely adorned by sacrificial fillets†—
Mothers of children now no more imperilled;
Youths and young brides hush, at such time ill-omened,
    Each lighter whisper.

Truly to me this holiday is sacred,
And its bright sunshine chases cloudy troubles.
I fear nor open feud nor stealthy murder,‡
    Earth yet holds Cæsar!

Up, boy, and bring the perfume and the garlands,
And wine that to the Marsian war bears witness,
If one jar, baffling Spartacus the Rover,
    Somewhere lurks hidden.§

* "Unico gaudens mulier marito." See Orelli's note on "unico," which some have interpreted in the sense of "unique" or "peerless;" Dillenburger, as "dear" or "beloved."

† Worn by the Roman matrons to distinguish them from freed women.

‡ "Nec tumultum,
Nec mori per vim metuam."

"Tumultum" here evidently means "intestine feud" or "popular outbreak;" "vim," "assassination," or "personal violence." With Cæsar is identified the prevailing security of law.

§ "The Marsic or Social war was continued from A.U.C. 663 to 665; and the Servile war, headed by Spartacus, lasted from A.U.C. 681 to 683; therefore the wine Horace wanted would have been sixty-five years old at least.

Go, and bid silver-tongued Neœra hasten,
Binding in Spartan knot her locks myrrh-scented;*
But, if obstructed by that brute her porter,
    Quietly come back.

Nothing cools fiery spirits like a grey hair;
In every quarrel 'tis your sure peacemaker;
In my hot youth, when Plancus was the consul,
    I was less patient.†

ODE XV.

ON AN OLD WOMAN AFFECTING YOUTH.

The names in this poem are, of course, fictitious, and the satire itself is of very general application even in the present day. Its date is undiscoverable.

Mend thy life—it is time; cease such pains to be vile,
    Flaunting wife of the indigent Ibycus;
Fitter far for the grave, do not gambol with girls,
    Interspersing a cloud 'mid the galaxy.

That which Pholoë thy daughter may suit well enough,
    In thee, hoary Chloris, is horrible:‡
'Tis permitted to her to besiege the young rakes
    In their homes, with much greater propriety:

No Bacchante the timbrel excites with its clash,
    Than that daughter of thine can be livelier;
And her fancy for Nothus so warms her and stings,
    That no roe on the hills is more frolicsome.

There seems to have been something remarkable in the vintage of that period, so as to make it proverbial; for Juvenal, one hundred years afterwards, speaking of the selfish gentleman who keeps his best wine for his own drinking, says:—

  'Ipse capillato diffusum consule potat,
   Calcatamque tenet bellis socialibus uvam.'"
        —S. v. 30, 89.—MACLEANE.

* "Myrrheum crinem." The scholiasts interpreted this expression "myrrh-coloured." Orelli and other recent commentators support the interpretation "myrrh-scented."
† i.e., when Horace was in his twenty-third year.
‡ "Anus cum ludit, Morti delicias facit."—P. SYRUS.

What becomes thee the best is a warm woollen dress ;
 Get thee fleeces from famous Luceria ;*
What become thee the least are the lute and the rose,
 And the cask tippled dry with young rioters.

ODE XVI.

GOLD THE CORRUPTOR.

This ode is among Horace's most striking variations of the moral he so
frequently preaches—content *versus* gold.   But here he does full justice to
the power of gold as the corruptor.   I have not adopted for this ode the
forms of metre I have elsewhere employed for rendering odes in the same
measure (Asclepiadean, with a Glyconean in the 4th line), but one by which
I have not unfrequently rendered the Alcaic stanza, with the slight variation of a monosyllabic termination in the second verse, while the termination of the first verse is dissyllabic.

The brazen tower, the solid doors,† the vigil
Of dismal watch-dogs sentried night and day,
      Might have sufficed to guard
         From midnight loves imprisoned Danaë;

But Jove and Venus laughed to scorn Acrisius,
The timorous jailer of the hidden maid,‡
      Opening at once sure way,
         The god transformed himself into—a Bribe.

More subtle than the flash of the forked lightning,
Gold glides amidst the armëd satellites ;
      More potent than Jove's bolt,
         Gold through the walls of granite bursts its way :

* A town in Apulia now called Lucera.   In its neighbourhood was one
of the largest tracts of public pasture-land.   The wools of Luceria were
celebrated.
   † "Robustæque fores."   Orelli suggests "firmissimæ," and objects, not
without fine critical taste, to the interpretation of Forcellini and others—
viz., "*oaken* doors," as a descent in poetic expression, just after insisting on
"brazen tower."   Certainly, in line 9, Ode iii., "Illi robur et æs triplex,"
"robur" comes first.
   ‡ Acrisius shut up his daughter in a brazen tower from fear of the oracle,
who had predicted that she should bear him a son who would cause his
death.   He is therefore timorous or panic-stricken (pavidus) because of the
oracle.

So fell the Argive Augur with his kindred,*
Gain, tempting one, whelmed in destruction all;
  The man of Macedon†
   By gifts cleft gates, by gifts sapped rival thrones—

Gifts have ensnared a Navy's fiercest chiefs,‡
Care grows with wealth, with wealth the greed for more.
  O my Mæcenas! gem
   Of Roman knighthood,§ ever have I feared

To lift a crest above the crowd conspicuous—
Rightly; the more man shall deny himself,
  The more shall gods bestow.
   I do not side with wealth, but, lightly armed,

Bound o'er the lines, deserting to Contentment;
Owner more grand in means the rich despise,
  Than were I said to hide,
   In mine own granaries, all Apulia yields

Her toiling sons, want-pinched amidst heaped plenty :—
A brooklet pure, some roods of woodland cool,
  Faith in crops, sure if small—
   Are a lot happier, though he knows it not,

Than his who glitters in the spoils of Afric.
Though not for me toil the Calabrian bees,
  Nor wines in Formian jars
   Languish their fire in length of years away,

* Amphiaraus; his wife Eriphyle, bribed by her brother Polynices, persuaded him to join in the siege of Thebes. There he fell, ordering his sons to put their mother to death. Alcmæon obeyed, and finally perished himself in attempting to get the gold necklace with which Eriphyle had been bribed.

† Philip of Macedon.

‡ This is held to refer to Menas, *alias* Menodorus, commander of Sextus Pompeius's fleet. He deserted from Pompeius to Augustus, then again to Pompeius, and again to Augustus. He had been freed-man to C. M. Pompeius.

§ "Mæcenas, equitum decus." By this significant reference to Mæcenas as the ornament of knighthood, Horace associates Mæcenas with himself in the philosophy of contentment—Mæcenas, having always remained in the equestrian order, to which he was born, declining promotion to the senatorial.

Nor fleecy wools gain weight in Gallic pastures,
Yet Penury keeps aloof; nor, lacked I more,
　　More wouldst thou me deny :
　　　Widening my means by narrowing my desires,

I shall have ampler margin for true riches
Than if to Lydia adding Phrygian realms.
　　Who covets much, much wants;
　　　God gives most kindly giving just enough.

ODE XVII.

TO L. ÆLIUS LAMIA.

This personage was the son of the L. Æ. Lamia who supported Cicero in the suppression of the Catiline conspiracy, and appears during the civil wars to have espoused the party of Cæsar.　Horace's friend was consul A.D. 3; afterwards appointed by Tiberius governor of Syria, but not allowed to enter on the administration of the province.　He became, A.D. 32, "Præfectus Urbi," and died the following year.　Mitscherlich says: "His own good sense will easily show any well-bred gentleman (urbanum) that Horace here, in a well-bred, gentlemanlike way, offers himself as a guest; in plain words, hints that Lamia should ask him to dine."　On which the commentator in Orelli observes, with much feeling asperity: "In the whole poem there is not a vestige of this sort of gentlemanlike good-breeding, if gentlemanlike good-breeding it be, which it is permitted vehemently to doubt."　Evidently the commentator is an Italian.　A gentleman of that country would certainly dispute the good-breeding of any friend offering to drop in at dinner.

Noble Ælius, whose house hath its rise in that Lamus
From whom both the first and the later descendants
　　(As attesting memorials* record)
　　　The great name of Lamia inherit,

Thou canst trace back, indeed, to an absolute monarch,
Holding sway, it is said, over Formia's walled ramparts,
　　And the waters of Liris, that flow
　　　Into grassy domains of Marica.

To-morrow the east wind shall send us a tempest,
Which—if true be the crow, that old seer of foul weather—
　　Shall strew in the grove many leaves;
　　　On the shore,† many profitless sea-weeds.

* "Per memores—fastos."　"Family records," not the "fasti con-
sulares."—MACLEANE.
† The shore of Minturna, on the borders of Latium and Campania, where the nymph Marica was worshipped.

While thou canst, then, protect from the rains the dry
    faggots;
Spend to-morrow in resting thyself and thy household;
    Feast thy genius with wine—but not mixed;
      And do not forget a young porker.

ODE XVIII.

TO FAUNUS.

Faunus was not a stationary divinity. He was supposed to come in the spring, and depart after the celebration of his festival in December. From "parvis alumnis" (translated "young weanlings"), we may suppose this ode was written in spring.—MACLEANE. Ritter denies that by "parvis alumnis" young animals are meant; and contends that the words refer to young plants, transferred from the nursery to fields or orchards. Ritter also dissents from the general interpretation, which I have followed, that "Veneris sodali" is to be coupled with "crateræ." According to him, the companion of Venus is Faunus, the lover of the Nymphs, and not the wine-bowl.

Faunus, thou lover of coy nymphs who fly thee,
Enter my bounds, and fields that slope to sunlight;
Enter them gently; and depart, propitious
    To my young weanlings,

If tender kid, when the year rounds, be offered;
If to the bowl, Venus's boon companion,
Fail not libation due!*—With ample incense
    Steams thine old altar,

        * " Si tener pleno cadit hædus anno,
           Larga nec desunt Veneris sodali
           Vina crateræ. Vetus ara multo
           Fumat odore," &c.

As I have here adopted a novelty in the punctuation, suggested by Macleane, it is well to subjoin his reasons for the innovation. "I have not followed the usual punctuation, which makes 'fumat' depend upon 'si,' with a comma at 'crateræ,' and a period at 'odore.' Horace claims the protection of Faunus for his lambs in the spring on the ground of his due observance of the rites of December, which he then goes on to describe. 'Pleno anno' means at the end of the year when the Faunalia took place." Therefore the division in the poem at which, after the invitation to Faunus in the spring, Horace passes on to describe the festival in the winter, is more intelligible, and far less abrupt, by commencing it with the sacrifice on the altar.

Loose strays the herd on grassy meads disporting,
What time December's Nones bring back thy feast-day ;
Blithe, o'er the fields, streams forth the idling hamlet,
    Freed—with its oxen.

Fearless the lambs behold the wolf prowl near them ;
The woodland strews its leaves before thy footstep ;
And on his hard task-mistress Earth, exulting,
    Thrice stamps the delver ! *

ODE XIX.

TO TELEPHUS.—IN HONOUR OF MURENA'S INSTALLATION IN THE
COLLEGE OF AUGURS.

A. Terentius Varro Murena, adopted by A. Terentius Varro, whose name
he took, according to custom, subdued the Salassi, an Alpine tribe, and
divided their territory among Prætorian soldiers, who founded the town of
Augusta, now Aosta. He was named Consul Suffectus for B.C. 23. In B.C.
22 he was involved in the conspiracy of Fannius Cœpio against the life of
Augustus, and, though his guilt seems doubtful, executed. This is the
same person whom Horace addresses under the name Licinius, Book II.
Ode x., "Rectius vives Licini," &c. The metre in the original is the
second Asclepiadean; but I have found it easier to preserve fidelity to the
sense and spirit of the poem by employing one of the varieties of rhythm
which I have appropriated to the Alcaic.

You inform us how long after Inachus flourished
Royal Codrus, who feared not to die for his country ;
    What noble descendants from Æacus sprung,
    What battles were fought under Ilion the sacred ;

* " Gaudet invisam pepulisse fossor
    Ter pede terram."

"'Fossor' is put generally, I imagine, for a labouring husbandman, who
may be supposed to have no love for the earth that he digs for another."—
MACLEANE. This triple stamp is a dancing measure, which is likened to
the anapœst, where two feet are short and one long. Macleane quotes Sir
John Davies's poem (Orchestra) in explanation of this measure—

" And still their feet an anapœst do sound," &c.

But it is perhaps best understood by anyone who happens to have learned,
in the old-fashioned hornpipe, that step familiarly called "toe, heel, and
cloe,"—touching the ground lightly with the toe, next with the heel, and
then bringing down the whole sole of the foot with a stamp. I have
seen that step, or something very like it, performed in a village dance in the
south of Italy.

But you say not a word upon things more important—
What tho price one must pay for a cask of old Chian ?
    Baths,* rooms—where and whose ? What the moment
      to thaw
    Theso frost-bitten limbs in the sunshine of supper ?

Hillo, boy, there, a cup ! † Brim it full for the New Moon !
Hillo, boy, there, a cup !   Brim it full for tho Midnight !
    And, boy, there, a cup !   Brim it full—to tho health
    Of him we would honour !—Murena tho Augur.

Let the bowls be proportioned to three or nine measures,
As each comrade likes best ; ‡ tho true poet will ever
    Suit his to tho odd-numbered Muses, and quaff
    Thrice three in the rapture the Nine give to brim-
      mers.

But the Grace, with her twin naked sisters, shuns quarrel,
And to more than three measures refuses her sanction.
    Ho ! ho ! what a joy to go mad for a time !
    Why on earth stops the breath of that fife Berecyn-
      thian ?

And pray, why is that harp so unsocially silent,
And tho lively Pandèan pipe idly suspended ?
    Quick, roses—and more !   Let it rain with the rose !
    There's nothing I hate like the hand of a niggard.

---

* "Quis aquam temperet ignibus." Orelli considers this refers to the water to be warmed for the baths ; Ritter, to the water to be warmed for admixture with wine. I have adopted tho former interpretation, though I think it doubtful.

 † "Here, in a kind of phantasy, the poet transports himself with Tele-phus into the midst of the entertainment."—ORELLI.

      ‡ "Tribus aut novem
    Miscentur cyathis pocula commodis."

"The ' cyathus' was a ladle with which tho drink was passed from tho mixing-bowl to the drinking-cup. Tho ladle was of certain capacity, and twelve 'cyathi' went to the Sextarius. Horace says, in effect, 'Let the wine be mixed in the proportion of three cyathi of wine to nine of water, or of nine of wine to three of water.' . . . 'Commodis,' 'fit and proper,'—'cyathi,' that is, 'bumpers.'"—MACLEANE. The above seems tho best and most intelligible interpretation of a passage in which, if con-jectures were cyathi, tho commentators would have greatly exceeded tho number allowed to the nine Muses.

Let the noise of our mirth split the ears of old Lycus.
He is envious—our riot shall gorge him with envy.
  The ears of our neighbour, his wife, let it reach.
    No wife could suit less the grey hairs of old Lycus.*

Thee, O Telephus, radiant with locks of thick cluster,
Thee, with face like the star of the eve at its clearest,
  Budded Rhode is courting; I too am on fire,
    But me Glycera keeps in the flames, burning
    slowly. †

ODE XX.—Omitted.

ODE XXI.

TO MY CASK.

This poem appears composed in honour of some occasion in which Horace entertained the famous L. Valerius Messala Corvinus. No man in that great age was more remarkable for the variety of his accomplishments than this Corvinus. Sprung from one of the greatest consular families, he espoused the senatorian party in the civil wars, and attached himself especially to Cassius. He held the third place in the command of the Republican army, and at Philippi turned Augustus's flank, stormed his camp, and nearly took him prisoner. Subsequently he made terms with Antony, whom he left for Augustus, after Antony's league with Cleopatra—and at Actium commanded the centre of the fleet with great distinction. Besides his eminence as a commander and a statesman, he was conspicuous as an orator, a wit, a historian, and a grammarian. He also wrote poetry.—See Smith's Dictionary for fuller details of life, art. "Messala."

---

* The graduated process of a drinking-bout is most naturally simulated in these verses. First stage, the amiable expansion of heart in the friendly toast—the toleration of different tastes;—each man may drink as much as he likes. Secondly, the consciousness of getting drunk, and thinking it a fine thing;—joy to go mad. Thirdly, the craving for noise;—let the band strike up. Fourthly, a desire for something cool;—roses in ancient Rome—soda-water in modern England. Fifthly, the combative stage;—aggressive insult to poor old Lycus. Sixthly, the maudlin stage, soft and tender; complimentary to Telephus, and confidingly pathetic as to his own less fortunate love-affairs.

† Commentators have endeavoured to create a puzzle even here, where the meaning appears very obvious. Rhode runs after you (petit), who are so handsome—Glycera does not run after me, but keeps me languishing; the sense is consistent with the tone, half envious, half sarcastic, with which the poet always speaks of Telephus, the typical beauty-man and lady-killer.

Coeval with me, born when Manlius was consul,
Whatsoe'er the effects of thy life, while in action—
    Spleen or mirth, angry brawl or wild love,
        Or, O gentle cask,* ready slumber—

Under what head soe'er there be entered account of †
The grapes thou hast kept since in Massicus gathered,
    Thou art worth being roused on a day
        Of good fortune ; descend ‡ for Corvinus

Asking wines by age mellowed !   He will not neglect thee,
All imbued though he be with Socratical maxims.
    Father Cato, full often, 'tis said,
        Warmed his virtue with wine undiluted. §

Thou givëst a soft-pricking spur to the sluggish,
Makest gentle the harsh, and confiding the cautious.
    Chasing care from the brows of the wise,
        Thou unlockest their hearts to Lyæus.‖

Hope and nerve thou restorest to minds worn and harassed,
Add'st the horn that exalts to the front of the beggar ;
    Fresh from thee he could face down a king,
        Fresh from thee, brave the charge of an army.

Thee, shall Liber and Venus, if Venus come merry,
And the Graces, reluctant their bond to dissever,
    And the living lights gaily prolong,
        Till the stars fly from Phœbus returning.

* " Pia testa." The exact meaning of " pia " here has given rise to much critical disputation. Macleane says he knows no better translation than Francis's " gentle cask," for the meaning is to be derived from its connection with " facilem somnum.' Yonge adopts the same interpretation, " gentle, kindly,"—observing " it would be ' impia' if producing ' querelas, rixas,' " &c. I have translated " testa " cask, as a word familar to the English reader, but it here properly means the amphora, a vessel into which the wine was, as we should say, bottled.
† " Quocunque nomine," " on whatever account." On the technical meaning of " nomen," signifying " an entry in an account," see Mr. Long's note on Cicero in Verr. 11, 1, 38. " ' Lectum,' which Forcellini interprets ' selected,' rather applies to the gathering of the grape from which the wine was made. Massic wine was from Mons Massicus in Campania."—MACLEANE.
‡ " Descende"—i. e. descend from the place where it was kept (apotheca), in the upper part of the house.
§ " Mero," wine undiluted.
‖ " Retegis Lyæo." " The dative case, ' to' Lyæus, appears here to be employed rather than the ablative."—ORELLI.

ODE XXII.

VOTIVE INSCRIPTION TO DIANA.

Nothing more need be said of this ode than that it is one of the votive inscriptions common among the ancients, and that a pine-tree would be very fittingly dedicated to Diana. The attempts made to extract a story out of the occasion and the offering are preposterous. That which is chiefly noticeable in this and other poems by Horace, more or less similar, is the rare and admirable merit of terseness. The poet has sufficient reliance on himself to be sure that, however briefly and simply he expresses himself on a subject to which brevity and simplicity belong, his unmistakable mark will appear on the work.

Guardian of mountain-peaks, and forests—Virgin,
Goddess triformed—who, thrice invoked, benignly
Dost hear young mothers in their hour of travail,
        And from death save them;

Thine be this pine which overhangs my villa,
To which each closing year shall be devoted
A youthful boar, of sidelong thrusts indulging
        Vain meditations.

ODE XXIII.

TO PHIDYLE.

Jani and other commentators have supposed the Phidyle here addressed to be Horace's country housekeeper, and that Horace in this ode answers some complaint of hers that her master did not permit her to sacrifice in a manner sufficiently handsome. Orelli observes that Phidyle could not be Horace's servant, for she is represented as sacrificing according to her own choice and will. But this no servant could do: the act of sacrifice for the whole family belonged exclusively to the head of the establishment. The ode, if addressed to any individual at all—which it probably was not—would have been addressed, therefore, to some mistress of a plain country household.

If with each new-born moon thou lift to Heaven thy sup-
        pliant hands,
If with some grains of frankincense, fresh corn, and flesh
        of swine,
        My rustic Phidyle, thy rites
        Appease thy simple Lares,

Thy fruitful vines shall neither feel the south wind's poisoned
       breath,*
Nor mildew blight to sterile dearth thy harvests in the ear,
    Nor appled autumn sicklied airs
       Infect thy tender weanlings.

Let victims whose devoted blood shall tinge the Pontiff's
       axe
Pasture on snow-clad Algidus, mid oak and ilex groves,
    Or, fattening fast on Alban meads,
       Grow ripe for pompous slaughter : †

But not from thee thy homely gods ask hecatombs of sheep;
Content are they with what thou giv'st—content with rural
       crowns ;
    So twine thy humble rosemary wreath,
       And weave thy fragile myrtle.

The costliest offering softens not the household gods, if
       wroth,
More sure than a votive cake or grains of crackling salt,
    Provided that no sin pollute
       The hands which touch the altar.

ODE XXIV.

ON THE MONEY-SEEKING TENDENCIES OF THE AGE.

This ode, like those with which Book III. commences, appears written
with a design to assist Augustus in the task of social reform after the conclusion of the civil wars. Orelli ascribes the date to A.U.C. 725, 726,
Macleane to 728. It is more purely didactic than the first five odes of this
book—that is to say, it has less of the genuine lyrical mode of treating
moral subjects. If in that respect inferior to those odes—as regards the
higher range of poetry in the abstract—it is inferior to no ode in elevation
of sentiment.

---

  * " Pestilentem Africum," the sirocco.—ORELLI.
  † The flocks and herds that belonged to the College of Pontiffs were fed
on Algidus and the meadows of Alba Longa.

Though, as the lord of treasures which outshine
   The unrifled wealth of Araby and Indus,
The piles on which reposed thy palaces,
   Filled up both oceans, Tuscan and Apulic; *

Yet if dire Fate her nails of adamant
   Into thy loftiest wood-tree once hath driven,†
Thou shalt not banish terror from thy soul,
   Nor from the snares of death thy head deliver.

Happier the Scythians, wont o'er townless wilds
   To shift the wains that are their nomad dwellings;
Or the rude Getæ whose unmeted soil
   Yields its free sheaves and fruits to all in common; ‡

There each man toils but for his single year—
   Rests, and another takes his turn of labour;
There ev'n the step-dame, mild and harmless, gives
   To orphans motherless again the mother.

No dowered she-despot rules her lord, nor trusts
   The wife's protection to the leman's splendour.§
There, is the dower indeed magnificent!
   Ancestral virtue, chastity unbroken,

* In reference to the custom of building palaces out into the sea. Munro adopts the reading "publicum" for "Apulicum."

† "Si figit adamantinos
    Summis verticibus dira Necessitas
Clavos."

Various attempts have been made to explain the obscurity of this metaphor. I have adopted Orelli's interpretation, which he considers to be decidedly proved the right one by an Etruscan painting—viz., that while the rich man is busied in casting out the moles and raising the height of his palace, Destiny is seen driving her nails into the top of the building, as if saying to the master, "Hitherto, but no farther; the fated end is come to thyself." Macleane, however, prefers the interpretation of a commentator in Cruquius, who takes "verticibus" for the human head, the most fatal place for a blow. There is no disputing about tastes; but I confess I like this interpretation less than any. Whatever Fate is about to do with her adamantine nails, it seems necessary, for connection with the preceding lines, that she should fix her mark on the ambitious piles which the man is building—not on himself. And if she has driven her nails into his head, she might spare for that head the net or snare to which the poet refers in the line that follows.

‡ The habits of the Suevi, as described by Cæsar, Bell. Gall. IV. i., are here imputed, correctly or not, to the Getæ.

§ "Nec nitido fidit adultero." Macleane follows Orelli in considering that this means that she does not trust to the influence of the adulterer to protect her from the anger of the husband.

Shrinking with terror from all love save one;
  Or death the only sentence for dishonour.
Oh, whosoe'er would banish out of Rome
      Intestine rage and fratricidal slaughter,

If he would have on reverent statues graved
  This holy title, "Father of his Country,"
Let him be bold enough to strike at vice,
      Curb what is now indomitable—Licence,

And earn the praise of *after* time!   Alas!
  Virtue we hate while seen alive; when vanished,
We seek her—but invidiously; and right
      The virtue dead to wrong some virtue living.*

But what avails the verbiage of complaint—
  To rail at guilt, yet punish not the guilty?
What without morals profit empty laws?
      If nor that zone, which, as his own enclosure,

The Sun belts round with fires—nor that whose soil
  Is ice, the hard land bordering upon Boreas—
Scare back the avarice of insatiate trade,
      And oceans are the conquests of the sailor;

If dread to encounter the supreme reproach
  Of poverty, ordains to do and suffer
All things for profit, and desert as bare
      The difficult way that only mounts to virtue?

O were we penitent, indeed, for sins,†
  How we should haste to cast gems, gauds, gold, useless
Save as the raw material of all ill,
      Amid the shouts of multitudes applauding,

---

* These lines are, perhaps too boldly, paraphrased from the original in order to bring out more clearly the latent meaning, as suggested with pretty general acquiescence by Dacier and Sanadon; viv. "the envious man has a certain pleasure in regretting the dead because he can thus wrong or insult the living.

† I adopt the punctuation of Dillenburger, Orelli, and Munro—viz., that the full stop is at "bene pœnitet."—See note in Orelli to lines 49, 50.

Into the vaults of Capitolian Jove ;
  Or that safe treasure-house—the nearest ocean !
To weed out avarice dig down to the root,
  And minds relaxed rebrace by rougher training.

Look at yon high-born boy—he cannot ride !
  Horseback too rude for him—the chase too dangerous !
Skilful and brave—to trundle a Greek hoop ;
  And break the laws which interdict the dice-box : *

While his mean father with a perjured oath
  Swindles alike his partner and his hearth-guest,
Spurred by one passion—how to scrape the pelf—
  His worthless self bequeaths an heir as worthless.

The immoderate † riches grow, forsooth, and grow,
  But ne'er in growing can attain completion ;
An unknown something, ever absent still,
  Stints into want the unsufficing fortune.

ODE XXV.

HYMN TO BACCHUS.

Of this ode Orelli says, that it belongs more properly than any other ode
of Horace to the dithyrambic genus, any closer imitation of which was
denied to the language and taste of the Romans, as savouring of affectation
or bombast. Nowhere in Horace is there more of the true lyrical enthusiasm : the picture of the Bacchante, astonished by the landscape stretched
below her, is singularly beautiful. Dillenburger and Orelli conjecture the
poem to have been written A.U.C. 725-726 ; Macleane thinks it may have

---

* "Græco trocho." This hoop, made of metal, was guided by a rod like
our hoops nowadays. It seems to have been used in the thoroughfares, and
by youths as well as mere children. The laws against gambling were
stringent, and in Cicero's time it was an offence sufficiently serious for
Cicero to make it a grave charge against M. Antony that he had pardoned
a man condemned for gambling, as he was himself a habitual gambler.
Juvenal says that the heir still in his infancy (bullatus) learnt the dice from
his father.

† "Improbæ divitiæ." "Improbæ" has not here the sense of "dis-
honest" or "iniquitous," as it is commonly translated ; it means, rather,
"immoderate," "out of all proportion." Macleane rightly observes that
"improbus" is one of the most difficult words to which to assign its proper
meaning. It implies excess, and that excess must be expressed according
to the subject described.

been on the announcement of the taking of Alexandria, A.U.C. 724. It was evidently while some new triumph of Cæsar's was fresh in the mind of the poet and of the public.

Whither, full of thee, O Bacchus,
　Am I hurried by thy rapture, with a spirit strange pos-
　　sessed ?
Through what forests, through what caverns ?
　Underneath what haunted grottoes shall my voice be
　　heard aloud,

Pondering words to lift up Cæsar
　To his rank 'mid starry orders, in the council-halls of
　　Jove ?
O for utterance largely sounding,
　Never yet through mouth of poet made the language of
　　the world !

As the slumberless Bacchante
　From the lonely mountain-ridges, stricken still with
　　wonder, sees
Flash the waves of wintry Hebrus,
　Sparkle snows in Thracian lowlands, soar barbarian
　　Rhodopë,

Such my rapture, wandering guideless,*
　Now where river-margents open, now where forest-
　　shadows close.
Lord of Naiads, lord of Mænads,
　Who with hands divinely strengthened, from the moun-
　　tain heave the ash :

Nothing little, nothing lowly,
　Nothing mortal, will I utter !　Oh, how perilously sweet
'Tis to follow thee, Lenæus,
　Thee the god who wreathes his temples with the vine-
　　leaf for his crown !

　　　　　* " Ut mihi devio
　　　　Ripas et vacuum nemus
　　　　Mirari libet."

Some of the MSS. have " rupes " instead of " ripas," and that reading is adopted by Lambinus and Muretus.　Dillenburger, Orelli, Macleane, Munro, and Yonge agree in preferring " ripas," as having the authority of the best MSS.　Assuming this latter reading to be right, it renders more appropriate

ODE XXVI.

VENUS.

This ode has been generally supposed to be written when Horace had
arrived at a time of life sufficiently advanced to retire from the service of
the ladies, and Malherbe, the French poet, had it in his eye when, at the age
of fifty, he made farewell visits to the fair ones he had courted till then, and
informed them that he resigned his commission in the armies of Cytherea.
But I think with Macleane that the ode represents nothing more than a successful gallant's first refusal; and that to apply it to Horace himself, or to
assume, from the opening, that he was getting into years, and about to
abandon lyrical poetry, is to mistake the character and scope of the ode.

I have lived till of late well approved by the fair,
And have, not without glory, made war in their cause;
   Now the wall on the left side of Venus * shall guard
     `My arms, and the lute which has done with the service.

Here, here, place the flambeaux which lit the night-march;
Here, the bows and the crowbars—dread weapons of siege,†
   Carrying menace of doom to the insolent gates
     Which refused at my conquering approach to sur-
     render.

the previous description of the Bacchante's amaze in seeing all the landscape
expand before her. The poet then comes on the river-bank as he emerges
from the forest, the country thus opening upon him, and again closed in.
So in Schiller's "Der Spaziergang" the poet plunges into the wood, and
following a winding path, suddenly the veil is rent. The passage is well
translated by a lamented friend, Dr. Whewell:—

"Lost is the landscape at once in the dark wood's secret recesses,
   Where a mysterious path leads up the winding ascent;

Suddenly rent is the veil; all startled, I view with amazement,
   Through the wood's opening glade, blazing in splendour the day."

I cannot help thinking that Horace had in his mind an actual scene, as
Schiller had in the Walk—that it was in some ramble amidst rocks, woods,
and water, that the idea of this dithyramb occurred to him. We have his
own authority for believing that, like most other poets, he composed a good
deal in his rural walks,—"circa nemus uvidique Tiburis ripas operosa parvus
Carmina fingo."

  * In the temple of Venus, on the left wall, as being most propitious.—
MACLEANE. The left side, as the heart side, is now, in many superstitious
practices derived from the ancients, considered the best for divinations connected with the affections. In chiromancy, the left hand is examined in
preference to the right, not only for the line of life, but for the lines supposed to prognosticate in affairs of the heart.

  † The torches to light the gallant to the house he went to attack, and
the crowbar to burst open her door, are intelligible enough. What is

Regal goddess who reignest o'er Cyprus the blest,
And o'er Memphis, unchilled by the snow-flakes of Thrace,
   Lift on high o'er that arrogant Chloë thy scourge,
     And by one touch—but one—fright her into sub-
      mission.

ODE XXVII.

TO GALATEA UNDERTAKING A JOURNEY.

We know nothing more of Galatea than the ode tells us, by which she appears to have been a friend of Horace's meditating a journey to Greece. Upon the strength of a line in which he asks her to remember him, an attempt has been actually made to include her in the catalogue of Horace's mistresses; whereas the poem, in the digressive introduction of the glorious fate which awaited Europa, might much more plausibly be supposed to intimate that some lover or spouse of very high degree was reserved for Galatea at her journey's end. The beautiful picture of Europa's flight and remorse is among the instances of Horace's exquisite adaptation of the dramatic element to lyrical purposes.

Let the ill omen of the shrilling screech-owl,*
Or pregnant bitch, or vixen newly littered,
Or tawny she-wolf skulked down from Lanuvium †
    Convoy the wicked ;

Let the snake break ‡ off their intended journey,
If their nags start, when arrow-like he glances
Slant on the road—I, where I love, a cautious
    Provident Augur,

meant by "arcus," "the bows," is by no means so clear. The weapon may be merely symbolical (Cupid's bow and arrows), or it may have been the arbalist or cross-bow, and used to frighten the porter.—See Orelli's note.

  * "Parræ recinentis." Macleane observes that it is not determined what this bird "parra" was, or whether it is known in these islands. I venture to call it, as other translators have done, the screech-owl, which is still, in Italy as elsewhere, deemed a bird of bad omen. Orelli treats of the subject in an elaborate note, which, however, decides nothing. Yonge says, "I believe it is the owl."—See his note.

  † "Rava decurrens lupa Lanuvino." The wolf runs down from the wooded hills round Lanuvium, because that town was near the Appia Via, leading to Brundusium, where Galatea would embark.—MACLEANE, ORELLI. "Rava lupa." What exact colour "rava" means is only so far clear that Horace applies it both to a lion and a wolf. Orelli says the word is properly applied to the colour of the eye, and is between black and tawny, as in many animals.

  ‡ "Rumpat." I follow all the best recent editors, English and German, with

Ere the weird crow, reseeking stagnant marshes,
Predict the rain-storm, will invoke the raven
From the bright East, and bid the priestlier prophet
        Promise thee sunshine.*

Go where thou mayst, be happy; and remember
Me, Galatea !   May no chough's swart shadow
Darken thy path—and not one green woodpecker
        Dare to tap leftward.†

But see with what fierce tempest—prone Orion
Rushes on baleful !   I have known the breakers
In Hadria's gulf ; and with what fawning smoothness
        Sins the pale west wind.

To feel the blinding shock of rising Auster,
The howl of dark seas lashing shores that tremble—
This we wish only to the wives and children
        Of our worst foemen.

Europa, thus to the fair bull deceiving
Trusted her snowy form ; thus, ensnared in
The widths of ocean, eyeing its dread monsters,
        Paled from her courage :

She but of late in meads the wild-flowers culling
Weaver of garlands votive to the wood-nymphs,
Now beheld only through night's darkling glimmer
        Stars and wide waters.

Once reaching Crete, Isle of the Hundred Cities,
" Father," she cried, o'ercome with shame and sorrow,
" A daughter's name, alas, a daughter's duty
        I have abandoned !

the single exception of Munro, in reading "rumpat" and line 15, "vetet."
Munro prints "rumpit"—"vetet" showing good reason for his preference.
Introduction, p. xxxi.

    * The crow flying back to his pool or marsh indicated bad weather. The
raven croaking from the east was an omen of good weather, therefore the
poet summons the raven in time to forestall the crow. He calls the raven
"oscinem corvum." The epithet is technically augural. "Oscines aves"
were birds which the augurs consulted for their note, as they consulted the
birds called "præpetes" for their flight.

    † "Picus," a woodpecker or heighhould.—ORELLI. "The green wood-
pecker."—YONGE.

" What have I done ? what left ? *   The crimes of virgins
A single death does not suffice to punish.
Am I awake ? have I in truth committed
      Sin, and so vilely ?

" Or am I guiltless—duped by a vain phantom
Leading a dream out of the ivory portal ?
Wise choice, indeed,—here, lost in desert waters,
      There, culling blossoms !

" O that the bull were to my wrath delivered !
O for a sword to hack his horns, and mangle
The monster now so hated, though so lately—
      Woe is me !—worshipped.

" Shameless, my household gods I have forsaken,
Shameless, I loiter on the road to Orcus !
Would to the gods that I were in the desert
      Strayed among lions !

" While in these cheeks the bloom be yet unwithered,
And all the sap of the luxuriant life-blood
Make their prey tempting, may this fatal beauty
      Feast the fierce tigers.

" I hear my absent father, ' Vile Europa,
Why pause to die ?   More ways than one, O coward !
Here, at this elm-tree, strangled by thy girdle,
      Sole friend not quitted ;

" ' Or there, down yonder precipice, plunge headlong
Whirled by the storm-blast to thy grave in ocean ;
Unless, O royal-born, it please thee better,
      Sold into bondage,

" ' To card the wool of some barbarian mistress,
And share with her the base love of a savage.' "
While thus she raved despairing, Venus softly
      Neared her, arch-smiling,

---

* "Unde quo veni."   " ' Unde' implies not that she was so distracted
that she had forgotten from whence she had come, but what an exchange
I have made."—MACLEANE.

                            E E

With the boy-archer—but his bow was loosened;
And sating first her mirth, thus spoke the goddess :
" Thou wilt not scold when this loathed bull returning,
      Yields to thy mercy.

" Know thyself bride of Jove the all-subduing.
Hush sobs ; learn well to bear thy glorious fortune ;
Thou on one section of the globe * bestowest
      Name everlasting."

ODE XXVIII.

ON THE FEAST-DAY OF NEPTUNE.

It is but a waste of ingenious trifling to conjecture who or what Lyde was,
or, indeed, if any Lyde whatever existed elsewhere than in the poet's fancy.
The poem is very lively and graceful, and evidently intended for general
popularity as a song, without any personal application to the writer.

What, on the feast-day of Neptune,
    Can I do better? Up, Lyde ! Out from its hiding-
       place, quick,
Drag forth the Cæcuban hoarded;
    Make an attack upon Wisdom!   On to the siege of her
       fort !

See how the noon is declining,
    Yet, as if day were at stand-still, laggard, thou leav'st in
       the store
The cask which has lazily slumbered
    Since Bibulus acted as consul ; now is its time to awake.

Sing we, by turns, of King Neptune,
    And the green locks of the Nereids ; then to thy bow-
       shapen lyre
Chant us a hymn to Latona,
    And to the swift-footed Dian, and to her arrows of light ;

-----

* " Sectus orbis " literally means " half the world," as the ancients
divided our planet only into the two great divisions, Europe and Asia.

Then, as the crown of thy verses,
　　Chant to the goddess who visits, borne on her car by the
　　　swans,
Cyclades, Cnidos, and Paphos;
　　Night, too, shall have her deserts, and lullabies rock her
　　　to sleep.*

ODE XXIX.

INVITATION TO MÆCENAS.

No ode of Horace specially addressed to Mæcenas exceeds this in dignity of sentiment and sustained beauty of treatment. Horace's descriptions of summer are always charming, and though he rejects the prosaic minuteness by which modern poets, when describing external nature, make an inventory of scenic details as tediously careful as if they were cataloguing articles for auction, he succeeds in bringing a complete picture before the eye, and elevates the subject of still life by the grace of the figures he places, whether in the fore or the back ground. But he has seldom surpassed the beautiful image of summer in its sultry glow and in its languid repose which adorns this ode, in contrast with the statesman, intent on public cares, and gazing on Rome and the hills beyond from his lofty tower. It is unnecessary to point out the nobleness of the comparison between the course of the river and the mutability of human affairs, or the simple grandeur of the lines on Fortune so finely, though so loosely, paraphrased by Dryden; and so applicable to public men that it has furnished with illustrations appropriate to themselves some of the greatest of English statesmen.

Long since, Mæcenas sprung from Tuscan kings,
A vintage mellowing in its virgin cask,
　　Balms to anoint the hair,
　．　And roses meet for wreaths on honoured brows,

Wait at my home for thee.　Snatch leisure brief,
And turn thy gaze from Tibur's waterfalls†
　　The slopes of Æsula,‡
　　And parricidal Telegon's blue hills;

* "Dicetur merita Nox quoque nenia." The word "nenia" is applied to funereal dirges, and also, as Dillenburger observes, to the songs by which nurses rocked infants to sleep; and Orelli and Macleane suggest that such is the meaning of the word here.

† "Ne semper udum Tibur." I interpret "udum"-as referring to the cascades of Anio; it may mean the rills meandering through the orchards of Tibur.

‡ Munro has Æfulæ. "The f is found in some of the best MSS. of Horace, in the best of the scholiasts, as well as of Livy, as shown by Huebner in the Hermes, i. p. 426, who completes the proof by citing three inscriptions, one of them Greek, in which the gentile names, Aefulanus, Acfulanus, Αἰφουλανός, occur."—Munro's Horace, Introd. xxviii.

Desert fastidious wealth, and that proud pile
Soaring aloft, the neighbour of the clouds; *
  Cease to admire the smoke,
    The riches, and the roar of prosperous Rome.

Sweet to the wealthy the relief of change ;
Nor needs it tapestried woof nor Tyrian pall
  For simple feast, whose mirth
    In humble roofs unknits the brows of Care.

Now, hidden long, Andromeda's bright sire
Glares forth revealed : now rages Procyon,
  And the mad Lion-star,†
    As Sol brings back the sultry days of drought.

Now doth the shepherd, with his languid flock,
Seek streams and shades, and thickets dense, the lair
  Of the rough Forest-God ;
    And silent margins miss the wandering winds.

All rest save thou, intent on cares of state
And fears lest aught against thy Rome be planned
  In farthest east, or realm
    Of Persian Cyrus, or by factious Don.

The issues of the Future a wise God
Veils in the dark impenetrable Night,
  And smiles if mortals stretch
    Care beyond bounds to mortal minds assigned.

That which is present heed, and justly weigh ;
All else flows onward as the river runs—
  Now, in mid-channel calm,‡
    Peacefully gliding to Etruscan seas ;

* The lofty tower or belvidere of the palace built by Mæcenas on the
Esquiline Hill, whence Nero looked down on the conflagration of Rome.
  † This fixes the season to the beginning of July, when Cepheus, a northern
star below Ursa Minor, rises. Cepheus was mythically King of Æthiopia,
and father of Andromeda. Procyon rises about the same time, and is
followed, eleven days afterwards, by Sirius. Leo completes the picture of
summer heat.
  ‡ Orelli has "æquore"—most of the MSS. "alveo,"—which last reading
is adopted by Ritter, Yonge, and Munro.

Now, when wild torrents chafe its quiet streams,
Rolling, along with its resistless rush,
   Loosed crags, uprooted trees,
     And herds and flocks, and the lost homes of
     men,

While neighbouring forests, and far mountain-peaks
Mingle their roar. Happy * indeed is he,
   Lord of himself, to whom
     'Tis given to say, as each day ends, "I have
     lived : "

To-morrow let the Sire invest the heaven
With darkest cloud or purest ray serene,
   He mars not what has been,
     Nor from Time's sum blots out one fleeted hour.

Fortune, exulting in her cruel task—
Consistent in her inconsistent sport—
   Shifts favours to and fro,
     Now to myself, now to another kind.

I praise her seated by me ; † if she shake
Her parting wings I give back what she gave,
   And, in my virtue wrapped,
     Make honest Poverty my dowerless bride.

'Tis not for me, when groans the mast beneath
Fierce Africus, to gasp out piteous prayers,
   And bargain with the gods,
     Lest gainful bales from Cyprus or from Tyre

* " Cui licet in diem
Dixisse Vixi."

See Orelli's note against the usual interpretation of this passage. The
meaning is,—"Happy the man who at the end of each day can say, ' I have
lived.' " Ritter connects "vixi" with all the lines that follow to the end
of the ode—a construction which, I suspect, few critics will be inclined to
favour. Munro stops the connection at " vixit."

† " Laudo manentem." Orelli says that there is extant a rare coin of
the time of Commodus, inscribed " Fortunæ Manenti," in which a woman
is represented *seated* holding a horse by the halter with her right hand—
in the left a cornucopia. I have availed myself of this image in translating
" manentem."

Add to the treasures of the greedy deep ;
Then from the wreck my slender boat * the gale
    And the Twin-star shall speed,
      Safe with one rower through Ægœan storms.

ODE XXX.

PREDICTION OF HIS OWN FUTURE FAME.

This ode appears clearly intended to be the completing poem of some
considerable collection of lyrical pieces, forming in themselves an integral
representation of the idiosyncrasies of the poet in character and in genius,
thus becoming his memorial or "monumentum." It is therefore generally
regarded as the epilogue, not to the Third Book only, but to all the first
three books, after the publication of which, Horace made a considerable
pause before he published the Fourth. There is a great difference in tone
between this and Ode xx. Book II., addressed to Mœcenas. That ode, half
sportive, half earnest, seems written in the effervescence of animal spirits,
and might have been called forth in any moment of brilliant success. But
this is written in dignified and serious confidence in the firm establishment
of the poet's fame. It is unnecessary to defend Horace here from the
charge of vainglory, to which a modern poet, arrogating to himself the
immortality of fame, would be exposed. The manners of an age decide the
taste of an age. The heathen poets spoke of the immortality of their verses
with as little scruple as Christian poets speak of the immortality of their
souls. Not to mention the Greek poets, Dillenburger gives a tolerably long
list of passages from the Latin—Ennius, Virgil, Propertius, Ovid, Martial—
who spoke of their conquest over time with no less confidence than Horace
here does. The metre in the original is the same as that of Ode i. Book I.,
which perhaps strengthens the supposition that the poem is designed to
complete a collection which that ode commenced.

I have built a monument than bronze more lasting,
    Soaring more high than regal pyramids,
Which nor the stealthy gnawing of the rain-drop,
    Nor the vain rush of Boreas shall destroy ;
Nor shall it pass away with the unnumbered
    Series of ages and the flight of time.
I shall not wholly die!   From Libitina †
    A part, yea, much, of mine own self escapes.
Renewing bloom from praise in after ages,
    My growth through time shall be to fresher youth,
Long as the High Priest, with the Silent Virgin,
    Ascends the sacred Capitol of Rome.‡

* "Biremis scaphœ," a two-oared boat, rowed by a single rower.
† Venus Libitina, the Funereal Venus—Death.
‡ Viz., "while the Pontifex Maximus shall, on the ides of every month,

From mean estate exalted into greatness—
  Where brawls * loud Aufidus with violent wave,
And arid † reigned o'er rustic subjects, Daunus—
  I, in the lips of men a household name,
Shall have my record as the first who wedded
  To Roman melodies Æolian song.
Take airs of state—the right is earned—and crown me,
  Willing Melpomene, with Delphic bay.

THE SECULAR HYMN.

Religious games, called Ludi Tarentini, Terentini, or Taurii, had been held in Rome from an early period of the Republic. Their origin is variously stated, though the most probable mythical accounts agree that they were instituted and devoted to Dis and Proserpina in consequence of a fearful plague—whether by one Valerius in gratitude for the recovery of his three children, or in the reign of Tarquinius Superbus, in order to propitiate those formidable deities. In the latter case the plague had affected pregnant women, and their children died in the womb; and sterile cows (Taureæ) being sacrificed, the games were called Ludi Taurii. By these accounts it would seem that the games were connected with the health of offspring, and by all accounts that they were instituted in honour of Dis and Proserpina. To those eminent scholars who hold to the Etrurian origin of the Tarquins, "the Tarenti and Taurii are but as different forms of the same word, and of the same root as Tarquinius" (Smith's Dict., art. "Ludi Sæculares"). If so, the deities honoured were doubtless Etrurian—not Greek nor Roman—though the Romans subsequently identified them with divinities familiar to their own worship.

Be that as it may, during the Republic these games appear to have been only celebrated three times, at irregular intervals in no way connected with fixed periods or cycles (sæcula).

When Augustus had completed (A.U.C. 737) the second lustre, or the ten years for which the imperial power was first confided to him, it was very natural that he should wish for the solemnity of an extraordinary festival at once popular and religious; and probably also the desire of establishing a dynasty would give rise to the idea of rendering this solemnity regular, but at far-distant dates; thus associating indirectly the duration of the

---

go up to the Capitol to offer Sacrifices to Vesta, her virgins walking solemnly in the procession, as they did, while the boys sang hymns in honour of the goddess. With a Roman this was equivalent to saying ' for ever.' "—MACLEANE.

    * " Mantua Virgilio gaudet, Verona Catullo,
        Pelignæ dicar gloria gentis ego."
                          —OVID, Amores, iii. 15, 17.

† " Pauper aquæ Daunus," " Daunus scant of water." The epithet is thus, by poetic licence, applied to the legendary king, which, in plain prose, belongs to the country he ruled, i. e., the southern part of Apulia, as the Aufidus flowed through the western.

Empire with the welfare and existence of Rome. The custodiers of the Sibylline books, who had been increased from two to ten, and subsequently, probably by Sulla, to fifteen (quindecimviri), were ordered to consult those oracles, and they reported that the time was come to revive the old Tarentine games. They introduced, however, certain innovations, such as the cyclical or secular period, for their celebration (pretending that such periods had been always observed, or at least enjoined), and the substitution of Apollo and Diana for Dis and Proserpina. The latter change seems natural enough. Diana had among her attributes those of Proserpina, and Apollo was the deity whom Augustus especially honoured as his patron god. Dis and Proserpina were no longer in fashion, and were probably never very popular with the genuine Romans; while, as the festival was not designed, like the old Tarentine games, for the averting of some national calamity or mortal disease, but rather to attest the blessings enjoyed under the Empire, and implore their continuance, the direct invocation of the infernal divinities would have been very inappropriate; and, indeed, their powers as averters of evil had become transferred to Apollo and Diana (as the sun and moon), who were also the bestowers of good. Sacrifices were, however, offered to Dis and Proserpina on the first day of the ceremony among other gods, in the list of whom they are placed last. Still it may be seen in the following Hymn that much of the original character of the Tarentine or Taurian games was retained, however modified to suit altered circumstances. Diana is especially implored to protect mothers and mature their offspring. Augustus approaches the altar with white steers for sacrifice, as cows had been sacrificed to Dis in the Taurian games (though, as black animals had been offered to the infernal deities in time of calamity, the white colour of the steers was significant of the change to celestial divinities and the felicity of the period), and the games commenced in the Tarentum, *i. e.*, the same ground that had been consecrated to the Tarentine games. The nature and order of the ceremonies, which lasted three days and three nights, was entrusted to Ateius Capito, a celebrated jurist and antiquary, and Horace was requested to compose the principal hymn on the occasion. The games were held in the summer of the year B.C. 17. They were repeated four times during the Empire, but not at the periods enjoined by the Quindecimviri under Augustus, viz., in cycles of 110 years. The second took place, A.D. 47, in the reign of Claudius; the third, A.D. 88, in the reign of Domitian; and the fourth in the reign of Philippus, A.D. 248. For further particulars of the ceremony the general reader is referred to Smith's Dict., art. "Ludi Sæculares;" and for the mystical belief that the world was moving in a cycle, the completion of which constituted the Magnus Annus, when all the heavenly bodies returned to their original relative places, see Orelli and Macleane's introduction to the Secular Hymn. As the length of the ten sæcula which constituted the great Platonic year of the universe was not defined, but declared from time to time by prodigies from heaven, so this belief may account for the irregular periods in which the Secular Festival was held during the Empire.

When Horace boasts (Lib. III. Carm. xxx.) that he shall be spoken of as the first who adapted Æolian song to Italian measures, he must mean something more than the mere introduction of Greek lyrical metres into the Italian language. In this task Catullus had preceded him. He nowhere mentions Catullus; and though that omission has been ascribed to jealousy, there is no evidence of so envious a defect in Horace's general character. He bestows lavish praise on the eminent poets of his own time; and a jealous poet is more apt to be jealous of living contemporaries than of defunct predecessors. Nor is it to be forgotten that, if Horace confines his boast to the mere introduction of Lesbian metres, the Sapphics of Catullus must have been sufficiently fresh in popular recollection to afford his enemies one of those opportunities for confuting a boast and turning it into ridicule which are not voluntarily courted by a man of such good sense and of such knowledge of the world as Horace is allowed to have been.   And it is not to the Alcaic metre, but exclusively to the Sapphic, as connected with his name, that he refers, Lib. IV. Carm. vi.

> " Ego dis amicum,
> Sæculo festas referente luces,
> Reddidi carmen, docilis modorum
> Vatis Horati."

Horace's boast, then, is only to be justified by the supposition that although Catullus had preceded him in the adoption of the Sapphic metre, he had not adapted it to song—had not incorporated it in the popular form of lyrical music—and Horace had done so, and been the first to do it.

I apprehend, therefore, that Horace's vaunted originality consisted in being the first by whom the borrowed metres were set to Italian music—the first by whom, through arts not before divulged, the words were to be united with musical strings (" Non ante volgatas per artes Verba loquor socianda chordis "—Lib. IV. Carm. ix.), and thus popularised in banquet-halls and temples as national songs (Lib. III. Carm. xi.).   It seems to me that in this sense he says) he is pointed out as " Romanæ fidicen lyræ " (Lib. IV. Carm. iii.), " fidicen " being a word especially applicable to a musician, and only metaphorically to a poet.

That several of the odes were not adapted to singing does not invalidate this supposition.   Such will be the case with every copious lyrical poet, who may, nevertheless, like Moore, have achieved his main popularity through the adaptation of his verse to musical accompaniment and national airs.

Whether the music to which the measures employed by Horace were set was composed by himself in whole or in part, or by others, is a question on which there are no data for legitimate conjecture.   If by himself, one might suppose that some record of the fact would be preserved by Suetonius or the scholiasts.   On the other hand, if composed by another, it seems strange that a poet of character so grateful as Horace's should have refrained from all mention of one to whom he was under no mean obligations for the popularity his verses had acquired, and with whom he must have been necessarily brought into frequent and familiar intercourse.   It may, however, be said, as sufficient reason for such silence in either case, that a Roman of Horace's day would not have held the art of a musical composer in high account.

The writers who have sought to elucidate the obscure subject of ancient music consider it probable that nothing like the modern system of musical rhythm existed among the ancients, and that, since there is no mention of *notation* distinct from the metre of the song, the time was marked by that metre where the vocal music was united with instrumental (Burney's " History of Music ;" Hawkins's " Hist. of Music ;" Smith's Dict., art. " Musica ").   By this the reader can judge. for himself whether Horace's task in timing the music to his own rhythms would not have been comparatively easy; and whether, if it were thus easy, it would have been considered worthy of commemoration by his contemporaries, or been preserved in such brief records of his life as were consulted by Suetonius, or known to the scholiasts.

At all events, Horace appears, on account of the Secular Hymn, to have superintended the rehearsal of the recitative as " διδάσκαλος," according to the custom of dramatic and lyric poets of Greece ; and (Lib. IV. Carm. vi.) the young girls who take part in the chorus are enjoined not only to preserve the Lesbian metre, in which the hymn was composed, but to remember " pollicis ictum," the beat of his finger in marking time.

Regarded only as a poem, the Secular Hymn, though it deserves higher

praise than Macleane and other critics have bestowed on it, cannot be said
to equal the genius exhibited in many of the odes, especially in Book III.
But if set—whether by Horace himself, or by others whom he more or less
schooled and directed—to some music which became a grand national air,
such as "God save the King," or "The Marseillaise," we can readily
account for the special pride with which he refers to it, and the increased
rank which it appears to have won for him in popular estimation.

In the Secular Hymn, and in some of the Sapphic odes of the Fourth
Book, Horace more conforms than he does in the first three books to the
Greek usage, in the variation of the cæsura and the introduction of the
trochee in the second place. I have judged it necessary, for the solemnity
of feeling which is instilled into this poem, to add another foot to the fourth
line in the translation.

O Phœbus, and O forest-queen Diana,
Ye the twin lustrous ornament of heavën,
Though ever holy, in this time most hallowed
   Be most benign to prayer !

For duly now, as Sibyl verse enjoins us,
Pure youths, with chosen virgins linked in chorus,
To Powers divine o'er the Seven Hills presiding,
   Uplift the solemn hymn.

O Sun, the nurturer,* in bright chariot leading
Day into light to hide it under shadow,
Born still the same, yet other, mayst thou never
   See aught more great than Rome !

Blest Ilithyia,† mild to watch o'er mothers,
And aid the timely coming of the new-born,
Whether thou rather wouldst be as Lucina
   Or Genitalis hailed,

 * "Alme Sol." This epithet is to be taken in its proper sense as derived
from *alo*, Sun the Nurturer—MACLEANE.
 † "Ilithyia." This name, here applied to Diana, is equally applicable to
Juno, and, in the plural number, to the minor deities attending on childbirth.
There appears to me, if I mistake not, a singular beauty which has escaped
the commentators in the choice of names here given to Diana. Ilithyia and
Lucina (the one Greek, the other Latin) are names which Diana shares with
Juno, and therefore, as applied to childbirth, imply the children born in
sacred wedlock. The name "Genitalis" is that which Diana shares with
Venus, and therefore implies the offspring of chaste if ardent love. Thus,
"whether thou preferrest the name of Lucina or Genitalis," would mean,
"whether thou preferrest the name that associates thee with Juno or that
which associates thee with Love."

Goddess as each, mature our offspring ; prosper
The law that guards the sanctity of marriage,*
And may it give new blossom and new fruitage
    To the grand parent-stem !

So that as each eleventh solennial decade
Round to its close, this sacred feast renewing,
In song and sport, assembled Rome may hallow
    Three days and joyous nights.

And ye, O Parcæ, who have sung prophetic
Truths,† which, once said, the sure events determine,
Fixed as divine decrees,—a glorious future
    Join to the glorious past.

Fertile in fruits and flocks, let Earth maternal
With spikëd corn-wreath crown the brows of Ceres ;
Pure from all taint let airs and dews of heavën
    Nourish the new-born life.

Mild, all thine arrows sheathed within the quiver,
Hear thy boy-suppliants, merciful Apollo ; ‡
Hear thy girl votaries, crescent-crownëd Luna,
    Queen of the clustered stars.

If Rome be your work—if beneath your safeguard
A band of wanderers, Ilion's scanty remnant,
Ordained to change their city and their Lares,
    Have held this Tuscan land—

* The Julian law (de maritandis ordinibus), for the discouragement of
celibacy and the regulation of marriage, was among the social and moral
reforms aimed at by Augustus, and passed the year before the celebration of
the Secular games. It appears to have been a law well meant, but in
some respects singularly unwise and impracticable. The unmarried person
could not succeed to a legacy unless he married within a hundred days after
the bequest. Fancy poor Horace himself condemned to decide between
forfeiting the bequest of a villa at Tarentum or marrying some Glycera or
Pyrrha !
† Viz., the oracular Sibylline verses.
‡ This line seems to refer to the new statue of the Apollo of Actium set
up by Augustus in the Palatine temple. In the Apollo of Actium invoked
by Augustus before his battle with M. Antony, the bow is bent—in the
Apollo of the Palatine the bow is laid aside for the lyre and plectrum.—See
MACLEANE's excellent note on this line.

They, unto whom, through Troy that blazed unharming,
Pure-souled Æneas, his lost land's survivor,
Opened free path, and heritage more ample
    Than aught relinquished gave ;—

Gods, grant to docile youth worth's upright manners—
Gods, grant to placid age worth's calm contentment—
Grant to the Roman race growth, power, and riches,*
    And all that can adorn !

Bless him who nears with milk-white steers your altars,
Whose blood flows bright from Venus and Anchises ;
Still every foe in battle may he conquer,
    And after conquest spare.

Awed by our arms, and by the Alban lictors,†
Now the Mede owns our power on land and ocean ;
Now Ind and Scythia, she of late so haughty,
    To Rome for pardon sue.‡

Now Faith and Peace, and antique Shame and Honour
Flock fearless back, and Virtue long-neglected ;
And with them comes their sure companion Plenty,
    Rich with o'erflowing horn.

May he adorned with fulgent bow—the Augur,
Phœbus, the darling of the nine Camenæ—
He the mild Healer, lifting the sore burden
    That weighs down weary limbs §—

---

* " Remque prolemque." " Res " seems here used in its double signification of power and riches. The nearest approach to its sense in a single
word would perhaps be the old Anglo-Saxon " weal."

† Viz. by our military prowess and civil justice.

‡ " Responsa petunt." " Responsa " here has many significations, the
choice of which may well baffle a translator. It may mean replies to
proffered amity and submission—it may mean the opinions given by a juris-
consult to his client, or the mandates of the imperial government to its
dependants—or it may mean replies to the prayer of the barbarians to be
admitted to the protection and equity of the Roman laws, or the responses
vouchsafed by an oracular or godlike power to a suppliant for relief or
pardon. The last construction is adopted in the translation.

§ Apollo is here addressed in his fourfold capacity : 1stly, As the god of
power, but adorned rather than armed (as at Actium) with his bow ; 2ndly,
As the prophetic seer or augur (the religious attribute) ; 3rdly, As the
beloved of the Muses—i. e., the patron of peaceful arts and letters ; 4thly,
As the divine healer, which may, perhaps, here be used in a latent significa-

If shrines in Palatine he views with favour,
The coming lustre bless, and link it onward
To those yet brighter, through all time prolonging
   Rome and the Latian race.

And oh, may She who holds the sacred hill-tops
Of Aventine and Algidus, Diana,
To the Fifteen,* and to her own young vot'ries,
   Lend an approving ear!

So we, the choir of Dian and of Phœbus,
Versed in their praise, take home with us hope certain
That, heard by Jove and each divine Immortal,
   These words are felt in heaven.

tion, healer of the pains and wounds of the civil wars. Possibly all these attributes may have been symbolised in the pedestal of the statue, or on the walls of the Palatine temple, to which direct reference is made in the following stanza.

 * "Quindecim—virorum," the elect Fifteen who had the custody of the Sibyl books, the charge of the Secular games and solemnities, and in fact, were the priesthood of Apollo. — See Smith's Dictionary, art. "Ludi Sœculares."

BOOK IV.—ODE I.

Franke, in his "Fasti Horatiani," assumes the first three books of the Odes to have been composed between A.U.C. 724 and 730, in which latter year, or in the beginning of 731, they were given to the public, in the interval between Horace's thirty-eighth and forty-first year. Horace then appears to have devoted himself chiefly to his Epistles, and not to have published the Fourth Book of Odes till A.U.C. 741, when he was in his fifty-second year. It is said that Augustus had expressed a desire for its publication, as comprising the odes (iv. and xiv.) in honour of the victories of Drusus and Tiberius. These two odes are indeed unexcelled, even by the finest in the three preceding books; nor are most of the others below the standard of Horace's matured genius. The first ode was, he says himself, written in his fiftieth year. Macleane, in common with some other commentators, conjectures that it may have been an imitation from the Greek, and adds, "that he may have published it to fill up his book, not as a prologue to it, as many of the chronologists say,—for what is there in this ode that bears that character?" Not much, indeed, unless Horace wished to apprise his readers that they are not to expect in this book the lighter gallantries which had place in the former books. This book, indeed, only contains two love-poems besides the first—viz., the tenth and the eleventh; and one is glad to think that the tenth (omitted in the translation) was merely an artistic imitation or translation from the Greek.

Wars long suspended, now
Urgest thou, Venus? Spare! O spare! I pray;
I am not what I was
Under the reign of good Queen Cinara.

Mother of loves so sweet,
Thyself so cruel, cease to subject him
Whom the tenth lustre finds
No longer pliant to thy soft commands:

Go where, with blandishing prayers,
Youth calls thee back; hearts easier kindled seek,
And, borne on purple wings,
Greet Paullus Maximus * in banquet hours.

* If, as Estré observes ("Horat. Prosop."), this be the Paullus Fabius Maximus who was consul A.U.C. 743, the words "centum artium puer" could scarcely be applied to him, even in the widest sense in which the poets took the word "puer" or "juvenis." In fact he could not well have been younger than Horace. On the other hand, if, as some commentators, including Ritter, suppose, it was the son of this P. Maximus and the friend of Ovid who is meant, he would, it is true, have only been about twenty; but how could the line "pro sollicitis non tacitus reis," which refers to his eloquence as an advocate, apply to a youth of that age?

Noble and fair is he ;
Nor his the lips to pleading suitors mute ;
   Youth of a hundred arts
To bear thy conquering standards wide and far ;

   Whene'er some rival, rich
In gifts, he conquers, laughing, he shall place,
   By Alban waters, under citron roofs,
Imaged in marble, Thee.

   There shalt thou take delight
In spicëd balms, and songs commingled sweet
   With Berecynthian fife
And lyre—nor silent be the fluten reed.

   There, twice a-day, shall youths
Choral with tender maidens, chant thy name,
   As thrice, in Salian dance,
Quakes the green sod to feet that twinkle white.

   Me youth nor maid allures,
Nor the hope credulous of mutual hearts,
   Nor Bacchic contests gay ;
I wreathe my brows with vernal flowers no more.

    *   *   *   *   *
    *   *   *   *   *
    *   *   *   *   *

ODE II.

TO IULUS ANTONIUS.

Iulus Antonius was the second son of M. Antony the triumvir by Fulvia ;
the elder, Antyllus, was put to death by Octavian after the battle of Actium.
Iulus, then in his infancy, was brought up with great tenderness by his
stepmother Octavia, married her daughter Marcella, and rose to the highest
honours of the State—prætor, A.U.C. 741 ; consul, A.U.C. 744. His end was
tragical. He was either executed by Augustus or destroyed himself, A.U.C.
752, in the forty-second year of his age, on the charge of adultery with
Julia, to which crime he is said to have been induced by ambitious designs
on the Empire. Iulus possessed the literary accomplishments for which so
many of the Roman nobles in that day were remarkable. He was a pupil
of L. Crassitius, a celebrated grammarian, at whose school were instructed

youths of the first Roman families. According to the scholiasts, he composed not only works in prose, but twelve books in heroic verse upon
Diomed, which Acron styles "egregios;" though, as Macleane observes
with his customary good sense, "As it is most likely Acron never saw them,
his testimony is not worth much." Horace, however, in this ode pays a
high compliment to his poetic powers. The ode itself is a noble homage to
Pindar, and interesting for Horace's estimate of his own peculiar powers,
and his frank confession of the pains he took with his verses. The poem
was written during Augustus's absence from Rome for two years, when,
A.U.C. 737, the Sygambri, a fierce German tribe (whose name Jac. Grimm
derives from "sigu," victory, and "gomber," strong), had, with two other
tribes, invaded the Roman territory in Gaul, and defeated the Roman legate
Lollius with great slaughter. Augustus went in person into Gaul. The
German tribes retreated at his approach, gave hostages, and obtained peace.
Augustus, however, did not return to Rome till he had restored order in
Germany, Gaul, and Spain. As he was expected in Rome long before he
returned, the ode was probably written soon after the Sygambri had given
hostages and obtained peace, A.U.C. 738, or beginning of 739. It is commonly supposed that Antonius had urged Horace to celebrate the triumphs
of Augustus in Pindaric style, and that he modestly excuses himself from
that request. The tone of the ode favours this assumption, though it does
not leave it clear that Antonius had made such a request.

Iulus, he who would with Pindar vie,
Soars, with Dædalian art, on waxen wings,
And falling, gives his name unto the bright
   Deeps of an Ocean.*

As from the mountain-top a headlong stream,
Nourished by rains beyond familiar banks,
Seethes, and immense with might of deep-mouth'd sound,
   Rushes down Pindar.

All due to him Apollo's laureate crown,
Whether through daring dithyrambs he roll
Language, new-formed,† borne on the lawless wave
   Of his wild music;

Whether he sing of gods or god-born kings,
By whom the Centaurs with just doom were slain,
And dire Chimœra's flame was quenched; or those
   Palm-crowned in Elis,

Led as Celestials home; and chants the strife
Of steed or cestus; offering gifts, o'er Time
More potent than a hundred monuments
   Wrought from the marble;

---

 * As Icarus gave his name to the Icarian sea.
 † "Nova verba," "new forms of expression."

Or wails the youth snatched from a weeping bride,
And, in lamenting, lifts his force of soul,
Valour, and golden worth, unto the stars,
　　　Foiling black Orcus.

Ample the gale which buoys the Theban swan,
Whene'er to heights amid the cloud he soars.
I, like the bee of the Matinian hill,
　　　Gather the wild thyme,

With lavish labour hiving thrifty sweets ;
Lowly, by Tibur's grove and dewy banks,
I seek the honey that I store in song,*
　　　Kneaded with labour.

But thou, the minstrel of a grander lyre,
Celebrate Cæsar, when his laurelled brow
Looks from the car which, up the Sacred Hill,
　　　Drags the Sygambri ;

He, than whom never to this earth have Fate
And kind gods given, nor shall give, aught more great
Or aught more good, e'en tho' the ages rolled
　　　Back to the Golden.

Chant thou the games that honour the return
Of brave Augustus granted to our prayer;
The joyous feast-days, the hushed courts of law,
　　　Vacant of suitors.

Then, too, if aught that I can speak be heard,
My voice shall aid to swell the choral hymn,
And sing " All hail, thou fair auspicious sun,†
　　　Bringing back Cæsar ! "

* "Carmina fingo." "Fingo" corresponds to "πλάττω," which word
the Greeks used especially with reference to the making of honey.—ORELLI,
MACLEANE.
† " Et, O Sol
Pulcher! O laudande! canam, recepto
Cæsare felix."
It is uncertain whether "felix" refers to Horace, as "happy in the return
of Cæsar," or to the sun, forming part of the exclamation ; Macleane leaves
the choice to the reader's taste ; Vossius and others prefer the latter appli-
cation ; Orelli considers the former more tender. To me it seems more
F F

And while, O god of triumph, slowly on *
He moves in state, shout upon shout repeats
"Io Triumphc!" through the length of Rome;
　　　Frankincense steaming

Up to benignant gods.　Ten bulls, ten kine,
Acquit thy vow; a single steerling mine,
Fresh-weaned, and browsing into youth amid
　　　Prodigal pastures;

His frontal imitates the curvëd gleam
Of the young moon in her third night;—all else
Of tawny colour, on that front of snow
　　　Shimmers her signet.†

ODE III.

TO MELPOMENE.

The sweetness and dignity of this ode have been a theme of unqualified
praise to the critics.　It was evidently written after the Secular Hymn,
which gave authority and sanction to Horace's claim to be "Romanæ fidicen
lyræ."

----

according to the genius of lyrical composition to apply the epithet to the
sun.　We know already that Horace is happy in the return of Cæsar, otherwise he would not be joining in the procession and the hymn.

* "Teque, dum procedit, io Triumphe," not "tumque dum procedit,"
as in some of our popular editions.　It is the god Triumph which is
invoked by "io Triumphe."　Orclli prefers "procedit" to "procedis,"
which has good authority in the MSS. (see his note), and refers it to
Augustus: "O god of Triumph; while he, Augustus, proceeds, we," &c.
Macleane sees no reason for this preference, and adopts the text of Dillenburger, "procedis," which is also favoured by Ritter and Munro.　Yonge
follows Orelli.

† The conclusion of the ode has been, plausibly enough, blamed for a
discrepancy amounting to bathos between the gravity and elevation of the
preceding stanzas, and the familiar details of the steerling to be sacrificed—
"Desinit in vitulum mulier formosa superne" (STEINER).　Orelli, on the
contrary, thinks it conformable to poetic art, that the height of enthusiasm
should subside, as it were, in the placid anticipation of the destined
sacrifice.　Possibly Horace meant also, in describing the animal so minutely
as already reserved for the sacrifice, to imply how eagerly expected was the
return of Augustus;—the victims were already marked, the preparations
already made.

Whom thou, Melpomene,
Hast once with still bright aspect marked at birth,*
  On him no Isthmian toils
Shall shed the lustre of an athlete's fame;

  Him shall no fiery steed
Ravish to victory in Achaian car;
  In him no warlike deeds
Shall, from the hill-top of the Capitol,†

  Show to a world's applause
The glorious image of a conquering chief,
  With Delian leaves adorned,
Who crushed the swelling menaces of kings;

  Yet him shall streams that flow
Through fertile Tibur, and the thick-grown locks
  Of the green forest-kings,
Endow with lordship—in Æolian song.

  Me have the sons of Rome,
Sovereign of cities, deigned to enrol amidst
  The choir beloved of bards;
And now ev'n Envy bites with milder fang.

  O thou Pierian Muse,
That tun'st the sweet clash of the golden shell;
  Thou who, if such thy will,
Couldst make mute fishes ‡ musical as swans,

---

* "Nascentem placido lumine videris." The image here is taken from
astrology. To Melpomene is ascribed the influence of the planet ascendant
at birth, and by which, in technical terms, the "Native" (or new-born) is
"aspected."

  † "Neque res bellica Deliis
       Ornatum foliis ducem,
         Quod regum tumidas contuderit minas,
       Ostendet Capitolio."

"Ostendet" is a word borrowed from the ceremonies designed for pomp and
ostentation. The victorious general was shown at the Capitol, where he
returned thanks to Jove and the gods, deposited the spoils, and received the
homage of the world.—Torrentius, Dacier.

  ‡ This seems an allusion to the shell of the tortoise shaped into the lyre.

Thine is the boon, all thine,
That I am singled from the passers-by,
 "Lyrist of Roman song!"—
Thine that I breathe and please, if please I may.[*]

ODE IV.

IN PRAISE OF DRUSUS AND THE RACE OF THE NEROS.

When, A.U.C. 738-9, Augustus and Tiberius were in Transalpine Gaul, the fierce tribes of the Vindelici and Ræti (the first occupying a considerable range of country between the Danube and Lake Constance, the last neighbouring them to the south, and extending to Lake Como) made forays into Italy and Cisalpine Gaul, attended with great cruelty and massacre. Augustus sent against them Drusus, the younger brother of Tiberius, who was then in his twenty-third year. He defeated and drove them from Italy. It is clearly in honour of the victory under Drusus that the ode is composed. But as these tribes renewed their predatory incursions into Gaul, Tiberius was sent to the aid of Drusus with additional forces. Thus united, the two brothers reduced these and other tribes—such as the Genauni and Breuni—into the Roman province of Rætia (Rætia Prima and Secunda). It was in honour of this completed conquest, and of the part which Tiberius had in it, that Ode xiv. was composed, and, as may be reasonably supposed, somewhat subsequently to Ode iv. The opening of this poem is unusually lengthy and involved. It takes four strophes, or sixteen verses, before it disentangles itself of its similes, and reaches their application. I do not think that it deserves the blame some critics have attached to it for the slowness and complication with which the image of the young eagle is worked out; perhaps, indeed, the hesitating efforts of the bird before it gathers strength to attack dragons are artistically expressed in the labour of the verse. But I venture to doubt whether the poem would not have been better without the second simile of the lion-whelp, which has no novelty to recommend it, and is very inferior in picturesque vigour to the first one, while it is less appropriate to the eulogy on Drusus. The young eagle training itself to grapple with dragons that resist it, conveys an image of force against force ; but it is very little honour to a lion-whelp to conquer a helpless roe-deer or she-goat. "Caprea" means either, but Yonge appears to me right in giving the former interpretation to the word in this passage. Ritter vindicates the simile of the lion-whelp, observing that the illustration of the sheepfold and the dragons would not be appropriate to the Ræti, and that therefore the poet adds the image by which they and Drusus are comprehended.

Ev'n as the thunder's wingèd minister—
To whom, proved true to Jove's entrusted charge
    In gold-haired Ganymede,
        Heaven's king gave kingdom over wandering
        birds—

---

[*] "Quod spiro," "that I breathe the breath of song"—"quod movet me spiritus poeticus."—DILLENBURGER, ORELLI, RITTER.

Urged from his eyrie by the goad of youth,
And pulses glowing with ancestral fire,
    Learns from the winds of spring,
      When gone the rain-clouds, timidly to soar,

Till on the sheepfold rushes down its foe ;
Next, bolder grown, the hungering greed not less
    Of battle than of food,
      Drives him on dragons that resist his beak ;

Or as in gladsome pastures the wild roe,
About to die by fangs unfleshed before,
    Sees the fierce lion-whelp,
      Fresh from the udders of the tawny dam ;—

So the Vindelici young Drusus saw
Leading war home to their own Rœtian Alps ; *
    Whence from all time they learned
      To arm their hands with Amazonian axe †

I pause not now to ask ; nor is the lore
Of all things lore allowed ; enough that hosts,
    Victorious long and far,
      Vanquished in turn by a young arm and brain,

* "Videre Rœtis bella sub Alpibus." Macleane agrees with Orelli in adopting Bentley's emendation—"Rœtis" instead of "Rœti."—See Orelli's excursus to this ode, and Macleane's comprehensive note. Ritter and Munro have "Raeti."

    † "Quibus
    Mos unde deductus per omne
    Tempus Amazonia securi
    Dextras obarmet, quœrere distuli :
    Nec scire fas est omnia."

These lines are so little in poetic keeping with the noble earnestness of those immediately before and after them, that they have been summarily rejected by several editors, and Franke asserts them to be a silly interpolation. They are, however, justly no doubt, considered genuine by the best of the later authorities. Nor, indeed, are they inconsistent with Horace's habit of introducing a sudden change of playfulness or irony in the midst of his gravest verse. To me they seem evidently a satirical allusion either to some rival poem or to some prosy archæological treatise of his own day upon the origin or customs of the Vindelici ; and we lose the point because we have lost the poem or the treatise. Ritter vindicates the digression, and cites in precedent, Pind. Ol. I. 28-42.

Felt what the mind and what the heart achieve,
When reared and fostered amidst blest abodes,
    And with parental love
        A Cæsar's soul inspires a Nero's sons.

Brave and good natures generate natures brave.
In steer and steed ancestral virtue shows.
    Bold eagles never yet,
        Instead of eaglets, begot timorous doves.

Still training speeds the inborn vigour's growth;
Sound culture is the armour of the breast.
    Where fails the moral lore,
        Vice disennobles even the noblest born.

What to the Neros owëst thou, O Rome !
Witness Metaurus, routed Hasdrubal,
    And that all-glorious day
        Which chased from Latium the receding shades,

First dawn that laughed with vict'ry, since what time
Rode through Italia the dire African,
    As fire through forest-pines,
        Or Eurus over the Sicilian waves.

But from that day, labouring illustrious on,
Victory to victory linked, the Roman grew —
    Till in the shrines laid waste
        By Punic riot and fierce sacrilege,

Once more erect stood forth the gods of Rome.
Then thus outspoke perfidious Hannibal :
    " We deer, foredoomed as prey
        To ravenous wolves, our own destroyers chase,

" Whom 'tis our amplest triumph to elude,
And, hiding from, escape.   Race which, cast forth
    A waif on Tuscan seas
        From Troy's red crater, still had strength to house

" In cities ravished from Ausonian soil,
Its gods, its worship, and its grey-haired sires,
    Yea, and its new-born babes,
        The destined fathers of the men to be ;

" Even as the ilex, lopped by axes rude,
Where, rich with dusky boughs, soars Algidus,
    Through loss, through wounds, receives
      New gain, new life—yea, from the very steel :

' Not fiercer did the Hydra hewn, regrow
Against Alcides, chafed to be o'ercome ;
    Nor dragon-teeth, earth-sown
      In Thebes or Colchis, spring to armëd men;

"Merged in the deeps, more fair comes forth its star : *
Wrestle and win, it bears the winner down ;
    And widowed wives shall tell
      Of victors vanquished on the fields it fought.†

" No more to Carthage shall I send proud news ;
Dies, dies the power, the fortune, the renown
    Of the great Punic name ;
      Dies hope itself, for Hasdrubal is slain.‡

" There's nought the hands of men from Claudius sprung
Shall not achieve, with Jove their guardian god,
    Through the sharp stress of war
      Sped by the providence of heedful cares."

* "Evenit." Orelli, following Jahn, has "exiit"—a reading unsanctioned by more recent editors.
† "Prœlia conjugibus loquenda." Orelli considers that the line refers to the Roman wives speaking with exultation of the wars waged by their husbands. Ritter, on the other hand, powerfully supports the interpretation of Mitscherlich—viz., that the line refers to the widows of the slain. His argument seems to me convincing.
‡ Torrentius considers that here ends the speech attributed to Hannibal, and that in the last verse Horace speaks in his own person—an opinion which has had many followers, and is defended by Ritter. Orelli, supported by Macleane and Yonge, on the other hand, contends that the speech of Hannibal is continued to the close of the ode—firstly, because it is more complimentary to the Neros that their praise and predicted renown should come from the mouth of their foe; secondly, because it is more poetical to conclude the poem with the prophecy of Hannibal, and more in the spirit of Pindar, as Olymp. 4. and Nem. 4. Munro gives his authority to this reading.

ODE V.

TO AUGUSTUS, THAT HE WOULD HASTEN HIS RETURN TO ROME.

This ode, which Dillenburger rightly calls "dulcissimum carmen," may be taken in connection with the preceding and with Ode xiv. It was composed during the absence of Augustus in Germany and Gaul, and after the victories of Tiberius and Drusus. Augustus had been absent from September A.U.C. 738 to February 741. In the description of the blessings ascribed to the reign of Augustus, the security to life and property, the reformation of the previous licence of manners,—in short, the change from the calamities of civil war to the felicity of a government firm in maintaining order, and mild enough to be popular beyond all recorded precedent, Horace conveys his own vindication from the charge inconsiderately made against him for his attachment to the empire, and his enthusiasm for the emperor. And however adulatory the language he employs may appear to modern taste, it is no exaggerated expression of the common national sentiment in the times which had exalted Augustus to a share in the honours privately as well as publicly paid to the gods.

Best guardian of the race of Romulus,
And sprung thyself from deities benign,
Absent too long, fulfil thy promise pledged
    To Rome's high court *—return.

Bring to thy country back, belovèd chief,
The light : thy looks are to thy people Spring,
And where they smile, more grateful glides the day,
    More genial shines the sun.

As the fond mother with all passionate prayers
Calls back the son more than one year away,
By adverse winds beyond Carpathian seas
    Kept from sweet home afar,

Fixing intent upon the curving shore
The unmoving stillness of her wistful eyes ;—
So for her Cæsar, smit with faithful love,
    His country looks and pines.

Safe† plods the steer among the rural fields ;
The rural fields Ceres and Plenty bless ;

---

* "Sancto concilio"—the Senate.

† I.e., under the auspices of Augustus. "Rura perambulat." I adopt Ritter's interpretation that this refers to the ox at the plough, not roving through the pastures. Pales presided over pastures ; Ceres, named in the following line, over fields under the plough. The repetition of "rura"—

The wing'd ships fly through unmolested seas; *
Honour's fine dread of shame

Returns; no lusts pollute the modest home;
Licence is tamed by manners as by laws; †
Nor reads the husband in his infant's face
    A likeness not his own.

Fast by Crime stands its comrade Punishment.
Who fears the Parthian, who the frozen Scyth?
Who (Cæsar safe) whatever monstrous birth
    Germania's womb conceives?

Let fierce Iberia threaten war—who cares?
Each spends safe days on his own hills, and weds
His vine to widowed elms, then, home regained,
    Brims his glad cup to thee,

Blending with prodigal libation prayers; ‡
And, as Greece honoured Leda's starry son,
Or great Alcides,—with his household gods
    Mingles thy hallowed name.

"bos rura perambulat, Nutrit rura Ceres," condemned as a false reading by Bentley and other critics less illustrious, appears to me a peculiar beauty. "Faustitas" is another name for "Copia," "plenty."

* "Pacatum per mare." "Pacatum," "unmolested by pirates." The gratitude of the merchantmen and sailors to Augustus (then Octavian) for putting down piracy is very forcibly expressed in Suetonius, Oct. 98.

† Horace here refers to the "Lex Julia de Adulteriis," passed by Augustus, A.U.C. 737, and also to an improved standard of national manners. Dion Cassius (54, 19) implies that one reason for Augustus's expedition to Gaul (that is, absenting himself from Rome) was to get rid of scandal in regard to his alleged intrigue with Terentia, the wife of Mæcenas—which Macleane rightly dismisses as mere gossip. It is pretty clear, by these verses, either that Horace had heard of no such scandal, or that both he and Mæcenas regarded it with contempt. A poet of so exquisite a taste, and so consummate a knowledge of the world, would not have ventured on the line, "Nullis polluitur casta domus stupris," if such scandal were rife at that very time, or, at least, if any credit were attached to it; for thus the compliment would have been turned into a bitter irony against Augustus, and a cruel insult to Mæcenas.

‡ Literally "at his second course;" or rather, as we should say, "at dessert"—"alteris mensis." By a decree of the Senate, libations were to be offered to Octavian after the battle of Actium at private tables as well as in public banquets, and his name to be inscribed in hymns of praise as those of the gods.—DION. CASS., l. 1-19. It is to these national honours that Horace alludes whenever he speaks of Augustus as enrolled among the gods.

Live, O good chief, Rome's feast-days to prolong !
This is our orison at sober morn,
Our prayer with wine-dews on the lip, when sinks
    Underneath seas the sun.

ODE VI.

TO APOLLO.

This ode may be considered the prooemium to the Secular Hymn, A.U.C.
737, although evidently written after it. As that hymn celebrates Apollo
and Diana, so this ode appropriately commences with an invocation to
Apollo, whom Horace invokes (line 27) to defend the dignity of the Roman
Muse. The poet lingers specially on the praise of Apollo as the slayer of
Achilles; because, had he who spared not the babe in the womb survived,
Æneas, ancestor of Augustus, and the Trojan exiles who founded the Roman
empire, would have perished. Horace, then, after a brief reference to
Diana, turns, as choragus, to address the chorus of the Secular Hymn.

God, in whom Niobe's sad offspring felt
The stern chastiser of the vaunting tongue,
And Tityos vast, the ravisher,—and he,
    Phthian Achilles,

Almost the victor of high Troy (to thee
Unequal, over other force supreme);
Though warring with dread spear the Sea-nymph's son
    Shook Dardan towers,

As falls a pine beneath the biting steel,
Or cypress wrenched by Eurus from its root,
He fell, and wide and far on Trojan dust
    Stamped his great image.

The false horse, duping, in Minerva's name,
Lost Trojans mirthful at their feast of death,
With choral dances blithe in Priam's hall,
    Hid not Achilles.

His prey, alas ! he slew with open hand
His wrath, alas ! had given to Argive flames
The harmless infants ev'n within the womb,
    Smiting the unborn,

Had not the Father of the gods, subdued
By thee and Venus, with imploring prayer,
Pledged to Æneas by his solemn nod
    Walls more auspicious.

Tuneful Thalia's sovereign melodist,
Laving in Xanthian waves thy golden hair,
Support the honour of the Daunian Muse,
    Beardless Agyieus!*

Phœbus on me bestowed the soul, on me
The art of song, on me the poet's name.
† O noblest virgins, and O ye young sons
    Of noble fathers,

Wards of the Delian goddess, with her bow
Striking the flight of stags and lynxes still,
The Lesbian‡ measure timed and tuned by me,
    Guard unforgetful,

Chanting, with ritual due, Latona's son,
And her who kindles night with crescent beam,
Prospers the harvests, and the sliding months
    Speeds in their circle.

Say, maid, then wedded,§ "In that hallowed year
Which did the secular feast-lights re-illume,
Song dear to gods I sang—song taught by him,
    Horace the poet."

* The name of Agyieus seems here very appropriately invoked, because
Apollo takes that name from the Greeks, as presiding over the thorough-
fares of cities, 'quasi viis præpositus urbanis;' and all the streets of Rome
would have been alive with the festival and processions connected with the
Secular Hymn which the ode refers to.
† Here Horace turns to the chorus of the Secular Hymn.
    ‡ "Lesbium servate pedem, meique
        Pollicis ictum."
By "pollicis ictum" is meant the motion of the thumb in marking the
rhythm or time of the song, not the striking of the lyre.
§ "Nupta jam dices." Horace here admonishes those who were young
virgins in the chorus at the date of the Secular Hymn to remember, when
wedded wives, their part in the festival, with which he associates his
name.

ODE VII.

TO TORQUATUS.

The Torquatus here addressed appears to be the same Torquatus whom Horace invites to supper, Epist. Lib. I. v. Estré, considering there was no ground for Weichert's assumption that this person was C. Nonius Asprenas Torquatus, mentioned in Suetonius (in Vit. Augusti), expresses his surprise that the commentators had not thought of Aulus Torquatus, of whom Nepos speaks in his Life of Atticus, c. 11, who had served with Brutus and Cassius at Philippi, and was therefore Horace's old fellow-soldier. Macleane considers the poem to be one of Horace's earlier odes, and introduced to swell the fasciculus—or, as we should say, fill up the volume. I do not see much cause for that supposition. The sentiment is one habitual to Horace at every stage of his life, and it is in harmony with the tone of the epistle, published probably five or six years before the Fourth Book of Odes.

Fled the snows—now the grass has returned to the meadows,
    And their locks to the trees;
Now the land's face is changed, dwindled rivers receding
    Glide in calm by their shores.

Now, unrobed, may the Grace intertwined with her sisters
    Join the dance of the Nymphs.
"Things immortal, hope not!" saith the Year—saith the Moment
    Stealing off this soft day.

Winter thaws, Spring has breathed; quick on Spring tramples Summer,
    And is gone to his grave;
Appled Autumn his fruits will have shed forth, and then
    Dearth and winter once more.

But the swift moons * restore change and loss in the heavens,
    When we go where have gone
Sire Æneas and Tullus,† and opulent Ancus,
    We are dust and a shade.‡

---

* "Damna tamen celeres reparant cœlestia lunæ." Macleane appears to me right in differing from Orelli, who refers "damna cœlestia" to the changes of the moon. "'Tamen' shows that the changes and deteriorations of the weather and seasons are intended, and 'celeres lunæ' are the quick-revolving months," i.e., without metaphor, time brings back the seasons—time does not bring back us men when we once vanish. Moschus in his idyll on the death of Bion has a somewhat similar idea.

† Ritter has "Tullus, dives et Ancus," not "dives Tullus," observing that there is no just cause for calling Tullus rich, whereas the riches of Ancus were celebrated. Munro adopts Ritter's collocation.

‡ I.e., dust in the tomb, and a shade in Hades.

Who knows if the gods will yet add a to-morrow
    To the sum of to-day ?
Count as saved from an heir's greedy hands all thou givest
    To that friend—thine own self.

When once dead, the resplendent* tribunal of Minos
    Having once pronounced doom,
Noble birth, suasive tongue, moral worth, O Torquatus,
    Reinstate thee no more.

Her Hippolytus chaste from the shadows of Hades
    Dian's self could not free ;
Lethe's chains coiled around his own best-loved Pirithous,
    Theseus' self could not rend.

ODE VIII.

TO CENSORINUS.

On stated times, as in the Kalends of March and January, it was the custom of the wealthier Romans to make presents to their friends. To this
custom Horace refers, sending his verses to Censorinus, as the most acceptable gift he could offer. C. Marcus Censorinus was a man of consular rank,
bore a high reputation, and died greatly regretted.

Goblets and bronzes rare, my Censorinus,
    I on my friends would heartily bestow;
I'd give them tripods, as Greece gave her heroes—
    Nor should the meanest of my gifts be thine,
Were I but rich in artful masterpieces
    Such as a Scopas or Parrhasius wrought,†
When one in stone, in liquid hues the other,
    Now fixed a mortal, now enshrined a god.

---

* "'Splendida,' an epithet more proper of the court and tribunal than
of the judgment (arbitria) given. . . . The choice of poetic figure by which
to enlarge the simple notion, 'cum semel occideris,' was probably suggested
by Torquatus's own profession as an advocate, alluded to in Ep. I. v. 8, 9."
—YONGE. Ritter takes the epithet as referring to the splendour which
surrounded the tribunal of Minos, enabling him more searchingly to in-
spect the souls whom he judged; and observes that the splendour is here
opposed to "tenebris," line 25.
† Scopas was a famous sculptor of Paros, according to Pausanias, flourish-
ing about 450 years B.C. Parrhasius, a painter, native of Ephesus, about
400 B.C. He was a contemporary and rival of Zeuxis.

Not mine that wealth,* nor do such dainty treasures
    Fail to thine affluence nor allure thy mind;
That which charms *thee* is song : song I can proffer,
    And set a value on the gift I bring.
Marbles inscribed with a state's grateful praises,
    Wherein great chieftains live and breathe again :
The flights † of Hannibal, his threats hurled backward,
    And impious Carthage perishing in flames,
Made not more famed than did Calabrian Muses
    Him who bore off from conquered Africa
As his own spoils—a Name.‡   Nor aught thy guerdon,
    If scrolls be mute upon thy deeds of good.
Though son of Mars and Ilia, what—had silence
    Been his worth's cold obstruction—Romulus?
The genius, favour, voice of powerful poets,
    Consecrate Æacus, from waves of Styx
Ravished to golden isles.§   The Muse permits not
    The mortal worthy of her praise to die;
Him the Muse hallows to the bliss of heaven.
    Thus in the longed-for banquet-hall of Jove
Sits resolute Hercules; the sons of Leda
    Thus—one twin-star—from Ocean's nether deep
Snatch tempest-shattered barks; and thus doth Liber,
    His brows adorned with the vine's lusty green,
Hear as a god our mortal supplications,
    And guide the votive prayer to happy ends.

* "Sed non hæc mihi vis." The sense is approached by our English idiomatic slang expression, "I am not of that force."
† "Celeres fugæ" means Hannibal's hasty recall from Italy (Liv. xxx. 20).—ORELLI.
‡ "Scipio Africanus." This passage has given infinite trouble to the commentators. Ennius (denoted here by the "Calabrian Muses") celebrated the elder Scipio. But Carthage was burned, not by the elder Scipio, but by the younger Scipio Africanus, many years after the death of Ennius; and it cannot be supposed that Horace was so ignorant as to ascribe to the elder Scipio the act of the younger. It was even proposed by Bentley to omit the seventeenth verse, referring to Carthage, altogether; but the line is in all the MSS. extant. Others suggest that two lines are wanting after the seventeenth, which would have removed the alleged confusion; and this theory is supported by the assertion that odes in this measure are so constituted as to be reducible to stanzas of four lines each, while this ode wants at present two verses necessary to establish that rule. But, as Macleane observes, "the rule itself is arbitrary, and a precarious foundation for such an assumption as the loss of two verses, of which no traces are to be found in the oldest MSS. and commentators." Macleane thinks "that the confusion is easily seen through by those who avoid the commentators and judge for themselves. . . . When Horace says that the defeat of

ODE IX.

TO LOLLIUS.

As the preceding poem was addressed to a man who retained unblemished a popular reputation to the last, and whose death was considered a public calamity, so this poem, which equally treats of the immortality it is the gift of poets to bestow, is addressed to one who, if we are to take for granted such historical records of him as are left, was the subject of merited obloquy in his later years, and died by poison which he administered to himself, to the great joy of his countrymen. And it was for the vices most opposite to the special virtues Horace here ascribes to Lollius—viz., for rapacity and corruption—that his character, rightly or wrongly, has been most defamed. His vindication has been, however, very ably attempted by Tate (" Vindiciæ Lollianæ"), and the evidence against him is generally considered to rest upon prejudiced and questionable authority.—See Estré, Hor. Pros. At all events it is clear that the vices imputed to him by his personal enemy, Sulpicius Quirinus, and Velleius Paterculus, the adulator of Tiberius, were not suspected by Augustus, with whom, even after his defeat by the Sygambri, A.U.C. 737, he retained eminent favour and influence, and who subsequently appointed him tutor to his grandson, Caius Cæsar. If Lollius could deceive Augustus as to his real nature, it has been shrewdly observed that he might well deceive Horace. The exact date of the ode is unknown, but it has the appearance of being written after Lollius's defeat and recall; at all events, it was published not long after it, and is therefore an evidence of Horace's generous desire to soothe and sustain his friend in a time of reverse, and, no doubt, of unpopularity. The latter part of the poem is in Horace's noblest style of sentiment and expression. Ritter maintains that Epistles ii. and xviii., Lib. I., are addressed to the Lollius of the ode; but most critics consider them to be addressed to his eldest son.

Hannibal by the elder Scipio, and the destruction of Carthage by the younger, do not hold up their name more nobly than the Muse of Calabria, —who does not supply in his own mind, 'which was employed in doing honour to the elder'?" To me the meaning seems clear enough. Just as Horace, Lib. I. Carm. xii. v. 46, makes the name of Marcellus, who took Syracuse, stand for all his family, and include the young Marcellus, so he here makes the name of Africanus stand for the whole family, and include especially the younger Scipio. Or, as Ritter expresses it, the fame of the elder Scipio, recorded by Ennius, was revived in the destruction of Carthage by the younger.

§ " Virtus et favor et lingua potentium
Vatum divitibus consecrat insulis."

" 'Virtus et favor' are generally taken, like 'lingua,' as belonging to 'potentium vatum,' so that 'virtus' is ' vis ingenii, facultas poetica.' I doubt the accuracy of that interpretation; I think it rather means that though Æacus was virtuous (and he was much celebrated for his justice), his virtue would not have raised him to the skies but for the applause won for him by the poets. The causes, therefore, are his virtue and the public esteem ('favor'), and the poet's praise that made his virtue known."— MACLEANE. This interpretation is very ingenious, but as it is opposed to that accepted by the general body of Horatian commentators, I do not admit it in translation, though, like all the suggestions of this eminent critic, it merits respectful attention. I may add that Ritter also separates " virtus" and " favor" from " lingua potentium vatum."

Lest, perchance, thou believe that the words which to music,
I, whose birth was where Aufidus rushes far-sounding,
    Linked by arts not before me divulged,
      Are but sounds that are fated to die;

Remember, that though the first throne be great Homer's,
There are muses not tuneless, Pindaric and Cæan;
    With Alcæus, yet threatening and fierce;
      With Stesichorus, stately and grave.

Time destroys not what once sported loose in Anacreon;
To this day breathes the love, to this day glows the ardour
    Which the girl of Æolia consigned
      To the strings of her passionate lyre.

Spartan Helen was not the sole woman inflamed by
An adulterer's sleek locks; or seduced by the glitter
    Of the vestments embroidered in gold,
      And the graces and pomp of a prince;

Teucer bent not the first skilful bow of the Cretan;
Troy was more than once harassed by valiant besiegers;
    Other chiefs, besides Sthenelus strong,
      Or Idomeneus mighty, achieved

Deeds as worthy as theirs of a Muse to record them;
Not the first was Deiphobus keen, or fierce Hector,
    Who has met, without flinching, the blow,
      In defence of his children and wife.

Many brave men have lived long before Agamemnon,
But o'er them darkly presses the slumber eternal;
    All unwept and unknown, wanting Him—
      Making names ever sacred *—the Bard!

Little differs worth hidden from worthlessness buried;
In the page I shall speak, and the page shall adorn thee;
    I will let not, O Lollius, thy toils
      Fade in livid oblivion away.

---

* "Vate sacro." "Sacro" here has the sense of making sacred, consecrating.

In the converse of life thine the provident wisdom,
Thine, the temper unmoved by the changes of Fortune,*
   Whatsoever her smile or her frown,
     Neither bowed nor elate,—but erect;

The avenger of greedy and fraudful Corruption,
The abstainer from Gold, which draws all to its magnet—
   Consul not of the one year alone,
     For thy mind must be always in power   .

Whensoever an arbiter, faithful to justice,
Over what is expedient exalts what is honest,
   Awes the briber with one lofty look,
     And through hosts clears, victorious, his way.†

It is not large possessions themselves that are blessings;
More rightly called ' blest,' he whose claim to the title
   Is the wisdom which puts to their use
     All the gifts that he owes to the gods,

* "Secundis
Temporibus dubiisque rectus."

Rectus needs, I think, the paraphrase in the translation, "neither bowed nor elate;" not with head arrogantly lifted up in prosperous nor dejected in doubtful fortune. I agree with Orelli and Macleane in considering that the lines refer to the defeat of Lollius in Germany; and it seems that not only Horace here emphatically seeks to pay tribute to the steadfastness and integrity of his friend's character, but in the concluding stanza to vindicate his courage, and intimate that he was the last man who would have feared death.

    † The meaning of these lines seems explained by reference to Lib. III. Od. ii. lines 19, 20,—

" Nec sumit aut ponit secures
Arbitrio popularis auræ ;"

i. e. Lollius is not the mere official consul of a single year—he never lays down the insignia of his majestic virtue. It seems to me that the image is still continued through the lines,—

" Per obstantes catervas
Explicuit sua victor arma."

The lictors dispersed opposing crowds to make way for the consul; and "arma" here may signify their axes. Yonge renders the passage yet more symbolically, in this eloquent paraphrase: "The soul has an independent dignity so long as, true in principle and judgment, it rejects corruption, and bursts in a moral victory through the host of vices." Ritter insists on construing the lines literally, and refers them to Lollius's military administration of his province.

He who hardens his soul to reverse and privation—
He who looks upon death as less dread than dishonour—
　　Never fears, for the friends of his love
　　Or the cause of his country, to die.

ODE X.—Omitted.

ODE XI.

TO PHYLLIS.

As Horace had before (Lib. III. Od. xxviii.) invited Lyde to the feast-day of Neptune, so he here invites Phyllis to celebrate the birthday of Mæcenas in the Ides of April. The date of the ode cannot be determined, though it may be reasonably conjectured that when he speaks of Phyllis as his last love, he was of an age correspondent with the period at which the Fourth book was published. Nevertheless this is no sure index; for, as Macleane shrewdly intimates, most men promise the woman they woo that she shall be the last love. To those who insist upon giving literal individual personality to the fictitious names Horace introduces into his poems, this poem would seem written at a much earlier period, since Telephus, that universal ladykiller, is still described as "juvenis." But we have already seen that "juvenis" by no means necessarily signifies a youth. I do not believe, with Macleane, that Telephus is altogether a poetic fiction: neither am I satisfied with the grounds upon which Ritter identifies the Telephus of Ode xiii. Book I., and xix. Book III., with Heliodorus, the grammarian and Greek scholar mentioned Serm. i. 5, 2, and assumes that another person is designated under that name in this ode. Nothing is more likely than that among Horace's gayer companions there was some one very good-looking gallant, celebrated for his *bonnes fortunes* among the freed-women of Rome, whom the poet always designates under the name of Telephus. It is observable that there is considerable consistency in the way in which Telephus is mentioned in Horace, with a good-humoured, half-envious admiration for personal gifts, and whom, on the single occasion (Carm. xix. Lib. III.) in which the handsome gentleman seems disposed to bore with an unseasonable display of learning, he puts back into his right place as reveller and gallant, with a certain superiority, such as, when it came to a display of learning, a Horace might be disposed to assume towards a Telephus.

I've a cask of rich Alban wine full in my cellar—
It has passed its ninth year; in my garden, fair Phyllis,
There is parsley for chaplets, and O, in profusion,
　　　　Ivy too, ivy,

Thou art dazzling whenever that binds up thy tresses.
All my house laughs with plate; clasped around with chaste
    vervain,
Lo, mine altar stands thirsting the blood of a lambkin
        Soon to be sprinkled.

And all hands are at work; here and there run the servants,
Men and maids, helter-skelter; the flame mounts in flicker,
As it whirls the smoke cresting the point of its summit
        Round and around it.*

But that now thou may'st know to what mirth I invite thee,
'Tis in honour of Ides, not ungrateful to Phyllis,
'Tis the day that halves April the month we devote to
        Venus the sea-born.†

Day, indeed, that by me should be solemnised duly—
Scarce mine own natal day I hold equally sacred,
Since it is by its light, year on year, my Mœcenas
        Sums up life's riches.

Come, that Telephus whom thou art seeking (poor Phyllis!
He's a youth above thee) is now chained to another.
She is wanton and rich, and she holds him in bondage,
        Pleased with his fetters.

Phaëthon, burnt in his chariot, deters from ambition,
Wingèd Pegasus spurning Bellerophon earth-born
May admonish thee also by this solemn lesson,
        ' Seek but what suits thee;'

Deeming Hope, when it flies out of reach, is forbidden,
O set not thy heart where the lots are unequal.
Come, with me be contented, of all loves my latest;
        Love with thee endeth.

---

    * "Sordidum flammæ trepidant rotantes
          Vertice fumum."
"'Vertice' is the top of the flame, which flickers as it whirls the dark
smoke on its crest—a spiral flame, culminating in a column of smoke. It
seems as if Horace were writing with a fire burning before him, and caught
the idea as he wrote."—MACLEANE.
   † In astrology the Star of Venus rules the month of April.

After thee never more woman's face shall inflame me;
O, be cheered, then, and come; let me teach thee such
          measures
As the voice which I love into sweetness shall render;
          Song lessens sorrow.

ODE XII.

INVITATION TO VIRGIL.

It is a vexed question among commentators whether the Virgil here
addressed be Virgil the poet. Yonge says that the general authority of
critics is against that identification. Macleane is disposed to favour it, and
it is not without other and very eminent defenders.

The main objections to the assumption are—1st, the chronological one.
Virgil was dead many years before the publication of the Fourth Book; but,
in answer to this, it is said that, in making up the collection composed for
Book IV., Horace might have included poems composed at a much earlier
date. Dillenburger considers that this ode was written in youth, and published in the final book of the Odes, as if Horace wished to refresh and
record the memory of his friend.

2nd, It is asked, "How can Virgil the poet be called the client of noble
youths?" To this it has been replied, that the youths referred to might
be the stepsons of Augustus, or (more generally by Dillenburger), that the
phrase means nothing more than the familiarity with persons of high
station, such as Agrippa, Pollio, and others.

3rd, That an injunction to lay aside the care or study of gain (studium
lucri) is very inappropriate to the liberal and generous character assigned to
the poet. But here again it is said, that it is absurd to take literally what
is obviously written in jest. If a man, the most indifferent to gain, had, for
instance, informed us that he thought he could sell an olive crop well, or
that he had found a good investment for his money, we might very well
say to him, "Put aside those mercenary thoughts of gain, and come and sup
with us." There would be at once a jest and a compliment in the irony of
the implied accusation. That the Virgil addressed must be a vendor of
perfumes, because he is asked to contribute a pot of nard; or a banker or
negotiator, because he is exhorted to put aside the care of gain—and a
scholiast in a Paris MS. inscribes the ode, "Ad Virgilium Negotiatorem,"—
is a conjecture less plausible than that he was a physician of that name to
the Neros, or a relation of C. Virgil the praetor, Cicero's friend.

Orelli and Yonge quote with approval Gesner's remark, "That there is
nothing in the poem itself which pertains more to the poet Virgil than to
any other friend of Horace's." On the other hand, it has been said that the
mythological imagery and the description of Spring with which the poem
opens, are addressed with appropriate felicity to the Poet of the Eclogues
and Georgics.

The question does not seem to admit of positive solution one way or the
other. The reader must judge for himself whether it is probable that
Horace included in the Fourth Book a poem that, if addressed to Virgil the
poet, he must have written many years before; and whether if he did thus,
as Dillenburger contends, seek to revive the memory of his early friend, it
would have been in a poem of a comparatively light character, and so wholly
free from any reference to the loss he had sustained.

Now Thracian breezes, comrades of the spring,
Temper the ocean and impel the sails;
Frost crisps not now the fields, nor rage the floods,
    Swollen with winter snows.

Now builds her nest the melancholy bird
Yet moaning Itys; she, the eternal shame
Of Cecrops' house for vengeance too severe
    On barbarous lusts of kings.*

Swains of sleek flocks on the young grass reclined,
Chant pastoral songs attuned to piping reeds,
Charming the god who loves the darksome slopes
    And folds of Arcady;

These, O my Virgil, are the days of thirst;
But if, O client of illustrious youths,
Calenian juices tempt, bring thou the nard,
    And with it earn my wine;

One tiny box of spikenard will draw forth
The cask now ripening in Sulpician † vaults,—
Cask large enough to hold a world of hope,
    And drown a world of care.

Quick! if such merriments delight thee, come
With thine own contributions to the feast;
Not like rich host in prodigal halls—my cups
    Thou shalt not tinge scot-free.

* "Quod male barbaras
Regum est ulta libidines."

Most authorities, Orelli amongst them, take "male" with "ulta"—viz., that the bird, whether Philomela or Procne, avenged too cruelly (nimis atrociter) the guilt of Tereus. I have translated accordingly, but am by no means sure that "male" should not be taken, as Macleane suggests, with "barbaras"—viz., the too barbarous, or evilly barbarous, lusts of kings. The bird is the eternal reproach to the house of Cecrops, not on account of the severity of her vengeance, but on account of the atrocity of the crimes she avenged. Most commentators of authority agree that the bird here meant is the swallow, not nightingale. Ritter understands by "flebiliter" the swallow's inarticulate twitter.

† "Sulpiciis horreis." The Sulpician wine-vaults were famous, and the scholiast Porphyrion says they were still the great magazines for wine and oil in his day, under the name of the Galban cellars. Ritter considers that Orelli is mistaken in supposing that Horace intimates that he will *buy* the wine there; and maintains that he refers to his own cask, which had been warehoused in the Sulpician magazine.

But put aside delays and care of gain,
Warned, while yet time, by the dark death-fires; mix
    With thought brief thoughtlessness; in fitting place
        'Tis sweet to be unwise.

ODE XIII.

TO LYCE, A FADED BEAUTY.

No subject of inquiry can be less interesting to a critic of good sense than that on which so many learned disputants have wasted their time—viz., who among the ladies celebrated by Horace were real persons or imaginary; and who are to be admitted into or rejected from the genuine catalogue of his loves? We have absolutely no data to go upon. There is no reason, except that he chooses to apply the same name to both, to suppose that the Lyce over whose ruined charms he now exults was the Lyce of whose cruelty he complains, Lib. III. Od. x.; nay, I believe that most recent scholars are pretty well agreed that the ode last mentioned was an artistic exercise, imitated from the Greek serenades. But, so far as mere conjecture from internal evidence may be allowed, the present ode seems to have in it a tone of earnestness which warrants a belief that the Lyce addressed was a real person. In the three concluding stanzas, the bitterness of sarcasm is tinged with a certain melancholy pathos which appears to indicate the memory of a former passion; and the direct reference to Cinara—to whom all interpreters agree in considering Horace was attached (whether or not he celebrates her under names of the same metrical quantity, Lalage, Glycera, &c.)—gives a peculiar air of individual truthfulness to the poem. Be this as it may, the ode is remarkable for its eternal applicability to a type in female character, and is replete with beauties of expression. The image in the last stanza is extremely striking. The simile is so simple that one might fancy it would have occurred to any poet, yet it is so expressed as to be quite original.

They have heard my prayers, Lyce, the gods;
The gods have heard, Lyce; thou'rt old,
    Yet still, setting up for a beauty,
        Thou wouldst tipple and frisk with the young;

Courting, maudlin, with tremulous chant,
Laggard Cupid: he's absent on guard
    O'er the bloom on the cheeks of young Chia,
        Whose lute is more sweet than thy song.*

---

* There is an opposition between Lyce's tremulous quaver, "cantu tremulo," and Chia's musical skill, "doctæ psallere," which can only, perhaps, be made clear by some slight paraphrase, as is attempted in the last line of the stanza, in translation.

For he roosts not on oaks without sap ;
Hollow teeth and dry wrinkles he flies,
    He is chilled by the snow of grey tresses,
      And thus has retreated from thee.

Sparkling gems, and the purples of Cos,*
Cannot back to thee bring the dead years
    Rapid Time has interred in our annals,
      For all men to number their graves.†

Whither fled is the beauty ? alas !
Where the bloom ? where the movement of grace ?
    Of that—O of that—what is left thee,
      Breathing loves, which stole me from myself,

Blest successor to Cinara thou,
Gracious form,‡ for arts pleasing renowned ?
    But to Cinara few years were conceded,
      By the Fates who have Lyce preserved

To be rival in age to the crow,
That the young, glowing yet, may behold,
    As a subject of mirth, in those ashes
      The fallen remains of a torch.

* Horace speaks of the robes from Cos in Sat. I. ii. line 100, as so transparent that they left nothing to conceal.

† "Tempora, quæ semel
Notis condita fastis
Inclusit volucris dies."

"Horace means to say that the days she has seen are all buried, as it were, in the grave of the public annals (as Acron says), and there any one may find them, but she cannot get them back. It is a graphic way of identifying the years, and marking their decease, to point to the record in which each is distinguished by its consuls and its leading events. 'Notis' merely expresses the publicity and notoriety of the record by which the lapse of time is marked."—MACLEANE.

‡ "Notaque et artium
Gratarum facies ?"

"'Facies' does not mean the face alone, but the whole form and presence. 'Facies autem totam corporis speciem significat.'"—DILLENBURGER. See, too, Orelli's note.

ODE XIV.

The introduction to Ode iv. in this book has, sufficiently for the purpose, sketched the outline of the events which led to the composition of this ode. As the former was devoted to the praises of Drusus, so the latter commemorates the subsequent and completing conquests of Tiberius, and refers all to the honour of Augustus in the establishment of his empire, and the consummation of his fortunes and his glory.

By what care can the Senate of Rome, and Rome's
          people,
With a largess of honours sufficiently ample,
     By what titles, what archives to time,
          Eternise thy virtues, Augustus,

Prince supremest, wherever the sun lights a region
That man can inhabit ?   What in war thou availest,
     The Vindelici lately have learned,
          Free till then from the law of the Roman.

By no even exchange in the barter of bloodshed,*
Drusus, leading thy hosts, overthrew the fleet Breuni—
     The Genauni—implacable race—
          And the citadels piled upon Alps

Horror-breathing ; then Nero the elder completed
Glories due to thine auspice in one crowning battle ;
     Closed the raid of the savage, and crushed
          The grim might of the giant-like Ræti.

All conspicuous he rode where the fight raged the
          fiercest,
Wasting down, to what wrecks ! that array of stern
          bosoms,
     Self-surrendered as offerings to death,
          In the stubborn devotion to freedom.

---

* " Plus vice simplici." This does not mean "more than once," but, as the scholiasts interpret, "with double loss to the enemy ;" or literally, as Macleane renders it, "with more than an even exchange"—*i.e.*, of blood.

Through the foe went his way, as the blast o'er the
　　billows
When the Pleiads are cleaving the rain-clouds asunder,
　　And the snort of his war-horse was heard
　　　In the midst of the lightnings of battle.*

As when Aufidus, laving the kingdoms of Daunus,
Bursts in wrath, and in form of the wild bull,† his
　　borders,
　　And prepares the dread deluge he drives
　　　O'er the fields that are rife with the harvest,—

So in storm, through that barbarous array swept the
　　Nero,
Mowing, foremost to hindmost, ranks serried in iron,
　　Till a victor he stood, without loss,
　　　On a ground that was strewn with the foemen;

But he owed to thyself the resources, the counsels,
And the gods. From the day that her port and void
　　palace,
　　Suppliant Egypt threw open to thee,
　　　Had thy reign reached its third happy lustre,

When, in crowning thy wish and completing thy glory,
Fortune ended the wars which her favour had pros-
　　pered,‡
　　And established in triumph the peace
　　　Of a world underneath thy dominion.

---

* "Medios per ignes"—*i.e.*, "per medium ardorem belli" (COM. CRUQ.).
† "Tauriformis Aufidus;" literally, "tauriform" or "bull-formed
Aufidus." The image is applied to many rivers by the Greek and Latin
poets. Macleane suggests that the branches of so many large streams at
the mouths of rivers might have suggested the idea of the horns; but it
seems to me that the comparison to the bull in general applies to the blind
and senseless violence of the animal, who runs on indiscriminately trampling and destroying everything in his way—just as the inundation of a
torrent does.
‡ Horace, here addressing Augustus, ascribes it to him as his crowning
victory that he has at last got the wish of his heart, which was peace—the
peace of the world, subjected to the Roman Empire. The victory of
Tiberius was on the fifteenth anniversary of the day on which Augustus
entered Alexandria, and, thus terminating the civil war, became supreme.

Thee the dauntless Cantabrian, before never conquered;
Thee the Mede and the Indian, and Scyth, the wild
        Nomad,
    Mark in wonder and awe, guardian shield
      Of Italia, and Rome the earth's mistress.

Thee the Nile, unrevealing the source of its waters;
Thee the Danube; and thee the swift rush of the Tigris;
    Thee the monster-fraught ocean, which roars
      Round the birthplace remote of the Briton;

Thee fierce Gallia, the land for which death has no
        terror,
Thee Iberia, the stubborn, hear hushed and submissive;
    The Sygambri, exulting in gore,
      With meek arms piled in trophy, adore thee.

ODE XV.

TO AUGUSTUS ON THE RESTORATION OF PEACE.

This ode is the appropriate epilogue to the Fourth Book, of which the
poems that celebrate the Roman victories under Drusus and Tiberius constitute the noblest portion. If it be true that the book was published on
account of these odes, and at the desire of Augustus, Horace would naturally conclude by a special reference to the beneficial issues of the wars
undertaken by Augustus, and from the final completion of which in Gaul,
Germany, and Spain, he had just returned to Rome. Horace here begins by
saying, that when he wished to sing of these wars, Phœbus checked him.
But Phœbus does not forbid him to sing the triumphs of peace; and, with
a lively lyrical abruptness, he therefore at once bursts forth:—

        "Tua, Cæsar, ætas
    Fruges et agris retulit uberes," &c.

That the poem was composed immediately after the return of Cæsar, and in
connection with Odes iv. and xiv., is, I think, made clear by its own internal
evidence. War is finished, and Augustus is celebrated as the triumphant
establisher of law and order, and the author of the national prosperity, and
the improvements, social and moral, which result from the security to life
and property bestowed by a government at once firm and beneficent. He
is here the descendant, not of Mars and Ilia, but of Anchises and Venus the
gentle.

Of wars and vanquished cities when I longed
  To sing, Apollo checked me with his lyre,
    Lest I launched sails so slight
    Into so vast a deep. Cæsar, thy reign

Has given back golden harvests to our fields ;
Our standards, torn from Parthia's haughty walls,
    Restored to Roman Jove ;
        Closed gates of Janus, vacant of a war ;

To righteous order rampant licence curbed,
Thrust from the state the vices * which defiled,
    And, in their stead, recalled
        The ancient virtues to their fatherland,†—

Virtues from which have grown the Roman name,
Italia's might, fame, and majestic sway,
    To the Sun's Orient rise,
        From his calm bed in our Hesperian seas.

Cæsar our guardian, neither civil rage ‡
Nor felon violence scares us from repose,
    Nor ire which sharpens swords,
        And makes the wars of nations and their woes.

Neither the drinkers of deep Danube break
The Julian Laws, nor Scyths, nor Seres fierce,
    Nor Persia's faithless sons,
        Nor wild men cradled on the banks of Don.

So, with each sacred, with each common day
(Prayer, as is due, first rendered to the gods),
    'Mid blithesome Liber's boons,
        Gathering our women and our children round,

Let us, as did our fathers in old time,
Honour with hymns and Lydian fife brave chiefs :
    Sing Troy ; Anchises sing ;
        Sing of the race from gentle Venus sprung.

---

* " Emovitque culpas." This refers to the moral reforms undertaken by
Augustus, such as the Julian law, " de adulteriis et de pudicitia."
† " ' Veteres artes.' 'Artes' here means 'virtues,' as in Book III.
Od. iii. ' Hac arte' (ἀρετῇ), as prudence, fortitude, justice, temperance."
— ACRON.

‡ " Non furor
Civilis aut vis exiget otium,
Non ira, quæ procudit enses,
Et miseras inimicat urbes."

Three causes of fear are removed : "Furor civilis," "civil war;" "vis,"
" personal violence ;" " ira," "foreign wars."

THE EPODES.

INTRODUCTION.

ORELLI, Dillenburger, and Macleane concur in accepting Franke's date for the publication of the book of Epodes— viz., A.U.C. 724, when Horace was thirty-five years old. The poems contained in the book appear to have been written between 713 and the date at which they were published ; and, no doubt, many of them were known to Horace's friends before publication. It is to these Epodes that Horace refers in the boast, Epist. i. 19-23, that " He first introduced the Parian iambics, following the numbers and the spirit of Archilochus " (of Paros). Their title of Epode was not given to them (any more than that of Ode was given to the poems classed under that name) by Horace himself. Such designations are the inventions of some long-subsequent grammarian.

These poems are not lyrical in point of form, though they are occasionally so in point of spirit—especially, I think, the 13th Epode. They serve as an intermediate link between Horace's Odes and his earlier Satires.

The first ten Epodes are all in the same metre—alternate trimeter and dimeter iambics ; they admit spondees only in the uneven places, and there is but one instance (ii. 35) in which an anapæst is admitted.

In the translation, the metre selected for the more important of these Epodes has been employed in the version of a few of the graver odes—viz., the ordinary form of blank verse converted into a couplet by alternate terminations in a dissyllable and monosyllable.

In the lighter of these first ten Epodes—viz., Ep. vi. x.— I have thought that the variation of a more easy and rapid measure was necessary to represent the lively spirit of the Latin.

EPODE I.

TO MÆCENAS.

This epode is generally supposed to have been composed when Augustus had summoned the leading public men, whether senators or equites, to meet him at Brundusium prior to the expedition against Antony and Cleopatra which resulted in the battle of Actium, A.U.C. 723. The poem warrants the assumption that Mæcenas had been then appointed to, or offered, a naval command; but it seems (Dio. 51, 3, and Seneca, Ep. 114, 6), that Augustus decided on retaining him at home to watch over the affairs of Italy, and maintain order at Rome. Mr. Dyer, in the "Classical Museum," vol. ii., p. 199, and subsequently in Smith's "Biographical Dictionary" (art. "Mæcenas"), contends that the poem refers to the Sicilian expedition against Sextus Pompeius, A.U.C. 718. Macleane objects to this supposition—"that the language of affection is too strong for the short acquaintance which Horace had then enjoyed with Mæcenas, and that there is evidence in the poem itself of the Sabine farm having come into Horace's possession when he wrote it; but that this did not occur till after the publication of the First Book of Satires is certain, and it is generally referred to A.U.C. 720."

So thou wilt go with thy Liburnian galleys,
    Amongst, O friend, those giant floating towers;
Prepared to share all perils braved by Cæsar,
    And ward them off, Mæcenas, by thine own.
But what of us, to whom, while thou survivest,
    Life is a joy;—thee lost, a weary load?
Shall we, as bidden, take our ease contented?
    Ease has no sweetness if not shared with thee;
Or shall we bear our part in thy great labour
    As fitting men of no unmanly mould?
Yes, we would bear; and thee o'er Alpine summits,
    Or through the wastes of guestless Caucasus,
Or where the last pale rim of the horizon
    Fades on the farthest waters of the west,
Follow with soul undaunted. Dost thou ask me
    How, weak in body, and unskilled in war,
My toil could lighten thine? I should be present
    With terrors less than those the absent know;
Ev'n as the bird more dreads for her young nestlings,
    If for a moment left, the gliding snake;
Not that her presence could avail for succour,
    Albeit she felt them underneath her wing.

Gladly in this or any war a soldier
    Would I enlist, for hope of thy dear grace;
Not that, attached by ampler teams of oxen,
    My ploughs may struggle through the stubborn glebe—
Not that my flocks should, ere the dog-star parcheth,
    Change hot Calabria for Lucanian slopes *—·
Not that for me some villa's pomp of marble
    Should shine down white upon luxuriant vales,
Touching the walls with which the son of Circe †
    Girded enchanted land in Tusculum.
Enough, and more than I can need, for riches,
    Thanks to thy bounty, is already mine;
I am no Chremes, hoarding gold to bury ‡—
    No loose-robed spendthrift lusting gold to waste.

EPODE II.

ALFIUS.—THE CHARMS OF RURAL LIFE.

This poem, in which a glowing description of country life and its innocent attractions is placed in the mouth of the rich usurer Alfius, is one of the happiest examples of Horace's power of polished and latent irony. Macleane thinks that the poem was originally written in praise of rural life, and that the last lines were added to give the rest a moral. "At any rate," he says, "the greater part of the speech must be admitted to be rather out of keeping with the supposed speaker." This alleged want of keeping does not strike me, nor do I believe that the last lines were "an afterthought." The idea is in complete harmony with the substance of Satire i. Book I., in which Horace says that the miser is never contented with his own lot, but rather extols those who follow opposite pursuits :—

    " Nemo ut avarus
  Se probet, ac potius laudet diversa sequentes; "

but that nevertheless the nature of the man returns to him; and if you offered to let him exchange with the person he envies, and so be happy, he would not accept the offer. The same idea is expressed more briefly, Book I.

---

    * The wealthy proprietors sent their flocks in summer from the hot Calabrian plains to the wooded hills of Lucania.
    † Telegonus, son of Circe by Ulysses, said to have founded ancient Tusculum on the summit of the hill, the slope of which is occupied by the modern Frascati, and to have there introduced the magic arts of his mother. The lines in the original are slightly paraphrased in the translation, in order not to lose to the English reader the poetic idea associating Tusculum with legendary enchantment, which the words "Circæa mœnia" would have conveyed to the Latin.
    ‡ " 'Chremes.' The allusion is, perhaps, to a character in some play of Menander."—MACLEANE.

Ode i. lines 15, 35—"The merchant, terrified by the storms, lauds the ease of the country, but very soon refits his battered vessels." That a rich money-lender might at some moment feel and express very glowingly an enthusiasm for country life 'is natural enough; we have instances of that every day. No one praises or covets a country life more than a rich Jew or contractor. We do not know the occasion which may have suggested the poem; but nothing is more likely than that there was a report that the famous usurer was about to buy a country place and retire from business; and on the strength of that rumour Horace wrote the poem.

"Blessed is he—remote, as were the mortals
    Of the first age, from business and its cares—
Who ploughs paternal fields with his own oxen
    Free from the bonds of credit or of debt.*
No soldier he, roused by the savage trumpet,
    Not his to shudder at the angry sea; †
His life escapes from the contentious forum,
    And shuns the insolent thresholds of the great.
And so he marries to the amorous tendrils
    Of the young vine the poplar's lofty stem;
Or marks from far the lowing herds that wander
    Leisurely down the calm secluded vale;
Or, pruning with keen knife the useless branches,
    Grafts happier offspring on the parent tree;
Or in pure jars he stores the clear-prest honey;
    Or shears the fleeces of his tender sheep; ‡
Or, when brown Autumn from the fields uplifteth
    Brows with ripe coronal of fruits adorned,
What joy to pluck the pear himself hath grafted,
    And his own grape, that with the purple vies,
Wherewith he pays thee, rural god Priapus,
    And, landmark-guardian, Sire Silvanus, thee : §

* "Solutus omni fenore"—"who neither lends nor borrows upon usury:" so Torrentius and Orelli. Macleane says the words would equally suit any other person besides a city usurer, and would mean that in the country he would not be subject to the calls of creditors, and need not get into debt. This interpretation is perhaps too loosely hazarded. An illustrious Horatian critic, to whom the translator is largely indebted, observes that "solutus" evidently refers to usurious bonds, and is so employed in the Satires; and suggests, as a more literal translation, "Unshackled by the bonds of usury."

† "Nec horret iratum mare." This does not apply to the sailor, but to the trader or merchant—"nec mercaturam exercet."—ORELLI.

‡ "Aut tondet infirmas oves." Baxter strangely interprets "infirmas" as "sickly" (aegrotas); Orelli as "feeble" (imbecillas). Voss translates it "zarter," and so far agrees with Macleane, who considers it a purely ornamental expression.

§ "Pater Silvane, tutor finium." Silvanus, whose more usual attribute

Free to recline, now under aged ilex,
  Now in frank sunshine on the matted grass,
While through the steep banks slip the gliding waters,
  And birds are plaintive in the forest glens,
And limpid fountains, with a drowsy tinkle,
  Invite the light wings of the noonday sleep.

"But when the season of the storm, rude winter,
  Gathers together all its rains and snows,
Or here and there, into the toils before them,
  With many a hound he drives the savage boars;
Or with fine net, on forkëd stake suspended,
  Spreads for voracious thrushes fraudful snare,
And—joyful prizes—captures in his springes
  The shy hare and that foreigner the crane.
Who would not find in these pursuits oblivion
  Of all the baleful cares which wait on love?
Yet, if indeed he boasts an honest helpmate,
  Who, like the Sabine wife or sunburnt spouse
Of brisk Apulian, in the cares of household
  And of sweet children bears her joyous part;
Who on the sacred hearth the oldest fagots
  Piles 'gainst the coming of her wearied lord;
And in the wattled close the milch-kine penning,
  Drains the distended udders of their load;
From the sweet cask draws forth the year's new vintage,
  And spreads the luxuries of an unbought feast:
Such fare would charm me more than rarest dainties—
  Than delicate oyster of the Lucrine lake,
Or (if from eastern floods loud-booming winter
  Drive to our seas) the turbot or the scar.
Not softer sinks adown the grateful palate
  The Nubian pullet or the Ionian snipe,*
Than olives chosen where they hang the thickest;
  Or sorrel, lusty lover of green fields;

is the care of corn-fields and cattle, is here made to undertake the protection
of boundaries, which properly belonged to Terminus.
  * "Afra avis"—"attagen Ionicus." What bird is meant by the "Afra
avis" is a matter of uncertainty. Yonge says it is the guinea-fowl—
Macleane inclines to the same opinion; but we know little more of it than
that it was speckled. The "attagen" is variously interpreted woodcock,
snipe, and, more commonly, moorfowl. The Ionian snipe is to this day so
incomparably the best of the snipe race, that I venture to think it is the
veritable "attagen Ionicus."

H H

Or mallows, wholesome for the laden body,
  Or lambkin slain on Terminus' high feast,
Or kidling rescued from the wolf's fierce hunger.
  How sweet, amid such feasts, to view the sheep
Flock blithe from field to fold, see the tired oxen
  With languid neck draw back thei nverted share,
And home-born * labourers round the shining Lares
  Gathered—the faithful swarm of the rich hive ! "
Thus said the usurer Alfius, and all moneys
  Lent till the mid-month—at that date calls in,
And, hot for rural pleasures, that day fortnight
  Our would-be farmer—lends them out again.†

EPODE III.

TO MÆCENAS IN EXECRATION OF GARLIC.

Horace appears to have been tempted to eat, when dining with Mæcenas,
some dish over-seasoned with garlic, unaware of the prevalence of that
ingredient, or unprescient of its effects. Some commentators, whom Dillenburger follows, suppose this to have been a kind of compound salad called
"moretum," in which cheese, oil, milk, and wine contributed their motley
aid to the garlic. This, however, was a primitive rustic comestible not
likely to have been found at the table of Mæcenas. Whatever the dish
might have been, Horace seems to have considered the recommendation of
it a bad joke, and he takes revenge upon the chief criminal, garlic, in the
following humorous anathema.

The commentators in general assume that Horace could not have taken
the liberty to refer to Terentia in the concluding lines, "Manum puella,"
&c., and that the poem was therefore written before Mæcenas's marriage,
probably A.U.C. 719 or 720. Ritter, on the contrary, denounces with much
indignation the idea that Horace could impute the indecorum of so familiar
an intercourse with a freedwoman to a man of the grave occupations and
dignified position of Mæcenas, and insists on applying "puella" to Terentia,
in which case the poem would be written shortly after the marriage of
Mæcenas, which Ritter chooses to date, A.U.C. 725 (i. e., a year after Franke's
date for the publication of the Epodes).

If e'er a parricide with hand accursed
  Hath cut a father's venerable throat,

---

* "Positosque vernas, ditis examen domus." This is a picture of the
primitive rustic life, in which the labourers, familiarly with the master,
gathered at supper round the Lares.—COLUM. xi. 1, 19. "The home-born
slaves cluster round the master, as the bees round the queen-bee."—
RITTER.

† "Omnem redegit Idibus pecuniam,—
    Quærit Kalendis ponere."
The ides, nones, and kalends were the settling days of Rome.

Hemlock's too mild a poison—give him garlic;
  O the strong stomachs of your country clowns!
What deadly drug is raging in my vitals?
  Was viper's venom in those fraudful herbs?
Or was Canidia, armed with all her poisons,
  The awful cook of that infernal feast?
Surely Medea, wonderstruck with Jason,
  As of all Argonauts the comeliest chief,*
Smeared him with this soul-sickening preparation,
  Which quelled the bulls to the unwonted yoke.
In this she steeped her present to the rival,
  From whom, avenging, soared her dragon-car.
Never such heat from pestilential comets
  Parched dry Apulia, thirsting for a shower;
Less hot that gift which, through the massive shoulders
  Of sturdy Hercules, burned life away.
Jocose Mæcenas, 'tis no laughing matter:
  If e'er thou try it, may thy sweetheart's hand
Ward off thy kiss; and sacred be her refuge
  In the remotest borders of the bed.

EPODE IV.

AGAINST AN UPSTART.

All the scholiasts agree in considering that the person satirised in this ode was the freedman Menas, lieutenant to Sextus Pompeius, who deserted to Augustus A.U.C. 716. Modern critics have objected to this assumption, and their objections are tersely summed up and answered by Macleane in his prefatory comment on the ode. In some inscriptions Vedius Rufus has been named instead of Menas. Ritter maintains the accuracy of this identification, and affirms that it was no other than Vedius Pollio, a Roman knight, who had been originally a freedman, mentioned by Seneca, Pliny, and others.—See Ritter's note.

---

* "Ut Argonautas præter omnes candidum
    Medea mirata est ducem."

"Posteaquam Medea Jasonis ceteris omnibus Argonautis pulchrioris forma capta est, sic construe, 'non vero Jasonem candidum mirata est præter omnes Argonautas.'"—ORELLI. Macleane prefers the construction which Orelli prohibits, but I like Orelli's the best.

As tow'rds the wolf the lamb's inborn repugnance
    Nature makes my antipathy to thee,
Thou ` on whose flank still burns the Iberian whip-
    cord,*
    Thou on whose limbs still galls the bruise of chains,
Strut as thou wilt in arrogance of purse-pride,
    Fortune can change not the man's native breed.
Mark, as along the Sacred Way † thou flauntest,
    Puffing thy toga, twice three cubits wide ‡—
Mark with what frankness indignation loathes thee,
    Seen in the looks of every passer-by ! §
"He, by Triumvers so inured to lashes,
    As tired the public crier to proclaim,‖
Now ploughs some thousand fat Falernian acres,
    And wears the Appian Road out with his nags;
In public shows, despite the law of Otho,¶
    He takes a foremost place and sits—a knight.

---

* "Ibericis funibus." These were cords or ropes made of "spartum," usually said to be the Spanish broom and employed for ships' rigging. "It may be added, in favour of the theory which makes Menas the hero, that the mention of Spanish ropes seems to imply that the person had suffered on board ship, if not in the country itself, since, as Pliny tells us, ropes of spartum were especially used in ships; and the only way to give point to the epithet is to suppose it had reference to Spain itself, or to the fleet."—MACLEANE.

† The Sacred Way, leading to the Capitol, was the favourite lounge of the idlers.

‡ "Cum bis trium ulnarum toga." According to Macleane, this applies to the width of the toga, not the length, as commonly translated: I follow his interpretation, but it is disputed.

§ "Ut ora vertat huc et huc euntium
    Liberrima indignatio."

I think with Macleane that this appears rather to mean the open indignation which made the passengers turn their looks *towards* him, than turn *away* in disgust, which is the construction of the scholiasts. Yonge suggests a totally different interpretation : "See how a free" (*i. e.*, unreserved, undisguised) "scorn *alters* the *countenance*" (ora vertat) "of all who pass along."

‖ The Triumviri Capitales had the power of inflicting summary chastisement on slaves. When the scourge was inflicted, a public crier stood by and proclaimed the nature of the crime.

¶ Fourteen rows in the theatre and amphitheatre, immediately over the orchestra, were by the law of L. Roscius Otho, A.U.C. 686, appropriated to the knights. As the tribunes of the soldiers had equestrian rank, if the person satirised were one of them, he could therefore take his seat in one of the fourteen rows, despite the intention of Otho, which was to reserve the front seats for persons of genuine rank.

What boots the equipment of yon floating bulwarks,
  Yon vast array of ponderous brazen prores?
What! against slaves and pirates launch an army,*
  Which has for officer,—that man—that man!"

EPODE V.

ON THE WITCH CANIDIA.

None of Horace's poems excels this in point of power—and the power herein exhibited is of the highest kind ; it is power over the passions of pity and terror. The degree of humour admitted is just sufficient to heighten the effect of the more tragic element. The scene is brought before the eye of the reader with a marvellous distinctness. A boy of good birth, as is shown by the *toga prætexta* and *bulla* which he wears, has been decoyed or stolen from his home, and carried at night to some house—probably Canidia's. The poem opens with his terrified exclamations, as Canidia and her three associate witches stand around him. He is stripped, buried chin-deep in a pit, and tantalised with the sight of food which he is not permitted to taste, till, thus wasted away, his liver and marrow may form the crowning ingredient of the caldron in which the other materials for a philter have been placed. That it is for an old profligate, whom Canidia is resolved to charm back to her, that the philter is prepared, adds to the vileness which the poet ascribes to the hag. This epode was probably composed about the same time as the 8th Satire of the First Book, in which Canidia and Sagana are represented seeking the ghastly materials of their witchcraft, and invoking Hecate and Tisiphone in the Esquilinian burial-ground. The poem has little of the graces of expression which characterise Horace's maturer odes, and in one or two passages the construction is faultily obscure ; but the grandeur of the whole conception, and the vigour of the execution, need no comment, and compensate for all defects.

The scholiasts say that Canidia's real name was Gratidia, and that she was a Neapolitan perfume-vender. That she was ever a mistress of Horace's is a conjecture founded upon no evidence, and nothing extant in Horace justifies the assumption. This poem was written when Horace was young, and he could scarcely have remembered, except in his childhood, Canidia more lovely than he invariably represents her.

"But O,† whatever Power divine in heaven,
  O'er earth and o'er the human race presideth,‡

---

* The slaves and pirates are supposed to refer to the fleet of Sextus Pompeius.

† "At, O deorum," &c. The word "at," thus commencing the ode, is significant of the commotion and hurry of the speaker, and also brings the whole scene more vividly before the reader. The poem begins, as it were, in the middle of the boy's address to the witches, omitting what had gone before.

‡ "Regit," not "regis"—"presides," not "presidest." The boy does not invoke the gods ; he is addressing Canidia. It is but a disordered exclamation.

What means this gathering? why on me alone,
  Fixed in fierce stare, those ominous dread faces?
By thine own children, if, indeed, for thee *
  Lucina brought† to light true fleshly children—
By this vain purple's childish ornament ‡—
  By Jove's sure wrath—why are thy looks as deadly
As the stepmother's on the babe she loathes,
  Or wounded wild beasts, glaring on the hunter?"
As the boy pleaded thus, with tremulous lip,
  From him fierce hands rent childhood's robe and bulla,
And naked stood that form which might have moved,
  With its young innocence, a Thracian's pity.

Canidia, all her tangled tresses crisped
  By the contracted folds of angry vipers,
Spake, and bade mandrakes, torn from dead men's graves,§
  Bade dismal branches of funereal cypress,
And eggs and plumes of the night screech-owl, smeared
  With the toad's loathsome and malignant venom,
Herbs which Iolcos and Hiberia send, ||
  From soils whose richest harvest-crops are poison,
And bones, from jaw of famished wild-bitch snatched,¶—
  Bade them all simmer in the Colchian caldron.**

  * Here he addresses Canidia.
  † Ritter, Yonge, and Munro have "*adfuit.*"
  ‡ "Per hoc inane purpuræ decus precor." This is the "toga prætexta"
which was worn by free Roman children, together with the "bulla," a small
round plate of gold suspended from the neck. Both were relinquished on the
adoption of the "toga virilis," about the age of fifteen.
  § "Sepulcris caprificos erutas," the wild fig rooted up from graves.
  || Hiberia here does not, as elsewhere, mean Spain, but a region, now part
of Georgia, east of Colchis. Iolcos was a seaport of Thessaly.
  ¶ Why bones snatched from the jaws of a hungry bitch should have the
virtue that fits them for ingredients in the witches' caldron is not clearly
explained by the commentators. It is not only the angry slaver of the
famishing bitch robbed of her food that gives the bone its necromantic value
—there is virtue in the bone itself. The dog meant is one of the ownerless
wild dogs that prowled at night for food, and haunted burial-grounds such as
the Esquiline, where the lowest class of the poor were buried so near the
surface of the ground that their remains could be easily scratched up, and
the bone adapted for the caldron would be a human bone. So, in the "Siege
of Corinth"—

      " And he saw the lean dogs beneath the wall
        Hold o'er the dead their carnival,
        Gorging and growling o'er carcass and limb." &c.

  ** "Flammis aduri Colchicis." The materials thus collected by the
witches are not burned as fuel in the magic (Colchian) flames, but are boiled

Meanwhile, bare-legged, fell Sagana bedews
    The whole abode with hell-drops from Avernus,*
Her locks erect as some sea-urchin barbed,
    Or wild boar bristling as he runs.   Then Veia,
Remorseless crone, loud grunting o'er the toil,
    With her fell spade the yawning death-pit hollows,
Wherein they bury the yet living child,
    And twice and thrice each long day mock his famine.†
Chin-deep (as waters on their brim suspend
    The swimmer) plunged, lingering he lives in dying,
To gaze upon the food denied his lips,
    Till the parched liver and the shrivelled marrow
Shall into philters for vile love consume,
    When once, yet staring on the food forbidden,
The glazing eyeballs waste themselves away.
    If idle Naples and each neighbouring city
Rightly believe, the Ariminian hag,
    Unnatural Folia, failed not that grim conclave,
She who could draw the moon and subject stars,
    With her Thessalian witch-song, down from heav̈n.

To them, with thumb-nail pressed to livid tooth,
    Which gnawed and mumbled it, spake dire Canidia.
What said she, or what horror left untold ?
    " Ye of my deeds sure arbiters and faithful,
O Night, O Hecate, who o'er silence reign
    In darksome hours to rites mysterious sacred,
Now, now be present ; now on hostile homes
    Turn wrath invoked, and demon power revengeful ;
Now, while amid the horror-breathing woods
    Lurk the wild beasts, couched languid in soft slumber,
Dogs of Sabura,† up ! bark loud ; let all
    Mock the old lecher, with a nard anointed

as materials for the philter, of which the marrow and liver of the unhappy child are the completing ingredients.
   * From the fount Avernus.

       † " Longo die bis terque mutatæ dapis
           Inemori spectaculo."
" Longo" belongs to "die," and not to "spectaculo." " Inemori" is not found anywhere else ; the ordinary form is " immori."—MACLEANE.
   ‡ " Sabura," one of the most populous and one of the most profligate streets of Rome. Canidia prays that the barking of the dogs may rouse the street to mock the old man, skulking to other mistresses than herself, and

Than which none subtler could these hands complcte.
But how?* what's this? Have they, then, lost their
virtue?
The barbarous Medea's direful drugs,
Wherewith she wreaked her wrongs on that proud rival,
Great Creon's daughter, yea, consumed the bride
By venom steeped into the murderous mantle,
And soared away destroying :—Me, nor herb
Nor root hath failed to render its dark secrets
Latent in inaccessible ravines.
The beds he sleeps on aro by me besprinkled †
With Lethe of all other loves than mine.
Ho! ho! yet struts he free,—at large,—protected
By charm of which more learned than myself.
Ah, Varus, ah! by no trite hackneyed philters
Ill-fated wretch, shalt thou rush back to me,
Thy truant heart no Marsian charms recover ‡—
A mightier spell I weave ; a direr bowl
Now will I brim, to tame thy scornful bosom.

thus scare him back to her. It seems clear from what follows that the nard
or unguent was composed by Canidia, though that is disputed by commentators, and the construction itself is obscure. It is this magical unguent that
is to cause the dogs to bark—see Orelli's note. Absurdly enough the
scholiasts assumed, on the authority of this passage (for what other authority
is there?) that Canidia was by profession a vendor of perfumes.
  * "Quid accidit?" The spell fails—the dogs do not bark. Varus does
not go forth into Sabura, nor come to Canidia. "Do the drugs of Medea
fail?" &c. "She speaks," says Macleane, "as if she had been actually using
the drugs of Medea."
          † "Indormit unctis omnium cubilibus
                Oblivione pellicum."
The sense of this passage is exceedingly obscure, and has been subjected to
various interpretations. I adopt that of Orelli, viz.—Canidia had smeared
the couch on which Varus slept with drugs to make him forgetful of all
women but herself; taking "unctis" with "oblivione," anointed with
oblivion—"omnium pellicum," "of all wantons." Still this construction is
not satisfactory, because, just before, Canidia supposes that Varus was out on
his rambles, from which the barking dogs were to scare him to her, and she
is surprised to find that he is quietly asleep.
          ‡ "Ad me recurres ; nec vocata mens tua
                Marsis redibit vocibus."
The Marsian witchcrafts were those in vogue with the populace. The sense
is not, as commonly translated, that his mind or reason (mens), maddened by
Canidia's spell, shall not be restored to him by the counter-charms of the
Marsian witchcraft; but that he shall run back to her, and that his mind or
heart will not be thus restored to her by her employment of any common
vulgar incantations. No, she is now preparing a mightier bowl (referring to
the victim present), &c.

Sooner the sky shall sink below the sea,
  And over both the earth shall be extended,
Than thou not burn for me, as in the smoke
  Of these black flames now burns this dull bitumen."
Then the child spoke, not seeking, as before,
  Those impious hell-hags with mild words to soften.
But pausing long, now in his last despair,
  Launched the full wrath of Thyestëan curses.*
"Witchcrafts invert not the great laws divine
  Of right and wrong as they invert things human;†

---

* "Thyesteas preces."   Curses such as Thyestes might have invoked
on Atreus, who slaughtered and served up at the banquet his brother's
children.

   † "Venena magnum fas nefasque non valent
    Convertere humanam vicem;
    Diris agam vos."

Of all the obscure passages in the poem this is the most obscure. The
contradictory interpretations of various commentators have not served to
render it less so. The translation most in vogue is that suggested by Lambinus : "Witchcraft (venena) can invert the great principle of wrong and
right, but cannot invert the condition or fate (or vicissitude in the fate) of
men," "valent" being understood in the first clause. Munro, Introduction,
p. xxviii., adopts the arrangement of Lambinus, with one point of difference.
"I do not think," he says, "'Magnum' can be joined with 'fas nefasque.'
I have therefore made it parenthetical where it seems to me to have much
force. The meaning is, 'venena (id quod magnum est) fas nefasque valent
Convertere, humanam vicem non valent.'"   Ritter takes "venena" as
poisons which may be beneficial as medicaments, or deadly, used with malignant purposes, and are thus "magnum fas nefasque;" and takes "humanam
vicem" as the retribution due to human deeds. Orelli, in an excursus,
gives, with his usual candour, not less than nine various interpretations, but
very decidedly pronounces himself in favour of that which I believe he
originates, and which is certainly a bold one. He assumes "magnum fas
nefasque" to be the subject, and that the sense is, "the great law of wrong
and right (divinæ leges), according to human sense (humanam vicem), cannot convert (soften and bend) witchcraft or the hearts of witches." Maclcane
says, I think correctly, "that if this view of the construction were adopted,
it would be better to render 'humanam vicem' 'on behalf of men or of
humanity.'"   Maclcane suggests two other interpretations (see his note),
which appear to me more open to objection. Yonge, following Orelli in the
main points, asks whether it may not be better to reverse the order, and take
"venena" for the nominative case—thus, "sorceries (and those who use
them) cannot change (i. e., turn aside or defeat) the divine law, as they can
men and men's law; therefore I appeal to them: such an appeal will draw
down a wrath implacable." He renders "humanam vicem" "in human
fashion," "after the manner of men." I have adopted the sense of this
interpretation. Witchcraft is a better word here than sorceries, which properly signify divination by lot. Two other interpretations have been suggested to me by eminent scholars : 1st, Witchcraft cannot distort (or
overthrow) the great rules of right and wrong in the interest of men (taking
"humanam vicem" in the sense, "hominum causa"). 2nd, Witchcraft
cannot overthrow the great law of wrong and right—human retribution.

So to those laws my dooming curse appeals,
    And draws down wrath too dire for expiation.
Mark where thus foully murdered I expire,
    With every night I haunt you as a Fury, *
Mangle your cheeks, a ghost with bird-like claws ;
    For such the power of those dread gods the Manes.
On your unquiet bosoms I shall sit
    An incubus, and murder sleep with horror ;
And at the last, as through the streets ye slink,
    Street after street the crowd shall rise against you,
Hither and thither hounded, till to death
    Stoned by fierce mobs, vile hags obscene, ye perish ;
By wolves and Esquilinian birds of prey
    Your limbs unburied shall be rent and scattered.
Nor shall my parents, who alas! survive
    To mourn me, lose this spectacle of vengeance."

EPODE VI.

AGAINST CASSIUS.

It is by no means clear who is the unlucky object of these verses. Acron says he was a satirical poet of the name of Cassius, upon the strength of which the scholiast in Cruquius assumes him to have been the not uncelebrated orator Cassius Severus, who was banished by Augustus, and died in poverty and exile about sixty-three years after the date of this ode. This supposition is not tenable, for Cassius Severus, as Orelli remarks, must have been a boy, or a youth of about twenty, when the ode was composed ; nor is there any authority on record that Cassius Severus was a poet. Other commentators have supposed the person meant was Mœvius or Bavius. If the right name be Cassius, nothing is known about him ; nor is it of any importance. Horace's invective, for what we know to the contrary, might have been as unjust and inappropriate as the lampoons of irritable young poets generally are. Ritter conjectures the person therein satirised to have been Furius Bibaculus, notorious for the bitterness of his iambics, and who included Octavian Cæsar in his attacks.

Why snap at the guests who do nobody harm,
    Turning tail at the sight of a wolf ?
O cur ! thy vain threats why not venture on me,
    Who can give back a bite for a bite ?
Like mastiff Molossian or Sparta's dun hound,
    Kindly friend to the shepherd am I ;

* " Furor "—literally, " a personified madness."

But I prick up my ears, and away through the snows,
 If a wild beast of prey run before;
But thou, if thou fillest the woods with thy bark,
 Art struck dumb at the sniff of a bone.
Ah, beware! I am rough when I come upon knaves,
 Ah, beware of a toss from my horns!
I'm as sharp as the wit whom Lycambes deceived,
 Or the bitter foe Bupalus roused; *
Dost thou think, when a cur shows the grin of his teeth,
 That I'll weep, unavenged, like a child?

EPODE VII.

TO THE ROMANS.

This poem is referred by Orelli (who rightly considers it composed at a comparatively early age) to the beginning of the war of Perusia, A.U.C. 713—14, to which period the 16th Epode is ascribed. Others refer it to A.U.C. 716, the expedition of Augustus against Sextus Pompeius, which is not very probable; others, again, including Franke, to the much later date of 722, the last war between Augustus and Mark Antony. Ritter contends that it relates to the war against Brutus and Cassius.

O guilty! whither, whither would ye run?
Why swords just sheathed to those right hands refitted?
Is there too little of the Latian blood
 Shed on the land or wasted on the ocean,
Not that the Roman may consign to flames
 The haughty battlements of envious Carthage;
Not that the untamed Briton may be seen
 In captive chains the Sacred Slope descending;
But that, compliant to the Parthian's prayer,
 By her own right hand this great Rome shall perish?
Not so with wolves; lions not lions rend;
 The wild beast preys not on his own wild kindred.
Is it blind frenzy, or some demon Power,†
 Or wilful crime that hurries you thus headlong?

* Archilochus, to whom Lycambes refused his daughter Neobule, after having first promised her to him. The poet avenged himself in verses so stinging, that Lycambes is said to have hanged himself. Bupalus was a sculptor, who, with his brother artist Athenis, ridiculed or caricatured the uncomely features of Hipponax, and his verses are said (though not truly) to have had the same fatal effect on the sculptor that those of Archilochus had upon Lycambes.

† "Vis acrior," "a fatal necessity;" equivalent to θεοῦ βλάψ.—ORELLI, MACLEANE.

Reply!   All silent; pallor on all cheeks,
   And on all minds dumb conscience-stricken stupor.
So is it then! so rest on Roman heads
   Doom, and the guilt of fratricidal murder,
Ever since* Remus shed upon this soil
   The innocent blood atoned for by descendants.

EPODE VIII.—OMITTED.

EPODE IX.

TO MÆCENAS.

The date of this Epode is not to be mistaken. "It was written when
the news of Actium was fresh, in September A u.c. 723. It was addressed
to Mæcenas, and it is impossible to read it and suppose he had just arrived
from Actium, where some will have it he was engaged."—MACLEANE.
   The fine ode, Book I. 37, "Nunc est bibendum," was written a year later,
after the news of the taking of Alexandria and the death of Cleopatra. In
both these poems it will be observable that Horace avoids naming Mark
Antony—some say from his friendship to the Triumvir's son Iulus, to
whom he addresses Ode ii. Lib. IV.; but at the battle of Actium Iulus
was a mere boy, and it is not possible to conceive how Horace was even
acquainted with him at that time.   There must have been some other
reason for this reticence, and it is quite as likely to have been one of
artistic taste as one founded on personal or political considerations; for
Horace does not mention by name Cleopatra, nor even Sextus Pompeius.
It is consistent with the dignity of lyric song to avoid the direct mention
of the name of our national enemy, especially if conquered.   In an English
lyrical poem on the Crimean war, we should scarcely think it strange if the
poet did not obtrude on us the name of Nicholas.

When (may Jove grant it!) shall I quaff with thee
   Under thy lofty dome, my glad Mæcenas,†
Cups of that Cæcuban reserved for feasts—
   Quaff in rejoicing for victorious Cæsar,
While with the hymn symphonious music swells—
   Here Dorian lyre, there Phrygian fifes commingling?
As late we feasted, when from ocean chased,
   The Son of Neptune fled his burning navies,‡

   * "Ut immerentis," &c.   "Ut" here has the signification of "ex quo,"
ever since.—ORELLI, MACLEANE.
   † "Beate Mæcenas."   The epithet "beate" seems here to apply to the
gladness of Mæcenas at the good news, rather than to his general opulence
or felicitous fortunes.
   ‡ "Neptunius dux," Sextus Pompeius, who boasted himself to be the
son of Neptune.   Though Horace speaks of the rejoicing at the defeat of

He who did threaten to impose on Rome
  That which he took from slaves, his friends—the fetter.
A Roman (ah! deny it after times),*
  Sold into bondage to a female master,
Empales her camp-works,† and parades her arms,
  And serves, her soldier, under wrinkled eunuchs.
Shaming war's standards, in their midst, the sun
  Beholds a tent lawn-draped against mosquitoes.‡
Hitherwards,§ then, Gaul's manly riders wheeled
  Two thousand fretting steeds, and shouted "Cæsar."
And all along the hostile fleet swift prores
  Back from the fight, and slunk into the haven.||
Hail, God of Triumph! why delay so long
  The golden cars and sacrificial heifers?
Hail, God of Triumph! from Jugurthine wars
  Thou brought'st not back to Rome an equal chieftain;
Not Africanus,¶ to whom Valour built
  A sepulchre on ground which once was Carthage.

Sextus Pompeius as if it were of late ("ut nuper"), it occurred between five and and six years before (A.U.C. 718). Fugitive slaves formed a large part of the force of Sextus Pompeius.

* This does not refer to Mark Antony himself, but to the Roman soldiers under him. The singular number is used poetically.

† "Fert Vallum." The Roman soldier carried palisades ("vallum") for an empaled camp.

‡ "Conopium." The mosquito net or curtain in use in Egypt, and still common in Italy and hot climates, placed in the midst of the "signa militaria"—i. e. the rising ground on which the military standards were grouped round the prætorium or imperial tent.

§ "At huc." The reading in the MSS. varies. Orelli has "at hoc," and takes "hoc" with "frementes Galli." I prefer Macleane's reading, "at huc," taking "frementes" with "equos;" "huc" thus means "hither," "to our side." Ritter has "ad hunc," contending that "ad" has the force of "adversus"—i. e. against Antonius, who is signified, though not named. Munro has also "ad hunc," observing that "it has most authority; but what Horace did here write it is impossible to say. 'Ad hunc' may = 'ad solem.'" As the lines refers to the desertion to Cæsar of the Gauls, or cavalry of Galatia, under their king Deiotarus, "at huc" seems the simplest interpretation.

|| "Hostiliumque navium portu latent
    Puppes sinistrorsum citæ."

Macleane considers the meaning of the words impenetrably obscure, from our ignorance of the Roman nautical phrases. He inclines to favour Bentley's supposition, that "sinistrorsum citæ" may be equivalent to "back water;" adding, "something of that sort, connected with flight, I have no doubt it means."

¶ "Neque Africanum," not, as some would have it, "Africano," as referring to the African war.

Routed by sea, by land, the Foe hath changed
　For weeds of mourning his imperial purple ;
Or spreading sails to unpropitious winds
　For Crete, ennobled by her hundred cities ;
Or by the south blast dashed on Afric's sands,
　Or, drifting shoreless, lost in doubtful seas.

Ho there, good fellow ! out with larger bowls,
　And delicate Chian wines, or those of Lesbos ;
Or rather, mix us lusty Cæcuban,
　A juice austere, which puts restraint on sickness ;
The Care-Unbinder well may free us now
　From every doubt that fortune smiles on Cæsar.

EPODE X.

ON MÆVIUS SETTING OUT ON A VOYAGE.

　The name of Mœvius has become proverbially identified with the ideal of
a bad poet; but, after all, the justice of this very unpleasant immortality
rests upon no satisfactory evidence.　Virgil, with laconic disdain, dismisses
him and Bavius to obloquy, and this poem is a specimen of Horace's mode,
in his hot youth, of treating a person to whom he owed a grudge.　But
poets are very untrustworthy judges of the merits of a contemporary poet,
whom, for some reason, or other, they dislike. If nothing of Southey be
left to remote posterity, and he is only then to be judged by what Byron
has said of him, Southey would appear a sort of Mœvius.　On the other
hand, what would Byron seem if nothing were left of his works, and, one
or two thousand years hence, he were to be judged by the opinions of
his verse which Southey and Wordsworth and Coleridge have left on
record ?　As to the severest things said of Mœvius by writers of a later
generation, and who had probably never read a line of him, they are but
echoes of the old lampoons, "Give a dog a bad name," &c.　If it be true,
as the commentator in Cruquius says, that Mœvius was "a detractor of all
learned men," and a cultivator of archaisms, or an elder school of expression, "sectator vocum antiquarum," it is probable enough that he incurred the resentment of Horace and the scorn of Virgil by his attacks on
their modern style, and that his adherence to the elder forms of Latin poetry
was uncongenial to their own taste.　For Virgil's contemptuous mention,
indeed, there might be some cause less general, if Mœvius and Bavius wrote
the Anti-Bucolica ascribed to them—i. e. two pastorals in parody of the
Eclogues ; and especially if Mœvius were the author of a very ready and a
very witty attempt to turn him into ridicule.　Virgil, reciting the First
Book of his Georgics, after the words, "Nudus ara, sere nudus," came to a
dead halt, when some one, said to be either Mœvius or Bavius, finished
the line by calling out, 'habebis frigore febrem."　Whoever made that
joke must have been clever enough to be a disagreeable antagonist.　One
thing, at all events, seems pretty evident—viz. that Mœvius must have
had power of some kind to excite the muse of Horace to so angry

an excess. Had he been a man wholly without mark or following, he could scarcely have stung to such wrath even a youthful poet. Be that as it may, this ode has all the vigour of a good hater, and there is much of the gusto of true humour in its extravagance. The exact date of its composition is unknown, but it bears the trace of very early youth. Grotefend assigns it to A.U.C. 716, when Horace was twenty-seven.

Under ill-boding auspices puts forth the vessel
    Which has Mœvius—a rank-smelling cargo—on board;
Either side of that vessel, with surges the roughest,
    O be mindful, I pray thee, wild Auster, to scourge!
On an ocean upheaved from its inmost foundations,
    May the dark frowning Eurus snap cables and oars;
And may Aquilo rise in his might as when rending
    Upon hill-peaks the holm-oaks that rock to his blast!
On the blackness of night let no friendly star glimmer
    Save the baleful Orion, whose setting is storm;
Nor the deep know a billow more calm than the breakers
    Which o'erwhelmed the victorious armada of Greece,
When, from Ilion consumed, to the vessel of Ajax
    Pallas* turned the wrath due to her temple profaned!
Ha, what sweat-drops will run from the brows of thy
        sailors,
    And how palely thy puddle-blood ooze from thy cheeks;
As thou call'st out for aid—with that shriek which shames
        manhood†—
    On the Jove who disdains such a caitiff to hear;
When thy keel strains and cracks in the deep gulf Ionic,
    Howling back the grim howl of the stormy south-blast.
But O! if in some desolate creek thou shalt furnish
    To the maw of the sea-gulls a banquet superb,
To the Tempests a lamb and lewd goat shall be offered
    As a tribute of thanks for deliverance from thee.

* It is cleverly said by one of the critics, that Pallas is appropriately enough referred to here as the avenger of the bad poetry with which Mœvius had insulted her.
† "*Illa* non virilis ejulatio." He speaks as though he heard the man crying.—MACLEANE.

EPODES XI. AND XII.—OMITTED.

EPODE XIII.

TO FRIENDS.

Of all the Epodes, this, of which the metre consists of a hexameter verse, with one made up of a dimeter iambic and half a pentameter, appears to have most of the lyrical spirit and character of the Odes. The poem, addressed to a party of friends in winter, suggests comparison with the 9th Ode of the First Book, "Vides, ut alta stet nive candidum," also a winter song; but the occasion is very different, and the spirit that pervades it not less so. Ode ix. Lib. I. has no reference to public troubles; unless, indeed, a reader should indorse the very far-fetched supposition that verse 7, "Permitte divis cætera," has a political allusion. Its main image is in the picture of an individual, and the happy mode in which, while yet young, that individual may pass his day. Its tone is cheerful, and with no insinuation of pathos. This epode, on the other hand, is evidently addressed to friends excited by anxieties and apprehensions in common. If it be allowable to draw a conjecture from the touching illustration of the fate of Achilles, doomed in the land of Assaracus to a stormy life and an early death, the poem might have been written between the date of Horace's departure into Asia Minor, in the service of Brutus, and that of the trials and dangers which closed at the field of Philippi, A.U.C. 712. Ritter, indeed, places its date in the interval between the death of Cassius and the battle of Philippi. It may, however, be observed, that if the invitation to the feastmaster to bring forth the wine stored in the consulship of Torquatus is to be taken literally, wine of that age could scarcely have been found in the commissariat of Brutus. If not written while in the camp of Brutus, it was probably composed between A.U.C. 712 and 716, soon after Horace's return to Rome, before the fortunes of his life, and perhaps his political views, were changed by the favour of Mœcenas, and while his chief associates would naturally have been among the remnants of the party with whom he had fought, and to whose minds (if there be anything peculiarly appropriate in the reference to Achilles) military dangers in a foreign land might still be the salient apprehension. It is evidently written some years before Ode ix. Lib I. Horace here classes himself emphatically with the young. In Ode ix. he addresses Thaliarchus, or the feastmaster, with the half-envious sentiment of a man who points out the pleasures of youth to another—who yet sympathises with those pleasures, but is somewhat receding from them himself.

Frowning storm has contracted the face of the heaven,
   Rains and snows draw the upper air heavily down;
Now the sea, now the forests, resound with the roar
   Of wild Aquilo rushing from hill-tops on Thrace.
Seize, my friends, on To-day—foul or fair it is ours—
   While yet firm are the knees, nor unseemly is joy;

And let Gravity loosen his hold on the brows*
   Which he now overcasts with the cloud of his scowl.
Broach the cask which was born with myself in the year
   Of the Consul Torquatus.† All else be unsaid ;
For, perchance, by some turn in our fortunes, a god
   May all else to their place in times brighter restore.
Now let nard Achœmenian afford us its balm ;
   Doubt and dread let the chords of Cyllene‡ dispel ;
Listen all to the song which the Centaur renowned
   Sang of old to the ears of his great foster-son :—
"Boy invincible, goddess-born, mortal thyself,§
   The domain of Assaracus waits thee afar ;
There the petty‖ Scamander's cold streams cut their way,
   And there slidingly lapses the smooth Simoïs.
From that land, by the certain decree of their woof,
   Have the Weavers of Doom broken off thy return,
And thy mother, the blue-eyed, shall never again
   Bear thee back o'er the path of her seas to thy home.
But when there, let each burden of evils ordained,
   From thy bosom be lifted by wine and by song ;
Soothers they of a converse so sweet, it can charm
   All the cares which deform our existence away."

* "Obducta solvatur fronte senectus." "Obducta," as if clouded with care and sadness.—ORELLI. Orelli interprets "senectus" in the sense of "morositas," "tædium," to which the word "senium" is more frequently applied. Macleane renders it "melancholy," in which sense, however, he allows it is used nowhere else. I think the right meaning is "gravity" or "austerity," in which sense it is employed by Cicero, De Clar. Orat. 76, "Plena litteratæ senectutis oratio."

† "Tu vina Torquato,"&c. Here he addresses himself to the master of the feast. Sextus Manlius Torquatus was consul A. U. C. 689, the year of Horace's birth—"O nata mecum consule Manlio," Lib. III. xxi. 1.

‡ "Fide Cyllenea,"—viz., the lyre, invented by Mercury, born on Mount Cyllene, in Arcadia. There seems to me too much beauty in the choice of the word, which introduces an image of Arcadian freedom from care—the ideal holiday life.

§ Achilles.

‖ Ritter supposes that the Scamander is here emphatically called small (parvi Scamandri flumina) antithetically to "grandi alumno"—the great hero who found the scene of his actions by a stream so small. Should this conjecture, exquisitely critical, if not too refined, be admitted, then "lubricus et Simoïs" must form a part of the antithesis insinuated; i. e., actions so great beside a stream so small—actions so vehement, and of renown so loud, beside a stream so smooth.

EPODE XIV.

TO MÆCENAS IN EXCUSE FOR INDOLENCE IN COMPLETING THE VERSES HE HAD PROMISED.

It is impossible to say whether the verses thus promised and deferred were, as commonly supposed, the collection composed in this Book of Epodes, or some single iambic poem. The context seems to favour the latter supposition. The beauty who inflames Mæcenas, so gracefully mentioned at the close of the poem, is, according to the scholiasts, certainly Terentia, whom Mæcenas was then either married to or courting. And that assumption is generally adopted by modern critics. Still it scarcely seems consistent with Roman manners, or with Horace's good breeding and knowledge of the world, that he should imply a comparison between his passing caprice for a public wanton, and the honourable love of a man of the highest station to the lady he had married, or was wooing in marriage.

Why this soft sloth, through inmost sense diffusing
    Oblivion as complete
As if with parched lip I had drained from Lethe
    Whole beakers brimmed with sleep ?—
Thou kill'st me with that question oft-repeated—
    Mæcenas, truthful man,*
A song I promised thee ; to keep my promise
    A god, a god forbids—
Forbids the iambics, for I have begun them,
    To shape themselves to close.†
Thus it is said, by love inflamed, the Teian
    Lost his diviner art :
And on the shell to which he wailed his sorrow,
    Music imperfect died.
Thou too art scorched ; enjoy thy lot ; no fairer
    Flame, shot from Helen's eyes,
Fired Troy :—me Phryne burns—a wench too glowing
    To stint her warmth to one.

---

* " Candide Mæcenas." " Candide " here has the signification of honourable or truthful. You kill me—you, a man of honour—asking me so often why I do not fulfil my promise.

† " Ad umbilicum adducere," is to bring a volume to the last sheet.—MACLEANE,

EPODE XV.

TO NEÆRA.

This poem may have been an imitation of the Greek, but as Horace pointedly introduces his own name as that of the complainant, it must be inferred that, at all events, he meant to be understood as speaking in his own person.   The probability is in favour of the supposition that it was the expression of a genuine sentiment, and addressed to a real person.   Maclenne pushes too far his sceptical theory that Horace's love-poems are merely artistic exercises, like those of Cowley.

'Twas night—the moon shone forth in cloudless heaven
   Amid the lesser stars,
When thou didst mock, in vows myself had taught thee,
   The great presiding gods ;
Closer than round the ilex clings the ivy,
   Clasping me with twined arms :
" Long as the wolf shall prey upon the sheepfold—
   Long as the seaman's foe,
Baleful Orion, rouse the wintry billows—
   Or the caressing breeze
Ripple the unshorn ringlets of Apollo,
   Our mutual love shall be ! "
Ah ! thou shalt mourn to find me firm, Neæra ;
   For if in Flaccus aught
Of man be left, he brooks not halved embraces ;
   Stooped to no second rank,
His love shall leave thee, and explore its equal.
   The heart, in which the pang
Of the last treason once make sure its entry,
   Is ever henceforth proof
To charms which perfidy has rendered hateful.
   And thou, O happier one !
Whoe'er thou art, in my defeat exulting,
   Be rich in herds and lands ;
And as for gold, I give thee all Pactolus ;
   Know all the lore occult
Stored by Pythagoras re-born ; in beauty
   Nireus himself excel ;
And yet, alas ! in store for thee my sorrow,
   Thou too wilt mourn
Loves with such case made over to another—
   My turn for mockery then !

EPODE XVI.

TO THE ROMAN PEOPLE (OR RATHER TO HIS OWN POLITICAL FRIENDS).

This poem is generally supposed to have been composed at the commencement of the Perusian war, A.U.C. 713—the year following the battle of Philippi, when the state of Italy was indeed deplorable, and the fortunes of Horace himself at the worst. He had forfeited his patrimony, and it was two years before he was even introduced to Mæcenas. At that time he would have been twenty-four. The poem has the character of youth in its defects and its beauties. The redundance of its descriptive passages is in marked contrast to the terseness of description which Horace studies in his odes; and there is something declamatory in its general tone which is at variance with the simpler utterance of lyrical art. On the other hand, it has all the warmth of genuine passion; and in sheer vigour of composition Horace has rarely excelled it.

Another age worn out in civil wars,[*]
   And Rome sinks weighed down by her own sheer forces,
Whom nor the bordering Marsians could destroy;
   Nor Porsena, threatening with Etruscan armies;
Nor rival Capua,[†] nor fierce Spartacus,
   Nor Allobroge,[‡] in all revolts a traitor;
Nor fierce Germania's blue-eyed giant sons;
   Nor Hannibal, abhorred by Roman mothers,—[§]
That is the Rome which we, this race destroy;
   We, impious victims by ourselves devoted,
And to the wild beast and the wilderness
   Restoring soil which the Romans called their country.
Woe! on the ashes of Imperial Rome
   Shall the barbarian halt his march, a victor;

[*] "Altera ætas," the preceding age being that of Sulla.
[†] "Æmula nec virtus Capuæ." Capua, after the battle of Cannæ, aspired to the "imperium" of Italy.—Liv. 23, 2.
[‡] "Novisque rebus infidelis Allobrox." This line is generally supposed to refer to the Allobrogian ambassadors, who, at the time of Catiline's conspiracy, promised to aid it, but afterwards betrayed the conspirators, and became the chief witnesses against them. The Allobroges, a Gallic people on the left bank of the Rhone, two years later broke out in war, and, invading Gallia Narbonensis, were defeated by the governor of that province, C. Pomptinius. The line may, however, be intended to designate the general character of this people, without any special reference to the conduct of their ambassadors in the conspiracy of Catiline.
[§] "Parentibusque abominatus Hannibal." Orelli and Dillenburger interpret "parentibus" as "our fathers," "the former generation." Doering, Ritter, and Macleane, interpret the word in the sense of "bella matribus detestata," c. i. 1, 24, in which latter sense the line is translated.

And the wild horseman with a clanging hoof
   Trample the site which was the world's great city,
And—horrid sight—in scorn to winds and sun
   Scatter the shrouded bones of Rome's first founder.*
If haply all, or those amongst you all,
   Who be of nobler nature, ask for counsel
How to escape the endurance of such ills,
   I know none better than this old example :
Leaving their lands, their Lares, and their shrines,
   To wolf and wild boar, went forth the Phocæans,†
One state entire, accursing the return ;—
   Go *we* wherever a free foot may lead us,
No matter what the billow or the blast,
   Welcome alike be Africus or Notus,
Are ye agreed ? ‡   Who can this vote amend ?
Why pause ?   To sea ! accept the favouring auspice.
Yet ere we part thus swear : When the firm rocks,
   In the deep bosom of the ocean buried,§
Rise to the light and float along the wave,
   Then, nor till then, return for us be lawful !
Back unrepentant we will veer the sail
   When Po shall lave the summits of Matinus;
When into ocean juts the Apennine ;
   When herds no longer fear the tawny lions;
When nature's self becomes unnatural,
   And, love reversing all its old conditions,
Tigers woo does, the kite pairs with the dove ;
   When into scales the he-goat smooths his fleeces,

---

* "Quæque carent ventis et solibus ossa Quirini." I have rendered the simple meaning of the line, but the literal construction is, that he shall scatter the bones of Romulus, hitherto free, in their secret place, from wind and sun. Elsewhere (Car. iii. 3, 16) Horace speaks of Romulus as rapt to heaven, according to the popular belief. Varro, according to Porphyrion, says the tomb of Romulus was behind the Rostra. Orelli suggests that Romulus (Quirinus) is not literally signified in the verse, but rather symbolically, as the ideal representative (*der ideale representant*) of the other Roman citizens, whose bones shall be scattered to wind and sun.

† "Phocæorum—exsecrata civitas." "Exsecrata" is used in a double sense, "binding themselves under a curse."—MACLEANE. The oath of the Phocæans, who left their city when besieged by Harpagus (Herod. i. 165) never to return till an iron bar they threw into the sea should float on the surface, is amplified in the oath which Horace suggests to his political friends.

‡ " 'Sic placet'—'placetne,' the usual formula. The poet fancies himself addressing a meeting of the citizens."—MACLEANE.

§ "In the deep bosom of the ocean buried."—SHAKESPEARE.

And quits the hill-top for the briny seas.
    So swear, swear aught that cuts us off for ever
From the old homes, and go, one State entire,
    Accursing the return. If all not willing,
At least that part which is of nobler mind
    Than the unteachable herd. To beds ill-omened
Let those nought hoping, those nought daring, cling.
    Ye in whom manhood lives, cease woman wailings,
Wing the sail far beyond Etruscan shores.
    Lo ! where awaits an all-circumfluent ocean—
Fields, the Blest Fields we seek, the Golden Isles
    Where teems a land that never knows the ploughshare,
And laughs a vine that needs no pruner's hand—
    Where the glad olive ne'er belies its promise,*
And the dusk fig adorns its native stem †
    There from the creviced ilex wells the honey ;
There, down the hillside bounding light, the rills
    Dance with free foot, whose fall is heard in music ;
There, without call, the she-goat yields her milk,
    And back to browse, with unexhausted udders,
Wanders the friendly flock ; no hungry bear
    Growls round the sheepfold in the starry gloaming,‡
Nor high with rippling vipers heaves the soil.§
    These, and yet more of marvel, shall we witness,

---

    * "Nunquam fallentis termes olivæ." The olive crop is still as fickle as the English hop crop—one good year for two bad ones is the accredited average. The olive crop, like the hop, was and still is often ruinous, from the speculative gambling which its uncertainty tends to stimulate. Horace says that which came home to every olive-grower when he speaks of an olive-tree that never deceived its cultivator.
    † Viz., ungrafted.
    ‡ "Vespertinus ursus."
    § "Neque intumescit alta viperis humus." Orelli, in one of those notes, exquisite for accuracy of perception, in which his edition is so rich, objects to the common translation of "alta humus"—mountainous or rising ground, in which vipers are not found. He suggests, on various Greek authorities, that "alta," in its sense of "deep," not "high," has the signification of "fertile" (we say a deep rich soil, in antithesis to a thin poor one) ; and to those who dissent from that interpretation, Orelli commends Jahn's proposed construction to take "alta" with "intumescit"—"swells high." Macleane indorses it. Orelli refers "tumescit" not to the sweltering venom, but to the undulous movement of the reptile, alternately rising and falling, so that the ground literally seems to heave, as the commentator in Orelli says he has himself noticed, in his solitary walks along the meadows and water-banks of Italy, which, but for the vipers, would have been exceedingly pleasant. In the translation it is sought to render this idea, drawn from the critic's personal observation, and which, as a friend suggests, is in

We, for felicity reserved; how ne'er
  Dank Eurus sweeps the fields with flooding rain-storm,
Nor rich seeds parch within the sweltering glebe.
  Either extreme the King of Heaven has tempered.
Thither ne'er rowed the oar of Argonaut,
  The impure Colchian never there had footing.
There Sidon's trader brought no lust of gain;
  No weary toil there anchored with Ulysses;
Sickness is known not! on the tender lamb
  No ray falls baneful from one star in heaven.
When Jove's decree alloyed the Golden Age,
  He kept these shores for one pure race secreted;
For all beside the Golden Age grew brass
  Till the last centuries hardened to the iron,
Whence to the pure in heart a glad escape,*
  By favour of my prophet-strain is given.†

EPODE XVII.

TO CANIDIA—IN APOLOGY.

This poem completes Horace's attacks on Canidia by an ironical pretence of submission and apology. I state in a note my conjecture that he was

---

curious accordance with a passage in Humboldt's "Aspects of Nature," where he describes the reptiles, snakes, breaking their way through the clay soil left by the inundations of the Orinoco, and lifting the ground into little heaps. Ritter finds fault with Orelli's interpretation, and contends that "alta" denotes the high grass and herbage of the soil.

* "Quorum" depends on "fuga"—flight from the iron ages. "Piis" has the signification of "pure from crime."

† It has been supposed by some that the description of these happy islands, and the idea of migrating thither, is taken from the account of the Western Islands, which almost tempted Sertorius to seek in them a refuge from the cares of his life, and the harassment of unceasing wars. This story, which is told by Plutarch in his life of Sertorius, is said by Acron to have been given by Sallust. But the general tradition of a happy land separated from the rest of the world was popular among the ancients from the earliest time, and Horace might have got the notion from Hesiod or Pindar. The poem, however, would assume a much deeper and more earnest character if we could suppose that the passage in question has a symbolical signification, and refers to the isle of happy souls in which Achilles was wed to Helen. In that case the latent meaning would apply to another world beyond this, and its moral would be, "Rather than submit to the ills and ignominy in store for us, let us take our chance of those seats in Elysium reserved for the pure."

really suffering from an illness when it was written. There is no reason to
infer with some, that, because he says his hair was turning grey, the verses
were written in later life. "But now at thirty years my hair is grey,"
says Byron. At what age Horace detected his first grey hair—and he
became grey early—no one can guess. The poem has all the character of
the early ones comprised in this book. It is the only Epode in which the
same metre (trimeter iambic) is adopted.

Now, O now, I submit to the might of thy science!
  Now behold, as a suppliant, I lift up my hands!
I adjure thee by Proserpine, and by great Hecate—
  I adjure the by all the most pitiless Powers—
I adjure thee by all thy weird black-books of magic,
    Strong in charms to call down loosened stars from the
      sky—
Dread Canidia, O spare me thy grim incantations!
  And O slacken, O slacken, thy swift-whirling-wheel! *
Evën Telephus moved the fierce grandson of Nereus,†
  Against whom he had marshalled, in insolent pride,
The host of his Mysians, and levelled his arrows;—
  Evën Hector the death-dealer (sternly consigned
To the maw of the dog and the beak of the vulture)
  Weeping matrons of Troy were allowed to embalm,
After Priam, alas! (his stout walls left behind him)
  At the feet of the stubborn Achilles knelt down.
So the rowers of toil-worn Ulysses, witch Circe
  From the spell that transformed them delivered, at will,
Giving back to limbs bristled ‡ the voice and the reason,
  And the glory that dwells in the aspect of Man.
Enough, and much more than enough, for all penance
  Have I paid to thy wrath, O thou greatly beloved—

* " Citumque retro solve, solve turbinem." All the MSS. have " solve."
Lambinus has " volve" without authority. " Turbo" is a wheel of some
sort used by sorceresses; "rhombos" is the Greek name for it. Ovid,
Propertius, and Martial mention it.—MACLEANE. This critic considers
that " retro solvere" means to relax the onward motion of the wheel,
which will then of itself roll back. I may observe that "turbo," which
means both a whirlwind and a spinning-top, probably implies the shape of
the witch's wheel, as being wide at its upper part (the hoop), and spiral at
the bottom.
  † Telephus, king of Mysia, opposed the Greeks on their expedition to
Troy, was wounded by Achilles, grandson of Nereus, and son of Thetis.
Achilles cured him by the scrapings of the spear with which he was
wounded.
  ‡ Previously transformed to swine. Bentley's reading of Circa instead
of Circe (the Latin instead of the Greek termination), founded on the state-
ment of Valerius Probus, is adopted by all the more recent editors.

O thou greatly beloved by huckster and sailor ! *
Fled away from my form is the vigour of youth,
And the blush-rose of health from my cheeks has departed,
    Leaving nought but pale bones scantly covered with skin.
And my hair is grown grey with the spell of thy perfumes ;
    From my suffering I snatch not a moment's repose.
Still the night vexes day, and still day the night vexes ;
    I can free not the lungs strained with gaspings for breath.†
Wherefore, wretch that I am, I confess myself conquered ;
    I acknowledge the truth I had dared to deny ;
Yes, the chant of a Samnite can pierce thro' a bosom,
    And the Marsian's witch-ditty can split up a head !
What more wouldst thou have ?   Earth and Sea !   I am hotter
    Than Alcides in fell Nessian venom imbued,
Or than Sicily's flame budding fresh in fierce Ætna.‡
    Dost thou mean, then, for ever to keep up this fire—
O thou warehouse of venomous fuel from Colchis,—
    Till I'm whirled, a parched cinder, the waif of the winds ?
What the death that awaits or the fine that redeems me ?
    Every penalty asked I will honestly pay :

* As the lowest of the low.

† "Neque est
Levare tenta spiritu præcordia."

The symptoms described are those of a real malady—emaciation, fever, sleeplessness, difficulty of breathing—a malady familiar enough to those who have experienced an Italian malaria. The whole poem seems to me to have the air of being written at some period of actual illness, in the attempt to draw amusement from humorous exaggeration of his own complaints, which is common enough among witty invalids. The nature of the poem would perhaps scarcely suggest itself to him if he were quite well in health at the time.

‡ "Nec Sicana fervida
Virens in Ætna flamma."

I take "virens" to have the same signification here that it has Lib. IV. Carm. xiii. 6, "Virentis doctæ psallere Chiæ "—*i.e.*, youthful, blooming or budding, in the spring of life. "Virens flamma" may be compared with Lucretius's "Flos flammæ." I agree, therefore, with Macleane, who follows Lambinus and the scholiast in Cruquius, in interpreting the meaning to be "the flame, always fresh and renewing itself," and having no more to do with the colour of the flame as of sulphurous green, which is the supposition favoured by Orelli and Dillenburger, than it has in the line quoted above, where it is certainly not meant to imply that Chia is "green." The emendation of "furens," suggested by Bentley on inferior MS. authority, and rejected by most recent commentators, would substitute a prosaic commonplace for a poetic image.

Speak ! a hunded young stéers ; or a couple of stanzas
  To be sung to a lute-string attuned to a lie,
I will chant thee as chaste, I will chant thee as honest ;
  Thou shalt traverse, a gold constellation, the stars.
Moved by prayer Castor's self, and the twin of great Castor,
  Gave back sight to the bard who had Helen defamed.*
So may'st thou, for thou canst, from this frenzy release
  · me—
  Mercy, thou, by no filth-scum paternal defiled †
Mercy, thou who didst never, an agëd wise-woman,‡
  From his grave the first day § rake a beggar-man's dust !
O thy breast is the kindest, thy hands are the purest—
  Not a doubt, Pactumeius is really thy son ; ‖
And whenever thou barest the pangs of a mother,
  'Tis to rise from thy bed with the bloom of a maid !

----

* "Infamis Helenæ Castor offensus vicem,
       Fraterque magni Castoris, victi prece."

The poet alluded to is Stesichorus, punished with blindness for libelling
Helen, and recovering his sight after writing an apology (palinodia), of
which a fragment remains.   Other writers ascribe to Helen the grace of restoring the poet's sight.   Probably Horace follows some other version of the
story lost to us, in attributing the restoration to her two brothers.   The
allusion to Castor and Pollux, twin stars, comes naturally enough after saying
that Canidia shall become a constellation herself.

† "Obsoleta."   This word, as Macleane observes, is applied in an un-
usual sense.   It usually signifies " that which is gone to decay," "out of
use;" and so it comes to mean that which is spoilt and worthless (in which
sense Macleane implies that he would take it here).   Orelli, I think, better
explains it as "inquinata," "deformata."   I apprehend that "inquinata,"
in the sense of " stained," or " defiled," is the right meaning—as in Seneca
(Agam. 971, a line which appears to have escaped the commentators on the
passage), "Dextera obsoleta sanguine."

‡ "Neque in sepulcris pauperum prudens anus."   Macleane, in his note
on Canidia, Epode iii. p. 280, observes, that Horace says Canidia is not an
old woman, and refers to this very line as proving it.   It proves just the
contrary.   Horace, speaking in the most obvious irony, had before asked if
he should celebrate her with a lying lyre, and all he is now saying about
her is, of course, to be read in the opposite sense.

§ "Novendiales pulveres."   This has been variously interpreted ; but
Orelli and all recent commentators agree in accepting the general authority
of Servius, Ad. Æn. 5, that the ashes were buried the ninth day after
death—the body having been burned on the eighth.   Probably enough the
poor were not kept so long above ground ; but the phrase " novendiales "
might have come into conventional usage as signifying the first day of
burial.   It means, at all events, fresh buried, while warmth was yet in the
ashes—that being essential for the purposes of witchcraft ; and the ashes
were scattered and reduced to powder for those purposes.

‖ "Tuusque venter Pactumeius."   It would seem that the person,
whoever she might have been, represented by Canidia, was rather sensitive

CANIDIA'S REPLY.

" Why on ears locked against thee pour prayer unavailing ?
  Not more deaf to the sailor, stripped bare to the skin,
Are the rocks upon which, 'mid the darkness of winter,
  Breaks in thunder the reef of a merciless sea.
What, forsooth ! raise a laugh at the rites of Cotytto*
  Divulged ? Mock the Cupid of Cupids most free ?
As if thou wert high-priest to the witchcraft of charnels,
  And in safety might make a town-talk of my name !
What my gain to have squandered on beldames Pelignian
  My gold, and have mixed up the poisons most quick ?
Yet they are not so quick, but their work shall seem
    tardy †
To thy longings for death to escape from thy pain.
Ay, for this shall thy thankless existence be lengthened,
  That with every new day there shall come a new
    pang.
For reprieve sighed the father of Pelops the faithless,
  Hungry Tantalus, yearning in vain for the food ;
For reprieve sighed Prometheus, fast bound to the vulture,
  And doom'd Sisyphus upward vain-heaving the stone.
But reprieve is just that which Jove's law has denied
  thee.
Thou shalt wish, in the weary revolt from thy woes,
Headlong now to leap down from the height of a turret,
  Now to sheath in thy bosom the Norican blade,
Now to garland thy throat with a noose, but wish vainly.
  Conquered foe, on thy shoulders in state I will ride,
And the earth shall acknowledge my scorn and my triumph.
  What ! shall I who, as thou, curious fool, knowest well,

---

to the charge of sterility, or that, for some reason or other, she had palmed off a supposititious child (Pactumeius) as her own. In the former poem on Canidia, Horace had implied a doubt if she had any real offspring, " Si vocata partubus Lucina veris affuit." He now ironically appears to make it up with her, by declaring that Pactumeius is really her son. Ritter has Partumeius instead of Pactumeius.

  * The rites of Cotytto, of Thracian origin, were celebrated only by women, with one presiding priest.

  † " Sed tardiora fata te votis manent." There is dispute about the reading and interpretation of this passage. I adopt those sanctioned by Orelli and Macleane.

Mould and move human life in the wax of an image;
   Who can snatch with my chantings the moon from the
      sky;
Who can raise up the dead, though consumed into ashes,
   And can temper at pleasure the bowl of desire ;—
What! shall I bring mine arts to an end in lamenting
   That they have not the slightest effect upon thee?"

THE END.

BRADBURY, AGNEW, & CO., PRINTERS, WHITEFRIARS.

www.ingramcontent.com/pod-product-compliance
Lightning Source LLC
Chambersburg PA
CBHW032016110726
47901CB00004B/1105